BALLISTIC KISS

Also by Richard Kadrey

Sandman Slim

Sandman Slim

Kill the Dead

Aloha from Hell

Devil Said Bang

Kill City Blues

The Getaway God

Killing Pretty

The Perdition Score

The Kill Society

Hollywood Dead

Another Coop Heist

The Everything Box

The Wrong Dead Guy

*

The Grand Dark

*

Metrophage

*

Butcher Bird

BALLISTIC KISS

A SANDMAN SLIM NOVEL

RICHARD KADREY

HARPER Voyager
An Imprint of HarperCollins*Publishers*

This is a work of fiction. Names, characters, places, and incidents are products of the author's imagination or are used fictitiously and are not to be construed as real. Any resemblance to actual events, locales, organizations, or persons, living or dead, is entirely coincidental.

HarperCollins books may be purchased for educational, business, or sales promotional use. For information, please email the Special Markets Department at SPsales@harpercollins.com.

FIRST EDITION

Designed by Paula Russell Szafranski

Library of Congress Cataloging-in-Publication Data has been applied for.

ISBN 978-0-06-267257-5

20 21 22 23 24 LSC 10 9 8 7 6 5 4 3 2 1

For Michael Blumlein.

Doctor.

Writer.

Friend.

The cunning folk know the songs
of all the broken places.
—Hookland via David Southwell

I do believe in spooks. I do believe in spooks.
I do. I do. I do. I do. I do. I do.
—The Cowardly Lion, *The Wizard of Oz*

ACKNOWLEDGMENTS

THANKS TO MY agent, Ginger Clark, and everyone else at Curtis Brown. Thanks to my editor, David Pomerico, and the whole team at HarperCollins. Special thanks goes to David Southwell for insights into the wonder of Hookland. Also, Cassandra Khaw, Kace Alexander, AdriAnne Strickland, and Elsa Hermens.

BALLISTIC KISS

When you're trying to hold off a hellbeast you better have something bigger than a meatball sub. Especially if it happens to be your only weapon.

I mean, this isn't even a good sandwich. A good meatball sub should be hard to hold. A crunchy, saucy, meat-filled football. This thing is skinny as a ferret. Probably from a chain restaurant in some Fresno mall. Only I don't go to malls. Or, for that matter, Fresno. And, seriously, the only people who'd buy this crap hate themselves, and I'm merely into self-loathing.

The difference is subtle but important.

Anyway, back to the hellbeast.

A huge blob of bruised purple skin and teeth like rotary saws. Spidery legs waving like they're trying to hail all the cabs in New York. Only the legs have teeth too. Shouldn't a hellbeast have teeth *or* scary spider legs? Both just seems rude.

Speaking of killing, that's what about to happen to me.

I look around for something sharper than a sandwich,

but there isn't anything. Maybe I could throw some hoodoo at the fucker to at least slow it down, but I can't think of any. Mind's a total blank. So, I rip the meatball sub in half and throw each piece into each nostril on its wobbly snout. It rears back and shudders. Stops coming after me. This is my cue to run like hell to the nearest exit.

Only there aren't any. I can't even climb up out of the arena because it's one big fucking dome.

What have I gotten myself into? How did I end up here, and more important, how do I get out with no doors and no hoodoo?

As I sprint, I sort of half-remember that I used to be good at hoodoo on the fly. Like, maybe I don't have to do anything complicated, like a hex. Just bark the words and something will happen. What have I got to lose?

I turn and point a defiant finger at the blob's face. A mix of English and Hellion and maybe some kind of Narnia stuff I make up as I go.

Nothing.

Zip.

Then a light flickers in the air. A flame that spreads out from a pinpoint to the size of a dinner plate. Where it stops. And falls onto the ground.

That was embarrassing.

I go back to fleeing.

Run about a dozen steps, trip, and fall flat on my face. That's sure to scare the beast off. Real tough-guy stuff, coming up with a mouthful of dirt. The good news is that what I tripped over is the top of a femur. I drag it out of the arena floor and wait for the hellbeast like a fucking caveman. A cracked-out Fred Flintstone.

Finally, the spidery bastard sneezes out both halves of the sandwich. It looks as pissed as a big purple blob can and charges me. From what I can see, it only has one big red-rimmed eye in its wobbly head. As much as I want to run, I stand my ground until it's close enough.

Then I throw the femur as hard as I can.

It flies end over end and gouges right through the hell-beast's eye. Yellowish jelly sprays down its face and when it howls, the ground shakes. That's my cue—I start running again. There has to be a way out of here. But as I run around the edges of the arena, pounding on the walls, all I feel is well-worn bricks. That means someone used hoodoo to get us in here. Great. If I could fucking remember some, I could hoodoo my way out. I try to think. Really think. But all I come up with is Clint Eastwood in *The Good, the Bad and the Ugly* saying, "God is not on our side because he hates idiots."

The blob's shadow falls over me. Even though it's blind, its big nose must make it easy to track prey by smell. Then I remember something.

Shadows. Walking through shadows. I can do that. How? The Room of Thirteen Doors. Yes! It's all coming back to me. I have a way out of this demonic shit pit.

Then the hellbeast wraps its legs around me and rips me in half.

I WAKE UP screaming. My right hand hurts and my knuckles are bleeding.

Perfect. Another B-movie dream sequence to start the day.

Why can't I ever win in these things? Instead, it's always some *Jacob's Ladder* outtake, and I want to talk to the director because the script needs a rewrite.

Glancing around, I see that I've punched a hole in the bedroom wall. That's going to take some spackle. But who am I kidding? I break things. I don't fix them. On the other hand, the hole is annoying and a reminder of the nightmare. I grab one of the paperbacks on the floor and shove it into the hole. *The Black Dahlia* by James Ellroy. There. Good as new.

I've sweat through the sheets. No going back to sleep now, so I get up and wander into the kitchen to make some coffee.

It's a nice place that I'm in these days. Big. The décor is hilarious. There's orange shag carpet and an avocado-green sofa. Lots of warm early seventies colors. I keep expecting Mike and Carol Brady to wander in to have a key party.

The rest of the place is even stranger. The walls are circular and the furniture is round to fit against it. It's a lot like living in a flying saucer. Thomas Abbot—big boss of the whole California Sub Rosa scene—loaned it to me. I don't know if it was pity or a bribe or if he's just being a nice guy, but I sure as hell need it right now. I used to live above Maximum Overdrive, the last video rental place in L.A. Now I don't. It's a long dull story that has to do with my dying for a while and people moving on with their lives. I don't want to get into all that now—right now I need coffee. And maybe food. When did I eat last? I lose track of these things on my own.

While the coffee brews, I get some water and swallow a handful of pills. PTSD drugs from my friend Allegra. They're supposed to help with the nightmares and to keep my mood straight when I'm up and walking around. I don't know if they're doing anything. I don't feel any different. Any more relaxed or "less hypervigilant." I'm not sure what's so wrong with being hypervigilant. It kept me alive for twelve years in Hell and a year and a half in L.A. But I made a deal with Allegra, and she promised that they'd help me feel more human and get back into the world. I wouldn't mind that part.

The burbling sound of the coffeemaker is soothing after the dream. I wash the blood off my knuckles, but they're pretty much fine. I'm a fast healer.

My Colt .45 is spread in pieces on the kitchen counter. There are patches, cleaning solvent, gun oil, and a brush nearby. I run the brush back and forth through the barrel, trying not to think about anything but the smells and the feel of the metal in my hand. It doesn't work. The inside of my head is a mess.

I felt all right a couple of weeks ago. No more monsters. No more Wormwood. But I guess reality catches up with everyone. Two or maybe three weeks ago I got back from Hell after being stuck there for a year. Just long enough for people to forget about you.

Candy is gone. Half-gone anyway, living with her girlfriend Alessa in our old place above Max Overdrive. The store is doing great without me. Vidocq is deep into some kind of research, so he's not around. Brigitte is remote. I don't know what that's about. Hell, even Kasabian on his creaky metal body thinks I'm a loser. He's the one who gave me the pile of old paperbacks stacked up in the bedroom.

Look how far I've fallen. I'm actually reading to pass the time.

Then there's Janet. I don't know what the hell is going

on there. She's pretty and smart and it's nice talking to her. She works at Donut Universe, so I even get free apple fritters when I stop by, which I've been doing more frequently. Sometimes I think I should stop. Maybe tomorrow. Maybe not.

The phone rings, so I turn it over on its face. When the coffee is done, I pour a cup and drink it down, still a little too hot. That was dumb. My throat clamps shut and it makes me cough like an idiot.

I reassemble the Colt, load in a couple of slugs, and open the kitchen window. Put both shots dead center into a dusty pine tree on the hillside below. The jump of the pistol in my hand and the smell of the shots instantly brighten my mood.

The phone vibrates. Someone texted me. I ignore it. Pour more coffee.

I'm one step behind the world and it feels like I'll never catch up. Like I'm just going through the motions of my old life. You know that kid you were friends with in grade school who never grew up? You kept them around because they meant something to you once and they'd be lost without you. But they're a burden. Someone you have to apologize for and explain to your other friends. I don't want to need explaining. I'd rather be back in Hell than be anyone's eternal fool.

Yeah, these PTSD pills are going great.

The phone rings while I'm pouring another cup of coffee. Annoyed, I flip it over. It's Candy. I hesitate but see that she's the one who called and texted earlier. I have to admire that kind of obstinacy. So, I thumb the phone on. She speaks right away.

"Hey, you."

"Hey yourself."

"What are you doing?"

"I just shot some trees."

"Sneaking up on you, were they?"

"Plus, one of them owed me money."

She laughs a little. Says, "Why, the nerve. I once had to slap a rosebush."

"For what?"

"It stung me with a thorn."

"That's what thorns are for."

"Is that what thorns are for? I thought they were tiny hooks for mice to hang their hats."

"Now you know better."

"Poor mice. Nowhere to hang their hats."

"Poor rosebush. You should apologize."

"I will when you will."

"To a tree? Never. They have gardeners and birds on their side. What do I have?"

"Me," she says.

I don't say anything for a minute, thinking. Then, "You sure about that?"

She sighs. Then, "Look, I know things are weird. But don't ever think I don't love you."

"I didn't say I did."

"Didn't you?"

"Is that what you really called me to say?"

"No. I called to tell you to get out of the damn house," she says, kind of insistent.

I sip my coffee.

"I get out all the time."

"No, you come here, get movies, and go right back home.

Go *out*. See people. Go to Bamboo House of Dolls. Carlos misses you."

I pretend to consider it.

"Maybe. I'm way up the freeway these days. Bamboo House isn't walking distance anymore."

"Don't be a jerk. You stroll through a shadow and you're right there."

"Is that how it works?"

Candy sighs, not sad this time. Maybe exasperated. I do that to people.

"Okay," she says. "Here's another idea. Don't leave your house."

"I was already doing that and I'm really good it at. I could give lessons."

"Have a party."

"What kind of party?"

"You talked about having a movie night. Do that. Invite everyone."

"I don't know. It sounds scary and there are a lot of walls I haven't punched holes in yet."

"Listen, you goof. You go to the store. You get some drinks and some snacks. You put them on a table and people come over."

"It sounds easy when you say it."

"It *is* easy. You still have money, right?"

"Sure. Fifty grand I stole from Eva Sandoval."

"Then you can afford a cold-cut platter."

"What if no one comes?"

"Of course people will come. In fact, I'll ask them for you."

Maybe it's good I'm taking these damn pills. I get a weird

cold feeling in my gut. Like fear. Like panic. Yeah, I get scared, but panic? No.

Fuck this.

"I don't know. I mean, I just had the shag carpet cleaned. You should see it. It's like walking on an orange musk ox."

"That sounds like an invitation to me. You're having a party tomorrow night."

The panic feeling gets more intense.

"Tomorrow? That's really soon. I still have to get my hair done."

"Tomorrow at eight," says Candy brightly. "Drinks and snacks. Can you handle that or do I have to send you pictures to remind you what food is?"

"I remember food. It's the stuff you chew."

"That's right. The stuff you chew."

"Never cared for it."

"Tomorrow at eight."

"I'll have to get some new movies. Company kind of movies."

"Come by anytime. Kasabian misses you too."

"Now I know you're lying."

"I love you."

I feel dumb. I want to talk like a grown-up but all that comes out is, "Got to go. There's trees that need killing."

"See you tomorrow."

I hang up, considering the sound of Candy's voice. It has a weird kind of hold over me. It always has. How does she do that?

And then it hits me:

Oh fuck. What did I just agree to?

That panicked feeling again. Friends. Here. I'm so out of practice. What if I've forgotten how to talk and just grunt like a damn ape? And shopping. Aren't there services that'll do it for you?

"Hello, Foods 'R Us. I'd like some meat and crackers. Also, a life. You're out of those? Then just send bourbon."

I take a cup of coffee and the Colt to the living room and set them on the table with the remains of my old life. The black blade. A na'at—my favorite weapon when I fought in Hell's arena. And my most prized possession: a single Malediction cigarette that fell through a hole in my coat pocket. I found it just the other day and I'm saving it for a special occasion. I could probably find more smokes if I went back to Hell, but I'm done with the place for now.

I use some of the gun oil on the joints of the na'at. It's a Hellion weapon, so it doesn't take much maintenance, but it feels good to be doing something with my hands. I turn on *The Texas Chainsaw Massacre 2* where I left off last night. It's a minor piece of work but charming in its own grotesque way. I clean my weapons and let sounds of chain saws and screams fill the room. I know it's probably not good for me, what with all the nightmares, but old habits die hard.

I stay that way for I don't know how long. Cleaning the knife and na'at. Glancing at the Malediction, tempted by its tire-fire aroma. My mind clears and I finally relax.

Maybe Candy is right and I should stop by Bamboo House of Dolls. I could do with a drink and food that isn't cold cuts and mayonnaise. The thought of being back somewhere familiar, listening to Martin Denny on the jukebox, and seeing Carlos immediately makes me feel better.

Which is when the fucking phone rings again. For a minute I feel a twinge of relief, hoping it's Candy with a good excuse to cancel the party. Instead it's Abbot. My landlord. His calls, I can't ignore. I put the phone on speaker and say hello as I continue cleaning the weapons.

"Hello," he says. "How's the house treating you?"

"Just great, thanks. Is this the eviction call?"

"Why do you say that?"

"No reason in particular. I'm still a little surprised that the Sub Rosa is being so generous with me."

"You're an asset, Stark. A mess, but an asset. People understand that."

"Also, it's a good way to keep track of me."

"That's a definite plus."

When the knife and na'at are sparkling, I set them aside. Pick up my coffee. It's cold.

"Are you calling to see if I'm stealing the towels?"

"Steal away. Haven't you noticed that, like the food, they replace themselves?"

"Yeah. I thought you just sent elves over or something."

"That's the deluxe service. You're not there yet."

"So, what *is* the call about?"

When he speaks again his voice sounds tired and worried.

"A situation has come up where we might need your help."

"Hellions, monsters, or skateboarders? I'm good with a garden hose. I can get those kids off your lawn."

"Ghosts."

I smile a little.

"You're telling me the Sub Rosa doesn't have a party bus of necromancers and exorcists ready to go at all times?"

"Firstly, it's an entire infestation of ghosts. And secondly, we've tried all the usual methods and nothing's worked. That's why we might need your help."

"I kill things. I don't deal with things that are already dead."

"We both know that's not true. But the important thing is that you know Hellion hex systems. That's one thing we haven't tried."

Fucking perfect. The last thing I want is to be on Scooby-Doo patrol. But as long as I'm living here for free the Sub Rosa calls the shots.

"When do you need me?"

"The good news is that we might not. We're bringing in a coven from San Francisco. They have more experience with the unruly dead."

"Great. Have a latte and give them my best."

"I'll be sure to pass on your good wishes. We're going to give this another couple of days. But if they can't clean up the mess, I'll have to give you a call."

"As long as it isn't tomorrow night."

"What's tomorrow?"

"I'm having a movie night with the girls. We're going to do each other's nails."

"What movies are you watching?"

"I'm not sure yet. I'm thinking about *Con Air* or *Face/Off*."

"I've never seen those."

I almost spill my coffee.

"You've never seen *Con Air* or *Face/Off*? How are you allowed to even live in L.A.?"

"Goodbye, Stark. Have fun at your party."

"When your spooks are gone, go to Max Overdrive. Kasabian will set you up with some real movies."

"You know there's something called streaming, right?"

"Nope."

"Okay. I'll talk to you later."

I hang up and sit there for a minute. Abbot's a nice guy, but the idea of going back to work—and as a ghost janitor—is extremely unappealing. If he wanted me to punch some sewer monsters, fine. Set some kill-crazy vampires on fire, cool. I'd even pick up his dry cleaning. But hanging around with a bunch of incorporeal fuckups sounds downright depressing, and I don't need more of that right now. Plus, has Abbot ever seen a movie in his life? How can I work for a complete illiterate? It's undignified.

Talking to him wrecked my mood. There's no way I'm going to Bamboo House now. I'd spend the whole time grousing and I've been doing too much of that lately. I don't need to inflict it on Carlos or anybody else. Instead, I grab all the movies in the house and step through a shadow so that I come out in front of Max Overdrive. Maybe trading these in for some new discs will put me in a better mood. And if it doesn't, at least I'll only bother Kasabian.

I try to psych myself up so I'll go into the shop all smiles. Not let anyone know what a delicate flower I've become. But Hollywood is Hollywood, and on a hot day on the right corner you can smell the shit a block away.

There's a new pretend dive bar for young media bros near the corner of Las Palmas. Outside, a muscular guy in new leathers is doing a belligerent Tom Hardy impression—like the most deranged audition in history—and has backed a smaller guy against the wall, jamming a finger over and over into his chest. I can't tell if the smaller guy is a friend, a younger sibling, or a lover. He's definitely someone Tom Hardy is sure he can dominate. Tom keeps pointing to a shiny new Harley Roadster with all the bells and whistles. I get the feeling that the little guy wasn't sufficiently impressed and Tom is trying to scream awe into him. When Tom takes a breath, the little guy tries to slip away, but he's not fast enough. Tom gets hold of his arm and yanks him back hard.

So, I kick over the bike.

"Clumsy me. Sorry."

At the sound of crunching metal, Tom spins around. He lets go of the little guy and approaches me slowly, like his mind can't quite wrap itself around the carnage. Finally, he looks at me.

"Motherfucker, do you want to die right now?"

I put a boot on the bike and step over it, careful to leave a footprint on the pristine seat. When I'm kissing distance from Tom I look into his stupid, beer-addled eyes.

"Do you even know what death is, Tom?" I say. "It's dumb, and it's loud, and it smells bad; you're in Hell and you want to die to get away from it all, but you're already dead and there's nowhere to go. And what's worse is you know you're there because you deserve it, because you're such a fucking waste of skin and gristle. So no, I don't want to die. It's no fun and there's too many people like you there."

I'm not halfway through the sales pitch when he reaches for a knife. The little guy is still against the wall, too scared to make a run for it.

I say, "Why don't you let your pal go and I won't piss in your gas tank?"

Tom starts waving the knife around, all movie menacing. No way the little guy is going to run now. I know what he's thinking. He's worried that Tom is going to kick my ass and take it out on him later.

I slap Tom hard, and he takes a step back like he forgot that I have hands and can do things with them.

"It's okay," I tell the little guy. "He's not going to hurt you."

He takes a couple of steps. Looks at Tom and back to me.

Tom lunges at me with the blade. It's not much of a fight. He's as subtle as a one-eyed hippo. I smack his drunken hands away, bat the knife to the ground, and grab him by the throat. Lift him up so he's on his tiptoes. He does a funny little dance as he chokes.

I look at the other guy.

"Do you want him gone for now or forever?"

He hesitates. Then says, "Forever."

"Done."

"You're not going to kill him . . . ?"

I lift Tom up a little higher. He waves his arms around like he's trying to signal passing jets.

"There's too many people around," I tell the little guy. "But he won't bother you again."

He runs off.

When I drop Tom, he falls in a big leather heap. I get his knife while he's still trying to remember how to breathe and cut a hex into the palm of his left hand. A funny Hellion one you only use on people you find extra annoying.

The moment Tom catches his breath he's on his feet. Swings a big John Wayne roundhouse punch at my face. I stand there and let him connect. At which point, he screams. His hand has collapsed into a soft wad of hemorrhaging meat.

"You're going to want to watch your temper, Tom. From now on whenever you smack someone in anger, your bones are going to turn to chalk and come apart like just now. Don't worry. They'll grow back, just not a hundred percent. And each time you break them, they'll get worse and worse until there's nothing left of you but a sack of rattling skin. Understand?"

"What?" he peeps.

"Never mind. You'll figure it out."

I leave him there nursing his putty hand and head to Max Overdrive. People are streaming out of the shop. Others mill around on the sidewalk as I go inside. I'm surprised when the place is empty.

Kasabian glares at me from behind the counter.

"Your usual graceful entrance," he says.

"He started it."

He shakes his jowly head.

"We've *had* this discussion. You're a shit magnet. You attract trouble."

"And I made it go away."

He sweeps his metal hand around, gesturing to the empty shop.

"Look, dumbass You scared all our customers away. You're a walking calamity."

My heart is still pounding from the scene on the street. It shouldn't be doing this. I was in much worse situations in the arena and didn't break a sweat. But that guy got to me—and I wanted to hurt him. Bad. There's still more rage stuck in me than I wanted to admit earlier. I should talk to Allegra. Maybe try some different pills. Or maybe forget them altogether. What fucking good are they if all they do is jack up my heart rate and make me not want to hurt bullies?

I set the movies I brought with me on the counter, a little embarrassed that Kasabian might be right about my scaring everyone out of the place.

I say, "Let me pick up some new stuff and I'll get out of your way."

"Thank you. We got some new special titles in."

Max Overdrive is known in the underground-movie-fiend community for its "special titles." A nice little witch friend of Candy's has contacts in other dimensional realms where movies that don't exist in this world are common. It's the only reason the place is still in business.

I look past Kasabian at the racks behind him.

"What did you get?"

"Kubrick's *Napoleon.*"

I shake my head.

"Too big. Too serious. I want something for the party tomorrow night."

"I heard about that," he says.

"You're invited, you know."

He shakes his head slowly.

"I'll pass. I don't want to watch you beat up the hors d'oeuvres."

"What else did you get in?"

"Vincent Ward's *Alien 3.*"

"The one on the satellite with the monks who have to fight the xenomorph with wood?"

"The very one."

"Cool. I'll take that for me. But I still need something, you know, company friendly. *Con Air* or *Face/Off*."

Kasabian's eyes narrow at me.

"*Face/Off* is strictly for film nerds who want to scream at its awfulness."

I think it over.

"Maybe that's not the right mood."

"No, it's not the right mood for the people you invited. They just want something stupid and light and fun. Get *Con Air*."

"And maybe something old and funny to go with it?"

"Stay safe. *The Thin Man*. Or something straight-up funny. *His Girl Friday*."

"Can I have both?"

"Will you go away?"

"Watch my dust."

"Fine," he says. "You know where the regular stuff is. I'll get the Vincent Ward."

While I'm pawing through the forties comedy section, Alessa—Candy's girlfriend—walks out of the back room, a pile of invoices in her hand. She stops for a second. Probably wondering why the shop is empty.

I call over to her, "Hi. How are you?"

She looks at me, then to Kasabian. He raises his eyebrows a little and she turns back to me.

"Hi, Stark," she says. The way she stomps upstairs lets me know that she knows I'm the reason the store is empty.

Kasabian laughs.

"Man, she loves you."

"Fuck off. I'm over here trying to be a person."

He shakes his head, still laughing.

"Making friends everywhere you go."

I think Alessa hates me most because of my old connection to Candy. But I'm not trying to steal her away. I'm no homewrecker, and I wish I and Alessa could at least be in the same room together for two minutes. But she's only seen me in a crisis. Killing people and encouraging Candy to go Jade. I know she doesn't want that for Candy. I'm nervous about her coming to the party. So I'll be extra polite, wear a clean shirt, and try not to set anything on fire.

Kasabian takes my discs and puts them in a bag. I grab it and head for a shadow.

He shouts, "Try not to murder anyone between here and the wall."

AFTER I DROP the discs at the flying-saucer house, I step through another shadow and come out in the parking lot of a giant supermarket at the corner of where Sunset and Hollywood Boulevard meet. Back in the silent-movie days, when this area was wide open land, they shot some big epics here. This corner is sacred ground. I was in one of these stores a year or so ago but chickened out and ran away. Not this time. I'm going to shop the hell out of this place. I head into the grocery, all innocence and optimism. Grab a cart and venture into the consumer wonderland.

I'm not ten steps inside when a rent-a-cop starts following me. She doesn't have a gun, but I spot pepper spray and a Taser.

This again. I want to leave but don't. I'm tired of feeling like I don't belong anywhere. Besides, I don't have to do any hoodoo on the cop or anyone else. I have a pocket full of hundreds and I know the one most important rule in L.A.: money is the magic anyone can do. So, I stand my goddamn ground.

There's a young guy in a spotless apron giving out free samples near the frozen food aisle. I stroll up with the cop behind me as discreet as a pink elephant.

The guy with the samples flashes me the smile of a true believer and without pausing says, "Care to try a sausage?"

I pick up one of the little meat discs with a toothpick and pop it in my mouth.

"It's our brand-new extra-spicy chorizo with super jalapeños and a generous layer of pepper jack in the middle."

I watch him as he talks, like he's the most interesting guy in the world. Over his shoulder, I can see the cop's reflection in the glass doors of the frozen food cases. But as I stand there, fascinated by every word falling out of Sausage Man's face, the cop gets bored and wanders off. The truth is that the sausage is pretty good.

I say, "What's a super jalapeño?"

He falters for a second.

"It's like a regular jalapeño . . . only super."

I pop another piece of chorizo in my mouth and say, "I really like this."

Sausage Man beams like I just named my firstborn after him.

"It's one of our most popular new items," he says.

I think for a minute, tugging at a memory. Then, trying to

act like a normal person chatting with another normal person, I blurt, "It reminds me of manticore tail."

He blinks once.

"Manticore?"

"You know. Those big fuckers that graze along the Styx. Human head. Lion body. Scorpion's tail? Hard to kill, but they're good eating."

He smiles at me the way you smile at a rabid dog, hoping it will bite the guy across the room and not you. His eyes move around in their sockets, trying to spot the security guard. By then I realize what I've done and feel bad for ruining Sausage Man's day. To make it up to him, I grab two packages of chorizo and dump them in my cart. He flinches slightly when I grab the merchandise but never drops the professional smile. Someone needs to give this guy an Oscar. I can smell his fear sweat. I wish Candy were here. She'd know how to calm him down.

I just mumble, "Thanks for the meat."

"Come again," he says.

"Probably not."

He whispers, "Thank you."

I steer my cart down the closest aisle to show Sausage Man that I mean him no harm.

I've been in this building for five minutes and I'm already discouraged. I've been going to bodegas ever since I got back from Downtown. I forgot what regular grocery stores were like. Complete nightmares. I prefer the street markets in Pandemonium, where you eat whatever someone killed that day. Simple. But it's not like that here. I mean, look at this aisle. What am I supposed to do with seven hundred kinds of soup?

I don't even like soup. Why am I here? Who are all these people buying all this soup?

This store is a like a bad day in the arena. I've lost and all I can do is crawl away and try not to die.

But.

I said I'd go shopping and get stuff for the party. I can't walk out of here empty-handed, so I come up with a plan.

I start at one end of the store and walk along the head of every aisle grabbing the first bright and shiny thing that catches my eye. At the far end of the store, I check my haul. A jar of olives. Tuna. Canned asparagus. Refried beans. Spaghetti sauce. Frozen pie shells. Low-sodium instant ramen. Tarragon. And, of course, the sausage. I'm no cook, but that seems like enough to throw something together for a party. But I still need dessert.

I use the same method in the cake department. What do people like for dessert? I think about Donut Universe. All of their stuff looks fun. Cream or fruit filling dripping out of the ends. Whipped cream and maybe a cherry on top. That's the secret. Sweet, but cute too. I circle the cakes and cookies on display, but I'm not impressed. Then I hit a frozen case and spot the perfect thing—a yule log with a little Santa and reindeer on top. Christmas cake is festive as fuck. Everyone will be really surprised.

My last stop is the best: the liquor aisle. I don't know what everyone drinks, so I just grab a couple of bottles of everything and pile it into the cart. The bottles tinkle together gently, kind of like jingle bells. Now I'm sure the yule log was the right choice.

I pile all of my crap on the belt at the checkout stand and

the lady running the register sweeps her weird little scanner over everything. She raises her eyes a fraction of an inch when she sees all the booze but, like Sausage Man, remains a real pro. Finally, she looks up at me.

"That's five hundred and sixty-seven dollars and forty-eight cents."

I pull out a wad of hundreds and lay down six. She doesn't touch them for a second. Just reaches for a pen and draws a line on each bill. It takes me a minute to register what she's doing. Checking for counterfeits. She draws a second line like she doesn't trust the first. Holds the bills up to the light. Glances at me and shrugs. I'm starting to get annoyed. Finally, she pops the money drawer open and counts out my change. Out the corner of my eye I spot the security guard again. A kid at the end of the counter loads my goods into bags, then into the cart. Grabbing my change, I head outside.

Just for the hell of it, I stop in the parking lot and light a cigarette. It gives the security guard time to follow me and watch me load my haul into a car. Only I don't have a car, so I aim the cart at a shadow at the edge of the building. Just before I disappear, I turn and give her the finger. Then I'm gone.

Put that in your report, Miss Marple.

WHEN I GET home, I empty everything onto the kitchen counter, except for the liquor. I leave that in the cart and shove it into the living room. As I look over the food, it occurs to me that it might be a little more random than I first thought. I'm not sure this stuff is meant to go together, but I'm certain if I mix it with stuff from the refrigerator it'll be fine. Better than fine, even. Then it hits me—maybe I should have gotten something hot to eat. Made it a real dinner party. Is it Thanksgiving yet? That's like a party. But no. It's too early in the year. Maybe I can pay someone to cook a turkey for me tomorrow. I'll have to remember to check into that.

I put the yule log in the refrigerator and go into the living room to clear all the guns off the table. When that's done, I check the walls to make sure I didn't punch any more holes in them while I was asleep. Lucky me, they look good. I don't have to clean. Whatever little elves refill the fridge do that.

What else do people do for parties?

Fuck, I'm useless.

Maybe I should polish my boots? Will people even look at my feet?

Holy shit. How do people even have parties?

I wander around for a few minutes, picking up books and clothes. Toss them all in the bedroom. With the door closed, the place doesn't look half-bad. But I'm still skittish after being run out of the grocery. It's humiliating. I mean, I've killed every kind of hellbeast imaginable. I'm related to Wild Bill Hickok. Yet, all I could think of to do for revenge at the store was steal a shopping cart. I'm keeping it too. That will teach them not to screw with a natural born killer.

God, I'm pathetic.

I need some food and some coffee. I stare at what's on the counter, but none of it looks worth a damn. And the coffeemaker turned itself off, so the sludge at the bottom of the pot is cold. I'm as twitchy as a chicken on a hot plate. I need to get out of here and someplace safe for a while. But I'm not ready for really heavy drinking yet. That leaves one choice.

I step through a shadow and come out in the parking lot

by Donut Universe.

I spot Janet through the window. She's in the last booth along the front of the place, drinking coffee and reading a magazine. I go over and rap on the window with a knuckle; she looks up and smiles when she sees me. Uses the magazine to wave me in. I go inside and straight back to her booth.

It's after lunch, so the place isn't crowded. A business type in a suit, tie loose, yammering into his phone. A table of teenyboppers cutting school to load up on sugar. An old guy nodding off in a sunny booth near the back, his coffee and donut untouched.

Janet slides out of the booth when I get there and pecks me on the cheek before pulling me into the booth so I'm sitting across from her. Pecking me on the cheek is a regular thing now. We've had coffee a few times and dinner at a sushi place nearby. After dinner, she kissed me hard in the parking lot and I let her. I still feel guilty about it and haven't mentioned it to Candy. And I feel bad about Janet too. So far, I've been able to make excuses not to go back to her place or let her come to mine. How much longer can I do that without feeling like a heel? I already feel like an idiot.

"This is a nice surprise," she says. "You want some coffee or a fritter?"

I hold up a hand. "Nothing, thanks. I've had it with food for the moment."

She furrows her brow.

"You okay?"

The teenyboppers laugh and I glance over at them. All they need for a party is each other and some shoplifted beer. It must be nice.

I say, "I agreed to something stupid."

"What?"

"It looks like I'm finally having that movie night at my place tomorrow. Unless I burn it down to get out of it."

She perks up at that.

"Great. What time should I get there?"

It didn't really occur to me that I'd stopped by to invite her until I sat down. Sometimes my brain plays tricks on me like that. One half gets ahead of the other and suddenly I'm in a donut place asking a pretty girl to a party I wasn't sure I wanted to have a minute ago.

"I was thinking around eight."

She gives me a lopsided grin. "Eight is perfect. Should I show up naked or will there be other people?"

It takes me a second to make sure I heard that right.

"There will be other people."

She sighs.

"Oh well. Clothes it is then. Do you need any donuts? Because I can bring about a million."

I shake my head, feeling things getting complicated and wondering if I should burn the house tonight or tomorrow.

"I'm fine on food. In fact, I just picked up some snacks."

"Really? What?"

"You know. An assortment."

"Like what, specifically?"

"Tarragon."

She looks at me.

"Stark, have you ever even been to a party?"

The old man in the corner stirs in his half sleep and I long to be over there with him. Nodding off without a care in the world.

"I freaked out, okay?" I say. "There was a sausage guy and a security guard and soup. All this goddamn soup. I couldn't take it, so I grabbed some things and left."

Janet looks out the window with a hand over her mouth, suppressing a laugh. She tries to hide it and now I feel worse than before.

When Janet is done finding me hilarious she says, "Would you mind if I brought a couple of things? I mean, it's my first time at your place. You're supposed to bring a gift."

"Really?"

I think about all of my first times going into places since getting back from Downtown. I guess most of them had to do with chasing creeps or asking people hard questions, so, technically, not killing everyone when I walked into a new place was sort of a gift. That makes me feel better.

I say, "Bring something if you want, but I've got it covered. I'm going to find somebody to cook a turkey, so we'll have warm food."

"A turkey?" she says. "Like Thanksgiving?"

"Yeah. Everybody likes turkey."

Janet takes a sip of her coffee.

"Huh. Anyway, it will be nice to finally see your place."

"It's not really mine. I'm just kind of squatting."

"But you sleep there, right? You have stuff and no one is throwing you out any time soon."

"I have a few things. And no, I don't think so."

She raises and lowers her shoulders.

"Then it's your place."

I like the sound of that. My place.

"Then I'll see you at my place."

She checks her watch.

"I have to get back to work."

I slide out of the booth.

"Sure. Don't let me keep you."

Janet stands and gives me another peck, this time on the lips. She uses her thumb to wipe off the lipstick.

"See you tomorrow, Stark. I'm really looking forward to that turkey."

I go outside into the afternoon sun, feeling a lot better than I did leaving the grocery store.

But I'm having second thoughts about the bird.

I WALK BACK to Las Palmas. Tom Hardy and the bike are gone. All that's left of our time together is some scrape marks on the street and a small pool of gas. I must have cracked his tank. Good.

I don't go into Max Overdrive but cut into the alley next to it. Behind the dumpster is something wrapped in a dirty tarp, with stones holding the edges down. I kick the stones away on one side and toss back the tarp. And get my first look at the Hellion Hog in—how long? Well over a year. I would have loved to have it when I was back Downtown, traveling with the Magistrate and the Havoc. It would have burned all those chop-shop bikes and Frankensteined hot rods to the ground. Nothing can catch me on the Hog. I picked it up when I was playing Lucifer and running Hell. One hundred days of weirdness I never want to repeat in this life or any other.

The bike isn't the kind of thing you pick up at your local

dealership, or any custom shop on this plane of existence. The handlebars are wide, swept back, and pointed, like they're part of an aerodynamic longhorn. When you kick the Hog up high the engine burns cherry red. There isn't a speedometer because, as far as I know, you can't top it out. I was never able to, and I pushed it until Hell's asphalt bubbled and melted behind us. The point is, the bike is a motherfucker. Or it was.

Right now, it looks pretty sad. It's covered in streaks of dirt where humidity or maybe rain splashed up under the tarp and ran down the sides, leaving dried-up rivers of dirt and dust on the seat and body. There are cobwebs between the spokes on the wheels. Dead leaves and the shriveled carcass of a rat by the back tire. I brush some dust off the seat, swing a leg over, and sit down. Ugly as the Hog is, it still feels good. Like it's been waiting for me. Vibrating. Waiting to tear up the road again.

We'll see.

Someone—probably Candy—thoughtfully put a lock on the front tire. Even dead, she was always thinking of me. I can't stand the idea of going back into the store to ask for the key, so I take out the black blade and slice the thing off in one clean motion. Then I just sit there for a minute, getting a feel for the bike again. Also trying to figure out what the hell I'm doing. I'm too restless to go home and face the tarragon, but I can't think of anywhere I want to go either.

The Hellion Hog doesn't have a key because no one can ride it but me. I get a grip on the handlebars and kick the bike to life.

The sound is more like an explosion than an engine starting. The Hog stutters a few times, blowing out grit and whatever little bugs or hobos were unfortunate enough to nest in the pipes. I rev the engine a few times until the sound dies down to a steady jet-engine growl. With it still running, I climb off and shove the dumpster against the alley wall. Then I roll the bike around it so the front wheel is aimed at the empty street. I should have bought sunglasses while I was at the grocery. The sun coming off the water is going to be murder on my eyes, but it's a small price to pay to feel something like myself again.

I kick up the stand, shift into gear, and hit the gas. Come out of the alley like a torpedo heading west to nuke Venice Beach. The Hog rattles my bones and teeth. Shatters my eardrums. My heart is going about two hundred beats a minute and I can't quite catch my breath.

It's the best feeling in the world.

The Hog is massive, but I don't care right now. I lane-split through Hollywood traffic, scraping car doors and knocking off side mirrors—a jerk move, but I'm still upset about my shopping fiasco.

At a light, a guy pulls up next to me and points a pistol in my direction. A little pocket nine-millimeter. Adorable. He road rages at me like a jabbering gorilla. From what I can make out, he doesn't like my driving skills. Of course, he has a point, but he also has a gun, which makes me apologizing out of the question. Anyway, I'm faster than him. When he pauses to take a breath, I snatch the pistol out of his hand and drop it in my coat pocket.

When something like that happens, most sensible people back off and live to scream another day. Not this guy. He wants his gun back and steps out of the car to get it. But the dummy keeps one hand on the driver's-side door. So, when I kick it closed, his fingers get stuck between the edge of the door and the car body. The light changes and I leave him there with mangled purple fingers and a life lesson I can't quite figure out. But it will come to me.

To sum up, I got run out of a grocery store by Barney Fife, and I've had a knife and a gun pulled on me. Allegra would say it isn't healthy, but instead of putting me in a worse mood than this morning, today it's the opposite. I'm back on the Hog; I managed not to get shot, stabbed, or arrested; and I have no idea where I'm going. Just like old times.

I finally decide to head west, toward the ocean. That'll clear my head. I like the ocean. I don't get there much, but I like the noise and the waves. I just hate beaches. All those merrily colored coolers and people baking on towels. Zinc oxide on their noses and sand up their asses. College dudes in TOO FUCK TO DRUNK T-shirts and tan girls with bright bikini lines showing off the few inches of skin that aren't going to get cancer when it turn forty.

I blast up the 101 to the Ventura Freeway and all the way west to Las Virgenes Road, where I head south toward Malibu—land of blue skies, surfers, billionaire beach bunnies, showbiz has-beens, and dope dealer up-and-comers. Plus, the home of my favorite ghoul: Teddy Osterberg.

When I call Teddy a ghoul I don't mean he's a creep or anything. He's a real ghoul—he eats people. Mostly the dead. At one point he was going to eat me, but now he's dead, so fuck him and all his dirty little secrets.

Lucky for me and the local rich-kid wannabe gangbangers, no one in the Osterberg family wants anything to do with

Teddy's broken-down house *or* his graveyard collection. I forgot to mention that. Teddy collected graveyards. Brought them in from all over the world, set them up on his estate like trophies. At night, he'd dig up a body and have a feast. Sure, Teddy's place is in the heart of Malibu, but what Realtor is going to touch a place with this kind of history? And what are they going to do with all the bodies in all the graveyards? There are over a hundred corpses out here. Do you dig them up or pull a *Poltergeist* and just pretend you did? No, no one is touching Teddy's playground for a good long time. Which makes it the perfect little getaway for me when I need to clear my head.

The only sounds are the roar of the waves across the road and the low thrum of power lines at the top of the hill where Teddy's house stands. The low buzz and occasional crackle are oddly soothing. Like ghost whispers or electric blood pumping through miles-long veins. The sounds are another reason I like it here.

There's a large oak tree up the hill, so I take the short walk to get under its shade. The tree is surrounded by a circle of old tombstones. English. Each one two hundred years old or more. The markers are all jammed together like sliced bread. Someone didn't want them, but they didn't want to throw them away either. I don't know what the hell to make of them.

I'm still thinking about it when a shadow comes up behind me and a familiar voice says, "Shopping for yourself or a friend?"

I turn around to Samael and say, "Just admiring the view."

He comes closer to the headstones.

"I know a few of these names. Old-timers. But no judgment. Everyone ends up in Hell these days, so what does it really matter?"

"I didn't dream about Heaven when I was Downtown. I dreamed about L.A., but there were some days I'd have settled for the pearly gates."

"Funny. In all the time we've known each other you never said that before."

I look around at the other graves.

"I guess with Heaven closed to mortals, it's been on my mind. Poor slobs living so-called good lives, praying for Heaven and ending up eyeball-deep in shit with all the other losers."

"It sounds like you actually feel sorry for the righteous."

"Fuck the righteous. I just don't like con jobs. You angels built Heaven and Hell, but you don't want kids playing on your lawns, so you locked everybody out."

Samael raises a finger.

"I'm not on the side that wants to exclude mortals from Heaven. I'm fighting that faction and you know it."

"Sorry. I'm just in a mood."

"Because you lost your lady love?"

I walk across the unkempt lawn and Samael strolls with me.

"That's not it. Or it's just a part of it. When you got kicked out of Heaven, didn't you feel at least a little lost? I know it's not your style to admit feeling weak, but it's just you and me here. Didn't you ever have a moment where you weren't sure where you belonged?"

He takes a gold lighter and a pack of Maledictions from his jacket. Holds out one to me, lights it, then lights his own.

I'm hoping he'll offer me the pack, but he doesn't. Maybe my question bothered him.

"No," he says. "Not back then. Never during our exile from Heaven. We knew—I knew—that demanding free will for angels was a just cause. Father didn't agree, so he showed us the door. He was like that back then. Look at poor Adam and Eve. One mistake and out you go. But he's changed. You know that more than just about anyone. You've seen it happen."

I puff the Malediction and let its tasty poison fill my lungs.

"How is Mr. Muninn these days?"

"The war has taken its toll on him, as it's taken a toll on us all."

"Still a stalemate then. Heaven is locked. A no-mortal-soul zone."

"The fighting is a stalemate, but Father keeps talking. It's frustrating, but he's ever the negotiator. Ever the optimist."

"So, nothing has changed. The war is going to go on forever."

"Foreverish, maybe."

We stop by a cemetery full of graceful tombs and decorated sculptures. It looks Buddhist. Kids have left offerings of beers and Twinkies nearby. I'm sure they think they're being ironic, but I bet whatever spirits might haunt this forgotten place are grateful for whatever offerings they get.

Samael continues. "But no war truly lasts forever, even this one. The solution, like many things in life, is figuring out the right angle to approach from."

"It sounds like you're planning to trick Heaven away from the rebels."

At one grave, Samael lights a stick of incense he seemingly pulled from the air and stabs the end into a stone cup filled with sand.

"Nice trick," I say. "Is that how you're going to do the grift? Sleight of hand?"

He gives the grave a little bow and now I know he's showing off.

He says, "Would that be so bad?"

"How would you do it?"

"Who said anything about me?"

I look at him.

"Come on, man."

He starts to walk away.

"Well, if you're not interested . . ."

"I didn't say that. Let's hear your plan. Also, I'm going to need some incentive."

He comes back.

"Like what?"

I point my cigarette at him.

"First off, that pack of Maledictions in your pocket."

"Is that all?" he says, not making a move to give me the pack.

"No, but it's a start."

He takes out the pack and tosses it to me. I put it in my pocket and feel the pistol I took from my road rage pal. Having the damn thing annoys me, but I'll deal with it later.

"Okay," I tell him. "Let's hear your plan."

"There is no plan," he says. "Just a few scattered thoughts."

"Now you're being coy. You always have a plan."

He starts walking again.

"Have you ever heard of an angel named Zadkiel?"

"Nope."

"The angel of mercy, benevolence, and forgiveness?"

"Sounds like a lot of laughs, though. What's their story?"

"A millennium ago, give or take, Father gave her the keys to eternity. Dubbed her the Opener of the Ways. She can do something even Father can't do at the moment."

I look at him.

"Open the gates of Heaven?"

"Conceivably. Honestly, I didn't know her that well. She was always more of Father's crowd. Always fluttering about Earth. A bit of a shirker, which was the one thing I liked about her."

"What was she shirking?"

"When I said she was the Opener of the Ways, that was a bit misleading. Her main job was keeping doors closed so that things didn't bump into each other. Heaven, Hell, and Earth for example. But she also held apart different dimensions and realities. For a long time, she held the Kissi at bay."

Hearing the word "Kissi" makes me mad.

"You're saying this Zadkiel asshole could have kept the Kissi locked up, but she didn't?"

Samael nods.

"Exactly. A shirker, and a dangerous one at that. But on the other hand, if she can open the gates of Heaven, it makes the war moot. All the angels who want Heaven to remain pure can fuck off down to Hell and turn it into the priggish wonderland they so desperately want."

For the first time in what feels like a long while, I'm excited about something.

"Then all we have to do is get Zadkiel to do her key trick. How do we do that?"

"I haven't a clue."

And now I feel shitty again, but I don't want him to know that, so I get angry.

"No. I'm not doing this. I can't. Not right now."

"Come on. Join in the fun and help every mortal who's ever lived. Even the depressing ones like you."

I look at him.

"Careful with the guilt trips. I'm not all that thrilled with human beings right now."

"Don't you want to hear the rest, at least? Why she won't work with Father?"

"That's easy," I say. "She's missing."

Samael looks at me like a dog trainer whose favorite puppy just learned to fetch.

He says, "Good guess. But we have a clue as to where she is: Earth."

I give him a look.

"You want to narrow that down a little?"

"All right. The Pussycat Theatre on Hollywood Boulevard."

"That old porn place? That's been gone for a million years. How long ago did she disappear?"

"Forty-some-odd years now."

I knock some ashes from the Malediction.

"What the hell was the Opener of the Ways doing at a porn palace in the seventies?"

"I told you, she liked spending time with mortals. From what I understand, some of her friends had . . . exotic tastes.

Do you really think it's important?"

"Who knows? But maybe if we can figure out what happened forty years ago, we'll be able to find her. Only, even if there were any Pussycat Theatres around, what are the odds someone would remember her?"

"Virtually none," says Samael.

"Exactly. Case closed. See you around."

"You must be excited. Running off to solve the case already."

"I just said I wouldn't."

"You said you *couldn't*. Not the same thing."

I pick up a pebble and toss it across the graveyard.

"Why are you asking me to do this? Why don't you do it or get winged minions to do it for you?"

For the first time, he looks a little uncomfortable.

He says, "That's not really possible at this moment."

"It's Mr. Muninn, isn't it? If he isn't looking for her, why should I?"

His face softens a little.

"I know that you have your own problems. Bad dreams. Fists through walls. Questions about what's left for you on Earth. And then there's your donut friend. It must all be very confusing."

"It is and I don't want to talk about it."

"Of course. But if you ever do, you can always call. Anyway, I have to go before I'm missed. Good luck with your brooding or whatever it is you're doing out here."

"If you were me, considering my situation with Candy and whatever's going on with Janet, what would you do?"

Samael puts a hand on my shoulder.

"You're a mess, Stark. Give those women and yourself a break."

He heads back down the hill.

"Wait. What does that mean?" I yell.

He keeps walking but calls back over his shoulder.

"One more thing. You'll want to find Father's lost lamb soon. He's on the verge of giving up."

"What do you mean giving up?"

"The war. He has this idea that if he can stop the fighting now the rebels will be more reasonable in the future."

"What do you think?"

He gives me a sly look.

"You know what I think. Anyway, get cracking on the search. You have a week. Maybe a smidge more."

"I didn't promise anything," I say, but he's already vanished.

I sit down and lean against a marble Buddha. Finish my Malediction and smoke another, waiting for the sun to go down.

Mr. Muninn is giving up? That's insane. But Samael is right. Muninn would rather talk than fight, and if he thinks he's losing, maybe that's all he has left. Now that Samael has asked me to help, if I don't do it and Muninn gives up, I'll be as guilty as the old man when Heaven slams closed forever.

I don't like this pressure right now. And I can't help but wonder if Samael was being completely straight with me. He can talk around the edges of things and draw me into trouble he doesn't want to face himself.

And there's the rest of my ridiculous life.

Give those women and yourself a break.

What the hell does that mean? I should walk away from everything? Become a monk, watch movies, grow old, and complain about the old days when we had real movies and not 3-D holograms? I hate 3-D almost as much as I hate soup.

This whole setup bugs me and I keep wondering why an angel was watching porn on Hollywood Boulevard forty years ago in the first place. Maybe the Pussycat had extra-good popcorn. Or maybe, like Samael said, it was because of some exotic friends.

Goddamn it. Why am I even thinking about this? I have Candy and Janet to worry about. Not getting knifed by Alessa. And who the hell is going to cook a turkey for me? Whoever said Hell is other people was wrong. Hell is other people *in your house.*

I'm so fucked.

I hang around Teddy's playground just smoking and thinking until sunset. Finally, bored with myself and all the bullshit swirling around me, I fire up the Hog and head back to L.A. The only stop I make is on a cliff overlooking the Pacific. I throw the road rage pistol far out into the water. Let the fish have it. They have more sense than some people, including me.

It's a normal, boring ride back home. Then around Studio City, traffic slows. I pull off onto the feeder road that runs a little above the freeway. But just south of where Lankershim Boulevard meets the 101 something weird is happening. I stop the bike and look down on the scene.

Two stretch limos are parked in the center breakdown lane. Twelve, maybe fifteen people mill around in front of the lead limo. They're all in tuxes and ball gowns like they were on their way to a million-dollar wedding. The strange part is that none of them seem that upset to be stuck on the side of the freeway with traffic blasting exhaust and road grit all over their precious formal wear. In fact, it looks like they're having a party, passing around joints and bottles of champagne. After a few minutes, one couple—a man and woman—herd the partiers together for some kind of announcement. I figure they're giving the others an ETA on tow trucks, so I start to drive off. Only, then something *really* strange happens.

The couple move among the other wedding guests, standing behind them, looping something around their faces and tying it at the back. It almost looks like they're putting blindfolds on everyone. When they've trussed up the last guest, the couple lines them up along the edge of the median facing the road.

Then, one by one, they run straight into traffic.

The first few do surprisingly well, making it across three lanes before the first one—a blonde in a powder-blue floor-length gown—flies rag-doll-like off the front bumper of a Ford F-150 truck. When she finally hits the road, she flops around looking boneless, like a fashionable squid. But none of the wedding guests see her go down and they head straight into the speeding cars.

By now, tires are squealing as drivers hit the brakes. Metal crunches on metal as cars and trucks rear-end each other. But the batshit-crazy suicide prom keeps running. A few—the lucky ones—end up in places where cars have stopped or crashed into each other. They make it through the maze of metal by feel. One guy in a paisley cummerbund makes it across four of the five lanes before a Coke truck plows into the back of a Prius just as he's squeezing past. The Prius lurches forward, crushing the cummerbund's left leg between its front bumper and the rear bumper of the car ahead of it. The cummerbund lies there screaming, trying to crawl across the final freeway lane, leaving a crimson line on the road as he goes. Farther up the road, another guy is tagged by a speeding Porsche. He spins like a wind-up toy, arms and legs flying out at funny angles. What fucking amazes me is that the rest of the group makes it across all five lanes. Yeah, a lot of them are limping on broken legs, or holding on to bloody arms, but the crazy fuckers are alive enough to stumble onto the opposite shoulder of the road.

But the weirdness continues. When the last runner makes it to safety, the couple that started the whole thing dashes onto the road and heads to the bodies of the two extremely dead runners who didn't make it. As they reach each body, they pat it down, taking something from the man's breast pocket and the woman's clutch bag. Then they run across the road to join their friends. By now, everyone has their blindfolds off, and in their bloody, ripped-to-shreds clothes and broken bones, they high-five each other and hug.

It's then I notice what I didn't earlier: that there's another limo parked on the shoulder where the runners were headed. They limp and crawl inside and when the limo is packed, it blasts off out of there. Drivers run after it, screaming or throwing things. Some of them have pens and scraps of paper, but the car is long gone before they can catch a license plate (which I'm positive doesn't matter anyway). And the other two limos?

Well, they explode, sending dazzling red fireballs into the

night sky and blowing out the windows of nearby cars.

Whoever those suicidal blue bloods were, they planned everything perfectly. What their plan was, I'm not 100 percent sure. But they were all thrilled to make it to the shoulder, like it was just some kind of demented bar bet. And the ones who didn't make it? There's a small *whoomph* from each body and then they're burning too. Maybe the couple weren't taking things from the corpses but putting things on them.

Whatever kicks they were looking for, I think they found them. A lot of solid citizens are going to have strange stories to tell their insurance companies tomorrow. I don't know if what I just saw was a suicide pact or a human sacrifice, but to be honest, it's not my damn business. L.A. has more weird religions and suicide cults than any place on Earth. By this time next week, we'll be hearing about how they all drank poisoned Hawaiian Punch and ascended to a passing starship carrying Sun Ra and Amelia Earhart. Have fun on Venus or wherever it is you're going, you dapper maniacs. I have to get home and worry about my turkey.

THE NEXT DAY, I wander around the house like a penned bull. Bumping into things. Shoving furniture this way and that, then back again to its original position. I look around the cupboards for glasses so people can drink, and promptly break two of them.

This isn't like me. I'm not in high school or getting ready for my first kiss on prom night. I clawed my way out of Hell. This shouldn't be such a big deal. But these are my friends. I want them to have a good time, and I want to show them that I'm all right. The Blue Fairy came down and made me into a real boy and everything is fine, or at least not a disaster. But the more I try to fix the place up, the more of a wreck it becomes. I feel clumsy and dull witted. I want to punch something. I want to go somewhere and have a dumb guy hit me so I can hit him back. I need my heart racing, not my brain.

And on top of everything else, I have to worry about maybe helping Samael find a porn-addicted angel while helping Abbot hustle a bunch of dead people out into the street.

It's closing time. You don't have to go home, but you can't be dead here.

I know it sounds easy, once you know where the haunting is taking place. Only, ghosts can get cranky when you serve them with an eviction notice. Things get thrown. Timid spooks suddenly grow fangs. People get cursed. I once saw a dead society lady—pink Chanel dress, cute little Jackie Kennedy pillbox hat—throw a three-hundred-pound exorcist out a bay window into a kiddie pool full of blood. The red stuff was a nice touch on her part. The exorcist survived the fall just fine, but when he looked around and thought he was covered in his own guts, he took off faster than Speed Racer. Next time I saw the guy, he had a van and was doing Hollywood spook tours for gawkers from Kansas and Wyoming. And he'd never looked happier. He was smart. Some people know when to call it quits. Other people have nowhere else to go, so we shake down hellbeasts and shades, trying to keep a roof over our heads and bologna in the fridge. The point of all this is that I have a lot on my mind. Enough that I forget to get the goddamn turkey.

THE PARTY IS set for eight P.M. My phone rings around six

forty-five. It's Janet. For a second my heart races. Maybe she's going to cancel. Maybe everyone is going to cancel and I can sit quietly and eat tarragon on my own.

I say, "Hi. How are you doing?"

"I'm about to collapse. Come outside and help me."

"Outside where?"

There's a banging on the front door, like someone's kicking it.

"Is that you?"

"No. It's Buffalo Bill's Wild West show. Get in here. My back is about to break."

The entrance to the flying saucer house is through an abandoned nail salon. I open the door and there's Janet, grinning underneath a couple of giant donut boxes and two or three large paper bags.

"Help," she squeaks like a mouse on a life raft. I grab the heavy bags and let her carry the donuts inside. She takes a quiet look around the living room and says, "Nice. Where's the kitchen?"

"Over there on the left."

She's wearing knee-high black boots and jeans with a high-buttoned dark blue pinstripe vest with no shirt underneath. The vest shows off her upper-arm tattoos, something I haven't seen clearly before because all her shirts have had elbow-length sleeves.

Janet heads in and I follow her, setting the bags on the center island. Once everything is down she takes a deep breath and smiles. Gives me a peck on the cheek.

She says, "I might have gotten a little carried away."

I peek inside the bags.

"What is all this?"

Janet sniffs the air.

"How's the turkey? I don't smell anything."

"Yeah," I say. "That . . ."

She starts unloading one of the bags on the counter.

"I had a feeling. I didn't get any warm food, but I stopped off and picked you up a charcuterie platter."

"Charcuterie?"

"Meat. Cheese. Ever had a deli platter?"

"Sure."

"It's like that, only it doesn't suck."

She lays out a spread of thinly sliced meats and cheeses. More kinds of cheese than I've ever seen before. Some are really soft. I poke a plastic package and she swats my finger.

"No poking. Now, show me what you got at the store."

I point to the pile of crap over at the far corner of a side counter. She frowns as she paws through the mess. Finally, she picks up a jar of olives and comes back.

"We can do something with these."

"What about the rest of it?"

"Is there a shovel around here?"

"I don't think so."

"Too bad. I was going to tell you to bury it in a shallow grave."

For the first time since this party thing started I laugh and feel a little more relaxed. She points to the Donut Universe boxes.

"Here. Make yourself useful by laying those out on plates. I don't suppose you picked up some dessert?"

I've got her now.

"I sure did. You're going to love this."

I take her to the freezer and fling the door open.

"Check that out, smarty."

She just stares. Doesn't say a word.

Then, "Is that a yule log?"

"Isn't it great? Everyone loves Santa. And there's reindeers too."

"Stark, it's the middle of summer. That thing is practically old enough to vote and buy beer. Speaking of which, do you have any?"

"Beer?"

She sighs.

"Don't tell me you forgot beer."

"I got bourbon, vodka, gin, rum, aquavit . . ."

"But no beer."

I cross my arms.

"Did I mention they were mean to me at the store?"

"I know, and I wish I'd been there to give you your teddy bear and some warm milk, but you still need beer."

"I'll go get some."

"Too late."

Janet goes to one of the bags and makes a few passes over the top like a magician—and pulls out two six-packs of pricey Japanese lager.

"Voilà," she says.

I peek at all the loot in the other and lean back on the counter.

"I fucked this up pretty good, didn't I?"

She looks sympathetic.

"When was the last time you threw a party?"

It takes me a while to work it out. Eleven years Downtown, then a year back in L.A., then another year dead.

"Twelve? Maybe thirteen years?"

"I bet you were a different person then. Before whatever happened that gave you all those scars."

"Yeah. Pretty different."

"You'll get the hang of parties again. They're pretty easy when you stop panicking, which you clearly are."

I think for another minute.

"I've been shot, you know."

She frowns.

"Several times," I say. "Stabbed too. Poisoned. Set on fire."

"Is that true?"

"That and worse."

She takes a step back.

"I'm sorry, but why are you telling me this right now?"

"Because none of it freaked me out as much as trying to do something normal like throw a party."

Janet comes over and hugs me.

"You're such an enormous pile of neuroses. Just stop and tell yourself it's all going to be fine. We have plenty of time to pull this off. Just take a breath."

I do it.

"Now let it out."

I do that too.

"Now kiss me."

"How's that going to relax me?"

She gets her face closer to mine.

"Not everything is about you."

I kiss her and she kisses me and we take our time about it.

Finally, she pulls back.

She says, "There. Feel better?"

"I do."

"You just needed your mind on something else for a minute."

"You should be a psychiatrist."

"I don't think psychiatrists are allowed to kiss their patients."

"Too bad for them."

She bumps me with her shoulder.

"Come on. Let's finish setting up."

"Sounds good."

"Also, you need to explain that shopping cart over there."

I glance at it.

"I stole it from the store."

"We could have used it to carry stuff in."

"Yeah. I didn't think of it."

"I mean, it's what carts are for."

"Now you're making me feel bad."

"Why don't we put it away somewhere?"

I push it into the bedroom and close the door.

"Good," she says. "Now let's finish getting everything ready."

Once we have the food unpacked, laying it out goes pretty fast. We finish a little before eight and I pour us each a shot of bourbon. Janet asks what movies I got for the party.

"*Con Air* and *His Girl Friday*."

She sips her drink and says, "*His Girl Friday* doesn't have much of a score, but *Con Air* is fun. Songs like 'Sweet Home Alabama' and 'A Summer Place.' Trevor Rabin did the other music. Do you know him? He played in Yes for a while. Scored a couple of dozen movies at least."

I shake my head.

"Never heard of the guy."

"He's a little mainstream for me, but he's good at his job. That's what I want to do someday. Score movies. Maybe have an orchestra play my music. I'm in a little band that plays live soundtracks for silent movies. You should come see us sometime."

I look at her. Did we ever talk about this stuff? I don't think so.

"Why didn't you ever tell me this before?"

She laughs a little.

"I did. Over sushi. You were so worried about eating the food right and being a regular guy that you didn't hear a word of it."

"I'm sorry."

"It's okay. But stop worrying about being a regular guy. I get hit on by fifty regular guys a day. I like you because you're not regular. I bet your friends do too."

"Listen," I say, and pull a fistful of hundreds out of my pocket. "You spent a lot of your own money on this stuff. I want to pay you back."

She laughs again and takes one bill.

"Thanks, Daddy Warbucks. I stole the donuts, so they were free. This will cover the rest."

At eight, people start arriving. Carlos and Ray first. Then Brigitte. Vidocq and Allegra arrive together, which is nice to see. Candy gets there last.

She says, "Alessa couldn't make it. She has a headache."

"Too bad," I tell her. The headache is almost certainly a lie, but it's just good enough to get us both off the hook so we don't have to spend an awkward evening together.

Candy takes one look at Janet and goes over to her.

"Hi. I'm Candy."

"Hi. Janet," she says, barely getting the words out. She lets one arm dangle by her side while she nervously crosses her other arm over her chest.

"How do you know Stark?"

"From Donut Universe. There's some donuts in the kitchen if you're hungry."

"Thanks. I am a little."

More people introduce themselves to Janet and she's the same way with all of them. Suddenly quiet and nervous. That's the last thing I expected. I want to go over and save her, but Candy puts her hand on my arm.

"I like your friend," she says.

"Yeah. She's nice. A musician."

"Really? What's she play?"

I think for a minute.

"I'm not sure."

"She'll probably tell you eventually."

"Yeah," I say, keeping an eye on Janet, who looks like she wants to be anywhere else.

"I'm hungry," says Candy. "I'm going to check out the food situation."

"Okay. I'll join you in a minute."

"Terrific. Oh. One thing."

"Yeah?"

She goes to the kitchen and comes back with a napkin.

Points to the side of her mouth.

"You've got a little lipstick right there."

Now I feel as awkward as Janet looks.

"Thanks."

Candy winks and goes to look for food.

"Anytime, tiger."

Eventually, everyone drifts into the kitchen. When he sees the spread, Carlos's eyes get wide. He samples a thin piece of meat from the charcuterie board and nods. The he looks at me accusingly.

"Where'd all this come from? You sure as hell didn't get it."

I point to Janet.

"It was all her."

Carlos spreads some brie on a cracker.

"It's a good thing you know people like her and me. Otherwise you'd just be eating gas station sandwiches the rest of your life."

"I like your tattoos," says Ray. "Is that owl a symbol from *Twin Peaks*?"

Janet nods shyly.

"Yeah. It's my favorite."

"Mine too."

She smiles a little.

"It's probably why I work in a donut shop."

Vidocq pours a glass of wine for himself and one for Allegra. It's good to see them being nice to each other again.

Candy shares a smile with Brigitte and points her drink at me.

"You look a little jumpy tonight. You got the food. Did

you remember the movies?"

"Right outside."

"Smart man."

While Candy gives me an "I'm going to screw with you all night until you tell me more about this other girl" look, Allegra says, "How are you feeling? Still remembering to take your meds?"

"No problems. But we should talk about things in the next few days."

"Anytime. Just come by the clinic."

"Thanks."

We talk for a few more minutes before heading into the living room. Janet comes in last with the charcuterie platter and sets it on the living room table. On the sofa, Candy sits on my right. Janet is on my left, pressed against my side. I haven't felt this uncomfortable since I first got to Hell and was a freak show attraction.

I turn on *Con Air* and things relax for a while. People laugh at the right places and sing along with some of the songs. The moment the movie is over, Janet is up on her feet and pouring drinks for everyone. She makes a whole circuit of the room before sitting down again, looking more like a deer caught in headlights than the wisecracker who kissed me in the kitchen. She takes my hand for a second and squeezes it. I squeeze hers back and she seems to relax a little before moving her hand back to her lap.

Everyone chats, laughs, and eats. Except for Brigitte.

"Are you feeling all right?" says Candy. "You're so quiet tonight."

Brigitte shrugs and tries to smile. Instead her face turns

red. She puts her hand over her mouth and tears form in her eyes. Everybody shuts up.

Candy leans over and puts a hand on Brigitte's knee.

"What's going on?"

Brigitte takes a breath and wipes her eyes, smearing her makeup a little. She takes a breath and says, "They're trying to deport me."

"What?"

"I was with my lawyer this afternoon. He isn't sure if I'll be able to stay in America."

I say, "What happened? Did your visa expire or something?"

It's hard for her to talk, so she sits for a minute. Then she says, "My visa is fine. It's me who's the problem. My past."

"What does that mean?" says Candy.

I have an idea.

"It's the movies, isn't it? Some asshole bureaucrat found out."

She nods a little.

Janet says, "What movies?"

Brigitte looks at her.

"I was a sex worker for a time before I came to America."

"They're going to throw you out because you did some porn?"

She nods.

Candy says, "How did they find out?"

Brigitte looks disgusted.

"A man. Of course a man. He was one of the producers of my *Queen Bullet* series. I wouldn't marry him. The next thing you know, I get a notice in the mail. At first I thought it was a bad joke."

"Who is he?" I say. "I'll go have a word with him. He'll take everything back and you'll be in the clear."

She shakes her head.

"It's too late for that. He sent them evidence."

"This is bullshit. You helped save this city."

"Saved L.A.? How?" says Janet.

"Back when I met you, when the High Plains Drifters were taking L.A. apart? Brigitte came here to fight them. She taught me how to kill them."

Janet looks at Brigitte. "And they don't care you did that?"

"Evidently not."

She gets a couple of tissues from her bag. Candy goes over and sits down next to her.

"We'll figure this out," she says. "There are other lawyers."

Something occurs to me.

"I'm supposed to see Thomas Abbot. He's connected to every Sub Rosa in the state. He'll know a way out of this."

"You think so?" Brigitte says.

"He has pull with the governor, senators, everyone. There's always a loophole with these things. He'll find it."

Brigitte looks a little brighter at the thought.

"That would be wonderful."

"Don't worry about anything. I'll see him tomorrow and we'll get all this worked out."

Brigitte gets up and hugs me.

"Thank you. I don't want to leave. Not like this."

"No one is leaving anywhere," says Candy. "Stark will fix it. Right?"

"Absolutely."

Allegra says, "Maybe we should put a hold on the second movie for a while. Give everyone a chance to have a drink. Calm down a little."

I get my bourbon. "That's a good idea."

People get up and head back to the kitchen. When she isn't pouring everybody drinks Janet stands with me, munching nervously on a jelly donut, not talking to anyone. I was right to bring up Abbot. People relax knowing I'll get him involved. The bastard better be as connected as he claims. Candy, Allegra, and Brigitte huddle together, talking. I can't blame them. Janet is too shy to go over and all the men are smart enough to know that it was one of us who caused the problems, so we should just shut up and stay out of the way for a while.

When she finishes her donut, Janet wipes her hands and says to me, "That thing you said before. What's a Sub Rosa?"

I look at her.

We've been dancing around this topic since we met. Janet is smart enough to know that the people who cleaned up the mess with the High Plains Drifters aren't regular civilians you see in the street. She knows there's something special about me and the other people in the room. That's probably one of the reasons she froze up when everyone started arriving.

I say, "It's not that big a deal. Sub Rosa are people who can do tricks. Hoodoo. Magic. Whatever you want to call it. Thomas Abbot runs the operation. Keeps the lid on things."

"Are you like that?" Janet says. "Can you do magic?"

I look across the room. Carlos is giving me a look. I give him one right back.

"For fuck's sake, she's not dumb. Tell her the truth."

I don't say anything for a second. I don't have to.

Carlos points to me with a cracker covered in brie.

"Of course he's magic, darling. Look at his fucking face. He should have been dead fifty times over. Hell. He *was* dead for a while."

Janet looks at me.

"Wait. You were dead?"

Now I really give Carlos a look.

He shrugs.

"He makes it sound worse than it was," I say finally.

"The shit I've seen this man do," continues Carlos. "Those Vegas hotel magician *pendejos*, they'd piss themselves."

"Okay. You're done now, thank you."

Janet smiles at me, a little uncertain.

"Is everybody here Sub Rosa?"

I point to Carlos.

"Everyone except him. He's a bartender."

"Fuck you, Criss Angel. You try pouring two a hundred drinks a night."

"Who else?" says Janet.

"I dabble," says Ray. "But I'm not really Sub Rosa."

"You still helped save my life."

"Yeah. You were a mess when I met you."

Janet says, "Who else?"

I take a pull from my drink.

"Candy is the only other official Sub Rosa. But pretty much everyone here can do something . . . unusual."

"What can you do?"

I think about it.

"Mostly, not die. I'm pretty good at that. Except for the one time I wasn't."

Janet looks around.

"This is amazing. All these people."

"There's actually a lot of people like us. Some not even human. But we don't like to spread it around, so don't go talking about this. Okay?"

Janet shakes her head. "Not a word. But can you show me one trick? Please?"

"Perhaps you should show her something," says Vidocq.

Carlos says, "Yeah. Don't leave her hanging. Do your shadow trick."

"Yes. Please. Do something with shadows."

I swirl my drink for a minute and it set down.

"Okay. I'm going to do this one thing and then we're not going to talk about it anymore. Agreed?"

"Agreed," says Janet.

I walk to a shadow at the far side of the room and step through it. Come out behind Janet.

"Boo."

She jumps like she saw a rattlesnake.

"How did you do that? That was cool."

"It's just hoodoo. Nothing special."

Candy calls over to us.

"What the hell, Stark? Are you showing off for your girlfriend?"

I point to Carlos and Vidocq.

"They made me do it."

Candy scowls at them too.

"You've done your little trick. Stop it and eat a donut.

We're discussing important things over here."

"Sorry."

Their huddle breaks up a few minutes later and they come over.

Brigitte says, "If you don't mind, I'm not really in the mood for a party. I think I'll go home now."

I nod to a shadow.

"Want me take you the short way?"

She shakes her head.

"No thank you. I need some time to think. Candy will take me back."

And that's pretty much the end of the party. It wasn't quite the disaster I was afraid it might be, but I keep feeling I could have done more to make things better for people. Maybe the turkey?

Everyone says their goodbyes. Hugs and kisses all around. Then everyone is gone. Except for Janet, who takes the charcuterie platter back into the kitchen.

I follow her in and lean against the counter. I'm pissed that someone is playing games with Brigitte's life, but I'm also 99 percent sure that Abbot can make it stop, so I'm not as tense as I would have been without the meeting tomorrow. I've had a few bourbons so I'm not feeling too bad at all. I watch as Janet piles some half-eaten food onto an empty plate. She catches me looking and smiles.

"What?" she says innocently.

I set the plate on the counter and pull her in close.

"I feel it's my duty as the host to tell you what a pretty girl you are."

This time when I go in to kiss her, she pulls back.

"Can we talk about something?" she says, looking serious.

"Of course. Did I do something tonight? I saw you get quiet when everyone got here."

"Yeah. I was just a little intimidated by meeting all of your friends at once. They're all so interesting and I just go to school and work in a donut shop."

"But you're a musician. And besides, even if you just worked in a donut shop, you're as good as anyone here."

"Thanks. I'll be better next time."

"You don't have to be better. Besides, I'm supposed to be the awkward one. You're moving in on my job."

She flashes me a quick smile, then looks serious again.

I say, "What else is going on?"

"I'm going to say something and you might not like me anymore, but I need to say it."

"Unless you're a cop with a bench warrant, I'm going to like you no matter what."

"Some people have had a problem with it, so I just wanted to get it out there."

"Just say whatever is on your mind."

She looks at the floor before she begins to speak.

"When you call me 'girl' or 'she' this or 'her' that, well, I wish you wouldn't. I'm not a her or she or any of that."

"I'm not quite sure what you mean."

"Do you know what non-binary is?"

"No. What?"

"The simplest way to explain it is I think gender is dumb," says Janet. "I don't feel like a man or a woman or, really, even know what those things are. It all seems so made-up. Does that make sense?"

"I guess so."

"When someone calls me 'she' or 'her' they're just talking about some expectation of who I am because of how I look."

"That part I understand. So, not a she or a he either."

"Right. Gender just doesn't mean anything to me," Janet says. "Yeah, I was assigned female at birth, but mentally, emotionally, it doesn't mean anything."

"Non-binary."

"You can also just say 'enby.'"

"Enby. Okay. If not 'she,' what should I call you then?"

"'They' and 'them' works. I know that can be confusing at first, but I promise you it stops being weird pretty quickly."

"'They' and 'them.' I can do that. I'm still not sure I understand it all a hundred percent, but I'll try."

"That's all that matters."

I think about it for a minute.

"I think I'm a guy. He. Is that all right?"

"Of course. That's what I was trying to say. If it fits, that's perfect for you. It means you're who you feel yourself to be and what makes you happy."

"That makes sense."

Janet looks sheepish and says, "You still like me?"

"Of course. Why wouldn't I? Words are words. Names are names. None of that is going to change how I feel about someone. We are who we are."

"Some people—especially guys—don't handle it well. They think pronouns are stupid or that I'm going through a phase. But I'm not."

"Those guys sound pretty stupid."

I remember one of my guards when I was in the arena

Downtown.

"There was someone I knew once. Very far away. They speak another language there, but I think that person might have been non-binary too. Only they didn't call it that. They called it . . ." And I bark a Hellion word.

Janet laughs.

"Holy shit. Is that a real word?"

"Absolutely."

"It sounds like you farted through your mouth."

"That's how it feels too."

"Where is this magical fart kingdom?"

Now I'm the one who's uncomfortable.

"I don't know if I'm ready to talk about that yet."

"Okay."

"I'm not trying to be mysterious or hide anything. It's just that it's kind of . . ."

"Traumatic?"

"That's one word for it."

"Then tell me when you're ready."

"I promise."

"So, I guess if you're going to tell me something in the future it means we're going to see each other again?"

"It looks that way."

They kiss me and I kiss them back. For a long time.

I'm into it and then a second later I'm out of it. I see Candy's face clearly.

Are you showing off for your girlfriend?

I must tense up, because Janet gives me a questioning look.

"You okay?"

"Yeah. Just something popped into my head."

"Your friend Candy?"

"Damn. You're a mind reader too."

"It didn't take a mind reader to see that there was some history with you two."

"A lot actually."

"And you still haven't worked out how things are between you."

"Yeah."

"Does that mean I should back off and just bring you fritters and coffee?"

"You should definitely not do that," I said firmly. "I was gone a long time and she moved in with someone, but it's not like we're officially broken up or anything. It's confusing."

"I think her living with a lover gives you a certain amount of leeway in who you see."

"I think so too."

"But you still feel guilty."

"A little. This is all new to me."

"That's okay. It just means you're a nice guy who needs to work some shit out."

"Probably a lot."

They put a hand on my cheek.

"It's okay. I didn't think anything was going to happen tonight. If you had any game at all you'd have fucked me on the Bavarian creams when we were putting them out."

"Now it seems so obvious."

They look around.

"You want some help cleaning this place up?"

"No. It just sort of happens on its own and I don't ask questions."

"That's a nice setup."

I follow Janet into the living room.

We stand by the door kissing for a few minutes and this time I don't think about anything but Janet. When we open the door to leave they get a wicked look on their face.

"You like old movies?"

"I've seen a few."

Janet says, "If you want to see me again, just whistle. You know how to whistle, don't you?"

I say, "You just put your lips together and blow."

Janet does a low wolf whistle and closes the door behind her. *Them.*

I go back into the kitchen and pour myself another drink.

It's dumb for me to keep feeling guilty about Candy. She made her choice. She has her life. I need to get one of my own.

For a minute, I think about going after Janet. But I don't. Not tonight. I'm not quite ready tonight. And Samael's words are rattling around in my head.

Give those women a break.

This is ridiculous. I fought in the arena. Everyone in Hell was afraid of Sandman Slim. So why am I so nervous every time I kiss Janet? Does everyone know about enby but me? Am I that much of a shut-in? I need to get out more. Talk to people I'm not there to kill.

I bring the bourbon into the living room and watch *Alien 3* while eating the yule log.

Janet was right. I should have fucked her out on the Bavarian creams.

Them, not her.

Fuck.

This is going to take some time.

IT TAKES MOST of the night, but I finish all of the movies and half of the bourbon, and make a pretty good dent in the yule log. I have a vague dream where Samael talks about an angel named Zadkiel or something and how I have a week to save the world, like I'm Superman and the Pinkertons all rolled into one.

When Abbot calls, I'm hungover and in the middle of a massive sugar crash. It's like the little plastic Santa and reindeer from the log crawled into my head and are now bashing the inside of my skull with sledgehammers trying to get out.

I grumble something into the phone when I pick it up.

"You're still in bed?" says Abbot. "It sounds like you had a rough night."

"I did. Want to hear about my love life?"

"I'd rather be eaten by wolves."

"That's an option I hadn't considered. I'm guessing from the call that you need me after all."

"That's right. Come by at five."

"What time is it now?"

"Noon."

"No promises."

"This is serious, Stark, so don't be late."

I practically crawl into the kitchen. Drink a glass of water and a shot of bourbon. Finish it all with a not-quite-stale Bavarian cream.

I sleep a little before cleaning up. The neat-freak elves or whoever will eventually do it for me, but I want most of this stuff out of here now. Between Janet, Candy, and Brigitte's situation, last night was too much of a mess and I don't want it hanging around.

When it hits four thirty I shove some papers into the pocket of my coat and get on the Hellion Hog. It would be faster to get to Abbot through a shadow, but a ride will clear my head.

Since his boat sank a while back, Abbot has moved into a storage shed on a vacant lot in Westwood. Sub Rosa aesthetics are funny that way. Regular blue bloods like to show off their money with giant estates and palm trees that reach the sky. Sub Rosa are the opposite. The more their place looks like a hovel, the classier they are. Abbot's place looks like a shack fucked an outhouse and they had an ugly baby. I park the Hog on the grassless lot and go inside the shed.

That's where the shakedown begins. Abbot, being the Augur of all the California Sub Rosa, has a security detail as thorough and humorless as a black ops hit squad. We're doing fine until they try to take my weapons.

"That's not going to happen," I tell the head of the detail, a solid chunk of muscled beef in a business suit.

"Then you can't come in," he says.

I shrug.

"Fine. Tell your boss I was here—and early. When he fires you, I'm sure you'll find a lucrative career in grocery store security."

I head for the door but before I leave I shout, "Bye, Abbot," at the top of my lungs.

Outside, I don't even bother starting the bike. I light a Malediction and about two seconds later, three of the security kielbasas come out.

The tall one says, "The Augur would like you to come to

the meeting."

"And I get to keep my stuff?"

"He says that you may keep your weapons."

"Can I finish my cigarette first?"

"He'd prefer it if you came right now."

"Are you sure? Because this brand is really hard to find."

The big guy takes a breath.

"Look, man. I'm just doing my job. Don't be a dick."

He's right. I am being a dick, and I was a dick when I drove to Malibu the other day. I've probably used up my dick allowance for the month. I pinch off the lit end of the Malediction and put the unsmoked half in the pack, then head back inside the shack, the security meat close behind. The big guy from outside leads me into a marbled office the size of Indiana. Abbot is sitting at a large partners desk. Even so, he looks ridiculous in the enormous space.

"I'm glad you found a place to park your solid-gold blimp," I say. "Wouldn't want to leave that kind of thing on the street."

Abbot looks around and makes a face.

"It is a bit much, isn't it?"

"Not if you're the pope."

"Luckily, it's just a loaner."

"From Superman, right? I thought the Fortress of Solitude was farther north."

"Come on. We just talked about this," says the security guy.

I hold up a hand. "You're right. I just have an allergy to stuff like this. You don't?"

He glances at Abbot.

"I'm happy to protect the Augur wherever he is."

"But you wouldn't live in a place like this."

He looks straight ahead but mumbles, "Hell no."

Abbot laces his fingers together.

"Are you finished critiquing the décor, Stark? I told you this was serious."

"Ghosts, right? I still don't know why you want me. Are you telling me that between you and the wind chime squad from San Francisco you couldn't clear the place out?"

"That's exactly what I'm telling you."

"Huh. That's actually interesting. Still, what do you want me for?"

"No conventional thaumaturgic systems we've tried have budged the spirits. It's time for you to use Hellion methods."

I lean back in the chair.

"Why not? I finished all my movies and ate most of the yule log."

His eyes narrow.

"You have a yule log?"

"Yeah."

The guard tsks under his breath.

Abbot says, "Stark, it's summer."

"That's what people keep telling me."

He waves the yule log away and says, "The spirits appear about an hour after sunset. They're vicious. We don't know how many civilians they've killed or how many are still alive and in hiding. We've cordoned off the neighborhood with wards and charms, but the spirits are powerful. They keep pushing at the edges of the boundary. I don't know how long we can contain them."

"Hold on. Did you say they've taken over a whole neighborhood?"

"Yes. All of Little Cairo is off-limits to civilians and Sub Rosa. It's too dangerous for anyone but professionals."

I sit up straight again.

"But like I said the other day, I'm not a professional. I've chased a few spooks in my time, but not a whole neighborhood full."

"Try," says Abbot. "If you can hurt them, we might be able to bring a normal exorcism crew to finish them off."

I try to think of an argument against it, but I can't. The leather bully aside, I haven't seen any action in weeks and I can't keep punching holes in walls. Maybe getting out and killing something that deserves it will do me some good.

"When's sundown?"

Abbot looks at his watch.

"In a little over two hours."

"So, three hours until the party gets started."

"Exactly."

"Do you have any Spiritus Dei lying around? That stuff will kill anything."

He looks as the security guy.

"Matthew, would you bring him some from storage?"

He moves off.

I yell, "Don't be stingy, Matthew. Get a thermos full. Neither one of us wants me to have to come back here soon."

"Is there anything else you'll need?" says Abbot.

"If I do I'll let you know. And before I forget, I want to give you something."

I pull a folder from my coat and drop it on his desk. Abbot

opens it and looks surprised.

"What is this?"

"Bearer bonds. They're supposed to be valuable."

He looks through the thick pile.

"These look worth several million dollars."

"Good. Now here's the deal. I don't want the Sub Rosa spending that on marble condos like this place. Spread it around. Give it to people who need it. Charities or whatever."

He looks at me.

"Do I want to know where you got these?"

"Do you want me to tell you that the people who had them are dead?"

"No."

"Then don't ask."

Abbot lays his hand on the folder.

"This will be put to good use. I promise you."

"Good. I don't really trust any of the Sub Rosa overlords, but I do you."

"Thank you."

"Two more things—does this mean I can stay in the flying saucer house for a while?"

He holds his hands up.

"Consider it yours. Stay for as long as you like."

"Good. 'Cause I don't have anywhere else to go. Now there's the second thing."

"What's that?"

"A friend of mine. She goes by the name Brigitte Bardo. She's Czech and someone is trying to have her deported. She doesn't want to go and I don't want her to either. What can you do about it?"

Abbot thinks for a minute.

"I have friends in immigration. I can have them look into it for you."

"Don't look into it. Fix it."

"It would help if I knew her real name."

I write her phone number down on the folder with the bearer bonds.

"Call her and find out. She's been Brigitte for as long as I've known her and that's good enough for me."

Matthew comes back with a plaid thermos. I put it in a coat pocket and get up.

"Thanks. If there isn't anything else, I have a yule log to finish before sundown."

"Try to eat some real food, Stark. That's why we replenish the supply. It would be embarrassing for everyone if you got scurvy."

"But funny," I say, heading out. "Admit it. It would be fucking hilarious."

Matthew follows me.

I get on the bike and he says, "We have a deal?"

"What deal is that?"

"You don't come back unless the Augur calls you."

I take out the half-smoked Malediction and light it.

"We have a deal."

"Good," he says. He waves his hand, trying to blow the smoke away.

"What the hell are those things? They smell like you set a donkey's ass on fire."

"You really want to know?"

"Yeah. In fact I do."

"You're not going to believe me."

"Try me."

"They're called Maledictions and they're very popular in Hell. The Devil gave them to me."

Matthew thinks about it for a minute.

"See, my first reaction was that you're being a dick again. Then I remembered all the stories about you."

"And you sort of believe me?"

"I sort of believe you."

I put out my hand and we shake.

"Matthew, try not to die any time soon. Hell is a garbage dump. It's getting worse and there's no end in sight. You and your friends, you don't want to go there."

"What makes you think I'm going to Hell?"

"That's the problem. Everybody, good or bad, gets dumped in Hell these days. So, check twice before crossing the street."

He looks at me.

"This is you being a dick again, isn't it?"

"I promise you it's not. I'm being a person right now. You, your family, your friends, don't die until we get some shit sorted out."

Matthew keeps looking at me, trying to figure out what the gag is. Finally, he waves me out of the lot.

"Don't come back soon."

I gun the Hog and take off, wondering if he believes me and knowing he probably doesn't. I hope he doesn't find out the truth the hard way.

Heading home, I pass the place where I saw the crazies run across the freeway. There isn't a sign of them anymore. Not a hubcap or a burn mark or a body. I still can't help wondering what it was all about. It looked like something you'd see Downtown. A punishment for jaywalkers—run through traffic for the next thousand years. But those people looked like they were doing it for kicks. If that's their idea of a good time, what do they do when they're depressed? Swim through hot tar?

CANDY CALLS LATER in the day.

The first thing out of her mouth is, "Did you talk to Abbot about Brigitte?"

"I just came from a meeting. He can fix things."

"You're sure?"

"Fixing things is what he does. How else do you think he keeps California in one piece? He'll know the people to lean on."

"I hope so," she says. Then, brighter, "Your party wasn't bad. Honestly, I was expecting kind of a disaster. The kitchen on fire. The living room flooded . . ."

"The roof caved in."

"Exactly. But you did all right."

"Janet helped with things."

"She seems nice."

"Yeah," I say, feeling my throat go a little dry. I don't want to talk to her about Janet right now. "Anyway, I'm glad you thought it was all right."

"I hope it doesn't sound terrible to say things like that. It's just that I worry about you on your own. You can get lost in your head and forget to come out for air."

"I'm fine. Really," I lie.

No one talks for a minute, then Candy says, "We should

get together. Just the two of us."

"For high tea and crumpets?"

"No, dummy. A date night. You and me."

"Alessa is all right with that?"

"She knows you and I still have a connection. We can talk about the details on our date."

Half of my brain wants to be happy but the other, more rational, part is wary of getting kicked around again. Still, I say, "That sounds great."

"Cool. What do you want to do?"

"Want to come on spook patrol with me? Abbot wants me to check out some ghosts in Little Cairo."

"Oh. An adventure," she says. "Just like old times."

"Just like old times."

"When?"

"Around seven thirty. Before the sun goes down and things get hopping."

"This is exciting. I've missed this."

"Me too. I'll come by the shop."

"See you then."

I go into the kitchen, pop one of my PTSD pills, and pour myself a bourbon, trying to drink away my nervousness.

It looks like I have a date.

I call Janet and we talk for a while. They want to get together, but I tell them I can't and about the job I'm doing for Abbot. But not about Candy. It's just all too complicated. I tell them we'll meet for coffee the next day and hang up. It feels like I'm experiencing some kind of slow-motion whiplash. First, I have a love life with Candy. Then she's with Alessa and I don't, so I don't have anything. Then I meet

Janet and it might be something. And now Candy wants to be alone with me. I haven't felt this popular since I was everyone's favorite punching bag Downtown. I hope I don't end up as bloody as I did then.

THE SUN IS starting to dip in the sky when me and Candy enter Little Cairo.

With its pyramid and Sphinx-shaped houses, the neighborhood was wildly popular with Hollywood types in the thirties and forties, but the Egyptian fad faded by the early fifties, so the fashionable set moved on. In the midfifties and sixties, Little Cairo became a hipster and hippie hangout. The place was a dump by the late sixties, which made it even more popular with the groovy people. Charlie Manson and the girls lived there for a while. Blasted on acid, Jim Morrison climbed to the very top of the Great Pyramid and promptly fell off. He didn't get a scratch. Little Cairo was remodeled in the ironic eighties and made a modest comeback. Now the neighborhood is mostly a curiosity stop for tourists, like Chinatown or snaky Lombard Street in San Francisco. Right now, Little Cairo looks like a drunk tornado stumbled through the place, tossing around cars and trees, peeling the skin off the pyramids and obelisks, and just generally shitting up the place quite nicely.

After a short look around, Candy says—in her best Bette Davis voice—"What a dump."

We stroll to the edge of the neighborhood and I do a little hoodoo to reveal the wards and charms shutting Little Cairo off from the rest of the city. Abbot's crew did a good job. There's nothing getting in or out of here, and from the outside, the place looks normal, except for the police barricades and quarantine signs.

Candy and I sit on a curb. I take out a Malediction and she hands me a flask. I drink and pass it to her before lighting up.

She leans back on her hands and looks around. "I was wrong before. It's not so bad here."

I almost choke on my cigarette.

"Are you kidding? This is where junkyards go to throw their junk."

She looks around.

"I've seen worse."

"Fresno?"

She bumps me with her shoulder.

"Hell, dumbass. Remember when you took me there?"

"Yeah. That was brilliant. I almost got you killed."

"You almost get everyone killed. It's one of your charms."

"Thanks, I guess?"

"What I mean is that even though things get scary, it's never boring with you."

I look at her.

"You're bored?"

"I didn't say that. I just mean that, with all of your problems, it's nice having you back in L.A. again."

"It's good being back."

"You never told me much about what happened when you were . . . gone."

"Dead. I was dead. You can say it."

"Right. You never talk about it."

I take a deep puff of the Malediction.

"I spent a year on the road doing nothing but killing every

single day. That's all there is to tell."

"I know there's more to it, but I won't press you."

"Thanks."

She turns and gives me a sly grin.

"Janet seems nice."

I knew this was coming. I drop my head onto my folded arms.

"She is. They is. They are."

"Interesting stutter you have there. Is there something you want to tell me?"

I look up as the light begins to fade. Hold out my hand and pull Candy to her feet. We stroll through Little Cairo's trash-covered streets.

I say, "It won't be long now."

"Until the spooks come out to play?"

"That's what I'm told."

We turn a corner and Little Cairo suddenly gets worse. Dried blood on the pavement. Overturned cars. Luggage and furniture thrown out of windows. Smart Abbot. He didn't tell me quite how bad it was so I'd have to see for myself. Smart, but an asshole.

Candy peeks in the windows of some houses as we walk. I wait in the street until she says, "Weird."

I go over to her and look into a wrecked living room.

Blood. Blood everywhere, especially on the walls.

"Abbot said the spooks had killed some people, but nothing like this."

I put a hand on Candy's back.

"You want to get out of here? You didn't sign up for mass murder."

"First off, no, I don't want to leave. But look beyond the blood. What else do you see?"

All I see is debris from destroyed rooms, but Candy shakes her head.

"Look in here. The dining room table and chairs aren't touched, but everything is ripped off the walls."

"Maybe the ghosts haven't gotten to the furniture yet."

"Maybe."

She goes around to the side of the house and says, "It's the same thing here. Pictures and mirrors are on the floor. The clothes are all shredded."

"The bed is a bloody mess."

"But it's not destroyed. And see that chair in the corner? It hasn't been touched."

"What do you think it means?"

"Let's look in another house."

We stick our heads in through the shattered windows in a couple more houses. They're about the same as the first ones. Some things utterly destroyed, but others untouched.

"See the connection?" says Candy.

"I think so. Beyond the blood, everything that's destroyed is personal stuff. Photos. Clothes. Mementos."

"Someone is very angry."

Shadows are getting long in the street.

"We'll know soon enough, I guess."

We move back out into the street, walking around piles of ripped books, smashed dishes, and flipped cars.

"She," Candy says. "They. Them. Sounds like someone is having pronoun problems."

I scratch my ear.

"Have you ever heard of non-binary?"

She squeezes my hand and lets go.

"God, Stark. You're such a babe in the woods."

"This is so humiliating."

"What is? Meeting someone who's different?"

"No. My whole ridiculous life. I know everything about monsters but nothing about people."

Candy hugs me.

"It's going to be okay. It's funny how things change. Alessa and I have been together for a while now. You and me even longer. In a way."

"I'm not sure what you're getting at."

She lets me go and we walk some more.

"I mean, with the way things are with Alessa and me, if you wanted, you know, to get together with Janet, it's okay with me."

I stop and look at her.

"I'm not running off with Janet."

"What makes you so sure?"

"It's just not going to happen."

"Have you kissed her?"

I hesitate.

Candy nods, knowing. Keeps walking.

"I thought so. I have to admit that I was a little jealous seeing her pressed up against you at the party."

"It's nothing serious."

"Stark, let me be clear: I felt jealous, but under the circumstances I don't have any right to be."

I put my hands in my pockets. I don't want to be talking about any of this. So I say, "People feel what they feel. I know that much."

Candy stops and brushes a fly off my coat.

"I just want you to know that I love you and want you to be happy."

"I'm happy right now here with you."

"You don't look it."

"Happy-ish. Can we leave it at that?"

"Sure."

"Good. Because ghosts are going to show up in a few minutes and I don't want some dead psychos eavesdropping on my love life."

"Maybe they're not psychos. Maybe they're just, I don't know. Sad and acting out."

"Then I don't want to see them truly pissed."

With the sun gone, a couple of streetlights flicker on as Candy steps in front of me. When I bump into her she puts her hands around my neck and kisses me like she means it.

When it's finished I say, "What was that for?"

"I don't know. For taking me on an adventure? I love Alessa and the shop, but sometimes I miss fucking shit up."

"I'm always here for that."

We sit on a curb again and Candy takes my hand. We stay like that for a few confusing minutes.

Something moves in the air.

I say, "Did you hear that?"

"No. What?"

"I don't know. Let's get behind some cover."

There's a wrecked armoire leaning against a palm tree nearby. We get behind them.

The street is dim, lit only by the couple of functioning

streetlights.

Halfway down the block, a glowing pinpoint spins in the air. Soon it becomes a spectral rip that hovers just above the street. The rip expands, turning bright and hot, running down onto the pavement like molten glass. When the rip has dilated to the width of a bus, Little Cairo's dead explode out in a mad, furious rush.

There are a lot of different kinds of ghosts. Some are hard to tell from regular people until they pull their heads off or vomit maggots all over you. If those things happen you know you're dealing with a ghost—or possibly a parole officer. Anyway, these ghosts aren't the subtle kind. They're the kind that are dead and know it, barely here at all. Very pale and a little transparent, like people-shaped fog. But don't let that fool you. These see-through fucks have destroyed a dozen streets and emptied a whole neighborhood. Don't waste your pity on them. Save it for the poor assholes who are going to come home and find their secret porn stashes thrown all over the house. Then hubby or wifey gets to explain to the other what pony play is.

I throw a glamour on Candy and me. It makes us fuzzy and indistinct, kind of like the foggy ghosts. We follow the running horde to the edge of Little Cairo, where they slam headfirst into the wards. Some linger, clawing and gnawing at the barrier, while others run through the streets to continue wrecking the place.

Two even stranger things happen. We both notice an odd rhythmic murmuring coming from the direction of the spooks. Neither one of us can figure out what it is until Candy says, "It's singing."

I stare at the ghosts. None of their mouths are moving.

"It's not them, but there's definitely a sound coming from somewhere."

The other strange thing is even stranger.

One of the last ghosts is a tall black woman in seventies Stevie Nicks drag. Long flowing faux-Gypsy dress and beads. As she exits the spectral rip, she casually raises her hand in the air. Stars are visible above the dim streets. As her hand rakes over them they tremble, like I'm looking at the stars reflected in water.

I say to Candy, "Did you just see that?"

"Yes. What the hell was it?"

"I don't know."

I put a hand up to tell Candy to stay put and creep out into the street.

"Stark!" she whispers.

I look back and put a finger to my lips to quiet her. With my head down, I trot slowly to the edge of the spook parade. The glamour must be working because they don't do anything.

The ghosts who left the barrier spread out across Little Cairo, disappearing through walls and shattered windows. In no time, the street is full of the sounds of things breaking, being pulled off walls and out of closets and systematically destroyed. One house at the end of the block is just about gone. Doors off. Windows ripped out. Part of the roof collapsed. It doesn't look to me like there's much left to destroy there and the spooks seem to agree. Instead of going inside, a few of them get together and flip a Prius sitting in the driveway. These fuckers are stronger than I expected.

Candy creeps up beside me and holds on to my arm. Together, we follow several ghosts to different houses. It looks like she was right: one or two spooks run inside the house and tear the place apart—but selectively. Heading straight for bloodstained photos, paintings, small things on bedside tables, but leaving most of the other furniture alone.

"See? I told you," Candy says.

I nod and put up my hand again for her to be quiet.

When I look back, there's one lone ghost in the middle of the street by himself. He's short but handsome. Like Tom Cruise good-looking. He doesn't run like a maniac, just stands there trembling like he's cold or having some kind of seizure. A minute later he stumbles forward right under a streetlight and I get a good look at him.

"Holy shit. I know that guy."

"Is he a friend?"

"I mean, I don't know him know him, but I know who he is. He's Christopher Stein. An actor in the fifties and sixties. Mostly did B movies, but he was in a couple of big ones at the end. He was being groomed for the big time, but something happened and he dropped off the map."

"This is a hell of a place for a matinee idol to end up."

"He looks lost. Like he's not sure where he is."

"I don't know," says Candy. "That shaking could mean there's something wrong with him, but it could also just be rage. I've seen Jades get paralyzed like that before they change."

Soon, Stein moves off. He's shaking less now but still clearly tense. At the end of the block he turns left. Me and Candy follow him. He walks another half block before stopping in front of a house that looks like a half-excavated Egyptian royal tomb three stories tall. It's one of the few untouched houses on the street. Maybe it was just waiting for someone with a connection to it to come home.

Sure enough, after staring at the place for a minute or two, he stumbles forward, passes through a tall window, and disappears inside the place. I start after him. Candy stops me.

She says, "Where are you going?"

"After Stein. I get the feeling he's new here. Maybe if I can see what he wants it will give us a clue to what's really going on here."

"Why bother? Why not just do some magic and get rid of the ghosts right now?"

"I just want to see . . ."

"Oh my god. It's because he's a movie star. You want to hang around with a dead movie star."

"I just want to see what he does."

"You're such a terrible liar. Go on and follow your drive-in boyfriend. I'll stay here and shout if anything weird happens. Well, weirder."

"Thanks. I'll be back in just a minute."

I step inside the house through a shadow. Candy is half-right. I am a little curious about what a has-been star is looking for. Does he miss his Emmy or that tux he wore to the Oscars that one time? But it's funny when I get inside. The house doesn't look like anywhere I imagine an actor would live in, even a B one. It's just an ordinary house. There's nothing inside remotely movie related. No set photos or souvenirs. No scripts. It's just, well, a house. Boring, but decent furniture. A nice TV. There are some books around, but they're all just cheesy bestsellers. Also, there's no blood anywhere. Who lived here and what's Stein looking for?

On the other hand, maybe Candy is right. Maybe I'm getting distracted because I know who this guy is. Still, maybe if I can figure out what one spook wants I can figure out what they all want and send them home without getting rough.

Speaking of rough, Stein finally gets down to it.

The shaking stops and he goes right for the walls. Like the ghosts in all the other houses, he grabs paintings, hangings, and photos off the paneling, rips them up, and throws them in every direction. He knocks everything off a mantelpiece above a fake fireplace and crushes it under his expensive ghost shoes. The glamour continues to do its job. He either can't see me or he's too focused to care. When Stein starts upstairs, I follow him.

It's the same act there. He tears the bedroom apart, concentrating a lot on the bed itself. From underneath, he pulls out a chest full of cuffs, leather collars, and floggers. That's something, at least. Maybe he used to party here and, for some reason, has bad memories. I keep trying to remember how Stein died, but I don't have a clue.

When he's done with the bondage gear, he goes straight to the closet. It's all women's clothes. I get the feeling he must have known whoever lived here because he rips everything off the hangers and shreds it.

I haven't seen many angry ghosts in my time, but this is starting to get a little tedious. I mean, every spook here has the same act. Get in. Run for the barriers. Fail. Shit the place up. After that, well, I don't know about that yet. I haven't seen what they do when there's nothing left to break. With luck they go out the way they came, but from the sounds echoing in from the street, I don't think that's how this works.

After ten minutes of watching Stein go nuts, I'm fed up and decide to head out. There's nothing more to learn here. Except, he's ignored me enough that I get sloppy leaving the bedroom and step on some glass. The moment he hears it, he looks straight at me. I remember how these dead assholes can turn over cars, so no more fucking around. Sorry, pal. Whatever it is you're pissed about, you're not going to take it out on me.

The moment he steps in my direction, I bark some Hellion hoodoo.

And exactly nothing happens to him.

I try it again, turning up the volume a little. Still nothing. When he rushes me, I pull out some arena battle hoodoo and blast him right in the face. The whole house shakes. It doesn't even slow him, and the next thing I know, I'm sailing out of a second-floor window with Stein looking down at me as I fall.

Luckily, there's a small patch of lawn out front and, like every other lawn in L.A., it's overwatered, so the ground is a little soft. Still, it's a two-floor fall and I'm seeing stars and little chirping cartoon birds when I hit. Candy rushes over and helps me up.

She says, "What happened?"

"I laughed at his baby photos and he didn't take it well."

"Dummy."

The other bad part about being tossed out of a second story by one dead prick is that other dead pricks tend to notice. The moment I'm on my feet, every specter, wraith, and phantasm on the street starts in our direction. Then Stein slides through the front wall of the tomb house. My hoodoo didn't do much against him, but I wasn't going full out before. Now I'm fed up with these bastards, so I pull out my Colt and start blasting with bullets dipped in Spiritus Dei. The slugs take down every ghost they hit, but I don't have enough bullets for them all. By the time the Colt is empty, there must be a hundred dead things rushing at us. I have one last trick I can think of. Something that always works.

I conjure a ring of flame around Candy and me and explode it out like a fire bomb in all directions. Buildings shake. Windows blow out and palm trees catch fire. Once again, exactly zero happens to the ghosts bearing down on us.

"Do something! Something good!" shouts Candy.

But I'm out of ideas. The dead are practically on top of us.

From down the street comes the thud of car doors opening and closing, then the sound of squealing tires. The ghosts turn away from us and toward a Chevy SUV shooting down the street straight at us. Some jackasses who managed to hide from the spooks decide to make a break for it while the ghosts are distracted by me and Candy. It's not a bad plan, but they're not handling it well.

At the last minute, the Chevy tries to steer around the spook mob—which is now running for it—but the dunce behind the wheel cuts the top-heavy SUV too hard. It runs up onto the curb, bounces a few times, and almost turns over before the driver steers too hard the other way. The Chevy fishtails for a few yards, the driver hits the brakes at exactly the wrong moment, and the SUV tips over on its side, crashing into the street.

I grab Candy and take her through a shadow into the flying saucer house. Then, before she can say something, I go back to Little Cairo.

I have to give the driver and passenger credit; they're not giving up. The driver's-side door, which is now pointing straight up, opens in a flash and a man climbs out. Hands appear a second later from inside the SUV and he reaches down to pull another guy out. But it's no use. They're completely surrounded by a mass of grasping spectral hands.

My head is still a little funny, so some of the scene plays out like it's far away. Like I'm watching a movie. I start forward, but I'm dizzy, so I'm too slow and all I can do is wonder, if the first guy didn't stop to help the second one, would he have gotten away? Because now the ghost mob is all over them. That weird singing sound that follows them is louder than ever as they rip the two SUV guys to pieces. I can barely hear their screams. And there's nothing I can do to help them. I've seen enough stuff like this in my life that I don't want to see it again. I turn away.

And walk right into Chris Stein, who rushes me like a goddamn black-eyed banshee. I jump into a shadow and stumble out into the living room.

Candy stands nervously by the sofa.

"Were you able to help them?"

"The two guys?" It's our first night together in I don't know how long. What should I tell her? Do I want to leave her remembering this night as crazy excitement or blood sacrifice and carnage? Is that what I want her to always think of me? I hate lying, but I'll admit it, I'm scared of what the truth will do her. And us.

"They're okay. I got to them just in time."

"Oh good," she says, and drops onto the sofa. I sit down next to her and she rests her head on my shoulder, breathing hard.

She mumbles, "Well, that wasn't a regular night home."

I look at her.

"Please don't tell Alessa. She'll stab me in my sleep."

Candy reaches for the bourbon on the table. Takes a couple of good pulls before saying, "Are you kidding? She'd be just as mad at me. How's your head? That was a pretty good fall."

"I'm still a little dizzy and my shoulder is sore, but okay."

She hands me the bourbon.

I take a pull and say, "That haunting back there. It didn't feel right."

"What do you mean?"

"Like it wasn't an ordinary haunt. Those weren't regular ghosts. It didn't feel at all like the hoodoo I'm used to. Spells and hexes. It felt older. Weirder. Almost like . . ."

"Like what?"

"Angelic stuff."

"But you're part angel. Shouldn't you have been able to hurt them?"

"You'd think so."

Candy gets up and heads to the kitchen.

"Almost dying makes me hungry. How about you?"

"Don't you have to be getting back soon?"

She stops in the kitchen door and turns.

"Didn't I tell you? I'm spending the night. That okay with you?"

I look at her, waiting for a joke. But she's serious.

"More than okay."

"Cool. I'm going to make a sandwich."

"I'll be in in a minute."

"What are you going to do?"

"I'm still thinking about Stein."

"He did kick your ass pretty thoroughly."

"I just have this feeling that if I can figure him out, I'll figure out the whole haunting."

"You do that, Gandalf. I'm going to roast beef myself. I'll get you some too."

I take out my phone and call Abbot. He answers on the second ring.

"Stark. How did things go?"

"On a scale of one to ten, about a negative nine."

"What happened?"

"It was all really interesting for a while and then one of them threw me out of a second-floor window."

"What? Are you all right? Do you need a doctor?"

"I'm fine. I landed on my head. By the way, nice move not mentioning that they're bloodthirsty murder freaks."

"You saw the bloodstains, I take it?"

I lower my voice so Candy won't hear.

"I saw them rip two people apart."

He doesn't say anything for a second.

Finally, "Tell me everything."

"I think your people missed some civilians. Maybe a lot of them."

"The crews were very thorough."

"If I'm right, people are going run out of food and water and decide to make a run for it. These guys didn't get far."

Abbot says, "You're sure they're dead?"

"They're in about fifty pieces all over someone's lawn, so yeah, I'm reasonably sure."

"This is awful. I'll send a crew in the morning to identify the bodies."

I rub my sore shoulder.

"I should have known that if all your people couldn't clear out that bunch, it wasn't going to be easy. Maybe getting tossed out a window is what I deserved."

"Did you learn anything about them? Did you see any weakness?"

"Not so much a weakness as a familiar face. You ever hear of an old movie star named Christopher Stein?"

"No. Why is he important?"

"I'm not sure he is. But nothing anyone has tried on them has worked. I thought that maybe going after one of them would let me figure out the rest."

"How can I help?"

"Stein was murdered. I don't remember how or when, but I bet it was in Little Cairo. Maybe if I knew more about his case it would help. Can you get me his police report?"

"Of course. You'll have it first thing in the morning. Is there anything else?"

"Nothing now, but keep that doctor handy. I have a feeling this isn't the last window I'm going to fall out of before this is over."

"I'll make some calls about Stein's report. Take my advice and go easy tonight."

I look at Candy in the kitchen.

"Good advice. Talk to you later."

I go into the kitchen and Candy hands me a sandwich. While I'm eating it, she wanders around the apartment. I forgot that she hasn't spent much time here. I eat and let her roam. After a couple of minutes she calls to me.

"Stark."

"What?"

"Why is there a shopping cart in your bedroom?"

"I stole it."

"You're quite the outlaw these days."

"I get around."

A minute later she comes back into the kitchen. She's naked.

"Are you done with that sandwich or what?"

I drop it on the counter and we race to the bedroom. She wins because I bump into the shopping cart. When we're both inside, she pushes me onto the bed and climbs on top.

"If you and Janet haven't done anything, I'm guessing it's been over a year since you've been in a position like this. Think you still remember how this works?"

"You might have to show me."

"That was pretty much my plan. Now shut up and kiss me."

I do. We spend the rest of the night breaking a lot of the furniture. She even leaps into the shopping cart and I run her around the apartment. Back in the bedroom, she jumps from the cart and lands on the pillows. We knock over the splintered furniture and punch holes in the walls until almost dawn. By the time we go to sleep we're as wrecked as the room. I haven't been this happy in years.

CANDY IS ALREADY dressed when I wake up. She shakes me gently.

"I have to go. If you're too tired, I can call a cab."

I get up and pull on my pants and boots.

"Of course not. I can take you home."

She sits on the edge of the bed as I dress. Her heart rate is up a little. She's nervous. Wants to get home, but doesn't want to be a jerk about it.

As I pull on my shirt and coat she says, "Last night was a lot of fun."

"Even almost getting eaten by ghosts?"

She smiles.

"Even that."

I don't look at her when I speak.

"Are you saying 'see you later' or is this 'goodbye and never going to happen again'?"

She comes over and hugs me.

"Never goodbye. And tonight will happen again. But not for a while. Okay? Alessa and I are still working some things out."

It's not exactly the answer I was hoping for, but it's not bad.

"Sure. I'm glad she was willing to go along with it at all."

"It took a lot of talking. A lot of convincing that I wasn't running off to be some guy's straight wife, popping out babies and doing the dishes."

I frown.

"Is that what she thinks I want from you?"

Candy shrugs.

"I don't know. You're a guy and a dangerous one. She

doesn't have the highest opinion of men in the first place."

I hold my hand out to her.

"I'll wait. As long as it takes."

Candy smiles as I pull her into a shadow.

We come out in the alley next to Max Overdrive. She kisses me on the cheek before heading inside.

"I'll call you," she says.

"Great, but can I ask you for a favor? Some of Chris Stein's movies? Especially *Murdering Mouth*? That was his last A-list role."

"Give me a minute."

Candy is in the shop for a while. Stein was never big enough that he'd have his own section inside, so she'll have to paw through Westerns, noir, and a few other genres. I'm tempted to light a Malediction, but after I take the pack out, I shove it back in my pocket. I don't have too many left and I don't want to have to go Downtown and scrounge more in the middle of a war zone.

Last night was great, but no matter how much I wanted things to be different, I knew that Candy would leave in the morning. I just wish we'd had a chance for a cup of coffee or something. A moment of calm together before she took off. But beggars can't be choosers, and sometimes, they're lucky they even get to be beggars. For now, I'll go along with the rules and timetables that whatever it is we're doing requires.

Instead of a cigarette, I take out one of the pills Allegra gave me and dry-swallow it. Candy comes out of the shop and hands me a plastic bag.

"Did you take a pill just then?"

"A Tic Tac," I say.

She sniffs.

"Doesn't smell like one."

I look in the bag.

"These my movies?"

"Yep. Keep them as long as you like. No one has checked any of them out in at least a year."

"Thanks. I think these will be a help."

"I hope so."

Candy looks back at the shop, then back at me, and makes a small, uncomfortable face.

She says, "I should probably go."

"I'll see you around."

She kisses me gently on the lips.

"I'll call you."

She heads back inside the shop, giving me a small wave before she closes the door.

The rat carcass I found under the Hellion Hog is still lying on the ground where I kicked it. Now I feel a sudden kinship with the little bastard. He just wanted to check out the bike and now he's as dried out as beef jerky. I find a piece of paper, pick him up by the tail, and drop him on the metal dumpster lid. I'm tempted to toss him inside and burn it. Give him a real Viking funeral. But I don't want anyone calling the fire department and interrupting this tender moment, just me and my rodent pal. So, I just whisper a little hoodoo and he bursts into flames where he lies.

Adios, little rat. Enjoy Valhalla. Get drunk. Break some furniture with another cute rat. Shit changes. Is gone. Maybe comes back. But it's never the same. Try to remember and appreciate everything. Even the shitty parts.

"What the fuck are you doing, Stark?"

I look up and there's Kasabian with a bag of garbage in his metal hand.

"Oh. Hi. I'm burning a rat."

He blinks once.

"Of course you are. Silly question. Get out of the way. Sane people have work to do."

He starts to brush the smoldering carcass off the lid and I put out a hand to stop him.

"Hey. That's a friend of mine."

"Then can you and your friend be anywhere else right now? You're freaking me out a little."

"Sorry."

I whisper some hoodoo and the rat's body cools. Turns to ashes and blows away. I'm a little sorry to see him go. Kasabian tosses his garbage bag in the dumpster.

"Are you drunk?" he says.

"Not at all."

He walks away down the alley.

"Then go home and get drunk. And when you wake up, call Allegra. You need medical attention."

"I'm already seeing Allegra."

"Whatever pills she's giving you, you need more."

Before he goes inside something pops into my brain. I don't exactly know why, but it seems important, so I say it.

"I'm sorry I cut your head off."

He stops.

"What did you say?"

"Really. I'm sorry I cut it off."

"Is . . . is that supposed to make up for anything?"

"No."

"Good, because it doesn't."

"To be fair, you did shoot me."

"You scared me. Kind of like you're doing now."

"Okay. But don't shoot this time."

"Fine. But maybe don't be lurking over there when I come back out."

"Fair enough."

"Goodbye, Stark."

"See you around."

"See, every time you say that it sounds like a threat."

"It's not."

"And yet."

He goes inside and slams the door.

I get out my phone and call Janet. When they—good for me, I got it right this time—don't answer I leave a message, then step through a shadow and come out across town by Vidocq's apartment. I knock on the door a few times and when he sees me, he ushers me in like the fancy Frenchman he was two hundred years ago. It's always good to see him at moments like this. Vidocq is the closest thing to a real father I've ever had.

The apartment is a carefully arranged mass of chaos. Vidocq is an old-school alchemist and every flat surface is covered with books or strange lab equipment. Bunsen burners. Alembics. Long swirly glass tubes full of a green, viscous something. I swear that when I get close, the bubbles are little eyes that blink at me.

When I go to the kitchen he's poured two cups of coffee. He looks at me and holds up a pint bottle of whiskey.

"Isn't it a little early?" I say.

"Quite."

"Good point. Fill 'er up."

We sit in the living room and drink our spiked brew for a while.

Vidocq says, "Is this just a social call or is there something special on your mind?"

"Both, I guess. I've had so many questions since I've been back. Like, the first time I almost died, my angel half and human half split. I was two people for a while. This time, though, I was just fucking dead and no sign of any angels. What do you think it means?"

Vidocq gets up and brings back an ancient book that smells like wood smoke, old blood, and mildew. He opens it to a dog-eared page and points to a hand-drawn image of an anvil. It's surrounded on both sides with alchemical symbols and a long set of instructions written in Latin.

"Very pretty. What am I looking at?"

"The formula for Samvari steel. It's an obscure substance even among those who practice the craft. It's said that the formula comes from another plane of existence and was payment for some great, dark favor. What it was, I don't know. What I do know is this. The steel, once made into a weapon, had the power to kill both your human and angelic halves."

"But I'm back now. Shouldn't there be an angel me too?"

Vidocq runs his finger along a line of Latin and reads it out loud. It's all gibberish to me.

He says, "I suspect that your unusual death and peculiar resurrection have fused your dual nature into something inseparable."

"Is that good?"

"I have no idea."

"Where would a third-rate creep like Audsley Ishii get something like that?"

"A very good question and one, like your previous one, I can't answer."

I take a long sip of the coffee. It burns just right going down.

"All right. Let's forget the knife. What about my body?"

"You're referring to your left arm, I assume?"

I hold it up in the light streaming from a window.

"Right. It's my regular arm again. Not my Kissi prosthetic. When I was almost dead and you burned me, my body came apart and put itself back together. I was healed."

"A fortunate outcome if you ask me."

"I'm not complaining. But if the fire fixed my body, why not my scars? I still look like I went through a woodchipper."

"That's easy," says Vidocq. "Should I get another book for you?"

"Please don't."

"Very well. You are a Nephilim. The last of your kind. We don't have any trustworthy descriptions of previous Nephilim. We have no idea if their complexions were smooth . . ."

"Or scarred like mine."

"Exactly. It's my theory that you haven't really received the scars over the years, but that your scars are simply part of your divine nature. Like a sculptor chips away stone to reveal a face beneath, so your various injuries removed the flesh that obscured your true self. I'm sure this process will continue and that you'll acquire new scars in the future."

"I don't like the sound of that."

He sips his coffee and shakes his head. "And I don't care for the immortality with which I've cursed myself. All we can do is carry our burdens with grace."

When we finish our coffee, Vidocq goes to get us more.

I say, "It was nice seeing you and Allegra getting along so well at the party."

"Yes. Things are back to much the way they were before our troubles. However, she still refuses to live here with me again."

"Love is the worst."

"How are things with you and Candy?"

I stare into my coffee cup.

"It's complicated. We spent last night together, but I'm not counting on it happening again. At least any time soon."

"Still. Her feelings for you remain strong. She's loved you through life and death and now life again. That's more than most men get."

"I know you're right. But I just want things simple. The way they used to be."

Vidocq sits back and crosses his arms. The idea gets to him too.

Finally he says, "Nothing is ever the same the second time. It might be worse. It might be better. But it's never the same. And it's never as simple or innocent as it once might have seemed."

I look at him hard.

"I thought you French bastards were supposed to be romantics."

"You must be thinking of someone else."

"There's no secret formula for turning back time with people? Bring her enchanted posies that sing show tunes? Magic escargots that pick lottery numbers?"

He laughs a little.

"Trust me. I've looked for tricks in all my books and travels. Nothing can truly fix a fractured romance. And love potions just drive people mad."

"I was afraid of that."

He thinks for a minute.

"I liked your lady friend, Janet."

"It's nice, but a whole other kind of complicated. I mean she's great. And she gets me free donuts."

"At least there are some compensations."

"It's nice hanging out like this. You should come to my place. Just you and me. We'll drown our sorrows in movies and booze."

"I'd like that."

I say, "To whatever the hell it is we're doing with our lives."

We clink mugs. Then I remember what brought me here.

"What do you know about exorcisms?"

CHRIS STEIN'S POLICE report is sitting on the living room table when I get back. The folder is old and thick. There are coffee stains and some smeared inky fingerprints on the front. When I open it, the file smells musty. You can tell no one has so much as touched it in decades. I open it and start spreading papers on the table. There are interview transcripts. Medical reports. Police reports about the original call. Detective reports about local resident interviews. Hair and blood samples An autopsy report diagrams the exact angle at which Stein was cut in half.

Now I remember why his murder stuck in my brain. It wasn't so much that he was a hot young actor cut down in his prime, it was that he was the punk-era Black Dahlia. Sliced in two and left in a small long-gone park in West Hollywood. I go straight to the crime scene photos.

They're strange. I've seen plenty of human and inhuman bodies ripped apart and cut up, but seldom so neatly. The cut is so straight it's like someone put him on a worktable and pushed him sideways into a giant circular saw. But that can't be what happened. The flesh around the wound wasn't ripped or damaged the way a saw blade would do to it. In fact, the edges of the wound, Stein's internal organs, and his spine were smooth. Cauterized. Like someone cut him up with one of those hot wires you use on Styrofoam. Only I never heard of a foam cutter that goes through bone. From the reports, it sounds like a lot of people thought it was some kind of cult killing. Maybe he was trying to get out and they wanted to send a message to the other members not to run. A couple of detectives decided it was Satanic ritual abuse, an idea that would catch on big a few years later.

In the photos, Stein's right hand is balled into a fist. When I look closer, I realize that he's holding something. I drop the photo and paw through the other papers fast. Inside a plastic envelope I find it. A note. It was crumpled in Stein's hand, but someone smoothed it out. The night Stein was murdered it rained, so most of the ink is illegible. But the part he clutched in his mitt—the very bottom of the note—is still clear. In a neat cursive hand someone wrote, "Forever Yours Forever Mine." I don't know what that means, but it doesn't ring Satanic to me. The cult angle might still hold. It could be a code. Something you'd say to a fellow traveler to let them know you're on their side. Really, though, it reads more like a mash note to me. A love letter from a killer who was sorry for what they were about to do.

I read through the file for a couple of hours, especially the interviews. Stein's career was on a severe downturn by the time of his murder. Scattered parts in B- and C-grade films. Mostly quickie one-or-two-day jobs. He did a lot of local theater, keeping his hand in with the L.A. arts scene. There were stories that he was a member of the Hollywood sex party crowd, too, making side money hustling sparkly debutants and/or their handsome boyfriends. Nothing surprising there. It was the seventies by then. With access to the best cocaine and the prettiest bodies in the universe, who wasn't going to dive in? But 99 percent of the partiers were doing it just for kicks. If Stein was making money, combine that with drugs and sex and Hollywood careers that could topple if the right stories got out, and you have a great motive for murder.

But what kind of maniac turns a simple murder into a Vincent Price movie by chopping the victim in half and carefully cooking the wounds closed?

There's one other thing that hits me: Stein never lived in Little Cairo. Ever. And the park in West Hollywood where they found him was miles away from there. So much for my one brilliant theory.

When I can no longer stand the crime scene diagrams and witness transcripts—all of which amount to one big nothing—I get another bright idea.

I put on Stein's movies and go through them in chronological order, watching him go from bit player with a few lines to matinee idol playing second fiddle to bigger stars, to *Murdering Mouth*, his last big movie. It seems to me that the phrase "Forever Yours Forever Mine" is so stilted it might be from a movie. I check all Stein's roles on IMDb and it's not a title. But it still might be a line of dialogue in a cheap melodrama.

It takes all day, from the afternoon to sunset, to go through his fucking oeuvre, and by the time I get to the closing credits of *Murdering Mouth*, I'm pretty sick of Stein's chiseled good looks. What's worse, no one ever says "Forever Yours Forever Mine." I even freeze-frame the music credits of each film, hoping it might be a song title. Nothing. If the phrase is from a movie, it's none of this batch, and I'm sure not going to crawl through Stein's fifty-odd movie and TV credits. That means I'm right back where I started. A would-be star who fell off the map, was killed Roger Corman–movie style, hustled his way through the movie swinger world, and is now a murder-hungry ghost haunting a neighborhood he never lived in or had any connection to.

Maybe my whole "figure out Stein and you'll figure out the haunting" idea is garbage, but I'm not willing to give up on it yet. There's one more thing I want to see.

When I check my phone, Janet has texted me about classes and a band rehearsal but says that she—*they*—will call me later. That leaves me free to try out my new genius theory.

An hour after sunset, I pop back through a shadow into Little Cairo, the Colt reloaded and ready to go.

I throw on a glamour and just like last night, a little speck of light appears in the air and opens into a molten gate that oozes into the street. Then the weird singing starts and the ghost mob blasts into Little Cairo looking for action.

The shade of a teenage metalhead girl in a leather jacket covered in chains and silver studs grabs a pigeon that was dumb enough to peck through gutter trash. Metalhead Susie rips the bird's head off. But instead of blood coming out, bright sparks like electric fireflies fill the air. The dead gather around the flies, swallowing them or kissing them before tossing them into the air, where they blend with the overhead stars. When the fireflies are all gone, Susie tosses the bird's headless carcass into the air and it flies away like it's just another night in Birdtown.

I have no idea what any of this means. It's no hoodoo I've ever seen. After last night, I hang way back in the shadows and let the spook parade stream by on its way to bounce off Abbot's barrier again. Soon, I see Chris Stein. He does the strange little trembling act he did last night and wanders right back to the house he ripped up earlier. By the time he reaches the place the street is filled with the sounds of shades merrily tearing apart one pyramid, obelisk, and Sphinx after another.

Stein takes his time getting to the royal tomb and just before he goes inside, I walk right out into the open, where the streetlamps light me up.

I'm behind him now, and from my pocket I take out the note Stein had in his hand the night he died and say, "Forever yours. Forever mine."

He freezes. Doesn't move. I say it again.

"Forever yours. Forever mine."

He turns and takes half a step in my direction, like he's not sure what to do. So, I go to him.

"Forever yours. Forever mine."

I hold the note out at arm's length in front of me. Stein is doing the trembling thing again when I get to him. Still, he reaches out and takes the note.

For a minute he just stares at the crumpled paper. When he looks up at me, there are tears running down his spectral face. I actually feel a little sorry for the murderous fuck. He pulls the note to his chest and holds it here. His whole body and demeanor change. He's no longer rigid. No longer giving off crazy murder vibes. I was right. The paper is some kind of Dear John letter. When the tears stop flowing, he actually smiles a little. But just for a second.

He goes rigid again. Convulses once, then twice. Stein moves his hands out from his sides as a cut slowly crosses his midsection. When it's sliced him cleanly in half, a brightness leaks out from the wound, like he swallowed a spotlight. He grimaces. Grabs his stomach. Stumbles. But he doesn't let go of the note.

It's then that I notice how all sound on the street has stopped. No poltergeist crashes or bangs. When I look around, I see that's because every goddamn ghost in Little Cairo is in a circle around us that stretches from the edge of one side of the street to the other. When I look back at Stein, he's just a couple of feet in front of me.

He says, "Forever yours. Forever mine." And reaches for me.

I'm fast, but so is the dead man. He doesn't get hold of me, but he almost tears one of the sleeves off my coat. Okay. No fucking around this time.

I manifest my Gladius, my angelic flaming sword, and he backs away as the circle of ghosts closes in on us. I rush the spook line and hack my way through. As I swing the Gladius around me, ghosts blip out of existence before they can get hold of me. That's good to know. Angelic fire works on them. Now, if there just weren't a few hundred of the dead fucks in every direction, I might be able to kill them all. Right now though, I just want to get closer to the light, where there are good shadows.

None of the dead set follow me. They're too chicken. I hold my sword above my head and shout, "Warriors! Come out to play!" but none of them get the joke. These dead bores are as movie-deficient as Abbot.

Feeling a little cocky, I'm just about to the streetlight when the first overhead electrical cable falls. It lands in the street a few feet from me, dancing and hissing like a spark-spewing cobra. Then another falls. And another. The streetlight goes out.

Fuck.

I was hoping it wouldn't come to this, but it's time to try something else.

I grab a piece of parchment from my pocket. It's covered in runes, geometric designs, and weird glyphs in ink made from red vitriol and mercury—and it's supposed to send every one of these ill-tempered assholes straight to Hell.

I shout some Latin I don't understand and touch the edge of the parchment to the Gladius, setting it on fire. Keep chanting the Latin until the parchment is nothing but ashes.

Something shoots past my ear. It happens again. And then my face is on fire. I double up, suddenly in pain and bleeding everywhere. It's like a hundred invisible knives cutting me at once. When something almost takes my right eye, I figure it out.

Broken glass. It's flying at me from every direction, from every house with a cracked window and every car with a shattered windshield. In a few seconds, my coat is in shreds and I'm bleeding from a hundred places. Plus, I have to hop over the hissing electrical lines like I'm doing goddamn *Riverdance*.

And the ghosts aren't going anywhere.

So much for Vidocq's useless goddamn spell. Lesson learned: never trust books.

All the streetlights on the block are out and the glass keeps flying. Holding one hand up to shield my eyes, I spot a Porsche sitting in the driveway next to me. I run to it and slam the Gladius through the rear end. The gas tank goes up in a beautiful rolling orange Michael Bay explosion. The spooks don't like that and the whole fucking mob rushes me.

Too late, Beetlejuice.

I jump through a jittery shadow and stumble out a couple of doors down from Bamboo House of Dolls. A few of the regulars outside smoking start to say hello but shut up when they see me covered in blood and glass. It's the same thing inside. I walk to the far end of the bar and the last three stools are suddenly vacant. Before I can sit down Carlos jabs a finger in my direction.

"Don't you dare," he says, and hands me a bar rag. "Put that on the stool. I don't want you bleeding all over my furniture."

I spread it out and sit down. He sets an empty beer mug in front of me so I can drop the pieces of glass inside. I pick them out of my face, my arms, and my scalp. All over. It doesn't take long before the mug is full. A second later there's a shot of bourbon by my elbow.

He says, "Nothing changes, does it? You in here covered in blood and drinking until you're stiff."

"Sorry. I just didn't want to go straight home."

"No problem. Sandman Slim fucked up is what brings in the customers. You're doing me a favor. Not yourself, but I'm cool with that."

"That makes me your happy hour."

He smiles.

"And I don't even have to put out snacks."

I down the drink and he pours me another.

"Seriously though, what the hell are you doing to yourself? You sit in that weird house all day, then you finally come by for a drink for the first time in how long looking like you've been boxing a buzz saw."

"Ghosts. I was boxing ghosts."

"Tell me you won at least."

"I'm not dead."

"You couldn't prove it by me."

"I'll be healed up by morning."

"Your coat won't."

The sleeve Stein grabbed is almost torn off. There are a million little holes from the glass, and the collar and cuffs are shredded.

I ask Carlos, "Know a good dry cleaner?"

"I know a good coat shop, you cheap bastard."

"Give me the name before I leave."

"I'll write it down for you. Just, please, don't touch anything."

He moves off to serve other customers. As I nurse my drink, I become very aware that people are sneaking up behind me and taking bloody selfies. A shy girl barely old enough to be in here nervously holds out a coaster and a pen at me.

"If you don't mind . . . I've been coming here for weeks hoping to meet you . . . would you . . . sign this for me? If that's okay."

I stare at her for a minute. Every inch of me is sore. The palm of my right hand is sliced open from where I was protecting my eyes. I'm pissed about losing twice in a row to a bunch of dead people too dumb to stay dead. Plus, my coat is ruined. I'm about to tell her no when I get a look at what's she's wearing. It's a tourist T-shirt with I ♥ HOLLYWOOD on the front, only she's used a Sharpie to color the heart black, crossed out the "I," and written "Fuck" over it. Her shirt is the first thing that's made me laugh in a while. I push the pen out of the way and take the coaster. Set it on the bar and press my thumb onto it, leaving a big, bloody print on top.

"That work for you?"

She beams at me and speaks slowly.

"That. Was. So. Metal."

"I'm glad you liked it. Cool shirt, by the way."

"Yeah? I could make you one."

I hold up a hand to say no.

"Thanks, but it wouldn't last long. I'm hard on clothes."

"Your coat's kind of fucked up."

"You noticed."

She says, "What are you going to do with it?"

"I don't know. Throw it away, I guess."

"Do you think I could . . ."

I squint at her.

"You want my coat too?"

She digs at the floor with the toe of one boot.

"If you're just going to throw it away . . ."

Over my shoulder Carlos says, "Christ, Stark. Give her the damn coat. At least you'll be somebody's hero tonight."

I look at him, then back to Fuck Hollywood. After a minute, I put the na'at, black blade, Maledictions, and my lighter on the bar. It hurts to get the coat off and Fuck Hollywood reaches out to help me do it. When it's off, she immediately puts it on. She's not very big. It hangs off her like a potato sack.

"How do I look?" she says.

"You're monster movie Miss America," says Carlos, and Fuck Hollywood beams at me.

"Thank you so much."

I lean on the bar.

"It's fine. It's junk. But if it shows up on eBay we're going to have words."

"Never. I promise."

I nod and she half runs out of the place like maybe I'm going to change my mind and ask for the coat back.

"You made someone's night," says Carlos.

I hold up my bourbon.

"And you made mine."

"Tell me you're going home after this. You don't have a date or something stupid like that."

"That reminds me."

I check my phone and Janet has returned my call. They want to come over to show me something. I look at myself in the mirror behind the bar as I call them back.

"That might not be a good idea tonight. How about tomorrow?"

They hesitate.

"I can't. I have a late class."

There's something in their voice. Strange micro-tremors. I can't always tell on the phone, but I think they're lying.

I say, "Okay. How about the night after that?"

"That sounds great. Around seven?"

"Great. See you then."

I try to fit all of my gear in my pockets, but the black blade will shred my pants and the na'at is too big. Carlos gives me a canvas community-garden tote bag.

"You garden?" I say.

Carlos makes a face.

"Fuck no. That's Ray's thing."

"Tell him thanks. I'll get this back to him."

"You better."

My lungs suddenly feel too healthy, so I go outside for a smoke. Fuck Hollywood is down by the corner showing off my coat to her friends. She comes over and when I get a cigarette, she whips out a lighter and sparks it for me.

"Thanks," I say.

"My pleasure."

I take a good look at her. Her hair is shaved on both sides of her head, revealing matching dragon tattoos. She has a couple of lip piercings. A lot of ear piercings. Still, there's something innocent about her. Not dumb, just made brittle by this city. A little punk angel. Which reminds me of something.

"Your name isn't Zadkiel, is it?"

She gives me a crooked smile.

"No. What kind of name is that?"

"Forget it. A friend wants me to help look for her, but I don't even know where to start. I was hoping I'd get lucky."

"Sorry."

We stand there awkwardly for a minute until a couple of limos stop a block or so down. People pile out in evening gowns and tuxes. Some of them limp or have casts or bandages. They have to be the freeway weirdos from the other day.

I start down toward them and Fuck Hollywood tags along.

"Friends of yours?" she says.

"Not by a long shot."

The rear limo's license plate reads DETHSLT.

I say, "What does that mean? Detective somebody?"

"Maybe it's German. You know, 'de' something."

"Hmm. 'Deaths LT'? 'Limited'?"

"'Death slut,'" says Fuck Hollywood.

"It can't be."

Before we reach the limos, the drivers have pried up a manhole cover and the soiree is climbing down into the sewer. We watch the last giggling jackass disappear into the muck below.

I look at Fuck Hollywood and say, "What the hell is wrong with this town?"

She's beaming again.

"That. Was. So. Metal."

Too fucking metal for me tonight. I take my tote bag and go home.

I WAKE UP late the next day, sleeping off the cuts and the bourbon. By the time I wake up, all the cuts have healed and my head feels only slightly like a demolition site.

To tell the truth, I'm not motivated to do much of anything at the moment. Candy and Janet are both puzzles. I'm not getting very far with Abbot's ghosts. I hope if I can't get rid of them he won't take it out on Brigitte. Hellion hoodoo doesn't budge them and Vidocq's books are useless. And I don't know if I'm right concentrating on Stein instead of just sneaking into Little Cairo and picking off the spooks one at a time. But I still think I'm onto something. "Forever yours. Forever mine" sure got a reaction. I need to dig deeper.

I read through the Stein file some more, but the hangover makes it hard to concentrate.

What's going on with Janet? I'm still sure they were lying, but why? It's not like we're engaged or something. If they're seeing someone else, why not just say it? I'll ask them about it tomorrow face-to-face, when I'll know for sure if they're telling the truth.

Some combination of the headache and not getting anywhere with anything right now leaves me tense and nervous. By evening, I'm ready to punch more holes in the walls just for the sheer fun of breaking things.

I go for my PTSD pills in the bedroom, but the when I pop the top, the bottle is empty.

Goddammit.

I don't even know if they're working, but what if they are and I'll get worse without them? The last thing I want to do right now is go out, but now I have to. I don't have a coat, so I just stick the Colt in the waistband at my back and step through a shadow.

I come out in the grubby little mini-mall by Allegra's clinic. I knock on the door with EXISTENTIAL HEALING on the front. Allegra's receptionist and assistant—Fairuza—lets me in. She's a Lurker, one of the many nonhumans who live in secret all over L.A. Fairuza is a Ludere, with blue skin and short horns, a compulsive gambler, and, like all Ludere, constantly in a schoolgirl uniform.

"Hi, Stark," she says cheerfully. "In for a tune-up?"

I show her the empty bottle.

"A fill-up."

"Relax. You think you're the only pill popper around here? I get migraines and have a knee that should belong to an eighty-year-old lady."

"Yeah, but these are crazy pills. Supposed to keep me from running amok or something."

"How are they working out?"

"Great. I just saunter amok these days."

She checks the label on the bottle and goes into the exam room.

"Give me just a minute."

I drop into one of the plastic waiting room chairs. Skim through a couple of magazines. A sports one featuring 'roid rage all-stars, and a celebrity one with L.A.'s newest power couple on the cover. They look like white bread and mayonnaise sculpted into a focus group's idea of "attractive." Safe, boring, and utterly forgettable. Hurray for Hollywood.

They make me feel even twitchier, so I take out a Malediction.

Allegra steps in front of me and says, "Light that and

you're dead."

I put the cigarette away and get up. She gives me a hug and pulls me into the exam room.

"It's good to see you. I enjoyed your party the other night."

"Thanks. Maybe I'll have another sometime."

"I hope so."

"It was nice to see you and Vidocq together again."

She nods.

"It's taken some time and a lot of work. I guess you weren't around for most of it—"

"Because I was dead."

"Yes. That."

"Everyone tiptoes around it. I wish people would just say it."

"Do you? It seems like something that could be very triggering."

"I'm fine. Really."

Allegra looks at the empty bottle.

"We'll leave that for now."

She goes to a cabinet and refills my bottle with pills. Gets down a second bottle and hands me both.

I look at the new pills. They're white and tiny. Like something you'd give a sick cat.

"What are these?"

"Lorazepam."

"Which is . . . ?"

"It's an antianxiety medication."

I put my regular pills in my pocket but leave the lorazepam on the exam table.

"No thanks."

"Stark, stop trying to be such a hard-ass all the time. You need help. These will help."

I look around the room.

"You know, when Doc Kinski ran this place, he had all kinds of hoodoo meds. Salves and potions, divine light glass . . . Why is it all you ever give me I could get over the counter?"

She gives me a hard look.

"First off, you can't get any of these pills over the counter. And second, why do I give you these instead of one of Kinski's wonder drugs? It's because I think that it's possible you have enough magic in your life. Maybe you need to forget about Heaven and Hell and monsters and demons for a while and just think about yourself and getting well."

"And that's why you give me baby aspirin?"

"You're an addict, Stark. Something bothers you, you use magic. Something gets in your way, you blow it up or make it vanish. People. Things. Ideas. It's all the same. You depend on your 'hoodoo' for too damn much. So, shut up and let me try to help you."

Every single molecule in my body wants to leave. Slam the door or jump through a shadow. Get on the Hellion Hog and just go. Never come back. I don't like these pills. I don't like this clinic. And I don't like getting yelled at. Worst of all, I don't know if she's right or not. I'm not sure of anything right now. I want to go back to Little Cairo and just start killing things. Yeah, I'm blipping people completely out of existence. But they're dead, murderous trash, right? Killing ghosts isn't that bad, is it?

Allegra takes the pills off the exam table and presses them

into my hand.

"Please," she says. "Just try them. You start feeling too down or like you're going to lose control, take one. I promise they won't hurt you or make you into a Care Bear. You'll still be Stark. A pain in everyone's ass. By the way, where's your coat? You're never out of that. It's your security blanket."

I hold up a finger. "First off, I don't have a security blanket. Second, I gave the coat away."

"Why? You love that ratty thing."

"A few reasons, I suppose. But mostly because of all the blood."

She frowns and closes my hand around the new pills.

"Try these. Please. You need them."

I put them in my pocket.

"I'm only doing this as a favor to you. So you feel like you're doing your job."

"Sure," Allegra says. "I appreciate you thinking of my feelings."

We both laugh a little at that bit of bullshit.

She gestures to the exam table.

"Sit down for a minute."

I do and she shines a light in my eyes. Makes me say ah. Does that weird thing doctors do when they feel under your jaw. From a nearby drawer she takes a little gold compass-looking thing with six or eight hands and presses it to my forehead.

I say, "So, you *do* still use hoodoo."

"Of course. Where and when it's appropriate."

"What does that thing say about me? Do I need more fiber? Maybe trephination? They say it lets the demons out."

She takes it off me and stares at the twirling hands.

"It says you're a mess, but basically healthy."

"Do I still get a lollipop?"

She reaches into a fishbowl on the counter and tosses me a Tootsie Pop.

I unwrap it and stick it in my mouth.

"Blue. My favorite non-flavor."

She leans back and shakes her head at me.

"I sometimes wonder what you were like when you were a kid. Were you this stubborn? I bet you were a handful."

"Mom says I was the handsomest boy in the world."

"I bet you were. But that doesn't answer my question."

I shrug.

"I was like any kid. I could just do tricks other kids couldn't."

"What's the first bit of magic you can remember doing?"

"Are you my shrink now, too?"

Allegra says, "Nope. We're just a couple of friends talking."

I think for a minute.

"I don't remember much that far back. I remember Mom being sad all the time. And drinking. I remember my father being gone. Small mercies."

"No happy memories?"

"My father missing when he tried to shoot me."

I immediately regret it.

"Sorry. That was a stupid thing to say."

She purses her lips.

"It's okay. I shouldn't have pressed."

I rub the back of my neck.

"Can we talk about literally anything else in the world?"

Allegra takes a Tootsie Pop for herself, but she doesn't unwrap it. Just holds it.

She says, "Remember when we first met? Some of the crazy places you took me?"

"That, I remember."

"We had adventures."

"I remember that too."

She unwraps the Tootsie Pop and holds it by the stick.

"I miss that, you know. I love the clinic, but sometimes I feel so trapped here. You and Vidocq and Candy are off fighting monsters and here I am, waiting to bandage you up when you get back."

"It's funny. Candy said something like that the other night."

"What did you say?"

"Let's go have an adventure."

"Okay. Let's."

She catches me off guard.

"You don't have patients?"

"Not right now."

"What kind of an adventure did you have in mind? 'Cause I've had my ass kicked a lot recently."

"It doesn't have to be anything big. Griffith Park."

"What's in Griffith Park at night?"

"I don't know. Coyotes? Owls? Muggers? You want to hit something? Go hit one of them."

I get off the table. She really wants to do this and these days we never get to talk except for doctor-patient stuff.

"Okay. Griffith Park it is then."

Allegra goes out and tells Fairuza they're closing up. Once she's turned off the lights, I take her through a shadow.

We come out near the old zoo. It hasn't been in commission for years and is just a lot of empty cages.

She looks around.

"This isn't exactly what I meant. Who are we going to meet out here? Some fifteen-year-olds with beer?"

I look around.

"I like it here. It's quiet. The moonlight looks pretty through the bars."

Allegra puts a hand over her mouth.

"Oh my god. Was that a pickup line you used when you were a kid?"

"Yeah. What do you think?"

"You tell me. Did it work?"

"Usually."

She smiles, then points at me. "What are we even doing here? Let's go to the real zoo. The one that's not all spiderwebs and leaves."

I check the time on my phone.

"It's probably closed."

"Like that ever stopped you."

"I'm shocked, doctor. You want to go trespassing on county property?"

"I sure as hell do."

"Okay. It's not far from here."

We walk to the other side of the park, to the side that skirts the Golden State Freeway. It doesn't take us long, but as I predicted, the zoo is closed.

The front entrance is huge. Maybe fifty feet tall. Across

the bottom is a row of barred entrances, like the doors on animal cages. It's all wildlife and education inside, but the way in is pure showbiz. If it were still fashionable to have dancing bears and elephants doing handstands, they'd have them out front too. Inside the zoo, it's part Disneyland and part animal jail, but honestly, I think the animals have it easier. Their enclosures keep them a safe distance from frat shitheads eager for a selfie with a lion that's waiting to disembowel them. And the cotton candy kids. Sticky little demons. They're protected from them too.

I gesture to the locked gates.

"What did I tell you?"

"So what?" says Allegra. "Make with the magic and get us inside."

"You know they have video surveillance in there, right?"

"And you can take care of that too. Don't deny it."

"Yeah, but I also might blow the thing up. I'm not always good with subtle."

She grabs my hand and pulls me to the entrance like an eager kid.

"Come on, man. You promised me an adventure."

"I guess I could throw a glamour on us so we'd be harder to see."

"Yes. That. Do that."

While I'm thinking of a good one I say, "What is it you're so anxious to see?"

She doesn't say anything for a minute, then mumbles, "Giraffes."

"What's so special about giraffes?"

"No, dummy. Look over there."

I turn to where she's pointing—just as a pair of giraffes stroll past the entrance like they own the place. We run to the fence and watch them go. A second later they're followed by a small herd of camels trotting along as happy as can be.

"What the fuck?" says Allegra. "That can't be right."

"It's not."

I point farther down the zoo walkway.

A pack of wolves slinks quietly along after the camels as tropical birds flutter by overhead.

"Oh shit. Those poor camels."

She looks at me.

"You have to do something."

I look right back at her.

"Like what? Turn the wolves vegan?"

Allegra grabs the bars as zebras and coyotes shoot by. Howler monkeys crawl around the top of the entrance.

Allegra starts to say something and I hold up my hand.

"If you want to go inside now and play Noah, forget it."

I look around for a guard or a security van in the parking lot. Instead, I spot two limos. One has the license plate DTHSLT.

"Shit."

Allegra says, "Who's that?"

"Fucking maniacs. Rich maniacs."

"Wait. You mean people did this on purpose?"

"I think they do it for kicks, but this is the stupidest one yet."

"And they're inside?"

"Probably."

"Great. Let's crash the party."

"Are you crazy? Therere wolves running around."

"Yes. And you can handle it. Come on."

I take a breath. I don't know when I've seen her this excited.

"Doctor, is this a good idea? With me being in such a fragile mental state?"

She looks guilty.

"I know this is crazy and I'm asking a lot and, no, it's probably not good for you, but . . ."

"But what?"

"I always wanted to pet a tiger."

Beyond the gate an elephant walks by, followed by a small group of people in tuxes and evening gowns. Like in the freeway stunt, they're all wearing blindfolds. Allegra follows my gaze and spots the maniacs.

"There they are!" she shouts.

She looks at me sternly.

"Take me inside right now, Stark, or I will never forgive you."

"What if you get eaten?"

"You won't let that happen."

"Honestly, I'm annoyed. I just might."

She gets her face close to mine.

"You'd do it for Candy. Do it for me. Inside. Now."

"And you want me to find a tiger for you too?"

"No. We can find the tiger together."

I want to take her away from here, but I know she'll never forgive me if I do. I've felt bad sometimes about her having to play doctor and missing all the fun. I just didn't think she'd want to punch a gator this badly.

I take her hand and pull her into a shadow.

We come out just inside the front gate.

The animal party goes on and on. Otters hop along the grass edges of the walkway. Bats swoop for insects in the glaring overhead lights. Some woman in a hoop-skirt gown like a TV Southern belle grabs a fistful of porcupine quills when she trips. The porcupine takes off, more scared of the crazy screaming lady than she is of it. A gaggle of rich twerps in identical blue pinstripe suits get body-blocked into the trash cans by a couple of baby elephants playing chase. That's the best thing I've seen tonight.

"One of these idiots is going to get trampled."

Allegra says, "Nah. They must have minders or spotters or off-duty cops watching their backs."

"I doubt it. Like I said, they're nuts."

She pulls me out into the parade.

"Come on. Tiger me and we can go home."

"I still don't think petting one is a good idea."

"Do some magic for me, damn it. Make it think it's a pussycat for a minute."

"For a minute."

"That's all I need."

So, this is what the rich do nowadays. In the seventies it was all coke and sex parties. Now it's haute couture and death kicks. Why not? The rich have always had the dumbest ideas and enough cash to make them come true. I have no doubt that by the end of the night one or two of these creeps will pay off a zookeeper to let them take an endangered species home for a good old-fashioned monkey cookout.

I let Allegra pull me out into the melee.

In just the few minutes we've been here, the animals seem to have become more on edge. I think being out of their cages was weird enough that they were happy just to run around. Now they're settling back into their normal behavior. Especially the predators. Nearby, the wolf pack takes down a zebra. The animal's screams are awful and the scent of blood fills the dry night air. Startled by the sound, a small group of fancy maniacs bolts and tries to get away. Instead they fall all over each other like Keystone Cops, which would be funnier if a lot of them weren't crying and punching each other.

I say to Allegra, "You still want to be here?"

She looks nervous but says, "We've come this far."

"That will look lovely carved on your tombstone."

We brush past docile deer and peacocks, plus small gaggles of nervous, drunk partygoers with their hands out in front of them like they're playing Blind Man's Bluff. What bothers me is that we haven't seen the really heavy predators yet. Lions or tigers. They must be off somewhere waiting for the right moment to pounce. I like cats and don't want to hurt one, but I will beat a lion to death with a shark if it tries to take a bite out of me.

Allegra grabs my arm and pulls me down one of the winding side paths.

"There," she whispers, pointing.

About ten yards ahead of us is a holy-shit real-life goddamn tiger. It looks as big as a blimp and more hard-core than the Terminator. And it's in hunting mode—head down, haunches up, low to the ground. It's creeping toward a couple of blindfolded women in slinky silk designer gowns. Both wear long gloves and matching mink stoles. They hold hands as they go, each trying to help the other stay upright.

Part of me wants to grab Allegra and run, but another part wants to keep an eye on the women. A couple of panicking dumbasses punching each other or falling on a porcupine is one thing, but Tigger here means business and the Shining twins up there have no idea what's going on right near them.

"Can we get closer?" says Allegra.

"You go on. I'm fine back here."

"I really want to do this."

"Here's your chance."

"You're going to protect me, right?"

"Define 'protect.'"

"You're not going to let it eat me."

"Not all of you. That's a promise."

She takes a couple of steps closer to the cat. I'm still near enough that I can grab her if all hell breaks loose. But I'm more worried about the morons up ahead. I'd do something, except I remember something from TV or a movie. It's that tigers don't attack from the front. They're ambush predators. They attack from behind. As long as the Shining twins keep facing the tiger and don't get too close, they'll probably be all right. Besides, they chose to be here. I'm more worried about Allegra's doing something dumb. She closes in on the tiger, puts out a hand, then falls back with me again.

"I can't," she says. "I want to, but I just . . . and I want you to do some magic to make it tame, but then what's the point of petting a tiger?"

"Do you want to leave?"

She shakes her head.

"No. I'm going for it. You've got my back, right?"

"As long as I don't get scared and run away, sure."

She keeps her eyes on the cat.

"Okay. Here I go."

I keep my hand about an inch behind her back so I can grab her fast. I have a feeling that with the mood Tigger is in, the moment Allegra touches it we're clearing out of here and fuck the twins and the others. They want to be Tiger Chow? Let them. I'll drop Allegra at Vidocq's and head home for drinks with Cary Grant and *His Girl Friday*.

Allegra is just inches from the tiger's rear end.

Ahead, one of the Shining twins laughs. The voice bothers me. From behind them, a woman yells, "Wait for me, Janet."

She stops and spins around, turning her back on the tiger.

After that, it all happens fast.

I shove Allegra to the side and bark some Hellion hoodoo. The tiger crashes to the pavement with a deafening roar. The twins rip off their blindfolds. One of them I don't recognize, but the other is definitely Janet. Goddamn "I have a late class tonight." They take a couple of startled steps back when she—they—see Tigger. But it's not interested in them anymore. It knows I'm the one who fucked up its lunch. I get Allegra behind me, but Janet and the other woman are frozen where they are. There aren't any shadows deep enough here to get behind and snatch them free. I pull the Colt from my waistband, but Allegra grabs my arm.

"No! It's not its fault."

"I don't care."

"Please."

She gets hold of the gun hard enough that I'd have to fight her off to shoot. Besides, Tigger makes the choice for me.

It takes a couple of low, slinky steps in my direction, then bounds at me like a black and orange Mack truck. The truth is that as much as I don't want to lose an arm, I also like the thing. It doesn't want to be here with these jacked-up thrill seekers. It wants to be in a mangrove swamp somewhere, eating whatever the hell it is tigers eat out there. So, when it leaps, I don't bark a killing hex. I just blast it over us. But not too far. I don't want to crack Tigger's spine. Only maybe I should have. The bastard is so fast, it swings a big paw at me and hooks a claw into my right arm, ripping me from wrist to elbow. My blood hits the ground, and that just drives Tigger crazier.

A few yards past the cat a blindfolded guy is waving his hands like he's trying to guide a jet to the passenger gangway.

"What's going on?" he yells. "Is someone having fun without me?"

I suppose there are worse last words.

"Charlie! Run!" yells Janet.

It's over before I can do anything to stop it. Funtime Charlie is down on his back and Tigger is dancing in his guts. He doesn't even have time to scream.

"Do something," shouts Allegra.

I bark more hoodoo and knock Tigger into one of the empty animal enclosures.

Then I yank the Colt away from Allegra. When I grab Janet they stare at me like I have eight eyes and a donkey tail.

"Stark?"

I drag them both into a shadow I spot near one of the overhead lights.

We come out in front of Existential Healing. While Allegra

fumbles with her keys, I mumble some hoodoo, but the medicinal stuff was never been my specialty. The bleeding slows, but I'm cursing and more than a little pissed. Finally, Allegra gets the door open and we all pile into the exam room.

She bustles around getting her medical gear. I get on the exam table as Janet stands at the end looking like a scared kid who got caught shoplifting—and got someone they knew mauled by a fucking tiger.

Janet says, "Is he going to be all right?"

Allegra speaks in a clipped tone that lets everyone know she's angry.

"He will be if you stay out of my way. Go stand in the corner over there."

Janet does as they're told, now looking embarrassed and anxious for me.

Allegra cleans the rip in my arm with Betadine, then moves on to one of Doc Kinski's tricks: a blue-green salve that stops the bleeding quickly.

She says, "If this was a straight cut, the salve would close it completely. But that tiger really ripped you open. You're going to need stitches."

"So stitch me."

"I could use Myrmecoleon jaws. They're a medicinal arthropod Kinski kept. The jaws will hold the wound together. They hurt a lot more than regular stitches, but they have one advantage."

"What's that?"

She smiles at me.

"They don't leave a scar."

The rip is really starting to burn now.

"You're fucking hilarious. You should be on TV," I say. "Just sew me up."

"Regular stitches it is then."

Allegra goes to get the equipment, but she has to move Janet out of the way, scowling the whole time. When she's back, she shoots me up with painkiller and starts sewing my arm. Janet is still in the corner, now looking equal parts guilty and queasy.

"I'm so, so sorry about tonight," they say.

The more Allegra yanks my skin back together, the paler Janet gets. I watch their eyes flick from me to the blood on the floor.

I say, "You ever see a wild animal wound before?"

"It's my first time."

"Take a good look. You wanted to know how I got these scars? This is it."

"You fought wild animals?"

"For eleven years."

"I don't understand. Like in a circus or something?"

"No, and you don't get to quiz me. I quiz you."

When I try to sit up my blood pressure drops about a thousand points and my head feels like it's spinning around like Linda Blair's.

"Lie back down," snaps Allegra. "I don't want you fainting on me."

I do what she says, turning my head in Janet's direction.

"Why don't you tell me what you and your friends were doing back there at the zoo?"

"I can't. It's a secret."

"Are you fucking kidding me? You almost died tonight.

Someone else did. I got this arm, and Allegra could have been hurt."

They look at the floor.

"I promised."

"Were you part of the freeway thing too? And the sewer thing?"

They don't answer.

"That's what I thought. Fine. Keep your secrets. Tell me where to drop you and I'll find a new donut shop."

Their head snaps up.

"Please don't do that. Look, I'll tell you later. When we're alone."

Allegra glances in their direction.

"Janet, you seem basically like a nice person, but that was fucked up tonight, so I don't want to know your secrets."

"I'm sorry you got mixed up in it, too."

"That was my fault. That's on me."

I say, "Forget it. I took you there."

By now Janet is snow white, but as they watch Allegra work on me they actually manage to get paler.

After a couple of minutes of her sewing me and my gritting my teeth Allegra says, "There. You're done."

I flex my hand and manage to sit up.

"Thanks. Want me to drop you at Vidocq's so you can tell him a story?"

She throws away all the used gear and says, "What I want is for you to go home and rest. You've lost a lot of blood."

She leans against the exam table.

"With the amount of muscle damage you have I'm amazed you can move your hand at all."

"You know me. I'm a fast healer."

"Go home and call me tomorrow so I know you're all right."

"I'll be fine."

"Call me," she says firmly.

"I will."

"And take a lorazepam when you get home."

"Yes, doctor."

Janet says, "Thanks for helping him."

Allegra gives them a look. "Try not getting him killed again tonight."

I hug Allegra and pull Janet into a shadow.

WE COME OUT in the flying saucer house.

Janet swivels around like they can't believe they're back again.

"Your shadow trick is freaking me out a little."

"It'll do that the first couple of times. Right now, I need to take those pills Allegra gave me."

Janet pushes me down onto the sofa.

"You sit. I'll get you some water."

As they go to the kitchen I yell, "Bourbon. I want bourbon."

"I'll bring you both."

Janet returns a minute later with two glasses, one filled to the top and the other filled barely an inch.

"Kind of stingy with the bourbon," I say. "I can afford more."

"Maybe you should have the water instead."

"You hold on to that. It will be plan B."

I swallow the pills with bourbon and lean my head back to rest on the sofa cushions. Janet sits down next to me.

"Feeling better?" they say.

"I hurt like hell."

I flex the fingers of my fucked-up arm. Each muscle feels like a saw blade under my skin.

Janet sits back next to me.

"Silly question," they say. Then, "Please don't be so mad at me. You weren't even supposed to be there to get hurt. It was all a game."

"I'm not mad at you. I'm mad at me. I should have just killed the damn tiger."

Janet's eyes widen.

"Oh god no. They're endangered."

"So was I."

They let out a long breath.

"It was exciting seeing you do magic. I always knew you could do something, but when you did . . . wow."

"A lot of other people saw it too. That wasn't supposed to happen either."

They gently squeeze my good arm.

"What else can you do?"

I wave a finger in the air.

"Nope. I'm still interrogating you. Tell me about the stunts you've been pulling. If I saw two, I assume there are more."

They sit on the edge of the sofa.

"There have been lots. Usually they're just once a month or so but we've had some birthdays this month, so there've been more excursions."

"*Excursions.* Is that what you call them? Running blind

through traffic?"

"That's what Juliette and Dan call them."

"They're the ones in charge?"

Janet looks uncomfortable, like they're thinking. Or getting ready to tell another lie. But when they answer the question I watch their eyes and see they're telling the truth.

Janet blurts, "It's called the Zero Lodge. Because there's zero chance you'll get out of it alive."

"Cute. I guess it was true for the guy the tiger ate."

They stare up at the ceiling.

"Poor Charlie. Charlie Karden. He was nice. Funny. A champion marksman too, you know."

"Maybe he should have told the tiger. How did you even find out about the Idiot's Lodge?"

"Please don't call it that. And you have to be sponsored."

"Who sponsored you?"

"My old roommate, Cassandra."

"Was she the woman you were with at the zoo?"

Janet's brow furrows.

"No. She's dead. A crackhead stabbed her."

"On an excursion?"

They give me a defensive look.

"No. We might be a little crazy, but we're not stupid."

"The jury is still out on that."

They get up and walk around the room.

"You're still mad."

"More than a little. What about the cops?"

"You mean when things happen to people?"

"Exactly."

"Dan and Juliette handle that. They have people who . . ."

They wave their hand in the air.

I say, "Clean up their messes for them?"

"Something like that."

Janet picks up the glass of water and drinks it down.

I say, "Why do you do it? The stunts, I mean."

They shake their head and say, "I want to ask you some questions you've been dodging."

"Trying to change the subject?"

"Very much."

"Shoot."

"Tell me more about fighting wild animals."

I shrug. I must be messed up from the attack because the lorazepam can't be working yet, but I'm suddenly exhausted.

"I was somewhere very bad and very strange. They had me fighting all sorts of nasty things. Most you've never even heard of."

"Was it like a gang thing?"

"More like a prisoner thing."

They look surprised.

"In America?"

"You don't get to know that yet."

Now it's Janet's turn to look annoyed.

"So, you get to know about the Lodge, but I don't get to know about your fight club?"

"For the moment."

They give me a sly smile.

"What if I give you an incentive?"

They move around so they're straddling my lap.

"Nice try, but those funny pills are hitting me. I can barely keep my eyes open. Besides, I'm still kind of mad."

They lean over and whisper, "Angry sex is the best." Then they kiss my neck.

With my good arm, I move Janet back.

"There is no way this is happening tonight."

They lean their forehead against mine.

"You sure?"

"Ninety-nine percent."

Janet says, "I'll take those odds."

They kiss me and the room tilts.

I pass out with them still on top of me.

I DON'T KNOW what time it is when I wake up, but it feels late. My neck is stiff from sleeping all night with my head against the back of the sofa. Janet is curled up next to me, their head on a pillow and one hand draped across my knee. I slide out from under them and go into the bathroom. When I flex the fingers of my right arm, they ache, but the pain is manageable. Using the black blade, I cut off my bandages. The arm doesn't look too bad. The skin over the wound has knit back together. It's pink and puckered and ugly as hell but in another day it will be just one more scar and the tiger just one more stupid story.

"Holy shit."

Janet is behind me in the bathroom doorway. They grab my arm and look at it.

"How is that possible? Half of your arm was gone."

"You're exaggerating," I tell them. "And I'm a fast healer."

"You said that in the clinic. This is more magic, isn't it?"

I push her out of the bathroom.

"I have to brush my teeth and things. We'll talk about it

later."

Just before I get the door closed they say, "Are you still mad at me?"

"I'll decide after I've had some coffee."

"You take your time. I'll make it."

With them gone and my head clear, I finally have a chance to think about things. Or really, wonder about them. I never took Janet for the crazy type, but here we are. The Zero Lodge and people getting run over by cars and eaten by tigers. I'm going to have to keep an eye on her—them. I have enough crazy in my life. If Janet is too much, I might have to find a new donut place after all.

They hand me a mug of coffee when I walk into the kitchen. Then I remember something.

"Fuck. My coat."

"What happened to it?" says Janet.

"I lost it in Little Cairo. I feel weird without it."

They run their fingertips through my hair, straightening it.

"Let's go out," they say. "For saving me, I'll buy you another one."

"You're a student. You can't afford new coats."

"Who said anything about new? I'll show you where I get all of my Lodge outfits."

THEY TAKE ME to a used clothes shop on Melrose. We must spend an hour pawing through the merchandise. One of the salesclerks, a heroin-thin guy in turtleneck-and-beret beatnik drag, follows us around and hands me things. I don't know if he's trying to be helpful or just make sure the scarred guy doesn't rob the place, but he gets everything wrong. Janet rejects all of his coats without letting me try on anything.

"That's too long," they tell the guy. "Not a private eye coat. More like Johnny Cash."

I'm happy to let them argue. It leaves me time to walk around and examine all the hexed clothes and anti-hex charms. I thought I recognized the intersection when we came in. We're at the nexus point in a territorial dispute between Hollywood High and private school Sub Rosa brats. There's enough hoodoo power in this little shop to launch it to Mars. My guess is at least half of the clothes they're selling didn't end up in here because someone needed money. This is a turf war in leather jackets, lace gloves, and vinyl corsets. And the staff doesn't have a clue. They probably just get migraines and the occasional bout of night terrors when someone brings in something truly insidious. I could spend all day in here following the spectral lines of hoodoo power as the dopey kids battle it out over absolutely nothing.

In the end, Janet and Jack Kerouac save the day and I walk out of the shop wearing a comfortable frock coat with only a minimal number of curses attached. I blow them away with one little Hellion bark and, feeling more like myself again, take Janet for a ride on the Hellion Hog.

WE BLOW DOWN the coast to Malibu and I show them how to sneak onto Teddy Osterberg's estate.

"You enjoy hanging out with all these dead people?" says Janet.

"I've known a lot of dead people. Occupational hazard."

"It's quiet, at least. And the trees are nice."

"The landscape is whatever goes with whatever cemetery.

Trees here. A bamboo grove there. Tombs or a waterfall there."

"Are all these cemeteries real?"

"Every one of them."

"You know some odd people, Mr. Stark," says Janet.

"So I hear."

Janet comes over and bumps me with their shoulder.

"Still mad?"

"I'm mostly over it."

"Did you see Rodney's eyes when he saw your gun?"

"Rodney was the clothes store clerk?"

"Yep. He almost shit himself. Me, on the other hand, I like it."

I take the Colt out from under my new coat and hand it to them. They make a little shocked noise when they feel the weight.

"It's a cinder block," Janet says. "How do you hit anything with it?"

"It's not so bad. You get used to it."

"Show me how to use it."

I take it from them and shoot some acorns under an oak tree.

"Me next," they shout.

When I hand them the Colt they just stare at it.

"All of a sudden I'm not sure about this."

"Go ahead. See that tumbleweed near the tree? Shoot it."

Janet points the gun at the ground nervously and says, "I thought there were a lot of safety rules."

"There are. Don't point the gun at me and don't point it at yourself. That's pretty much it."

They aim the gun with two hands and pull the trigger. The Colt's kick knocks them backward a couple of steps.

"Whoa. I was *not* expecting that."

"Everybody says that the first time. Try it again."

Another shot. Another miss.

"The tumbleweed is too small," they say with a mock pout.

Janet points to the nearby tombstones.

"Why can't I shoot at them?"

I take the pistol away and reload it.

"Those people have been through enough," I say. "They deserve a decent sleep."

When I hand Janet the Colt back, I get behind them and correct their stance. Straighten their hips and adjust their shoulders. I hold on to their hand and help them aim.

I say, "Shoot."

They pull the trigger and the tumbleweed jumps back a foot. Janet lets out a loud whoop and leans back against me.

"That was great!"

"Nice job."

Still leaning into me, they adjust their hips to shoot again. But they lower the pistol.

Janet says, "Stark. Do you have another gun?"

"Nope."

She grinds her ass into my crotch.

"Then what's that pressing into me?"

Before I can say anything, they turn and kiss me hard. I kiss her back and take the gun away.

Janet smiles and takes off their shirt.

"I guess you're not mad at me anymore."

"Not too much."

No matter how many times movies and songs make getting undressed fast sound sexy, in my experience, it's anything but. Especially on a hill in an overgrown cemetery. There's nothing to do but muscle your way through it and forget about dignity. Just keep going and you'll get to the promised land.

I start to say something about it, but Janet pulls me down on top of them and there's not a lot of talking after that. I'm not saying we break any furniture, but we manage to rattle a couple of tombstones.

SOMETIME LATER, WE'RE lying on my new coat and Janet is making finger guns to shoot at the nearby tombstones. When they catch me watching them, they lean over and bite my shoulder. It's a nice moment and I don't want to ruin it, but I'm an expert at ruining moments.

"You should know, I bring trouble to people I get close to."

Janet laughs once and leans on her crossed arms.

"I'm not scared."

"You should be."

They sit up and say brightly, "In case you didn't notice, scared isn't my thing. What's fun if it isn't at least a little dangerous? Plus, I always have my knife."

They pull it from the side pocket on their jeans. It's a pricy Microtech automatic knife. Push a button and the blade flicks out in a fraction of a second. Push the button again and the blade is gone. I click it a couple of times and give it back to them.

"The blade's more than two inches. That's illegal in California."

Janet looks shocked.

"Please don't tell Mom."

They put the knife away and lean against me.

"Admit it. Knowing I have a knife got you a little hard just then, didn't it?"

"Maybe a little."

She grabs me.

"Liar."

AN HOUR LATER, I drop Janet off at Donut Universe. Before they go in, they drag me around behind the place and we kiss like a couple of high school idiots.

When we come up for air, Janet says, "You should come with me tonight."

"Where?"

"The Lodge. There's a meeting. We're not supposed to bring nonmembers, but after what happened last night, I think they'll make an exception for you."

I want to say they're out of their fucking mind. That I never want to get near those people. But I have to admit that at this point I'm intrigued by these suicide-kick creeps. I wouldn't mind finding out what makes them tick. And who knows? Maybe I'd get a chance to punch Dan and Juliette in the nose. I bet that would give dead Charlie Karden a laugh.

"Why do you like the Lodge so much?"

"Come and see."

I say, "What time?"

"Pick me up at eleven."

They go inside and I drive back to the flying saucer house,

trailing a cloud of gray cemetery dust from my brand-new coat.

At home, I'm still confused by the whole thing with Janet. What am I supposed to do now? I want to cut things off with them before they get more complicated. But after today, I know that's not going to happen. What am I going to tell Candy? Or anyone else? I'm in deep here. Deeper than I thought I was ever expecting. On the other hand, it feels good to be wanted by someone. But, seriously, what the hell am I doing?

To take my mind off all that and Samael's idiot angel rescue mission, I go back through Stein's folder, looking for anything I might have missed. Cop reports. Autopsy report. Witness reports. Photos. Then I find a second plastic envelope that was caught between a couple of sticky coffee-soaked report notes. It holds a small green address book. I take it out and thumb through it.

I recognize some names of actors, actresses, and directors. Theater addresses. Talent agency addresses. Some bars and clubs. All of the entries are written in very clean and precise block letters. Some of the names are coded with icons and colors.

Pace Ripley. A red dot.

Amber L. A green star.

JS & DP. Double red dots.

Kiki. A black heart.

One name catches my eye. Danny Gentry. He was a friend of Stein's and just a notch below him in the billing for *Murdering Mouth*. With no other clues and nothing better to do,

I dial the phone number.

After a few rings, someone picks up. When they don't say anything I say, "I'm looking for Daniel Gentry."

"Who are you?"

Judging from his voice, he was asleep. By the way he slurs his words, he might have been sleeping one off.

"I'm a friend of Chris Stein's."

"Who?"

"Chris Stein. The actor."

"I know who you're talking about. I just haven't heard from anyone who knew him in twenty years. What do you want?"

"Just to talk."

I hear a low grumbling sound; either he's moaning or he fell back to sleep.

"Gentry?"

"Look," he says slowly and deliberately. "I've talked to the cops. I've talked to the papers. I've talked to his friends. I don't have anything else to say about Chris."

"What if I don't ask questions? What if you just reminisce for an hour?"

"Forget it."

"I'll give you a hundred dollars."

"Two hundred," he shoots back.

"For two I get to ask questions."

"Prick. Fine."

He gives me the address and it's the same one in the address book. He's been in one place for a long time.

"When can we meet?"

"You think I have a busy schedule?"

"I'll be over in an hour. Be there."

"Where else am I going to be?"

I shower, try to beat the worst of the dirt out of my coat, and have a few cups of coffee before getting on the Hog.

GENTRY LIVES IN the Kiernan Arms on a side street at the edge of Burbank. The Arms was kind of famous in the days of the old studios. They put up writers and young performers not big enough yet to move closer into Hollywood. But the building looks like it hasn't been maintained since Fatty Arbuckle was the king of comedy. It used to be kind of elegant, but these days it's a dingy fortress. An anti-junkie electric gate to get into an outer area with a dry fountain. There's another buzzer on the door to get into the building. Barbed wire on top of the metal fence out front. The neighborhood isn't quite what it once was.

If the outside is bad, inside, the Arms is a pile of junk. Half the doors on the mailboxes along the lobby wall have been torn off. The elevator is out of service. There are shaky banisters on the stairways where someone painted right over the splintered wood. Each floor features at least one unlit side corridor. Gentry is on the fourth floor. That can't be an easy walk for a guy in his seventies.

Each apartment has a little suburban-style doorbell. I ring Gentry's a couple of times because the apartment next door is blasting some kind of teeth-grinding country pop loud enough to make the hall light fixtures shake. It takes Gentry a couple of minutes to open the door. When he does, he gets one look at my face and says, "Christ. It's Lon Chaney."

He doesn't say "come in" but just leaves the door open.

I follow him down a short inner hallway to a dusty living room.

"Not that I should complain about faces," he says as he settles down into a sagging easy chair. "Look at my mug. I used to be kind of a dreamboat. Not Steve McQueen or anything, but I did all right."

He's right about being past his dreamboat prime. His forehead is like a rutted dirt road. The rest of his face is oddly sunken. The cheekbones are flattened like there's plastic under the flesh. His lips are slightly crooked.

I say, "Is that because of a car accident?"

"You know it. Seat belts were for sissies back then, except one day the Mustang decides to wrap itself around a tree and my face is hamburger."

"That must have been hard for an actor."

He waves a dismissive hand at me.

"They put me back together the best they could, but I was never the same. These days, of course, surgeons work miracles." He laughs a rasping smoker's laugh. "Like some of the critics said back then, I was ahead of my time." He laughs again and holds out his hand. "You have my two hundred?"

I put two bills in his hand and he looks them over before putting them in his pocket.

The white walls of the apartment are lined with posters of his old movies. Photos of his palling around with celebrities from the sixties and seventies. Some kind of award plaque too far away for me to read. Next to that is a plastic toy Academy Award with his name on it.

"What do you think?" he says. "Not bad for a farm kid from El Paso."

His sunken face and the sun-faded memories are pretty sad, so I say, "It's impressive."

But Gentry isn't dumb. He says, "No. You think it's shit. I can tell. Let me ask you something, Johnny Handsome. How many movies did *you* star in? Me? Twenty."

I don't mind if he gets mad at me. I just don't want him to throw me out.

"No, really. It's interesting."

"Fuck you. Why don't you take your attitude and that face and crawl back to the freak show?"

I look at him hard.

"I paid you up front, so we're going to talk. And be honest, you didn't star in all those movies. You were a bit player who didn't get decent billing until the last four or five."

He purses his lips and the angles of his face go even more out of whack.

"That's four or five more than you, Clark Gable."

"You're right. I've never been in a movie and I never met a celebrity in my life. But you have and that's why I paid you two hundred dollars. So, let's talk about Chris Stein."

He picks up a pack of Marlboros from a little table by his chair, tears the filter off one, and lights up.

"What do you want to know?"

"You were friends for a long time."

He puffs out a stream of smoke and in the sunlight, he disappears for a few seconds.

"We were. Met soon after we each came to L.A. We were roommates for a while too, only we didn't let many people know because back then two good-looking guys together in a shitty little apartment, people might think we were fags."

This guy gets more charming by the second.

"So, what happened? You were both about to hit the big time."

"The accident," he says. "And coke. I couldn't leave the stuff alone. Got a bad rep. Between my face and the drugs, the doors slammed shut. And *boom*. That was that."

Gentry gestures to the Academy Award with his cigarette.

He says, "Chris gave me that, you know. He knew I was a better actor than him. I think he also felt bad because he gave me that last line of coke right before the accident."

A rising star and a ruined career. That sounds like a pretty good motive for murder.

"You must have held that against him."

Gentry looks surprised.

"Chris? No. It was my own damn fault. After the mess, Chris helped me out when he could. You know. Money and other things."

"What kind of things?"

"Calm down. I'm getting to it."

He smokes for a couple of minutes, shuffling through memories, and many good ones I bet. Finally, he straightens his shoulders.

"Even when I couldn't work anymore, I still loved coke. But I didn't have any money. Chris introduced me to people who helped out."

He holds up a Marlboro with yellow nicotine-stained fingers.

I say, "You started dealing?"

He nods.

"See, I still had my Hollywood connections back then.

And in the right light, I wasn't so bad looking. Better than you ever were."

"Forget about me. Tell me about your connections."

"Goddamn Chris stayed handsome 'til the day he died. Even when he was on the skids like me. Back then though, he was into the private party scene, if you know what I mean."

"No. I don't." I'm pretty sure I do, but I want to hear him say it.

He shakes his head. Exasperated.

"Sex and dope parties, asshole. By then it was the seventies and everything went. Swapping. Three-ways. Chicks with chicks. Guys with guys. No one cared and no one judged."

"And Chris was into it?"

"Eyeball deep. Chris liked pussy and cock, so he had a grand old time."

"And Chris got you into the scene because you were dealing?"

Gentry stabs a finger at me.

"I told you. I was still good-looking. I could have gotten in myself. But, yeah, dealing helped. Chris introduced me to everybody. He was a good guy who didn't forget his friends."

"Are you sure no one got jealous?" I say. "Maybe someone got nervous about a good-looking guy like him."

He disappears in a puff of smoke again.

"Not back in those days. And Chris had a short attention span. He never spent too much time with anyone except for this one special trick."

"Who was that?"

Gentry shrugs.

"Who knows? It was Chris's one big secret. Whoever it

was, they had a real hold over him. After the drugs knocked him out of the business too, the trick took care of him. Helped out with rent and food money. But never too much. They kept him on a real short leash."

I'm getting tired of this gossip column stuff. I knew half of this from his file and the rest from the internet. But I can't tell if Gentry is dumb or just angling for more money. I take out another hundred but don't give it to him.

"Is there anything else you can tell me?"

His eyebrows arch slightly.

"You mean anything less savory?"

"Sure, let's try that."

The laugh again.

"Chris learned to pick locks like a pro. He taught me how to do it too. Not that I did it much. Just picked up an item here and there to keep the lights on. You know."

"Of course."

"It's not like the cocksuckers in this building don't deserve it."

He gets up and bangs on the wall for a few seconds.

"Turn down that goddamn music," he yells. But the country pop keeps coming. He shakes his head at the noise and sits back down.

I say, "Where did Chris learn to pick locks?"

"From his trick."

"And you have no idea who it was."

He thinks for a minute.

"If you ask me, it was Jimmy Summers or Claire Hennessey. Ever heard of them? The son and daughter of some big-time producer pricks. A couple of real juvenile delinquents, those kids. But money up the ass."

I wait for him to say something else. He doesn't, so I speak up.

"What does 'forever yours, forever mine' mean?"

"Is that a line from a movie?"

"That's what I thought, but I can't find it anywhere."

"Well, there you go."

He goes back to smoking and ignoring me. He has his money. Why not?

"That's everything you know?"

Through the smoke, he squints at me.

"What is it you're looking for?"

I think about it for a minute. Successful Hollywood people, hangers-on, and forgotten actors. Sex parties, drugs, and a secret lover. It's great stuff for a drive-in movie, but I'm not sure what good any of it does for me.

"I really don't know," I say.

Gentry beckons me forward and speaks quietly.

"You know, at one of the parties, I saw Elvis eat a peanut butter and banana sandwich off a certain starlet's tits. Balanced it right on top. For an extra hundred, I'll tell you who."

"I'd rather pay you not to tell me."

He leans back in his chair.

"Suit yourself, but it's a funny story."

"I bet. Can you think of anybody who might know more about Chris toward the end? Maybe even the party scene itself?"

"That'll cost the hundred you're holding and one more on top."

I take out a second bill but don't give him that either.

"Avani Chanchala," he says. "You heard of her? Famous real estate developer. She was heavy into the scene and she liked Chris a lot. Or at least his cock. But don't tell her I sent you. She owns the building and might evict me."

I give him the two bills and a third one besides.

When I say, "Thanks," he doesn't say anything back, just sticks the money in his pocket with the rest. I want to be annoyed, but the last thing I see on my way out of the apartment is that plastic Academy Award, and I can't help but feel sorry for the guy.

THAT NIGHT, JANET gives me an address way the hell up in the Hollywood Hills. It takes nearly an hour of driving around those endlessly winding roads to get there. Then, when I see the place I want to turn the Hog around and head down again.

Where we've arrived is one of those overdesigned glass-walls-and-a-pool L.A. houses that sticks fifty feet out over the canyon below, supported by nothing by a couple of steel beams. Ridiculous, defiant architecture. Who spends a few million dollars on a house that's guaranteed to collapse into a pile of kindling one day? Adrenaline junkies, I guess. Which makes a stupid kind of sense, because that's who we're here to see.

The front door is unlocked, so we go in. Janet shows me around, points out the view, the expensive *Architectural Digest* furniture, the art on the walls. I'm thinking, This is all going to look very pretty on fire one day, but I smile and keep my mouth shut. After the grand tour upstairs, they take my hand and lead me down a steep flight of stairs into a basement cut into the granite hillside.

There are maybe twenty people downstairs. They all give me the once-over when we come in. But they aren't what interests me. What gets my attention are the smells and the one lone Gloomy Gus in the corner. The Zero Lodge has its own trash wizard. It's the stink of his potions that grabbed my attention. Trash wizards are civilians with no real hoodoo power who taught themselves some tricks from old books and maybe a few hexes they bribed from a dumb Sub Rosa kid. Trash wizards are generally harmless, except this one has a Black Sun wheel on the wall behind him. The Black Sun is ancient, hard-core hoodoo that supposedly gives mystics power over the physical world. Nazis love Black Sun garbage, but this bunch doesn't look political. They're dummies just out for a good time, and I bet the junkyard Merlin is right there with them.

On the wall to the left of Merlin is what looks like hunting trophies mounted on plaques. Skulls of some hellbeasts and even a few Lurkers. I'm getting a bad feeling about what these creeps are really into.

Janet is holding my arm and feels me get tense.

"What's wrong?"

I nod in the direction of Merlin.

"The trash wizard in the corner and the dead stuff on the walls. Either someone here paid a lot of money for that stuff or you shouldn't be around these kinds of kicks."

Janet squeezes my arm.

"Relax. It's just some heads. It's like you said, Dan and Juliette probably just bought them. I mean, do you even know if they're real?"

"I guess not."

"Then don't take everything so seriously."

They kiss me on the cheek.

"Okay."

The rumpus room walls are bare stone scraped smooth. On a set of shelves in the corner are what look like excursion supplies. Blindfolds. Barbed wire. Bolt cutters. Medical kits. A few guns. Next to all of that is an impressively well-stocked bar. Recessed lights in the ceiling give the room a soft glow, but there are candelabras all over the place, like it's a TV séance show. For ten bucks a minute you can talk to your dead grandma or George Washington. I'm thinking of leaving again when a familiar face comes at me from out of the crowd.

"Hi, Stark. What are you doing here?" says Manimal Mike.

I look at the cast on his arm.

"Hi, Mike. It's good to see you in one piece."

It's his right arm that's injured, so he puts out his left to shake, but I already have my right hand out, so it's all an awkward mess. The silliness of the moment cuts through my mood.

Manimal Mike is a Tick-Tock Man. A craftsman who builds intricate mechanical familiars for rich Sub Rosa. I have a feeling his broken arm is costing him a lot of money in lost work.

Mike points a finger of his broken mitt at me.

"You're not thinking of joining the Lodge, are you?"

"We'll see. I'm not sold yet."

"I think Kenny put him in a bad mood," says Janet.

Mike looks over at the trash wizard.

"Kenny? He's all right. I mean, he can't do fancy magic like you, but he can pull off some cool tricks."

I fake-smile.

"Neat."

Janet elbows me gently in the ribs.

"The Lodge is the best," says Mike. He looks at the woman by his side. "Isn't that right, honey?"

She puts out her hand.

"Hi. I'm Maria Simon and I'm here with this goon."

Mike practically glows with happiness.

Maria looks a little young for him. Twenty-three or twenty-four. She's got a willowy Audrey Hepburn–in–*Breakfast at Tiffany's* look. Maybe she's good for Mike. He's more cleaned up than usual. No grease stains and his fingernails aren't crammed with dirt and metal shavings. Plus, he might have put on a few pounds.

She says, "The Lodge isn't for everyone. Are you the adventurous type?"

I scratch my nose.

"I'd rather be at home doing needlepoint."

"Stark, you said you'd listen," says Janet. They take my hand in theirs and say, "Stark's super adventurous. He's the one who saved me at the zoo."

"I should have guessed that was you," says Mike. "Poor Charlie."

"Yes. Poor Charlie," says Maria.

Now I'm annoyed again.

"Everybody keeps saying poor Charlie, but no one says where he went. What happens to the ones who get lost on your little excursions?"

Mike says, "We don't know. Dan and Juliette handle things like that."

I stage-whisper, "You don't think anyone's buried down here, do you?"

"I hope not."

"I think it's better not to know," says Maria. "I remember years ago when we were all high at the Masque club, Brendan Mullen said, 'If everyone knew where all the bodies were buried, no one would dance for fear of treading over some poor bastard's face.'"

The three of them laugh at that.

I don't.

Janet looks at me. "Some members of the Lodge are police, ambulance drivers, or work in the coroner's office. And Dan and Juliette know more besides."

I look back at Janet.

"And you're okay with them making people just disappear?"

Janet looks like she's getting tired of my questions.

"Look. It's not like anyone makes anyone do anything. You're allowed to skip excursions every now and then."

"As long as you have a good reason," says Mike.

I say, "And Dan and Juliette get to decide what's a good reason."

"Naturally."

"Did you take a night off after you broke your arm?"

"In fact I did. Right, baby?"

He gives Maria a big, dumb smile.

She says, "We spent the night at home. He couldn't even

cut his food, so I fed him steak like a baby."

"You know babies who eat steak? Those sound like some cool kids."

"Stop it," says Janet. "You know what she means."

"I'm just kidding."

"Of course," says Maria.

"When do I get to meet the Pope and Mrs. Pope?"

"In about ten seconds, I think."

"They're here," says Janet.

Everybody turns to the stairs as a couple makes a grand entrance.

Dan Perkins is in a silk shirt and pants with the sleeves rolled up. Business casual. He has gray hair and slightly funny eyes. Really, he looks less like a businessman than a gray-haired anthropology professor who's dipped into the school's ayahuasca supply one too many times.

Juliette Stray is a bleach-blond Mamie Van Doren knock-off. She kisses cheeks left and right as she moves through the crowd. A big smile masks someone trying to look way too nice for it to be anything but protective coloring—like the pretty stripes on a coral snake. Better keep an eye on her. If things go bad, she'll be the one who puts the knife in.

While Juliette plays social butterfly, Dan comes right over to me. He looks me up and down as we shake.

"You know, we don't usually allow outside interference in our excursions," he says.

I look him over too.

"I don't remember asking anyone's permission."

"And that's why we asked Janet if you'd like to stop by tonight."

I turn to Janet.

"This wasn't your idea? They told you to do it?"

They say, "I was going to ask Dan and Juliette if I could bring you anyway."

Juliette finally joins us, pecking me on both cheeks.

"It's true," she says. "Janet brought you up and we insisted on meeting the hero."

Dan says, "I understand that you're interested in joining our little social club."

"Not really. She's interested in me joining."

Damn it.

I look at Janet.

"Sorry. *They're* interested in me joining."

"It's okay," Janet says. "You're trying."

"Here's the thing," says Dan. "We usually have a pretty extensive vetting process."

Juliette says, "To see if the applicant is a true adventurer. But you already proved you're up for an interesting time."

Dan picks right up the moment she stops talking, like they've rehearsed the whole thing.

He says, "I take it you're Sub Rosa?"

Surprised, I say, "Does that get me extra brownie points?"

"A few actually."

"Still," says Juliette. "Ambushing a dumb animal is one thing."

Dan continues, "How are you when something intelligent can look you right in the eye?"

I don't like where this is going.

"You want to thumb-wrestle?"

"Something like that, but not me."

I look at Juliette.

She smiles and takes Dan's arm.

"You should be so lucky."

The Lodge members, when I look them over, are a dull bunch. Rich and poor. Fat and skinny. Some nervously not wanting to look me in the eye. Others staring daggers. There are a few buff gym rats in the group, but no one looks particularly dangerous. Besides, a lot of them still have casts and bandages from the freeway stunt.

I half-smile at Dan.

"You don't mean Janet, and I could knock over most of this bunch with a well-aimed Twinkie."

"Not any of them, either."

"Look, unless you have a gorilla in the guest room I'm leaving."

"In fact, we do. But not the guest room. Through there."

There's a metal door like a bank vault across the room. Whatever is behind it is set deep into the granite of the cliff the house stands on.

I glance at Janet and they nod eagerly at me.

Turning back to Dan and Juliette, I say, "Whatever you have planned, let's get going. Don't take this the wrong way, but for adrenaline junkies you're kind of boring."

Juliette ushers me to the vault door and purrs in my ear.

"I hope this will be more to your liking."

Dan holds it open for me and slams it shut the moment I'm inside. The room is completely black.

His voice comes through an intercom.

"Remember. No tricks."

"I'm not afraid of the dark, Danny."

"Then let there be light."

About a million watts of light floods the room, blinding me for a few seconds. There's a mechanical click from somewhere and something smashes me against the wall. When I shove back I'm suddenly flying through the air before crashing across the room.

The fall makes my not-quite-healed tiger arm hurt, which doesn't help my mood. But I can see now and what I get a look at makes me even madder.

The clowns don't just have a trash wizard. They have their own private vampire down here. And she looks hungry. I mean, it's not like vampires scare me. I've killed plenty and my blood is toxic to them, so I'm safe. It's just such a rich-asshole L.A. thing to do to have your own pet vampire with video cameras around the room so they can watch me on pay-per-view.

I say, "This isn't a nice way to treat a guest, Danny."

The intercom says, "Finish up fast and we'll have drinks after."

Fuck these people. I'm going to rip this thing in half and then I'm going push this goddamn house off the cliff.

When the bloodsucker comes at me, I pivot and smash it with my elbow hard enough to knock its fangs to Argentina. Only, its teeth stay put and she gets her hands around my throat and shoves me up against the wall. I grab both of her wrists and drive my heel into her knee hard enough that the crack of bones echoes off the walls. But that doesn't stop her for a second. A moment later, her knee has healed and she's still choking me.

This isn't how this was supposed to go. There's something

off about this vampire. I blame the trash wizard. He's given her some Black Sun protective hoodoo that's pumped up her strength and healing powers. Still, I'm not dead yet.

I keep my hands on her wrists and fall backward, bashing the vampire's head into the rock wall. When I step away to catch my breath she hops right back up. Half of her forehead is crushed, but she's hopping around fresh as a goddamn daisy.

There's a rack of weapons on the far wall. The vampire grabs a mace on a chain and swings it at me. Each time she misses, she gouges big chunks of stone from the floor and wall. I look at the weapons rack but don't see anything I like. I don't know if it's against the rules or not, and I don't care. I reach into my coat and pull out the na'at.

I extend it into a spear with a razor cutting edge. The next time the vampire swings at me I thrust with the na'at, cutting the chain on her mace. The spiked ball bounces off into a corner, which leaves her with a wooden stick. No hesitation now. I shove the na'at straight into her chest and through her heart.

But the fucker doesn't die.

She should be ashes by now, but she just stands there grinning at me. Mad, I make a dumb move. I thrust the na'at again, but the vampire sees it coming. She leaps high into the air and comes down with her knee right into my chest. I fall over backward with her on top of me. At this point I stop fighting. I should have used my best weapon right away, but I was annoyed and—I'll admit it—wanted to put on a show for Janet. Now, though, I'm done.

I shove my arm right into the vampire's face and let it bite me. Getting a mouthful of my blood for a vampire is like pouring acid down its throat. Sure, it hurts when her fangs go into my wrist, but it will be worth it to watch her burn.

Only instead of dying, she keeps sucking down more and more of my blood. This isn't possible. What kind of hoodoo did Kenny use on this dead piece of meat? The trash wizard has more skills than I would have guessed. I have so much respect I might kill him when I'm finished with Vampirella.

I punch her in her dented forehead hard enough to stun her for a moment. While her eyes spin around, I get my feet under her and push, launching her into the air. But she comes to while she's flying and lands flat on her feet. Without a moment's hesitation, she grabs a billhook from the weapons rack and charges me. I wait for her.

And wait.

Until she's just over an arm's length away.

Then I manifest my Gladius and cut off her head.

Black Sun hoodoo or solid weapons skills, they don't help now. Though when she drops the billhook she's still strong enough to claw at the air where her head used to be. But only for a few seconds. Then she ashes out like so much dirt on the killing floor. I look up at the cameras that have been monitoring the fight.

"Open that door, Dan, or in about ten seconds I'm coming through and taking more heads."

Bolts hiss and slide back and the door opens. Dan is there. He wags a finger at me.

"I'm not sure that flaming sword of yours is technically in the rulebook, but it *is* in the spirit of the fight, so I'm giving you a pass this time."

I grab him by the collar and toss him at Kenny.

"Let *that* pass too."

I let the Gladius go out and walk over to Janet. The crowd backs up.

They put their arms around me and say, "That was amazing, but please don't hurt anyone else."

"They better play nice."

"They will." She whispers in my ear, "I'm going to fuck your brains out tonight. You won't be able to ride your bike until Christmas."

I give them a squeeze, but I'm still too irritated to do anything more.

I go over to where Juliette is helping Dan.

"What did you do to that shroud eater in there? How did you protect it?"

"You're not the only one with a bag of magic tricks," says Juliette.

Dan continues, "We've used more than a few over the years."

He turns to the room.

"Isn't that right?"

People nod and laugh quietly. I don't spot any Sub Rosa among the goon squad, but that doesn't mean they don't have some on retainer. And then there's smug Kenny, the trash wizard. The Lodge has any number of connections to the baleful magic world.

I'm sweating and twitchy for another fight.

"Do I have to break anything else around here? Because I could use a drink."

"In a few minutes," says Dan.

"After what you did at the zoo and now with poor, departed Caroline," Juliette says, glancing back at the other room, "I think we can welcome you into the fold."

"Congratulations. You're a member of the Zero Lodge," says Dan.

"Where there's zero chance you'll get out alive," purrs Juliette.

There's polite applause from the others. Manimal Mike gives me a big thumbs-up with his good hand.

Dan turns to the room.

"We're planning a new excursion soon. A very challenging one."

"What is it?" I say.

"You'll see," says Juliette. "But no tricks without permission."

"They're right," says Janet. "Where's the kick if you can just poof us out of danger any time you want?"

I wipe some vampire dust off my coat.

"Fine. No poofing."

"Yay," they say quietly.

It's clear now that this bunch—and Dan and Juliette in particular—are into far weirder stuff than an armor-plated vampire and some danger games. But the fact they put such a powerful charm on the vampire is interesting. I'll stick around for now to protect Janet. But I'm not sure how long I can stand the rest of these fools.

Janet shoulder-bumps me, all excited.

While Juliette pours drinks at the bar, Dan addresses the room.

"To celebrate Manimal Mike's birthday, there's going to be an excursion Monday. We'll travel somewhere out of town and you'll work in teams of two."

Juliette hands me the drink and says, "Each team will get one canteen of water. That's all I'll say for the moment. Now, let's have a drink to James Stark, our newest member."

I raise up my glass and Juliette leads me around to glad-hand the rest of the dopes.

What the hell have I gotten myself into?

Janet holds me tight and rests their head on my back as I drive them home. It's a good feeling, but since we left the Lodge, my mind has drifted elsewhere.

When I let them off in front of their building, they take hold of my coat sleeve and say, "Come up, Mr. Stark?"

I have to frown.

"Can I take a rain check? There's something important I need do."

They let go of my sleeve and say, "Aww. You're no fun. Fine. Go do your important thing. But tomorrow night. Me and you. Doing it 'til dawn. Understood?"

I can't help but smile.

"I'm looking forward to it."

"You better be."

That feeling of wanting to flee comes back. Guilt. What am I going to tell Candy?

Janet waves and goes inside while I gun the Hog and head for the movies.

THE DEVIL'S DOOR drive-in is surrounded by a high black wall covered in flaming and horned dancing girls. There are eyes over the entrance and teeth around the edges so that when you enter, it's like you're driving right down the Devil's gullet. Flicker owns the place.

I don't know her real name and I don't know anyone who knows. All anyone is sure of is that she's Chinese and comes from heavy Sub Rosa money. She's a geomancer—a land witch. All of her strength is concentrated in certain patches of ground. Power spots that only she and a few other magicians know about. The Devil's Door sits right on top of her personal spot.

The guy selling tickets at the door waves me through and I head straight for Flicker's office behind the concession stand. I like it back here. It's a childhood movie memory. The sky overhead and everything smells vaguely of hot dogs.

I knock on the door and Flicker yells, "Come in."

It's dark inside. The only illumination comes from an old Philco Predicta TV. She's watching *The Tingler* with someone or some*thing* else. I mean, it's person shaped but completely black. No face or anything else. It's like a kind of human void next to her on the battered red sofa.

I say, "You have a fifty-foot screen to watch movies on outside, but you're in here with a twenty-inch black and white TV?"

"Twenty-one," she says without ever taking her eyes off Vincent Price on the screen. "The set is from 1960. The movie is from '59. They're kind of made for each other, don't you think?"

She finally looks at me, her eyebrows raised.

"I can't argue with that," I say. "Who's your friend?"

Flicker glances at the void next to her.

"I don't know. They just stop by sometimes to watch movies."

"They don't make you nervous?"

"Why should they? They bring their own popcorn. It's no big deal."

"I guess we've both hung out with worse."

"Much."

"And this is your patch. Who's going to cause trouble here?"

"I seem to remember a certain almost-dead man and his friends starting a bonfire."

"We had your permission for that."

"True. I'd never seen anybody stroll in and out of a fire like that before."

"Thanks again. I owe you for that and I won't forget."

She shrugs and eats some popcorn. "I know," she says. "Besides, it was a pretty neat trick to watch. It gave me a few new ideas on how to use land."

The movie ends. Vincent Price pays for his evil deeds and all is right with the world.

Flicker's void friend gets up and stretches.

"Same time next week?" she says. The void nods and gives her a little bow. It bows to me and softens into kind of a liquid state and flows into the darkness behind the sofa.

"Neat trick."

"I wish they would teach it to me," she says. "I have a family reunion next week that I'm not looking forward to."

"My condolences."

"I'll live. So, what brings you around tonight? I haven't seen much of you recently."

"I've been kind of hiding out."

"Birth's not easy on anyone and rebirth is worse."

"Maybe it's that. The whole world seems out of whack."

"This movie outside is almost over. You should stick around for the next one. *Blood for Dracula*, the old Andy Warhol monster flick."

I hold up a hand.

"Thanks, but I've had enough of vampires for one night."

She picks up some cigarettes from the desk and we go outside to smoke.

I light her up, then my Malediction. She takes a big puff and blows a smoke ring.

"You're not here for the movies and you look very much alive. What can I help you with?"

"It's not for me. This time it's for the whole city. Including you."

"Go on."

"There are some ghosts in town who won't stay put. Ghosts with a violent streak. They're trapped in Little Cairo right now, but the wards won't keep them there forever. Even if you lock down the Devil's Door, they'll sure as hell get your customers. I don't think you want to spend forever sitting here watching movies with your void pal."

"That doesn't sound fun at all."

"Then you'll check out the ghosts with me?"

"Of course. If the city locked down and I couldn't get to Burrito King every now and then I'd go mad. When and where do you want to meet?"

"Sunset tomorrow. I'll pick you up."

"I'll be here."

The end of *Flesh for Frankenstein* is playing on the big screen. I watch for a while as Udo Kier chews the scenery just right as the doctor.

"I love that guy."

Flicker blows another smoke ring.

She says, "He's even better as Dracula. I'm telling you, you ought to stick around."

"Some other night when you have something soothing, like werewolves or zombies."

"It's James Whale's birthday soon. We're having a festival. *Frankenstein. Bride of Frankenstein. The Old Dark House* and some others."

"I'll be here."

"Bring Candy."

I hesitate.

"We'll see."

"Oooh. That sounds interesting."

"I'll tell you about it tomorrow."

"Sunset. See you then."

I head back home and write down what Gentry told me. I've got a date with a real estate agent tomorrow, only she doesn't know it yet.

IN THE AFTERNOON I meet with Avani Chanchala. At least that's the name she goes by. I checked her out online but couldn't find out much more than a business address. That means Chanchala might be her real name, but it might not. Real estate in Hollywood is just an extension of show business. Real estate isn't just land, it's dreams. Sell the image. Not the dirt. It's liable to have a few bodies buried in it, but that possibility just makes it more charming and colorful—and expensive. People here change their names and appearance all the time, depending on the audience. Chanchala could be legit, but there's every chance she's really Susie Smith from Glendale.

The front door to Chanchala Abodes is locked, so I go in through a shadow. There's a reception area but no secretary. It's like they're begging me to loot this place. I go to the big office and open the door.

"Knock knock."

The office is nice but spare. It reminds me of pictures Candy showed me of Tokyo work spaces. All very pretty. Uncluttered. Lots of dark wood and light. But that kind of thing feels different in L.A. Less like an elegant Japanese aesthetic than someone ready to change with the times at a moment's notice or just grab what little there is and head for the hills.

Chanchala is looking over some papers. She takes off her glasses and says, "Well, you're certainly not Mr. Block."

I sit on a cushy chair by her desk.

"A client?"

"My two o'clock."

"Then I'll get right to the point. I want to talk about Chris Stein."

She cocks her head.

"And who are you again?"

"I work for Thomas Abbot. You know who that is?"

She sits back and looks uncomfortable.

"I've heard the name."

"I bet you have. I hear that you've sold property to the Sub Rosa."

Chanchala puts her hands on the desk.

"How did you know that?"

"I didn't. I just made it up."

"Cute. Chris was a century ago. Why are you asking questions now?"

"Because he's back. A part of him is at least."

"What does that mean?"

"You were in the party scene with Stein way back when. Tell me about it."

She picks up a pen and taps it impatiently on the pretty desk.

"If you're here to insinuate something, you can turn around and leave right now."

But her pupils have gone wide. I struck a nerve. Time to bear down on it.

"I'm here to ask questions, not call people names. Tell me about Chris and money."

She shrugs.

"When he needed money I introduced him to people who might be willing to pay for his services. I never made a dime off of him, you understand."

"Of course. Were Jimmy Summers and Claire Hennessey customers?"

She makes a face.

"God no. They were playmates. He did them for free."

This isn't getting me anywhere. Time to circle back to Gentry's stuff.

"Tell me about the parties. Toward the end. Did anything change?"

She laughs, but it's a sarcastic stage bark.

"You're talking about the sex magic angle."

"Exactly," I lie.

"I thought it was silly, but it *was* the seventies. Anton LaVey was all the rage. Black candles, pentagrams, Aleister Crowley, and pretend sacrifices? They gave the parties a new frisson."

"But you didn't believe any of it."

"Not a word."

"But you were there."

"Of course."

"Even after Stein was murdered?"

She looks uncomfortable again.

"Chris wasn't so much into the parties anymore. He'd changed. Gone a little over the edge. Maybe it was the coke. Still, he was busy being paid for his services. And, of course, he had his regular."

"The one who paid his rent but kept him on a short leash."

"That's the one."

"And it wasn't Hennessey or Summers."

"Definitely not."

"'Forever yours, forever mine.' Does that mean anything to you?"

"Not a thing."

There's a tiny Zen garden in a box on her desk. The sand is curved into gentle waves. I pick up the tiny rake, look it over, and toss it back in, ruining the design.

"What did you mean when you said Stein had gone over the edge?"

She shifts her shoulders nervously.

"Chris was always eccentric and a risk taker, but he went a bit mad about it. Breaking and entering. Stealing cars."

"I heard he could pick locks."

"Yes. But there were other things too. He'd set fires in abandoned buildings and not run out until the very last minute. He said he belonged to a club. He tried to get some of us to join. No one did, of course."

Something clicks in my brain. Something bad.

"Did he say 'club' or 'lodge'?"

"I suppose it could have been 'lodge.'"

"The Zero Lodge?"

"Maybe."

"Did he ever mention Dan Perkins or Juliette Stray?"

"Ha! Those nuts." The laugh is genuine this time. "I sold them their house. But no, it couldn't have been them. They weren't even in the city back then."

"And that's all you know?"

She picks up the rake and begins fixing the sand in her tiny garden.

"That's everything."

I crane my head around the expensive-looking office.

"I can see why you didn't need to make money off Stein. This is a nice setup."

A thin smile.

"I like it."

"Who else would know about Stein, hustling, and sex magick and all that?"

"Why should I tell you that?"

"Because a bad word to Abbot about your working as Stein's pimp is going to cost you money."

She stops raking and looks at me.

"I told you. I didn't make any money from Chris. I was a friend."

"But a good word from me could get you closer to Abbot and steady Sub Rosa customers."

She thinks things over for a moment. Then she writes something down on company stationery and starts to push it across the desk but grabs it back at the last minute. Once she's torn her name off the paper, she gives it to me. It's a name.

"What's this?"

"A name."

"Lisa Thivierge. The director?"

"Lisa hasn't directed anything in forty years. Hollywood has a way of forgetting about women when they have the temerity to grow out of their twenties. She can tell you more, though. But she's old. Be gentle with her."

"There's no address."

"Lisa went into seclusion. No one has seen her in over ten years. Longer, now that I think about it."

"Any idea who might know where she is?"

"None."

"Do you have a phone number?"

"Nope."

I put the paper in my pocket.

"Thanks, I guess."

"If you find her, don't tell her I gave you her name."

"I'm hearing a lot of that lately."

I get up and head for the door. Before I get there, she calls to me.

"I expect a good word to Abbot."

"I'll give him the word all right."

I have mixed feelings as I drive the Hog home. I don't

like Chanchala and I'm bothered by Chris's having to hustle for money. But an ex-actor's options can be limited in L.A., especially if they aren't as good-looking as they used to be. Chanchala's setting him up with clients bothers me because she's lying when she says she didn't make any money. Chanchala might not have made cash at the time, but she got connections that would pay off big in her real estate business. But Chris—should I feel bad for him? Maybe he enjoyed the work. We all do what we have to to survive. And if Brigitte taught me anything it's that sex work is work, every bit as real as selling real estate to the absurdly wealthy.

What troubles me more is Stein's connection to the Zero Lodge, where, as everyone likes reminding me, you have zero chance of getting out alive. Did he try to break away from them? But even if he did, he died in '79. Why is he back now? It makes me mad, but on the off chance someone knows something I'll stick around Dan and Juliette's playpen a while longer. At least Janet will be happy.

After sunset, I take Flicker to Little Cairo through a shadow.

She grins and looks like she doesn't even notice that the neighborhood is a war zone.

She says, "I haven't been here in years."

"You know the place?"

"We used to play Pharaohs here."

"What's Pharaohs?"

"It's like King of the Hill, but with pyramids."

"Kids."

"How much time do we have?"

"They come an hour after sunset, so soon now."

"That's plenty of time for what we have to do."

"Set up an ambush?"

"No," she says. "Prepare the ground for whatever's going to happen. You prepare the ground right and it can help you."

"What does 'prepare the ground' mean?"

"I'm a geomancer. A child of the King Below. Just as you're a child of the Hum. And a Black Lane Walker, too."

"Can you say that in English?"

Flicker points a finger toward the sky.

"Look up. What do you see?"

"Power lines."

"And if it was completely dark?"

"Stars?"

"I still think you'd still see the power lines. You're a child of the Hum. And a powerful one. A lord of the city, electricity, and human creation."

"I guess that makes sense. What's a Black Lane Walker?"

She chuckles.

"Your life, Stark. I mean, look at it. You live with one hand in this world and the other one grasping the next. Black Lane Walkers don't have an easy time of it."

"I can't argue with that part. But come on. The King Below. Child of the Hum. That's not L.A. That's fairy-tale stuff."

"Nothing in L.A. is just a tale. It's just the past remembered differently."

She touches the pavement.

"Nothing yet."

"Is that good?"

She shrugs.

"It's not anything."

I start to light a Malediction. Flicker takes it from my hand and puts it back in the pack.

"No fire. That will pull them right to you."

"Thanks. So, who's the King Below?"

"Someone with whom I have an understanding."

"Wait. You're not talking about Lucifer, are you?"

Flicker makes a face.

"Of course not. I mean the king below our feet. Land. Soil. The thousands of miles of stone between here and the center of the Earth. We drive and build and walk on him without giving him a thought. We owe the King offerings as much as any god."

"Can he stop earthquakes?"

"He *is* the earthquakes. They're his restless dreams."

"Has he tried Benadryl?"

"I thought you of all people would understand."

Flicker turns and walks away.

"I'm sorry. It's just that I can barely deal with Mr. Muninn and the mess in Heaven. Now I have to worry about getting the damn earth mad at me?"

"Just give the King Below a thought or an offering every now and then and you'll be fine."

"Like what?"

She kneels on a lawn and calls me over. After she digs a shallow hole, she pulls something from her pocket. It's a churro.

"Flour and cinnamon grown from his soil."

"You're fucking kidding. I never pegged you for a pagan."

She keeps digging.

"I'm as pagan as they come."

"But not a hippie Wiccan."

"And you're not just another dumb punk. We all find our place in the world however we can."

She buries the churro and pats down the dirt.

I say, "Is that what the ghosts are doing? Finding their way in the world?"

"The ghosts—most Stay Belows—are really pretty simple. They're like lost children. Instead of fighting them, find out what they want. Boredom can bring the dead back as much as trauma."

"Trust me. These ghosts aren't bored. They're having a grand old time. And the one I'm looking for is definitely traumatized. Not just murdered. Cut in half."

"A Black Dahlia?"

"Worse, he was famous for about ten minutes."

She shakes her head.

"That's a lot of pain to deal with."

"You think that's what brought him back?"

"I doubt it. But now that he's back he's acting on all that anger and fear."

We walk side by side down the street. I pick up a hubcap and Frisbee it back onto a lawn with an overturned Miata.

"Do you think it might be deliberate?"

Flicker looks at me.

"The manifestations? I doubt it. But the calling, yes. It's just that something went wrong."

"I'm convinced that Chris Stein is the center of this."

"You're probably right. As a Black Laner you have good

instincts for these things. I think that Stein is probably the magnet. The other Stay Belows simply follow him."

"Why do they sing?"

"They can't help it. It's their offering to the world for intruding. Plus, it calms both them and the land."

I look around.

"It's dark and no ghosts yet."

Flicker gets on her knees and presses her palms to the pavement.

I kneel down beside her.

"What are you doing?"

"Listening for them."

"With your hands?"

"They're Stay Belows. You can feel them before you see them. Get down here like me and put your hands on the ground."

I do what she says.

"Do you feel anything?"

"Nothing."

"We fed the King. This is your city. You have power. Open yourself up and let it out."

I kneel there for a minute trying to feel or see or hear something.

"Still nothing."

"All right. What *do* you feel?"

"A little shaking. Vibrations from street traffic."

"Stark, we're at least two blocks from any main street."

"Huh. How about that?"

"Yeah," she says.

"It's getting stronger."

"It is. Get ready."

"Ready how? What am I supposed to be doing?"

"Getting out of their way."

It's the same as always. The pinprick of light appears in the air. Melts. Widens.

"The Thurl," says Flicker.

"What's that?"

"Thurl. It's just a hole. But one where you can fall into the Otherworld or it can fall into ours."

"Can you close it?"

"Not without knowing what opened it."

I pull Flicker back as the drill continues. The spooks blast from the Thurl like a horror show hurricane. At the end of the mob comes Stein, looking as hangdog and confused as ever.

"There's the birthday boy."

She says, "Don't forget. We're in their territory now. To them, we're the ghosts."

Around us, the Stay Belows who don't rush Abbot's barrier get to work smashing the neighborhood into little bite-size pieces. There's a crash at the head of the block as an entire Sphinx falls onto its side.

It catches me by surprise and I curse, which is dumb. The spooks, who were busy a moment before, now turn and come for me and Flicker.

"Say the word and I'll take us out of here," I tell her.

"We're all right. I told you the King Below is looking out for me."

She raises her arms and the street seems to soften to quicksand. It rises and hangs in the air like waves waiting to crash on a beach, blocking the approaching spook mob. Then it's just me, Flicker, and Stein. He's ten or so yards away, but I know he recognizes me because he runs right at me, all fury and death. I've tried being nice, but I'm not putting up with this shit again. I manifest my Gladius and wait for him.

Flicker pushes me out of the way and begins to sing. It's a strange, old, high melody. Sad. Like a love song to a dead lover.

Stein slows his run.

She keeps singing.

He slows even more.

He barely shuffles the last few feet. Stein stops and sways back and forth to the melody.

When his eyes close Flicker says, "Why does he hate you like that?"

"It's something I said to him. 'Forever yours. Forever mine.' I don't know what it means."

"Interesting."

She takes a couple of steps toward Stein and says, "Forever yours. Forever mine."

Stein stops his swaying and makes a low animal growl.

Flicker keeps going. I keep my Gladius out.

"Forever yours. Forever mine."

Stein is shaking, but he doesn't move.

"Forever yours. Forever mine."

Stein snarls like a rabid dog.

Instead of running like a sensible person, Flicker opens her arms to him and says, "Forever yours. Forever mine."

When she's right in front of him, Stein puts his arms around her. Flicker embraces him.

They just stand there like that for a few minutes, Stein's head resting on her shoulder. I stay on guard for the slightest sign of anger from dead boy.

Eventually, Flicker steps back. She touches his face and comes back to me. Stein shuffles into the dark looking as sad and lost as ever. I let the Gladius go out.

I frown at her.

"What the hell was that?"

"It's definitely a woman he's looking for," Flicker says.

"That's something at least."

"There's more. He said, 'Zadkiel.' Does that mean anything to you?"

I've never felt dumber. Of course it was an angel who killed him. Sliced him in half and cauterized the wound by killing him with her Gladius. Was Zadkiel Stein's secret lover? The one who paid his rent but refused to let him stray too far? Did he know who she was? Did he try to break things off or was it something else?

"Stark? Does 'Zadkiel' mean anything?"

I nod.

"Everything."

In the distance, Stein is shaking again, not like when he leaves the Thurl. More like an animal tensing for a fight.

"I think our boy is getting agitated."

Flicker says, "We should go and let them get on with what they came to do."

She raises her hands again, and the pavement flows back to normal, like nothing happened.

"We can't just leave," I say. "The wards aren't holding. They're going to break out and do this to the whole city."

Flicker shakes her head.

"All the more reason to get in good with the King Below."

As she says it she hands me another churro.

I say, "You've been waiting to spring this on me all evening, haven't you?"

She smiles.

"A little bit. Are you going to do it?"

I use the black blade to rip a hole in a nearby lawn. Drop in the churro and cover it over with dirt.

"Am I supposed to say something?"

"'Thank you' is always nice."

"Thanks, King. You're a pal."

As I slip the blade back in my boot I think of all the strange hoodoo I've seen tonight and it makes me wonder something.

I say, "Do you know anything about angels?"

"Not a thing. Why?"

"I have an angel problem, but I don't know how to start or even if I should. Considering the source, it could be some kind of game."

"What do your instincts tell you, Black Lane Walker?"

"That I'm being played and should figure out what kind of game it is before I get in too deep."

"Then maybe you should."

"Maybe I should." I shake my head to clear it and say, "You ready to get out of here?"

Flicker gives me a look like she feels a little sorry for me.

"Come back to the Devil's Door and relax for a while where there are people."

"What are you playing?"

"*Road Warrior* and *Zardoz.*"

"Let's go."

I GO OVER to Janet's place early the next morning and they drag me straight into the bedroom, which isn't a bad start to the day. The Zero Lodge picks us up in a blacked-out van around ten. Everyone else in the van is dressed in evening gowns and snappy suits. Janet looks great in a secondhand tux. I'm the only one in regular everyday clothes. Apparently, I'm expected to look like a headwaiter if I'm going to stick around with these people. This is getting better and better. But Janet holds my hand, chatting happily with the other Lodge members as they try to guess what today's fun is going to be. Lava wrestling? Volleyball in a minefield? Maybe Manimal Mike taught them to play Billy Flinch but Dan and Juliette didn't want brains splattered on the basement walls.

After a couple of hours of driving, the chitchat has worn down to an occasional grumble, and even the Lodge hard core are getting restless. We finally stop around noon and pile out of the cattle car, straight into the desert.

It has to be over a hundred degrees. We're at the bottom of a dry canyon surrounded by dead and dying scrub and spindly trees that rise up from the dusty road where we're parked and straight up the steep canyon walls. There doesn't seem to be anything else in any direction.

Dan and Juliette come out of the front of the van back here with us cows. Trash wizard Kenny gets out of a second identical van.

Dan says, "I hope everyone had a good night's sleep last night and a pleasant trip out from the city. Today's excursion is going to be a real adventure. Juliette and I spent quite a lot of time setting it up."

"We sure did," says Juliette, doing her best Jayne Mansfield impression. "I almost broke a nail."

The line gets some polite titters.

She goes on, "You all look lovely today, except for our newest member, but I'm sure he'll get the hang of things."

She smiles in my direction and I give her a nod because it would upset Janet if I gave her the finger.

While she was talking, Dan hauled a plastic storage box from the back of the van and set it on the ground in the middle of the group.

"Are you ready to see what's inside?" he says. "It's essential to today's excursion."

A few of the old-timers yell, "Open it!" and whoop.

Dan does it with a flourish like he's going to reveal he stole the crown jewels. Instead, what's inside the box is a lot of canteens, maps, and what look like oversized wristwatches.

Fuck. It's a nature hike. Flicker should be here. This is her scene. Not mine.

Juliette tosses the first canteen and map to me and straps one of the watches on my wrist.

Dan says, "Today's adventure, boys and girls, is a kind of race, but not against each other. It's against the forces of nature itself."

Juliette keeps handing out the gear, smooth as a Beverly Hills cobra.

"You'll be working in teams of two. One will have the map and one will have the canteen. It doesn't matter which of you wears the timer. But you don't want to lose it because the timer is the most important piece of equipment you'll have."

When she's done handing out gear, Juliette says, "The excursion is simple. There's a route drawn on each of your maps. That's how you'll climb from where we are now to the top of the canyon. The canteen is, well, your canteen. Don't use it up too quickly because it's a long way to the top."

"As for the timer," Dan says, "a hike up a hill didn't really seem like quite enough of a challenge—until we found this particular canyon. You see, there's going to be a controlled burn here later today. You see all the brush and trees? By tonight they'll all be ash. And that's where your timer comes in."

Juliette says, "It goes off when the burn starts. If you're not at the top by then, you're going to want to shake a leg or get cooked like a Christmas goose."

"There's a prize for the first couple out and, I'm afraid, a penalty for the last. One final little challenge. Right, Ken?"

The trash wizard doesn't say anything. He just holds up a doctor's bag that could contain anything from a ham sandwich to a nuke.

Dan gives us all a grin.

"Does everybody understand the rules? Remember, you have to stick to the route on your map. There's also a penalty for any couple that uses another couple's route."

Juliette raises a start pistol over her head.

"You better have the idea by now, kids, because three, two, one . . . Go!" she yells, and fires the gun. Ten couples sprint away in ten different directions like lambs off to slaughter.

I walk in the direction of our route until Janet grabs my hand and pulls me.

"Come on," they say. "It's a race. If we're first we'll win

the prize."

I pull her back a little.

"Calm down. This isn't running weather. It's got to be over a hundred."

From behind us Juliette yells, "A hundred and fifteen."

Janet waves to her.

"We're fine," they say, but still pull me in a slow trot.

I have the map, so when we come to the bottom of the hill I take the lead on the trail. I have to admit I'm surprised at first. The climb isn't that bad and unless the fire is going to start in the next hour or so, we should make it out of the canyon in plenty of time. Janet comes up beside me and snatches the map out of my hands.

"Hurry up, Grandpa. I want that prize."

They run up the trail and I lope along behind them.

When it's 115 degrees out, enthusiasm will only take you so far before reality sets in. After an hour of walking, the trail becomes more difficult. The ground is all loose gravel and stones. There's nothing you can do but trudge through stuff like that, a step at a time. Each misstep sends you sliding back down the trail a few yards so that you have to climb the same damn ground again. Over and over. Finally Janet gives in and says, "I have to stop a minute."

I took off my coat a half hour ago, so I'm happy for a break. They hand me back the map and take a swig from the canteen.

"Fuck!" Janet yells, and spits out a mouthful of water.

I take the canteen and smell it.

"Salt water."

"What a shitty thing to do," they say.

"Dan and Juliette let a guy get eaten by a tiger and you're surprised they spiked the water?"

"When you put it that way, I guess not."

"You know, I could make it good water. It's easy hoodoo."

Janet snatches back the canteen and puts the top back on.

"Absolutely not. No tricks today. We do this like everybody else. Promise me."

I look around, less than not at all happy with the situation.

"Promise me."

I turn to them.

"Fine. No tricks. No hoodoo. No rabbits out of the hat."

"Thank you."

"We should get going. We still have a ways to go."

Janet spits out one last mouthful of salt and we head back up the trail.

A few minutes later, she points past me.

"Are those coyotes following us?"

I look and they're right. On the other side of the scrub, four coyotes lope along beside us.

I say, "Don't worry about them. They're not going to bother us."

"Are you sure?"

"I mean, if we die they'll eat us in a hot second. So my plan is not to die. Is that your plan, too?"

They smile.

"That's my plan."

We keep climbing. I hate the situation, but it's even worse for Janet. They're wearing high heels. They tried taking them off a couple of times, but the heat coming off 115-degree rocks was worse on their feet than the shoes, so they had to keep them on. I can tell they're in a lot of pain and still distracted by the coyotes because they don't even notice when their foot comes down just a few inches from a sidewinder ducking under a rock. I pull them away, but the damn snake gets their ankle. They scream, but I pull them up the hill a few yards to get clear of the snake.

When I lay them down, their ankle is already swelling.

"It burns," Janet gasps.

I pull their shoe off and look at the wound.

"It's not as bad as it could be. It didn't get its fangs in too deep. Let me fix this. I know some easy hoodoo."

Janet grabs my shoulder and squeezes hard.

"No tricks. No tricks."

"You could lose the damn leg or even die."

"Then help me."

I set my coat next to them and give them the sleeve.

"Here, bite down on that. This is going to hurt."

I get the black blade from my boot and cut the wound open more. Janet screams into the coat as blood gushes out. I squeeze the wound to get out as much of the venom as possible. Finally, I lean over and suck out blood from the wound, spitting it out fast. Even so, my lips tingle with poison. I have no idea if what I'm doing is helping. I've just seen it in a hundred Westerns and I can't use hoodoo, so it's better than nothing.

In a few minutes, the swelling seems to have stopped. I cut one of the sleeves off my shirt and tie it around their leg to stop the bleeding. Janet is still and ice white. Their pupils are pinpoints in the sun.

I help them up into a sitting position.

"Do you think you can hold yourself up on your good leg?"

Janet looks at me, bleary.

"I'll try."

I get them upright, but the moment they try to stand, they collapse again.

I look up the hill. The top isn't that far away, but on this shitty ground, even on two feet, it would take forever.

On my wrist, the timer pings. A minute or so later, a plume of black smoke climbs into the air on the other side of the canyon.

I pull Janet into a sitting position again.

"We have to go," I tell her. "I'm going to get you out of here."

They put their hand on my cheek.

"No tricks."

Goddammit.

"Fine. But this isn't going to be fun for anyone."

I get them up and carry them in my arms like Tor Johnson carried poor Mona McKinnon in *Plan 9 from Outer Space.*

The hill gets steeper and the gravel looser as we climb. It takes another hour to reach the top. We're breathing in lungfuls of black smoke by then. I'm sweating like a pig doing the Tour de France and stagger the last few yards on trembling legs. By now, I don't even know what kind of shape Janet is in.

To their credit, asshole Dan and Juliette come running when they see us. I set Janet on the ground and grab Dan by his stupid lapels.

"Rattlesnake. Tell me you have antivenin."

Juliette is already kneeling by Janet, a medical kit open on the ground.

Dan pats my arm.

"It's going to be all right. Juliette knows what to do."

When I check, Juliette is giving Janet an injection. That done, she takes off my shitty tourniquet and examines the wound.

"See?" says Dan. "My angel has nurse training, just for moments like this."

I let go of him.

"Okay, but if she loses that leg, I'm taking one of yours."

Dan just smiles.

"I believe *they* is the correct pronoun in this case. Not *she*. You're going to want to work on that before they're back on their feet."

Shit. Not only did I call Janet the wrong thing, but I got told off by the ringmaster of this psycho circus. He's going to have a chuckle with Juliette about that. I go back and kneel down next to Janet.

Juliette says, "Think you can carry them like a person for a minute and not a sack of potatoes?"

"Where do you want them?"

"I've turned on the air-conditioning in the van. Put them in there."

"We need to get them to a hospital."

"They're stable for now and should rest."

"If you're not going to take them, I will."

"You might want to speak to them first."

I carry Janet to the van and lay them down near the air-conditioning vent in the back. When they open their eyes I say, "I'm getting you to Allegra's right now."

They put their hand onto my hand.

"No tricks. You promised."

"Fuck that, you need a doctor."

"Dan and Juliette have a private clinic."

I push some hair from their face.

"Does that mean you've been hurt before?"

They pat my arm.

"It's okay. I'm feeling better. Let me rest."

I sit down next to them.

"I wonder how Manimal Mike and Maria are doing."

"You should go check on them."

"I'm not leaving you alone."

"Ask Juliette. She'll come and sit with me."

"I don't trust her."

Janet shoves me weakly.

"Go check on Mike and Maria. And, Stark?"

"Yes?"

"I mean it when I say no tricks. If you do anything, I won't like you anymore and you'll have to find a new donut shop."

I look outside. The wind has changed and smoke is blowing in this direction. The air stinks and the sky is giant swirls of jet black. I get out and tell Juliette that Janet wants her.

She looks at me with something that might be sympathy or might be a suppressed laugh.

"Of course, dear. I'll take care of everything for you."

"They said you know a clinic."

"They're waiting for us right now. We'll be leaving soon."

She heads for the van and I walk around the Lodge members. It's getting hard to breathe, but most of them seem to be back. I spot Mike and Maria at the top of a trail. Another couple is struggling to get up the last section of their climb. The woman's hair is wild, blowing in the wind that's pushing the smoke in our direction. She's practically dragging her partner, a little guy whose jacket and shirt are in tatters.

I grab Mike.

"Are they the last ones?"

Mike nods.

"Yeah. I wouldn't want to be them. Dan will be getting their penalty ready."

"He's still going to do it? Look at them. They're already half-dead."

Mike shakes his head.

"I know."

He holds out a canteen.

"We were the first ones up, so we got the prize. Fresh water. Want some?"

"Can I give it to Janet?"

"Of course," says Maria. "I'll take it to her."

"Thanks."

As the last couple struggles up the hill, Dan and Kenny lay down long mats on either side of the trailhead. They look like Astroturf. And they're covered in razor blades. The way the two suckers below are crawling along the trail, there won't be anything left of them to get out of the canyon. On top of that, flames are creeping quickly up the trail behind them. Razors or not, they don't have any choice but to keep crawling or they'll be burned alive. Lodge members are gathered around the trailhead screaming at them to move faster.

I could make this whole thing stop right now. Just mutter a few words of Hellion and the fire is out. The razors are gone. But I made a promise. Should I save these fools and lose Janet? I stand there like a dunce, weighing everything against everything else. The couple struggling up the hill chose to be here, and as much trouble as they're having, they're staying well ahead of the fire. The only thing they have to get by now is the razors. If they have any brains, they can strip down and pile their clothes on top. Sure, they'll get cut, but they won't be hamburger when they get to the road.

I look around. What the hell is wrong with these people? This is like Hell for halfwits. The ones who can't tell the difference between a martini and a flaming poker up the ass.

Then things get even worse.

Dan and Kenny haul a live goddamn sheep from the second van to the top of the trail. It bleats once when it gets a face full of smoke but doesn't bleat a second time, because trash wizard Kenny slits its throat. Even the lodge creeps lurch back at that. A couple of people throw up when Kenny disembowels the animal, leaving its belly open wide. Then junkyard Merlin pours a potion onto the entrails and whispers some dime-store hoodoo.

A few seconds later the guts begin to quiver and coalesce into *something*. A pile of wet meat that pulls itself up onto something like legs and opens a pair of quivering jaws to show rows of shattered bones that have formed into sharp, broken teeth.

Then the gut thing springs into the air, past the razor mats, and lands behind the crawling couple. It's hard to see what's happening through the choking smoke, but the screams tells everyone what they need to know. Through breaks in the darkness, it's hard to see much more than a spreading wet redness on the trail. The screams don't last too long and when the wind takes the smoke in another direction, all that's visible down the hill is Kenny's beast shoving gobs of someone else's flesh into its crooked mouth.

I told Janet no tricks, but it's hard not to grab the Colt and put a few rounds into what passes for its head.

The fire surrounds Kenny's monster and moves up fast behind it. The thing crawls up the trail toward us, trying to keep ahead of the flames. That's it then. Even if Janet hates me, if that thing makes it to the top, I'm killing it and will find somewhere else to get fritters.

In the end, I don't have to do anything.

As the glop monster reaches the razor mats, Dan goes to the top of the trail with a Glock in his hand and pumps six shots dead center into the thing. It lets out a startled wail and instead of turning away, it actually crawls faster, practically eviscerating itself as it drags its leaking body over the razors. Dan shoots it a couple of more times, but that's just icing on the cake.

The fire has caught up to the crawler. By the time it's at the top of the mats, it's a mass of twitching meat slowly roasting in a blazing furnace. The heat forces everyone back from the trail.

"Get in the vans," shouts Dan.

No one needs to hear it twice. The filthy mob piles inside and we speed away. No one says anything, not the whole two hours it takes to get back to L.A.

BECAUSE WE'RE NOT married and I'm not a family member,

the clinic won't let me stay with Janet overnight, but I arrive bright and early the next morning to get them out of there. They look good. No longer fish-belly white. And they can walk on the bad leg, though with a slight limp.

When we reach the parking lot Janet says, "Where's your bike?"

I just take their hand and pull them into a nearby shadow.

We come out in the flying saucer house. Janet drops down onto the sofa and I bring them a glass of water so they can take a Vicodin.

When they're done they say, "I like that thing you do with shadows."

"I'll tell you more about it, but right now I need to ask you something. You said I'd understand why you like the Lodge once I saw it. But I don't. What is it exactly that you get out of the place? You're not crazy like those other people. I just don't get it."

They reach for my hand and hold it loosely in theirs.

"I've been scared my whole life," Janet says. "I was born sick, without much of an immune system. I was afraid of people. Of my doctors. I was terrified of animals. I was afraid to leave my room. When I was older and got the right treatment, my parents wanted me to be a lawyer like my dad. But I always liked music. It got pretty abusive there before I moved out. Later, when I realized I was different, I got scared in a whole new way. I wasn't really a straight cis person. But I wasn't gay. I wasn't a man or a woman. I thought there was something wrong with me."

They squeeze my hand and I squeeze back.

"I'm sorry. I didn't know you'd had it so rough."

"It's why you teaching me how to shoot was a big deal for me. I might not have shown it, but I was terrified."

"You covered it up very well."

"I've had a lot of practice."

They look around the room, then back to me.

Janet goes on, "I'm well now, but I take a lot of medication and know that it could stop working at any time. Everybody is dying, but I'm dying a little faster than most. For me, the Lodge is a way to never fall back into my old patterns. I have to overcome the old fears when Dan and Juliette come up with their wild ideas. And after I've made it through one, there's no other feeling like it."

"Even after everything that happened at the canyon, you haven't thought about quitting?"

They shake their head.

"Not for a minute." Janet laughs and says, "Besides, it's the Zero Lodge. Quitting isn't an option."

I look at her.

"Did they threaten you?"

"Of course not. But there are things you don't understand yet."

"Like what?"

"It's like you and the shadow trick. I'll tell you, but not right now."

I think about it for a minute.

"Janet, I'm a killer."

They look at me like maybe they heard me wrong.

"For a long time, I was a private hit man. Since then, I've been pretty much freelance. At this point, I don't know how many *things* and people I've killed. And while I was doing all that killing, I found my way into the Room of Thirteen Doors."

They sit up straighter.

"Did all this happen here in L.A.?"

"Some."

"Where then? Stop being so coy about it."

I let go of their hand.

"It happened the same place I got all these scars."

"Where?"

"In Hell."

Janet flops against the back of the sofa, looking mad.

"Come on. For real."

"I'll tell you about it, but I'm going to need a drink first. Then, if you don't believe me and want me to not bother you anymore, I won't."

I come back with bourbon and explain the whole sordid story. From Mason to Lucifer to my escaping and coming back to L.A. To my surprise, Janet doesn't want me to take them home. I guess that means I'm stuck in the Lodge for a while. But at least I don't have to dance around the truth anymore. I don't know what any of this means in the long run, but for now, I'm happy we're both sticking around.

They lean forward to kiss me and I hear something funny. Like someone left the stereo on next door. Only there isn't anybody next door. And the song is strange and high and dangerously familiar.

The first ghost walks in from the kitchen. Two more come out of the wall by the bedroom. A fourth emerges from the front door.

"Stark, what's happening?" says Janet.

"Get down on the floor and stay there."

While I'm getting Janet down, the kitchen spook slashes my left arm with a sickle. I knock her back with a kick and go for the bedroom ghosts. They both have clubs, so I get low when I charge them.

I get the first spook around the waist and ram him into the second. They crash onto the shag carpet, but they're not really hurt. Spooks don't work like that. You can muscle them, kick them, knock them down, but unless you can convince them to go away or destroy them, you're stuck with the bastards.

I don't wait for the fourth spook to attack. I take a club from one of the bedroom ghosts and throw it. But I'm worried about Janet, so I get sloppy. The creep by the door sees the club coming from a mile away. She dodges it and throws a knife. I twist away—mostly. The tip catches me on the side, just above my kidney. By now the bedroom and spooks are back on their feet. I look over at Janet just as the kitchen spook makes a move for them.

No more fucking around. Even if I set the whole place on fire, that's just how it has to be.

I duck as the door ghost throws another knife and manifest my Gladius. Kick the coffee table out of the way and bring down the blade on kitchen spook's sickle arm. Then slice up again, cutting the ghost in two. It instantly blips out of existence.

One of the bedroom ghosts smashes me across the back with its club. It hurts like hell, but I swing the Gladius wide and take them both out with one slash.

The knife shade keeps tossing blades my way. I rush it, using the coffee table as a shield. Pin the spook to the wall and run it through the gut with the Gladius.

The room goes quiet. I look around for more dead killers. Make a circuit of the room with the Gladius, ready to burn anything strange out of existence. Check the kitchen. Check the bedroom. Nothing. I pull Janet from the floor and help them back onto the sofa.

"What the hell was that?" they say.

"Dead people."

"Ones you killed?"

"No. Just some random assholes."

"Does this kind of thing happen to you a lot?"

"It depends on your definition of 'a lot.' I told you before, bad things can happen to people who get close to me."

Janet looks at my arm and my back.

"You're bleeding."

"I'm hard on clothes."

"So you said."

There're holes all over the coffee table where the ghost knives embedded themselves. Another hole in the wall where the knife spook dodged the club I threw. Singe marks near the bedroom door where I took down the other two. All things considered, the place could be in worse shape.

I help Janet to their feet.

"Time for you to go home."

"Maybe you're right."

I take them back to their place. They don't ask me up this time.

Janet says, "Did you get that flaming sword in Hell too?"

"No. From my father."

"Your family is a lot more interesting than mine."

"I wouldn't mind them being a little duller. You're not going to work today, right?"

They nod.

"I thought about it, but after the snake bite and your Haunted Mansion ride, I think I'll take it easy today. But you're coming to the next excursion, right? Promise."

"I can't stand those people."

"Promise?"

It's clear Janet is going, and who's going to protect them if I'm not there?

"I promise."

My phone beeps. I check the screen. Abbot left me a message.

"Sorry. I have to go and talk to this guy."

Janet kisses me and says, "I never kissed a killer before."

"How do you know?"

"I never kissed anyone like you before."

They limp inside their building, blowing me a kiss before they close the door.

I go back to the flying saucer house and drag the coffee table back to where it's supposed to be. In the bedroom, I grab another one of Kasabian's cast-off paperbacks—*Personal Finance for the Power Entrepreneur*—and shove it in the hole where it belongs.

A lot worries me these days, but what has me right this minute is the certainty that the ghost attack was nothing more than a feint. Someone or something was just testing the waters. The spooks will be back and next time it's going to be worse.

I get some coffee, put my feet up on the wrecked coffee table, and call Abbot.

"How goes it with your assignment?" he says. Not even a hello. That's not like him. I need to give him something.

"I know a lot more about the Stay Belows than I did before."

"Stay Belows? Where did you learn a term like that?"

"You partner with people who can help. I do the same thing."

"What more have you learned about them?"

"Chris Stein is the key to the whole thing. The rodeo clown that all the bulls come after. If I figure out Stein, all the cows will wander home."

I hear Abbot take a breath.

"Whatever it is you're learning, whatever it is you're doing, do it faster. The spirits are cracking the wards. They won't hold forever. I've had to post people there already to look out for breaches."

"I'm going as fast as I can. I'm working a few angles."

"What angles?"

"Forever yours. Forever mine."

He doesn't say anything for a minute.

"Stark? What the hell was that? A spell? A hex?"

"It doesn't mean anything to you?"

"Nothing."

"Damn. I was hoping it might be a Sub Rosa thing. Something you blue bloods say."

"I can assure you that I've never heard anyone say 'forever yours, forever mine.' You think it's important?"

"It almost got me killed, so yeah."

I tell him about Stein's attacking me, then what Flicker said about Zadkiel.

"There's an angel involved? I knew you were the right man."

"I hope so."

Abbot says, "You think if you can figure out 'forever yours, forever mine,' you'll have everything you need?"

"I'm sure of it."

"Keep me in the loop. I have the whole Sub Rosa council ready to burn Little Cairo. I can only put them off for a little while longer."

"You can't do that. I told you. There are civilians in there."

"I can probably give you until the end of the week."

Samael and now Abbot. Everyone wants a present and they want it *now.* I should have kept the yule log. Merry Christmas and fuck you all.

"What about Brigitte's situation?" I say. "What can you do for her?"

Another breath on the line.

"Listen. I'm still looking into it, but your friend has lousy timing. Immigration is a hot topic right now. It's easier for the authorities to deport than to look at individual cases. The politics are just not on her side."

"Keep trying. I'm holding up my end of the bargain. You do the same."

"I'll do my best."

I was going to say something else. Something angry and stupid about Abbot, the council, and all the blue bloods on all the councils in the world. They hop from country to country without the Feds' looking at them twice. Their families too. If anything happens to Brigitte, I'm going to make a lot of them very sad.

Instead of being dumb I say, "You want me to go faster, get me an address on a Lisa Thivierge. She's an old movie director who went underground years ago. She'd be in her eighties by now."

"I'll look into it."

"One more thing. Do you know Avani Chanchala?"

"Of course. My in-laws bought their house from her."

"Lucky them. They're doing business with a pimp. You all are. Bye."

I hang up on him.

That was a waste of a conversation, but it gave me an idea.

I get a marker from a kitchen drawer and draw a wide circle on the marble counter, then a smaller circle inside it, and scrawl a few runes in the blank area between the two. Inside the inner circle, I scrawl the basic shape of L.A. County. It's not a map. It's more like something a kid would do when they're not potty training or making hand turkeys. But it's the best I can do without a paper map of the city. If I can pull off some location hoodoo, maybe I can get a sense of what neighborhood Thivierge might be hiding in—if she's even still alive.

I don't have an athame anymore, so I have to use the black blade as a platen, hoping it will point me in Thivierge's direction. Once the map is finished, I hold the blade above it and chant some Hellion hoodoo.

The blade moves instantly, but it doesn't point out a neighborhood. It pulls my hand into the air a couple of feet. Then it feels like something reaches right out of the marble and grabs me, plunging the blade hilt deep into the map. The marble countertop cracks and the whole house begins to shake.

An earthquake? Is it just my flying saucer or is it the whole city? The shaking goes on and on, getting worse by the second. The refrigerator slides away from the wall. Appliances jitter to the edges of shelves. Glasses and plates fly out of cabinets. And the earthquake just gets worse. To keep from falling I have to lean on the counter and hold the knife with both hands, hauling back on it with all my weight. Finally it pops out and I slam down onto my back, cracking my head on the marble floor.

Once the shaking stops I haul myself to my feet. The kitchen is a disaster, but there's a knot on the back of my head and I'm too dizzy to do anything about the mess. There's a scorch mark shaped like an obscure Hellion death hex in the center of the cracked kitchen counter. I grab the bourbon and kick my way through the debris to the living room. I have to turn the sofa upright to sit down.

All in all, it's a been a delightful twenty-four hours. Janet got bitten by a snake. I saw an intestine monster eat some people, then get cooked like bad brisket. I got my ass kicked by some third-rate spooks and now my nice kitchen looks like a drunk brontosaurus tried to fuck the dishwasher. If tomorrow is this much fun I might have to pack it in and go back to Hell. At least there all the houses there come pre-wrecked and I won't feel guilty about breaking this place.

I WAKE UP a few hours later. Still feeling guilty about the kitchen and whatever cleaner elves come by every day, I find a dustpan and shovel as much of the broken plates as I can out one of the windows, followed by the broken appliances. Someone told me it's what Martha Stewart does with her burned quiches, so I'm feeling pretty good about myself.

Candy calls about getting together and we decide to go to the Devil's Door drive-in.

I steal a T-Bird convertible from a vintage car lot in Beverly Hills and pick her up a little before eight. We speed over to Flicker's and find a space good and close to the screen. It's a strange feeling being out with people so many times these last few days. I've become so used to being alone that the feeling is a combination of relief and tension. At least with Flicker we were fighting monsters. And with Janet, we were trying not to die in the desert. But with Candy right now, it's just the two of us. No missions. No big agendas. Just us learning to be around each other again.

Flicker changed the movies and tonight it's a triple feature, *Frankenstein*, *Bride of Frankenstein*, and *Son of Frankenstein.* I've always felt bad that *Frankenstein* is my least favorite of the three, but tonight it's helpful because it gives me and Candy time to talk.

When I get the top down on the T-Bird Candy says, "How's the spook business?"

I light a Malediction.

"Better, I suppose. Flicker came along and showed me some of her tricks for dealing with the Stay Belows."

"She teach you to call them that too?"

"Yeah. She knew a lot more about the situation than I did, so I just played passenger while she did all the work."

"What did you learn?"

"That our dead pal had a girl, and I think she might be the

one who killed him."

"Any idea who it was?"

"An angel named Zadkiel. But I don't know why. If it was a simple angel problem, I could probably fix it. But it's not. There's someone else he's connected to. I'm sure of it. Someone secret. Someone with money. Maybe a thief or an ex-thief. I need to figure out who it is."

"Oooh. Catwoman!" says Candy playfully.

"I'm ready to believe anyone right now. Anyway, I'm tracking down more leads. Abbot is getting me an address."

She sits up, looking more serious.

"Is he going to help Brigitte?"

"He's trying. But it's bad timing with the Feds being so deportation happy right now."

"Fuck. You know, I'd like to find out who got her into this mess."

"Me too."

"If you find out, tell me so I can pay him a visit."

"We can go together."

"Hell yeah. Like old times."

"Like old times."

She brightens and says, "You should come by the store on Friday. Alessa's and my band are playing a little gig."

"I guess I haven't heard you play guitar since I came back."

Candy plays air guitar for a few seconds and says, "I'm a lot better than the last time you heard me."

"You had a year to practice."

"So, you'll come?"

"Will Kasabian let me in?"

She sits back in her seat and looks up at the screen. Dr.

Frankenstein and his creepy assistant are hauling a casket out of the cemetery.

"You let him get under your skin too much."

"Well, he does hate me."

"No, he doesn't. He gives you his books and tells you about our best new movies."

"That's just so I'll stay away."

Candy sighs.

"He just gets worked up sometimes. He gets scared."

"Yeah. Of me."

"Not just you. His body doesn't work right anymore. Sometimes his arms get stuck or his legs won't hold him."

"I'll tell Manimal Mike to come by and check him out."

"Mike already did. He says he can fix things, but it would mean taking Kas off his body for a few days."

I laugh.

"I bet I know what he said to that."

Candy nods.

"He started shouting and Mike left. Maybe you could talk to him . . . ?"

"He's not going to listen to me."

"You're probably right. But we have to do something."

I think about it for a minute, trying to come up with an angle. Some way to get Kasabian to make the right move. I start to say something about it, but what comes out is, "Listen. Janet and me, we've been—"

Candy cuts me off, still looking at the screen.

"I know. I mean, I guessed. It makes sense."

"I didn't go looking for it to happen."

"You don't have to explain anything to me. The way things

are, I know you get lonely."

"I suppose I do."

"You have such a hard time admitting things like that. You think you're still just Sandman Slim, the killer, and you don't need emotions."

I watch the screen for a minute with her.

"You think that's it? My head gets all scrambled when I try to figure it out. I mean, what about you and Alessa? How does she handle us being together?"

"She has a friend she sees sometimes too. We worked it out that as long as we're honest we can sometimes see special people."

I give her a mock-smug smile.

"I'm a special person?"

"Special jerk is more like it, but yeah."

"People are really complicated."

She looks at the sky.

"That's what makes it so great."

"Janet is complicated. More than I first thought."

Candy reaches over and takes my hand.

"Before you go on, promise me one thing."

"What's that?"

"I'm with Alessa and you're seeing Janet, and all that's fine. But please promise me that whatever happens with anybody else, we're always us. Connected. Can you do that?"

I look at her. Her eyes are still on the screen.

"You know I can."

"Then say it."

"Whatever else happens there's always us. Like you said when we first met, we're the funny little people . . ."

". . . who live in the cracks in the world," she says, and finally looks at me. "Thanks."

"Besides, who understands a monster more than another monster?"

I lean over to her and we kiss for a while.

When we come up for air, Flicker is standing by the car.

"Have you two got a minute?"

"Hi, Flicker," says Candy. "You should come by the store on Friday. My band is playing."

"Cool," she says. "I'll do that."

Then she looks at me.

"I have something for you."

Flicker hands me what looks like a small bundle of herbs, but it's too heavy for that.

"You serve salads at the snack bar now?" I say.

"No, smartass," says Flicker. "It's a distraction. If you want to talk to Stein alone or just corral all the Stay Belows, use the bundle. But get rid of it fast. It's nothing poisonous, but there's a stick of magnesium at the center. That stuff burns as bright as the sun. It'll attract any Stay Belows in the area."

"This is great. Thanks."

"Of course."

"I'll make sure Abbot pays you for this."

"Sweet," she says happily.

"How's the King doing?"

"Ask him yourself. You're friends now. As long as you respect him he'll be there for you."

"I still don't understand any of your hoodoo."

"The Stay Belows, the whole situation isn't based on your

magic. This is older stuff than that."

"I use Hellion magic. That's practically angelic and pretty damn old."

Flicker shakes her head.

"Hellion is a bastardization of angelic magic and a lot younger. What I do, what the King is, doesn't correspond to any of your systems. There aren't any spells. No bending the universe to your will. Sure, there are calls and incantations, even cries for help, but they're not to subjugate universal forces. When you work the old, old way, you *are* the universe and it moves through you. You just direct it here or there. It's really pretty simple."

I nod. "I don't think I could ever do that kind of hoodoo."

"Of course not. You're a Black Lane Walker. You do what's right for you. But that doesn't mean you can't ask for help every now and then."

"The King again."

"He can help you send them home. When you're ready, try making an offering."

"I'm not sure Mr. Muninn would approve."

"And where's Mr. Muninn now? Is he helping you? The King is *always* here. Right under your feet."

"I'll remember that."

Flicker wiggles her fingers at us and says, "Have fun, you two."

Me and Candy stay for all three movies, eat popcorn and concession-stand hot dogs. We make out between the features, and for the moment at least, it really does feel like old times.

JANET SEEMS A lot better the next night, though she still has a slight limp. That means, one more damn time, we get ready for the Lodge. They wrap their leg in an Ace bandage and say, "Tonight should be interesting."

"Another birthday excursion?"

"Yes. Rudy Morrello's. But don't worry. He's the last birthday boy for a while. After tonight, you won't have to see anyone for a month or so."

"You're one hundred percent sure you want to go back?"

They stand and put weight on their leg. It holds.

"One thousand percent," Janet says.

Not having to lay eyes on the doom twins—Dan and Juliette—for a few weeks sounds good, but I still haven't picked up anything new about Stein. And my only other lead—Lisa Thivierge—is still missing. Maybe it's time to stop being subtle with Dan and Juliette's flock and start pinning people against the wall until they tell me a story. But even then, anything they say will be second- or thirdhand. I haven't seen anyone old enough to have been in the Lodge in Stein's day.

Maybe Abbot is right. Maybe I should go back and kill the Stay Belows one by one with my Gladius. But the idea grates on me. The spooks didn't ask to be here. Stein drew them. Stein is the one who wants something and I want Stein. That means for now, I'm stuck with the Lodge.

Janet wants to ride the Hog to the doom twins' house, so we have to crawl up the hill in the dark, dodging coyotes and stoner kids in Daddy's Porsche. By the time we arrive at the mansion I'm in a dismal mood.

We go inside and it looks like any ordinary nouveau riche

L.A. cocktail party. When they see her, everyone rushes over to greet Janet. A lot of them are jealous of her snake bite and wish it had happened to them, because obviously, not getting burned alive wasn't enough of a high for them. A lot of the dummies are burned red from the desert sun, with hands and faces scratched by rocks and the coarse vegetation. Manimal Mike looks like hell, but Maria must be some kind of athlete. Not a scratch on her. There's a weird energy in the room. Giddy, but also wary. Seeing someone you know get eaten by a monster will do that to you. In a few minutes, Dan, Juliette, and Kenny arrive and greet everyone, especially the birthday boy, Rudy Morrello.

After a minute or two of adulation, Juliette raises her hands for quiet. When she speaks, she sounds like someone on TV trying to rope you into their pyramid scheme selling fake vitamins or wrinkle cream.

"After the great success in the desert, we thought we'd take things a little farther for the birthday boy. Tonight, Kenny is going to summon a full-fledged demon and capture it in a magic circle."

Dan picks up the pitch. "When they're ensnared, the demon becomes your slave and must answer all your questions—about the past, present, or future. Since it's Rudy's birthday, he'll have the honor of asking the first question."

Trash wizard Kenny, what have you been doing, you bad, bad boy? I want to run right then, but I know Janet won't leave. I think things over. Kenny *did* manage to summon the gut monster and enhance the vampire. Really, what Dan and Juliette are talking about is simple enough. Draw the circle. Do the hoodoo. It's mostly mechanics, really. If he sticks to his paint-by-numbers grimoire, even Kenny can't fuck it up.

As for the other Lodge members, the giddy tension in the room jumps up a couple of notches. Heartbeats pound like a gorilla banging on a trash can. There's the slightly metallic tang of fear sweat. But the crowd seems excited by their demon dream date. Mainly because they have to be. It's an animal thing, and a schoolyard thing. Never look afraid or whatever is coming for you will come twice as hard.

Juliette and Dan herd us ducklings down into the rumpus room. Kenny slipped away earlier and is already getting the ritual started. He takes a handful of salt and dribbles it out in a circle on the wooden floor. I push my way up front so I can check his work.

To my surprise, it's not a bad circle. Simple, but solid. It should hold any of the low-level bogeymen garbage Merlin can conjure. It's not like the ass has the power to call up a hellbeast or Qliphoth. At best, we might get the ghost of Bela Lugosi coming down from a bender.

I relax a little.

With the circle complete, Kenny begins a chant. Very quietly at first, then letting his voice rise with each repetition of the words. Like the circle itself, the chant is simple and pretty generic. Okay. Good. We're going to be all right.

With each round of the chant, Kenny gets louder. In a minute, he's practically shouting. Then something changes.

The little prick is going off script. I don't even recognize the language anymore. It's not English, Latin, Hebrew, or Greek. It sounds almost like someone trying to speak Hellion with a mouthful of marbles.

Oh shit.

Something explodes from the center of the circle, and the force of it knocks the first row of gawkers back a few steps.

The thing is about ten feet tall and squidlike. But not entirely physical. It's more like smoke, but not quite. The shape stutters and glitches like bad video. It flails its tentacles around like it's really pissed or trying to signal a waiter. It's a funny-looking thing.

The smoke squid's tentacles crawl across the ceiling, looking for a way out of the circle. It slams the edges with its thick body, looking for the slightest imperfection in the design. But it's stuck, and by the sound of its foghorn bellowing, it's not taking it well.

Good for you, Kenny. It looks like you actually pulled it off.

A moment later, the smoke squid gives up trying to bang its way out of the circle. It retracts its tentacles and just hangs in the air, like it's floating in dark water.

When the thing calms down, Kenny gets a round of applause. Even I have to give him a couple of claps for not getting us all killed in the first thirty seconds of the smoke squid's appearance.

Dan and Juliette escort Rudy Morrello right up to the edge of the circle. When he stops, the squid slowly turns its thick body around like it knows Rudy is there. While the rest of the Lodge stares in envy, the birthday boy looks like he's about to soil his nice suit.

Juliette says, "Is there anything you'd like to ask our captive?"

Rudy looks like he wants to run, but he's stuck between the doom twins and they're not letting him go anywhere.

"I'm . . . I'm not sure," says Rudy. "I had something, but I can't remember what."

Juliette puts an arm around him.

"Take a minute. Relax. I'm sure it will come back to you."

As Rudy stares, the smoke squid slams its tentacles at the edge of the circle, just a few inches from Rudy's nose.

Everybody jumps. Janet grabs my hand.

"Pass!" he yells. "I give up my turn. It's *my* birthday and I say that I don't have to go first."

"It's okay," says Dan. "You don't have to ask anything complicated. It can be who's going to win the World Series. When are you going to die. Even lottery numbers."

Rudy shakes his head furiously and pulls away from the doom twins.

"I need a minute. Let somebody else go first."

While they argue, I notice a few grains of salt on the interior of the circle move, like there's a gentle breeze coming from somewhere.

I say, "Hey, Kenny. What's that circle made of? Sea salt?"

He smirks at me like he was expecting the question.

"Of course it's salt," he says, "but I souped it up. The book says that silver is also a powerful spirit binder. So, for extra protection I added silver."

He looks so pleased with himself. A kid who just went around the block on his first two-wheeler. Too bad he's going to die.

Rudy finally pulls away from Dan and Juliette and plunges into the back of the crowd. Kenny steps up to take his place at the circle.

"*Pure* silver?" I say.

"Of course."

"You know that mixing too much silver with salt cancels the effects of both, right?"

He looks puzzled. "I've never heard that. You just made that up."

I grab Janet and try to pull them to the stairs, but it's too late.

Smoke squid manages to move enough of the circle out of the way that a tentacle blows through it and grabs Kenny around the neck. It pulls him into the air and shakes him like a terrier with a rat. His neck snaps and he's dead a second later.

I drag Janet back from the stairs to the vault room where I fought the vampire. I stay outside, but yell to the others as I go.

"In here, assholes."

Having honed their survival instincts through years of extreme craziness, Dan and Juliette are the first ones into the room before the rest of the Lodge shoves and claws its way inside. The smoke squid is out of the circle now, banging off the walls and shaking the whole building as it looks for a way out.

As the last few people make it inside the vault, Manimal Mike shoves Maria in ahead of him. Then some nervous creep pulls the door shut before Mike can get in.

The smoke squid grabs his arm and tosses him across the room like a dead flounder. Mike doesn't move after that, so the squid loses interest in him. To make sure, I shout some hoodoo at the thing and blast it into the wall a lot fucking harder than it tossed Mike.

The squid spins and comes after me, but I'm able keep it away with a stream of Hellion curses.

Whatever the thing is, it isn't dumb. When it realizes that it can't kill me, it shoots out its tentacles and probes the walls and ceiling for a way out. I pull the Colt and take aim at it with a Spiritus Dei–coated bullet. But as I'm squeezing the trigger, the smoke squid rips a set of heavy bookshelves off the wall and tosses them at me. I have to dodge it to keep from being crushed and by the time I have the Colt back up the squid is gone.

It turns out that the bookshelves were a con job. They were there to cover a passage cut into the rock wall. I want to ask the doom twins where the tunnel leads, but there's no time. All I can do is go after the squid and hope it's not hiding around the first turn to rip my head off. That would be embarrassing.

I hate chasing things that float or fly. I'm stuck on two legs, panting and sweating, while they glide around like Rocky the Flying Squirrel. I swear that I chase the smoke squid for at least twenty minutes before I get near it. We move down through a series of passages that open up into a huge cavern, which soon narrows into a wide tunnel.

I eventually catch sight of the squid. There are stalactites hanging from the roof of the tunnel. I shout some hexes, and one by one, they begin to fall. The third one comes down dead center on the squid, blasting its smoky body into a thin mist. I take a couple of shots at it with the Colt, but there isn't enough of the squid in any one place to hurt it badly. When it does coalesce again, it shoots out two long tentacles and latches on to one of my legs.

It drags me along the floor of the tunnel toward a black maw the size of a cement truck. When I try to shoot again, another tentacle knocks the Colt out of my hand. I have to wait until the last minute, when Smokey the squid thinks it's about to get lunch. Just before it tosses me like a peanut into its guts, I shout one of my old favorite bits of arena hoodoo—a massive pressure blast that hits like a cement truck.

The problem is, this close to the smoke squid, the blast could take me out too. There's a split second when the pressure hits and the squid lets go of me to dive into a shadow. Only I'm just a little bit off and the force of the tunnel blast rockets me through the shadow and into the Room of Thirteen Doors at the speed of a cruise missile. I hit the far wall and come to on the cool stone floor.

Once I'm sure all of my limbs are there and still working, I stumble out of the Room and back into the tunnel.

The doom twins and the other Lodge suckers are staring down at the two tons of goo that used to be the smoke squid. I come up behind Dan and Juliette as quietly as possible so I can rip out their spines in front of everybody.

Before I can get hold of them Janet screams my name and practically tackles me, holding me in a rib-crushing hug that goes on for a long time.

"I thought that thing ate you," they say.

"Nah. Turns out it was vegan."

Janet kisses me and when we pull away, I finally get a good look around at the tunnel.

My stomach knots up, because I know where I am.

What the hell is going on? I'm in the goddamn Jackal's Backbone. Only a few people are supposed to know about this place. It used to hold L.A.'s wandering dead. More important, it shares one of its walls with Mr. Muninn's secret cavern where he keeps his storehouse.

And if there's a secret passage here from Dan and Juliette's mansion, it means they know about the place. But do they know how powerful it is? They've probably been using it for their fucking excursions. That stops tonight.

I grab Dan and Juliette and drag them away from the others. No need for the rest of the kids to end up covered in their blood.

I bounce Dan off a wall, but Juliette just stands there looking bored. Once I get him back on his feet, I shove Juliette against the same wall and start talking very quietly and clearly.

"Do you have any goddamn idea how dangerous it is down here? There're things in these tunnels you don't want to know about. There're things *I* don't want you to know about."

I take the black blade from my boot and hold it to Dan's throat.

"Stark?" says Janet. "What are you doing?"

"I'm protecting you. I'm protecting these two losers. I'm protecting everybody."

"It doesn't look like it. Please put down the knife."

"Not until these two agree to get out of here and never come back. Or I'm putting their heads on the trophy wall upstairs."

For the first time, Juliette starts looking a little worried.

"Dan?" she whispers.

Dan's lips are bleeding and he has a nice cut on his forehead. But he doesn't look as scared as he should be.

"May I say something?"

"Keep it short."

He leans to the side and waves to the rest of the Lodge.

"Thanks, everybody, for a wonderful evening. We'll see you in a month for something truly spectacular."

Not very fucking likely. But it gets the mooks to leave. While the rest of the Lodge files out, I keep hold of the doom twins. I have a hundred questions for them. How did they find the place? What have they been doing down here? Who else have they told about the Backbone? But mostly, I'm just anxious to hurt them.

Janet takes hold of my knife hand.

"Please don't do this," they say. "Juliette and Dan have something to tell you. Please listen to them. It isn't just about you, but me too."

I don't like the sound of that, and I don't let the doom twins go. Out of the corner of my eye I can see a few Lodge members who haven't left, including Maria. Something weird is going on and Janet has a secret they haven't told me. The easiest thing to do would be to kill everyone and take Janet away, but that would put a definite crimp in our romance.

I'm about to let go of the doom twins when I say, "Just so we understand each other, if one of you runs, you both die."

They nod. Juliette pulls Dan away from the wall and says, "We wouldn't dream of running, would we, dear?"

Dan wipes away blood from his split lip with the back of his hand.

"I have a proposal for you," he says.

"I don't want your proposals. I want you out of here now."

"Please listen to him," Janet says. "I told you. This is about me too. About something bigger than any of us."

I look at them.

"What are you talking about?"

"The Lodge," says Dan.

"The Lodge Within the Lodge," says Juliette.

She looks past me.

"You're a member, dear. Explain it to him."

Janet is still leaning on my knife hand. I let her lower it.

"The Lodge Within the Lodge is special. It's not just excursions and games. It's about looking into the unknown. Expanding human consciousness. Looking into the world beyond the world."

I laugh a little.

"You want to see ghosts? You want to see Hell or Heaven? I can show you those things. You don't need these creeps."

"I don't want you to show them to me," says Janet. "I want to get to them on my own. Taking a helicopter to the top of a mountain isn't the same as climbing it. I want to climb, not to be dropped off like luggage."

"What do you think the excursions are for?" says Dan. "Just kicks? There are easier ways than that. The excursions are tests. Rites of passage to find the proper sort of people who can take part in the Lodge's real purpose."

"You get people killed."

"The weak ones, yes. But not you and not Janet."

"Do you understand now?" Janet says.

"Listen to them, Stark," says Juliette in a way that sounds like an ultimatum. "Join us in the Lodge Within the Lodge or go home. Or murder us all. Of course, you'll have to kill Janet too since they know about the Jackal's Backbone."

When I see the look on Janet's face, I put away the blade.

Janet comes over and puts their head on my shoulder. I drape an arm around them.

The doom twins look at each other.

"Does that mean you'll join us?" says Dan.

I think about it. The black blade is still in grabbing distance.

"Let me ask you something. You ever have any actors come through the Lodge?"

"Actors. Producers. Directors. You name it," says Juliette.

"Ever heard of one named Chris Stein?"

The doom twins look at each other.

Dan says, "The name is vaguely familiar. But he isn't one of our people."

"He'd be from around forty years ago. You have records that go back that far?"

"Yes, we do," says Juliette. "And you can see them."

"But only if you're one of us," says Dan.

I look over at Janet.

I want to see those records, but more than that, I don't want to lose Janet, even though I don't know what the hell it is we're doing. They're in over their head, too afraid of their past, and too in love with death to back out of things now.

I look over at Maria and say, "How's Manimal Mike?"

She smiles.

"He's all right. He just had the wind knocked out of him."

"Is he a member of this secret glee club?"

Maria nods. "You shouldn't judge things you don't understand."

"Wow. You could write fortune cookies."

I take a breath and look at the doom twins.

"I'm in, but you have to agree to one thing."

"What's that?" says Dan.

"No more scampering around in these tunnels."

"Done," says Juliette a split second after the words are out of my mouth.

"Actually, there's one more thing."

"What's that?"

"Stop killing so goddamn many people. You're making me look bad. This next excursion, take the ducklings to Disneyland or something."

"Also done," says Juliette.

Dan holds out his hand.

"Welcome to the Lodge Within the Lodge. I think you'll have a lot of exciting and mysterious times ahead of you."

Because I need more of that in my life.

CANDY CALLS THE next afternoon and I hope it's about what we said to each other at the drive-in, only it's anything but.

She says, "You should get over here right away. Kasabian was in a hit-and-run accident and he's in bad shape."

"He doesn't want to see me."

"He doesn't want to see anyone," says Candy, sounding even more anxious. "I mean, how many friends does he have? Alessa and I have tried talking to him, but he starts crying and gets embarrassed, which makes everything even worse. Maybe you can try talking to him?"

"He's not going to let me in."

"*I'm* going to let you in. Please."

This is exactly what I need right now. Kas getting weepy

about a couple of dents in his undercarriage.

"Okay. I'll be over in a few minutes."

I make it to Max Overdrive a half hour later and go straight into Kasabian's room.

He's laid out on his crummy little single bed. The covers are spattered with traces of blood. Kas has a serious black eye and his face is covered in welts and scratches. Worse, his legs are bent at weird angles and one arm is hanging on by a few thin strips of metal. I wait for him to go off at me, but he's too depressed to be angry.

"Come to see the dog-face boy?" he says. "That'll be a quarter, asshole."

"I only have hundreds."

He raises his good hand and lets it drop back down on the bed.

"You even fail better than I do. You get kicked around and end up rich. I try to buy a cruller and suddenly I'm the Elephant Man."

I sit on the wooden chair next to his bed.

"Does it hurt?"

"Look at me. Of course it hurts."

I hold up the bag I brought with me.

"You want a drink?"

"Some of that Aqua Regia crap? No thanks."

"No, this is good stuff. Remember a million years ago how you gave me my first Kurosawa movie?"

"You uneducated prick. Yeah, I remember."

I hand him the bottle from the bag.

"I'm returning the favor. Suntory Toki. Straight from Japan. The guy at the shop gave me a taste. It's smooth. Like having a fruit salad punch you in the face."

Kasabian examines the bottle.

"What's the gag? Did you spit in it or something?"

"Only a little."

Kas gives me a look, then fails miserably at opening the bottle. He tosses it to me.

"You do it."

I twist off the top and look around.

"You have a glass in here somewhere?"

"If it's good it doesn't need a glass."

Kas upends the bottle and takes a long drink.

"Not bad," he says.

"Not bad? It's better than anything you buy."

"Don't rub it in."

He sits there with the bottle propped on his chest looking already half-dead. I actually feel sorry for him.

"Did you see who hit you? I could stop by and have a word. Maybe shake some money loose."

"Some kind of SUV. You know, the big kind with wheels."

"Maybe I could get a potion from Vidocq. Something to help you remember better."

"Oh yeah, the French nutbag who turned himself immortal by mistake. You think I want to be immortal like this?"

"Okay. Maybe Allegra has something. I could at least get you some painkillers."

"That shit doesn't work on me. Believe me, I've tried. Norco. Oxy. Morphine. I even tried snorting heroin."

"You were using heroin?"

"Once, Mr. High and Mighty. Once."

"I'm not judging you. I just don't want you to OD."

He gives me a look.

"You sure about that?"

"Fuck you, crybaby. Give me back my whiskey."

"No way. This is the only good thing that's happened to me in years. Since that night Mason sent you to Hell."

"That wasn't a good night for me either."

Kas props himself up on his elbow.

"Yeah? Well right now look at you, then look at me. Who do you think came out ahead?" He takes a long pull from the bottle and says, "This is it, man. This is my life. I was a lousy magician, but I ran a good store. Now I can't even do that."

Kasabian thrashes around trying to sit up and spills whiskey everywhere.

"Calm down, Kas."

He stabs a finger at me.

"First Mason fucks me over, then you leave me nothing but a chattering head. A Halloween toy you throw away when all the candy's gone. My life is a fucking joke. So, no. *You* calm the fuck down."

Candy knocks and comes in.

"How are you boys doing?"

Kasabian smiles at her.

"We're great. How are you, princess?"

I don't like where this is going.

I say, "Kas, you want to yell at me, fine. But don't go after Candy."

He turns to me.

"Look at you, the knight in shining armor. How much good did that act get you? There she is. Standing there right in the doorway. Close enough to touch. She might as well be on the moon. You lost her, Stark. Sure, she goes on a little date with you every now and then just to keep you from blowing your brains out. You think it means anything? She's gone. She's got Alessa and the store and you've got nothing. Like me."

Candy says, "Please calm down, Kas. Let me get you a glass for the whiskey."

Kas doesn't hear her. His eyes are locked on mine.

"You got that big gun of yours with you? Of course you do. Come on. We'll go out together. Two losers no one will ever miss."

"I'm not shooting you and I'm not shooting myself."

"Then what good are you? Get out of here and don't come back. You too, princess."

Candy says, "Let me call Manimal Mike one more time."

"Fuck him and fuck all of you. Get out and leave me alone."

We leave and Kas slams the door behind us.

Candy slowly shakes her head.

"I've never seen him like this."

"I have. Those first few months after I took his head. This is my fault."

"Don't say that. He sent you to Hell. He shot you."

"But I'm still walking around and have a life. I took his head but kept him alive out of nothing more than spite. He has every right to hate me and there's nothing I can do to fix that or him."

"At least you tried. Now leave him to me and Alessa."

"Let me know if he gets worse. I'll drag his ass to Allegra whether he likes it or not."

Candy crosses her arms.

"See, that's exactly the kind of thing you can't do. What did you say the other night, about how you know everything about monsters but nothing about people? Well, if you want to help people, kidnapping them is a bad start."

"You're right. But if he gets to be too much to handle, call me. Maybe I can talk him into staying at the flying saucer house. Then he can yell at me and leave you two alone for a while."

Alessa comes over and stands behind Candy.

"Hi, Stark."

"Hi, Alessa."

"I heard you in there. Didn't turn out so well, did it?"

"You stopping by to rub it in?"

"No. To tell you it was a lot more than I expected from you. Like you meant what you were saying."

"You think I'm incapable of helping people?"

She gives me a wan smile.

"Most of what I've seen you do is kill people and get Candy and me in trouble. This was something new."

"Thanks, I guess."

"I do. As far as assholes go, you're not the biggest one I ever met."

"That I'll take as a compliment."

She heads back to the stairs that lead to the upstairs apartment.

"You should come to our gig on Friday."

"Thanks. Maybe I will."

When she's halfway up the stairs she shouts, "And bring back those movies. We have paying customers, you know."

"I won't forget."

Candy smiles at me.

"I consider that a breakthrough."

"I'm going to quit while I'm ahead and get out of here. Will you be at Bamboo House later?"

"You bet."

"Great. I'll see you tonight."

I go through a shadow to the flying saucer house.

I can't really blame Kas for what he said. He's basically right. His life has mostly been a mess. He was always a mediocre magician. Mason promised him power after he betrayed me but then never came through. And I thought I'd fucked him over like no one else could. But, no, it was some prick in an SUV who's off having it detailed right now to take out the dents and repaint the damage. No cop will lay a hand on the bastard, and what would we tell them anyway? "He ran a stop sign and hit a man with a hoodoo metal body"? That wouldn't fly with the LAPD. Even after he and Mason betrayed me and he shot me, I can't hate him. What I can do is find him a new body. Manimal Mike isn't the only Tick-Tock man in town. I have a few thousand dollars to spend. There are worse ways to go broke than helping out a fellow loser in the loser parade. Just another bug on God's windshield.

Even with Samael and Abbot's deadlines hanging over me, I need to clear my head after the tire fire of the last few days.

Don Tiare playing Les Baxter tunes is on the jukebox when I get to Bamboo House of Dolls with Janet. It's a busy night. Carlos pours us drinks right away, then moves off to serve other customers. Before any of the others get there, I pull Janet into a corner in the back of the bar. No chitchat with strangers tonight. No sneaky selfies. I just want a drink with friends.

"Tell me more about Brigitte," says Janet.

"What do you want to know?"

"You said she helped you fight the Drifters. Tell me about that."

"This city would be zombies and rubble without her."

"And you."

"Thanks, but it was mostly her. She was the boss and I just tried to keep up."

Janet looks at the happy, drunken crowd a little dubiously. It's a funny night. Maybe a tour group came in. The bulk of the crowd is civilians who probably heard rumors about Bamboo House or read a strange online review and have come down to rub elbows with L.A.'s most exotic citizens. After thinking for a minute, Janet turns back to me.

"It's not fair," they say. "Punishing someone for their past when they saved so many people."

"That's the problem. Not many people know what she did, and that means neither do the desk trolls who decide who stays and who goes."

"But *I* know what she did. She saved my life. You told me to go home, but you wouldn't have known what to do without her."

"True."

They swirl the ice in their glass.

"You're going to find whoever did this to her, right?"

"Absolutely. And Abbot's working on it too. I'm as mad about the situation as you, but for now, there's nothing to do but wait and see what happens from here."

"It's so unfair."

I lean against the wall and Janet leans against me.

"Fair has nothing to do with it. You should know that. Was it fair that you were born with a lousy immune system? Fair doesn't exist in this world. Just forget fair."

Janet looks sad.

I say, "Sorry. I'm just in a bad mood."

"Because of the ghosts?"

"Among other things."

We both know who I'm talking about. I wait for them to defend Dan and Juliette. Luckily, they don't.

"Poor Kenny," they say.

"Poor Kenny. Poor Charlie Karden. Poor whoever the hell those people were in the canyon or on the freeway. Is that really all there is to say about people getting killed for kicks?"

Janet frowns.

"You don't understand. It could have been any one of us. It would have been me if you weren't there. We signed up for this."

"That's fucked up, even for L.A."

"I didn't say I don't feel anything. It's just Lodge policy that mourning isn't part of the ethos. So, yeah, poor Kenny."

"He should have stuck to the hoodoo he knew. The creep could have gotten everyone killed."

"Still. What happened to him. It . . ."

"Wasn't fair? You're not not mourning too well. You've got too big a heart. You're too sympathetic to lost dogs."

"Like you?"

I bark and they hug me.

I want to remind them of how many times they could have

been killed and ask more about the Lodge Within the Lodge, but I can feel that this isn't the right time.

Allegra and Vidocq come in, followed by Candy and Alessa. Janet goes quiet, still nervous around the others. It'll pass. I hope.

With a full phalanx of L.A.'s most exotic, we muscle our way to the bar and clear an acre or so to drink. We're on our second round when Brigitte arrives, all smiles and waving. Carlos has a cocktail waiting on the bar before she even reaches us.

"You're looking chipper tonight," he says. "Did you get some good news?"

Brigitte sips her drink a couple of times.

"I'm going home to Prague," she says.

Candy goes over to her.

"What happened?"

Vidocq says, "So soon? Are the authorities forcing you out? There are things Stark and I can do to them that will make them change their minds."

Brigitte sips her drink.

"No," she says. "I'm leaving on my own. My lawyer said that if I leave voluntarily, I'll have a better chance of being allowed to return."

"How long will you have to go?" says Allegra.

Brigitte sets her empty glass on the bar.

"Just a little while. Five years maybe."

Carlos curses quietly in Spanish and gives her another drink.

She says, "You won't forget about me, will you?" She smiles . . . and then breaks down crying.

"It's not fair," says Janet, and gives me a "don't you dare say a word" look.

I say, "Brigitte, Abbot is still working on this. He'll come through better than any by-the-hour lawyer."

She shakes her head.

"My mind is made up. This is the safest way."

I don't know anyone stronger than Brigitte. She's been through so much in the last few years. She came here with nothing but a gun and some acting lessons. Had a few romances, more bad than good. She fell in love with Father Traven and then he died. She had a pretty successful cable action show and she's losing that, too.

"There's no one at the studio who can help?" says Carlos. "You're on TV. That's better than being on money."

That makes her laugh a little, but her face soon turns red again. No one says anything. What's there to say? It's stupid and brutal. I want to find whoever ratted her out and introduce them to Kenny's smoke squid.

Candy pulls Brigitte to her and in a second they're both crying.

What a pathetic bunch we are. Between just me, Candy, and Vidocq, we could rip a big smoking hole in this city. But here we are now, bullied by Feds and unable to even protect one of our own.

Janet has been nursing the same drink for the last twenty minutes. I really wish they'd get over their nervousness. They hand me their drink and walk to Brigitte.

"Marry me," Janet says.

Everyone looks at them like they're speaking Urdu.

"What?" says Brigitte.

Janet says it again. "Marry me."

Brigitte and Candy stare at her.

"I'm serious," they say. "You'll be the spouse of an American citizen and they'll have to let you stay."

Brigitte puts a hand on Janet's arm.

"That's very kind of you, but why would you do that? We've barely met."

"Because I owe you my life," they say. "When the Drifters were loose, you and Stark saved me. Now let me save you."

"It's not a terrible idea," says Allegra. "It should at least slow things down. I had a cousin in a green card marriage. They had to go through a lot of paperwork and a face-to-face with some snooty government bitch about where stuff is in the kitchen and each other's families. But those are all things you can memorize."

Carlos leans on the bar and says, "Ray is a minister in one of those internet churches. He can marry you and you can have the reception right here."

Brigitte's face is funny, caught somewhere between complete shock and vague relief.

"I don't know what to say."

"Say yes, dummy," I tell her. "I'd marry you, but I think I'm still legally dead. I should probably check on that."

Brigitte looks at Janet for a minute, like she's trying to figure out if the offer is legit.

Janet says, "My dad's a lawyer. He can help with the paperwork."

"Yes," Brigitte blurts out. "Yes."

"You'll marry me?" says Janet.

"I will."

They hug each other and Brigitte and Candy start the waterworks again. Everyone is hugging everyone and it's a complete mess. But the okay kind.

BY THE TIME we head for Dan and Juliette's it's late and I'm wrecked enough that I don't want to drive the Hog, so I take us through a shadow. My first night as a member of the Lodge Within the Lodge. If there's more initiation garbage—if they want me to beat up a yeti or fight another vampire—I'm killing the doom twins and going back to Bamboo House to celebrate.

Me and Janet head straight downstairs.

The rumpus room doesn't look as bad as I expected after the smoke squid. Someone did a nice cleanup job on the place. There are boards neatly nailed up over the entrance to the mountain tunnel. I'm guessing that Dan and Juliette didn't pick up as much as a dustpan. They must pay their cleaning people a fortune to keep their mouths shut.

The first person I see is Manimal Mike in a neck brace.

"Goddamn, Mike. Why are you here?" I say. "You look like hell."

He tries to smile, but the brace makes it like a grimace.

He says, "I'm fine. Maria's been taking good care of me. Besides, I wasn't going to miss your first night. Welcome to the big leagues."

He puts out his hand and I shake it.

"Thanks, but I didn't exactly love the minor leagues. What am I even doing here?"

"With Charlie Karden gone, there was an opening."

"Actually, you're filling two spots. Don't forget about my

friend Cassandra," Janet adds. "She brought me into the Lodge Within the Lodge before the crackhead killed her."

"But like I said before, what am I doing here?"

Dan comes over.

"You're going to transcend the human plane of existence."

"And go onto new ones," says Juliette. "The Land of the Dead. Other dimensions."

"Perhaps even time travel. The possibilities are limitless."

I shake my head.

"No offense, but I've already seen the Land of the Dead and it wasn't exactly fun."

"Did you have a guide?" says Juliette.

"You think they have docents in Hell? Someone to hand you headphones and point out the gift shop?"

Dan says, "There's your problem. We'll have guides taking us into these other realms so that we can explore in safety."

"Just like Virgil led Dante safely through the Inferno," says Juliette.

I look at her hard.

"You know that was a poem, right? Not a how-to book."

Janet says, "Calm down. Just listen to them and see what they can do."

"I thought Kenny was your trash wizard. Who's going to lead us into Valhalla now?"

"I will," says Dan. "Believe it or not, I have a fair amount of experience with these things."

"No offense, but Ouija boards aren't going to get you into the Land of the Dead and back out again."

"No offense taken."

Dan's smile never falters.

He says, "I'll make you a deal. We don't normally allow Lodge Within the Lodge members to quit. You know the saying."

"There's zero chance I'll get out alive. Yeah. I have the T-shirt and the mug."

Juliette says, "If you aren't impressed by what you experience tonight, you can walk out and you won't have to see us ever again."

"Just give it a chance," says Janet. "I know what happened with Kenny was awful, but we're not calling up demons or anything here. Just spirit guides."

"Will you listen to me? The Land of the Dead is a horror show."

"Then come with me for protection."

I look at Janet. They're so determined to show me the ragged edges of their world. I can't abandon her now. And I haven't seen the Lodge records yet.

But I hate this idea with all my being.

Nodding to Dan, I say, "Show me what you've got."

He takes an ornate box from a black altar covered in runes, charms, milagros, and dozens of other supernatural tchotchkes that I can't even identify. The box is old and heavy looking, like it's made of solid iron. There are snaky dragons and dancing skeletons on the top and sides. The designs look vaguely familiar. They're definitely Asian, but I can't quite place them. Dan moves slowly and deliberately, really putting on a show for a everyone. A Satanic priest crossed with Elvira, Mistress of the Dark. I'm already bored with his second-rate magic act when he finally opens the box and takes out a collection of bones, all delicately wired together.

It's a carved skull that's been carefully sectioned into several pieces like a 3-D puzzle. Each of the skull pieces is carved with more skeletons, some holding swords and some kneeling like they're in prayer. A collection of smaller skulls rings the top of the piece like a death crown. Loops of prayer beads hang down from the sides of the fractured assemblage. Now I remember—it's a Tibetan necromancer's mask, and I already don't like where this is going.

Dan carefully places the bones over his head.

He says, "I'd appreciate it if everyone knelt."

He gets down on the floor in the lotus position. I try not to roll my eyes, but everybody else gets down there with him, like we're going to play Spin the Bottle.

Juliette brings him a Tibetan horn made from a human femur. Dan gives the horn three good blasts, then starts doing a reasonably good imitation of a deep, overtone-laden Tibetan chant. This goes on for several minutes. Finally, he gives the horn three more blasts and plunges a long phurba—a three-sided Tibetan ceremonial dagger—into the ground.

I'm all prepared for nothing to happen, at which point I plan on stealing all of the doom twins' liquor and disappearing back to the flying saucer house.

But something does happen.

A pinpoint of light floats across the room, like a swollen firefly. It expands into a circle and something like molten glass pours out. Finally, when the ghostly Thurl is wide enough for something to come through, something does.

It's goddamn Kenny, all floaty and spectral. Like a prop from a William Castle movie. Even as a ghost he looks uncomfortable.

"Hi, everybody," he says. "I'm so sorry about what happened at the summoning. I guess Stark was right. I got out over my skis. Needless to say, I'm really embarrassed."

Juliette says, "It's all right, Kenny. You showed us wonders that we couldn't have imagined."

"Really? Thanks."

That cheers him up. As cheered up as a dead guy can get.

"What wisdom of the world beyond ours do you bring us?" says Dan.

"I'll tell you, but where I am, there are rules. Before I can answer your question, I'm going to need a sacrifice."

Juliette brings Dan a draped carrier that chirps quietly each time she shakes it. Dan pulls off the cover and there's a single white dove inside. Janet stiffens a little at the sight but doesn't move away.

Dan takes out the dove and cups it in his hands in Kenny's direction.

He says, "Please accept this, our sacrifice."

Quick as a snake, he snaps the bird's neck. It lets out one last long and sad chirp before its head drops limply by its side. That neck snap was fast and precise, something Dan has practiced. I bet the doom twins' compost can is stuffed full with the bodies of small, murdered animals.

Kenny's eyes snap shut and he shivers like someone just stuck an icicle up his spectral ass.

When he settles down, his eyes glow like the headlights on a Rolls-Royce.

"Excellent. Now, tell me what it is you wish to see."

"What you see," says Juliette. "Show us the Land of the Dead."

Dead Kenny holds his hands wide and an eerie landscape slowly forms around him. It's all shadows and blades, cleavers, kartikas, and every other cutting tool imaginable. I know the place intimately. The House of Knives in Pandemonium. Kenny made it all the way to Hell and the doom twins have pulled him back. I wonder how Kenny feels about that. For the first time, I have a little sympathy for the fool.

Kenny stands in the middle of the house as rotating pillars of blades pass around him, slicing him to ribbons, then pausing to let his body reassemble itself so the game can start all over again. His face contorts as much from his body's pulling itself back together as it does from the blades.

He says, "Behold Hell in all its ingenious glory."

"What else can you tell us?" says Juliette, completely ignoring that her pal is being deli-sliced over and over again.

"Parts are cold as the Arctic and some as hot as the sun. There are trenches and fissures full of blood. Everywhere is chaos and ruins. How long have I been trapped in here? A day? It already feels like an eternity, and I have all of eternity to look forward to treats like this."

"Can we come to you, Kenny?" says Dan excitedly. "Can we visit you in the Land of the Dead?"

"Kill yourself and find out."

They ignore that. "Can you show us other wonders? Anywhere outside the house? We want to see the vistas of the damned."

"I can show you everything—but again, there's a price."

"Name it. Anything," says Juliette.

Kenny turns to her, his face in mid-slicing.

"Another sacrifice. Each sacrifice you bring will help me

escape the horror of this house. The larger the sacrifice, the sooner I can leave. When I've done that, I'll show you all of Hell. Make a large enough sacrifice and I'll show you how to visit the Land of the Dead and return home safely."

"Thank you, my friend," says Dan. "We'll do as you say."

Kenny groans as a broadsword opens his belly the way he gutted the sheep.

"I have to go now. The bird wasn't much sustenance. Bring me something better next time."

Juliette says, "We will. Thank you. We'll see you soon, Kenny."

Poor, dumb Kenny fades and disappears into the thicket of the knives. His scream cuts off abruptly as the Thurl collapses.

The rumpus room is silent for a while. Then it's all looks of wonder and hushed whispers. Dan and Juliette kiss. Maria throws her arms around Manimal Mike and Janet grabs me in a big bear hug. I hug them back, but it's mostly to be polite.

These fucking children, playing with gasoline and guns.

Then next thing I know Dan is shouting, "A pit bull. No. A Rottweiler."

I say, "For what?"

"For the bigger sacrifice, of course."

"A Great Dane," says Maria, who seems a lot more into this scene than Mike.

Some Jed Clampett–in–a–turtleneck–looking prick says, "A Tibetan mastiff. Those are the largest dogs in the world."

"Perfect," says Dan. "I can get one tomorrow. Should I get more? We can fill the room with them!"

Juliette presses her forehead to his.

"You're thinking too small, dear heart. Forget dogs. What we need is a horse."

"Can you get a horse down here?" says Mike.

"Then we'll get a pony. That's probably better anyway. It's smaller and its blood is fresh and vital."

"I'm not sure a *small* horse is what Kenny is looking for," says Dan, and then the whole fucking room is debating what animal is small enough to fit down here but big enough to keep Kenny fat and happy. I tune it all out. Not only don't I care about their ridiculous plans, but I'm distracted by other things.

Like Kenny's entrance from Downtown. I've seen a lot of spirit manifestations over the years, but the one Dan pulled off was very specific. It's the exact same passageway I've seen too many times in Little Cairo. Could it be just a weird coincidence? Are Kenny and the doom twins reading from the same playbook as whoever called the Stay Belows back to this world? It's possible, but I have severe doubts.

The doom twins are so in love with death I can see them in the rumpus room night after night trying to get the hoodoo right. And they did it without even realizing it, opening a gateway and letting those murderous spooks into this world.

That all makes sense, but it still doesn't explain Chris Stein or why the haunting is in Little Cairo. When Juliette and Dan said they didn't know if he'd been in the Lodge they were telling the truth. I could see it in their eyes and hear it in the microtremors of their voices. So, how did Stein end up as the focal point for all those spooks? There's one thing I do know. I'm not going to find the answers here. These dummies have no idea what they're doing. That means someone else called

Stein. I'll take a look at their records, but I have a feeling I'm right back where I started.

Maybe not right back. Where did those spooks that attacked me in the flying saucer house come from? Me and Kenny weren't exactly friends. Did he figure out how to control the Stay Belows and send them for me? And did the doom twins know anything about it?

Janet says, "So? What do you think?"

"I could have shown you Hell without you killing the bird."

"Then do it."

"No."

"There's the problem. Kenny is the solution."

"Then why am I here?"

"You're a powerful presence," says Dan. "And you know more than you say. If things go pear-shaped, you won't let everyone die."

"Just you."

"That's a risk I'm willing to take."

Around me, the others are happily speculating on the best way to kill things for Kenny.

I turn to Janet.

"You're okay with the animal sacrifices?"

They whisper, "Not really. But Kenny is suffering. He said sacrifices would help him escape that terrible place."

I consider telling her that sacrifices don't work that way. They don't get you out of the House of Knives. I know this from personal experience. I still remember the blades ripping into me for the first time. It didn't even hurt—at first. The feeling was more an icy kind of shock. But the cold slipped away quickly and there I was with my insides twisting around whirling daggers. It was the first place the Hellions tried to get rid of me. Before the arena, it's where I discovered that I was hard to kill. But I can't tell Janet all of that.

Instead I say, "You can do what you want. I'm not murdering any dogs."

They hold on to my hand as I get up.

"Please don't make a scene."

I pull my hand away and turn to the doom twins.

"Thanks for the floor show."

I check Janet one more time to see if she—*they*—want to come with me. They turn away.

When I head upstairs, Dan calls after me.

"Leaving so soon? The evening was just getting started."

I stop by the door and smile at him and Juliette.

"There's one thing you should know. I don't kill animals. I kill people. And if anything happens to Janet, I'll kill you. Aside from that, stay away from me. All of you."

On the way out, I steal as much of the doom twins' liquor as I can shove into my coat.

THE NEXT AFTERNOON, I sit around with Vidocq at his place, my hoard of stolen booze spread out on his coffee table. I haven't spoken to Janet since last night, so that might be the end of that. I don't like to think about it, but then I don't like to think about being cool with people cutting up poodles for no goddamn reason. I want to think that Janet is better than the rest of the Lodge Within the Lodge crowd. I know it's a reach at this point, but I want to think that what Janet said was just a momentary bout of dementia. Still, not hearing from them makes me think that they've made up their mind about whose side they're on, and it's not mine. It's too bad. I lost Alice and mostly lost Candy but I'm still here. I suppose I'll get over Janet, but it's going to be a long, sad process finding a new donut place.

Vidocq says, "You're sure they were discussing animal sacrifices?"

"Dogs. Then a horse."

"*Mon dieu.* I've known alchemists who, when struggling with a seemingly unsolvable problem, turned to foul methods to obtain knowledge. But they never truly succeeded. One tainted morsel of information made them hungrier for more. And since it seemed to them that they had found a way of advancing themselves with little work, they turned from fools into monsters."

"Tell me about it."

Vidocq cups his hands like he thinks a hedgehog might fall from the ceiling.

"They would begin with small animals, eventually moving to larger and larger ones. When single beasts were no longer sufficient, they fell in with criminals, stealing whole herds to satisfy their growing desire for foul knowledge."

"Did it work? What happened to them?"

"The ones not arrested by the authorities turned darker and crueler in their desires. Some went mad. A few, realizing what they'd become, hung themselves. Some, however, simply became ever more monstrous. I remember one winter in particular. A deep cold had settled over Paris. The type that seems endless. Daily, there would be bodies in the street. The homeless. The foolish who walked into a storm after too much wine. It took some time, but contacts of mine in both the criminal and legal worlds told me that the greatest number of dead that winter were children."

"That stinks, but is it so strange? Aren't kids always the first to get hurt?"

"True. But the heads of children in a flood remained on their shoulders. Their hearts remained in their chests. You couldn't say the same for the dead children of Paris that winter."

"Human sacrifice?"

"The bodies and blood of children have powerful mystical properties. The younger the child, the more power it has. This is well-known in the world of dark magic. What was equally well-known among circles such as mine was that even contemplating hurting a child would lead you to the guillotine. Or worse."

"What's worse than having a sweaty cop cut your head off?"

"Us," Vidocq says.

He doesn't speak for a minute, lost somewhere in Paris a hundred years ago.

Finally, he says, "We were what the monstrous feared more than the police. The legitimate and sane alchemists and magicians of Paris. We did not take madmen and -women lightly. If we found a baleful wizard or witch before the police did, their end would be much slower and more terrifying than a quick death by the guillotine."

I take a sip of some expensive Scotch. It takes like burnt dirt.

"Dan and Juliette are nuts, but I don't think they're baby-stealing nuts."

"For now."

I watch a seagull fly by the window.

"Janet wouldn't put up with it. They'd tell me, even if we were on the outs like we are now. They're in over their head, but not so deep they'd let the doom twins feed Kenny a kid."

"I hope you're right. But power changes people. It creates a desire for more power. At a certain point it can become overwhelming and after certain acts people can find that there is no turning back."

Hearing all this, more than ever, I want to get Janet away from the Lodge crowd. Manimal Mike too. I hope Maria isn't leading him somewhere he can't come back from. Of course, I don't even know Maria, so I can't write her off yet. Maybe she was just caught up in the moment last night. But the others—Juliette, Dan, turtleneck guy, and the rest—they can't join Kenny in the House of Knives fast enough to suit me.

Vidocq says, "Tell me more about Little Cairo. Have you learned anything helpful from your restless spirits?"

I paw through the bottles on the table, looking for bourbon.

"A few things. Just not enough to matter. The Sub Rosa Council wants to wipe out the Stay Belows and my money is on that happening."

"A slaughter of the innocents."

"Not exactly innocent. I saw them kill people."

Vidocq raises a finger.

"Don't judge the dead so quickly. They are lost in our world. What they did could easily have been out of fear. Or for reasons we the living are simply unable to fathom."

"That's how Flicker talks about them. That they're mostly like lost children. She said that one of them, a guy named Chris Stein, was back because of a woman. A lost angel who's probably the one who murdered him. Samael wants me to find her too, but I keep running into brick walls."

"Love is a powerful force, even after death. It may not be revenge he's looking for, but forgiveness. For something he or she did."

"Does 'forever yours, forever mine' mean anything to you?"

Vidocq gives me a vague smile.

"I'm afraid not. The workings of the afterlife are more your specialty than mine."

"I just wish the fucking Stay Belows would stay below."

"You're a powerful magician, my friend. Surely you can handle a company of lost children."

Before I can answer, a firefly dot appears in the air across the room. It quickly expands into the Thurl that I've seen so many times lately. What's worse, the opening is directly in front of Vidocq's apartment door, blocking the fastest way out. Four armed Stay Belows walk out of the passage. The only encouraging thing about the situation is that they're all bunched up together.

Before they attack I yell, "Get behind me."

A smart guy, Vidocq does it.

"I have potions that can help dispel them," he says.

"Leave it to me right now."

I'm not fucking around with these dead bastards again, so I manifest my Gladius.

I don't know if ghosts can learn or there's a ghost gossip network, but they freeze in place. Then, one by one, they walk back into the glowing ghost gate.

I turn to Vidocq.

"What the hell just happened?"

"You frightened them. Apparently, even specters know about Sandman Slim."

"Maybe. Did I show you the ghostbuster kit Flicker gave me?"

As I pull the bundle from my pocket, something in the passageway moves.

Correction. Some *things*. Twenty or thirty Stay Belows charge at us all at once. Even with the Gladius, I can't handle that many.

Vidocq grabs a handful of his potion vials and throws them at the mob. As each vial breaks, the spooks fall back. But the effect only lasts a few seconds. Then they're rushing us again.

With nothing to lose but our asses, it's time for a field test.

I yell, "Close your eyes," and touch Flicker's bundle to the edge of the Gladius.

It bursts into brilliant, shimmering light. The smell of burning metal, sage, blood, and other acrid scents fills the room. I can't see but it must be doing something, because we aren't severely dead yet.

I drop the bundle on the floor, hoping it will keep the Stay Belows away long enough for Vidocq and me to get out of here. Even with his eyes closed, the tough old bastard is still throwing potions at the dead mob. I grab him and pull him into a wavering shadow cast by the bundle's painful light.

I lose my footing as we stumble into the Room of Thirteen Doors. When I'm back on my feet I realize that Vidocq is on the floor with half of a Stay Below on top of him, trying to sink its spook teeth into his throat. I can't use my Gladius without killing Vidocq too, so I bark Hellion hoodoo.

It knocks the Stay Below across the room, where it bounces off the Door of Dreams. I manifest the Gladius and as I'm about to send the fucker to oblivion, Vidocq shouts at me.

"Wait—can you hold the creature in place with magic?"

"Sure, but why?"

"So that we might learn from it."

I'd ignore anyone else, but not Vidocq. I bark a little more hoodoo, pinning the Stay Below to the floor. Now that it's helpless, it's kind of a pitiful thing. Half obliterated, cut off at the waist from the light in Flicker's bundle. What's with us now was probably saved by being dragged into the Room. Seeing it sliced across the middle like that, I can't help thinking about how Stein died. What a sad and frightening death it must have been for him. How much longer does he have before the Council and I will have to kill him?

I say, "Do something or let me put this fucker out of his misery."

Vidocq creeps over to the Stay Below and pours one of his potions into its mouth. The thing thrashes and shrieks on the floor. I have to bark more hoodoo to keep it pinned.

I say, "What the hell was that stuff?"

"Watch," he says. "With luck, in a moment we should see the creature's origin."

Something coalesces in the air. It's a low-res image, like something from an old-fashioned photo projector. Fuzzy, with the colors pale and faded. Over a minute or so the image sharpens enough that we can pick out details.

"What is that?" Vidocq says.

"It's Hollywood Boulevard. Can you read what's on that sign?"

Over the street is a wide expanse, like a billboard. It's covered in lights and blocky black letters.

"I see the word 'devil,'" Vidocq says.

"Me too. I think that's neon around the edge of the billboard."

"That's not a billboard. It's a marquee."

I squint at the apparition and see that he's right. As I creep closer to the Stay Below, the words come more into focus. I can see two words clearly now: "Devil" and "Jones."

I get even closer.

"It says *The Devil in Miss Jones.*"

"What is that? Some strange exorcism?" says Vidocq.

"No. It's an old porn movie. That's the marquee of the goddamn Pussycat Theatre on Hollywood Boulevard."

Vidocq frowns at me.

"How curious."

"That's a word for it. Are you sure your potion is working? That's the spook's origin?"

"I've been making this formula for over a century. It's never failed me."

"The lost angel was supposed to hang out there. Maybe this thing knew her? Or was part of the party scene?"

"*How curious.*"

"Is this thing going to tell us anything else?"

Vidocq shakes his head. "Perhaps if it was intact. However, in its present state, I doubt there's anything more than this impression."

"Okay then."

I manifest the Gladius and slam it into where the Stay Below's heart would be. It lets out a small gasp and blips out of existence.

Vidocq looks at me in wonder.

"A pornographic ghost. What does it mean?"

Pieces start falling into place.

"It means the angel who killed Chris Stein sent it. And I've seen that portal enough that I'm sure Dan and Juliette are helping them."

"If that's true, your friend Janet is in great danger."

"That's the problem. They love it."

I call their number, but it sends me straight to voicemail. Perfect. They're blocking me. At least I can leave a message. I tell them everything that's happened and what I've figured out, but before I can get it all out a text from Janet comes through. It's short and to the point:

LEAVE ME ALONE

My first instinct is to go through a shadow, grab Janet, and make them listen to me. But something Candy said comes back to me. "If you want to help people, kidnapping them is a bad start."

I try to tell myself this is different. It's not kidnaping. It's just talking about something important. But I'd probably have to hold them down to do it, and if that's not kidnapping—or worse—then I don't know what it is.

I put the phone in my pocket and, after checking for spooks, take Vidocq back to his apartment.

When I get home to the flying saucer house I punch a few holes in the wall. I want to go up into the hills and kill Dan and Juliette, but I can't do that. Not yet. Then Janet would be lost forever. Instead, I take some of Allegra's PTSD pills and turn off the lights. Flop down on the sofa and try to think.

Janet is in danger. Samael wants his angel. The Council wants their ghosts. Which crisis am I supposed to handle when they're all part of the same damn shit storm?

I'm not good with defeat, especially when it feels like there's a price on my head. But for the first time in a long time I have absolutely no idea what to do.

A FEW HOURS later, my phone buzzes. I grab it, hoping it's Janet. But it's a text from Abbot. The Stay Belows are starting to breach the wards around Little Cairo. His people have seen civilians, so they know the place is inhabited. Not that they care. The end of the text reads:

YOU HAVE 36 HOURS.

More good news.

I give Flicker a quick call and ask her to help Abbot's people reinforce the quarantine around Little Cairo. She agrees, which maybe gives everyone an extra day to live.

I toss the phone on the coffee table and it buzzes one more time. When I check it, there's an address in Benedict Canyon and a name: Lisa Thivierge.

I RIDE THE Hog up winding roads into the hinterlands of Benedict Canyon to a Gothic-style mansion right out of a thirties Universal horror movie. Dr. Frankenstein's summer home, or where a friendly neighbor chains up Lyle Talbot during the full moon. Even the name Lisa Thivierge is living under—Janet Lawton—is a gag: the name of the ingenue in the old Ed Wood movie *Bride of the Monster.* I like Thivierge already.

Thivierge first made her name in the late fifties as one of the few women directors in Hollywood and, along with Ida Lupino, one of the only women allowed to direct action movies. She was successful for years, but then she dropped out of the business and out of sight. No one seems to know why. Now here she is hiding in this monster-movie mansion. It's like some kind of decades-long practical joke.

Still, there are two things about the house that aren't funny. The first is the protective wards and charms around the windows and the front door. I move the doormat a few inches with my boot and find a line of red brick dust to keep out intruders.

The other peculiar thing about the house is the industrial air conditioner hidden behind a small stand of trees. The damn thing is the size of a pickup truck. Unless Thivierge plays a lot of hockey, the air conditioner makes no sense at all.

Before I ring the bell, I put on a glamour. Something blandly handsome, like a local TV weatherman. Thivierge is in her late eighties. There's no way she's going to let a stranger with my face into her secret tree fort. When I'm satisfied with my utterly forgettable face I ring the doorbell.

After a few seconds, an intercom crackles at me.

"Hello? What do you want?"

The voice is young and strong. Definitely not Thivierge's.

"Ms. Lawton doesn't know me, but I'd like to speak to

her."

"I'm Ms. Lawton's personal assistant. If you don't have an appointment, you need to go away before I call the police."

That escalated fast. But two can play that game.

"I'll go away, but tell Ms. Lawton I know her real name is Lisa Thivierge."

There's a long pause this time, like maybe the voice is conferring with someone.

The intercom crackles again.

"Ms. Lawton isn't interested in talking to you. Now, you need to go away."

"I have a feeling I got Ms. Thivierge's attention and that she's listening right now. Isn't that right, Ms. Thivierge?"

There's another pause before the voice says, "I'm calling the police."

With nothing to lose I say, "Forever yours, forever mine."

A second later, the front door opens.

The assistant is young and blond. At first glance I think she's heavyset, but I'm wrong. She's wearing an insulated bodysuit. An arctic breeze drifts out of Thivierge's front door into the sunny California sky.

The assistant looks me over.

"Are you with TV or the papers?"

"You think I'm a reporter? Is that what this is about?"

"It's about maintaining Ms. Lawton's privacy."

"First, stop with the 'Ms. Lawton' stuff. If she really was Lawton, you wouldn't have opened the door and LAPD would be taking me away in cuffs."

"If you're not a reporter, what do you want?"

"I already told you. Forever yours, forever mine. I want to

talk to Ms. Thivierge about it."

"She doesn't want to talk to you."

"I don't want to talk to anybody, but I have a job to do."

A phone to the left of the door rings. The assistant has to take off a glove to pick it up.

"Yes. I see. All right then."

She hangs up and steps away from the door.

"Come in," she says. "Ms. Lawton will see you after all."

I was right about the air conditioner, at least. The moment I set a foot inside Thivierge's Halloween castle, I'm freezing.

"I'm Maggie, Ms. Lawton's personal assistant."

The look she gives me isn't quite a sneer. It's more like she opened a garbage can and found a dead skunk inside. She holds up a hooded parka.

"Put this on."

I button up my coat against the chill.

"I'm fine."

Maggie puts the parka back on a wall peg and offers me a heavy scarf. I shake my head. Until I know exactly what's going on here, I don't want anything that might be charmed or get in my way in a fight.

"Suit yourself," Maggie says like I just refused a poison antidote.

"If we're done with the fashion show, can I see Thivierge now?"

"Ms. Lawton is in the back room by the garden. Follow me."

The rooms I walk through remind me of Danny Gentry's place, only a lot richer and a lot classier. Movie posters on the walls. Awards on the bookshelves. Lots of photos with lots of important people. What's funny, though, is that's there's a light coat of dust on everything, like no one's set foot in these rooms in a long time.

By the time we get to the back, where Thivierge is waiting, I'm beginning to regret not taking the parka. My hands are going numb and I can see my breath.

Finally, Maggie stops by a room sealed like something you'd see on a space station. The wall around the door is covered floor to ceiling in heavy, silver-backed insulation. The door itself is sealed with a kind of airlock, so that nothing that's going on out here is going to contaminate what's going on in the next room.

I touch my cheek and realize I can't feel my face anymore.

Maggie smiles at that and says, "Please don't upset her. She's fragile."

"I'll be like cotton-candy kisses."

Maggie gives me a look and opens the door. An even deeper winter blast smacks me and I can't help but shudder.

The crap I do to make a living.

I wait by the door and listen as Maggie seals it up behind me.

Across the room is an old woman in a wheelchair who looks like she was carved out of a glacier. A living ice sculpture for some billionaire's New Year's party. We stare at each other for over a minute.

Finally, I say, "Thanks for seeing me, Ms. Thivierge."

"All of a sudden you're polite. Did your mother teach you to be nice to old ladies?"

"No, ma'am. She taught me how to make her martinis."

That gets me a brittle laugh. She points to a sofa that's

covered in puffy insulated material. I sink six inches when I sit down.

"So, you found me out and tracked me here," Thivierge says. "Big deal. If it's money you want, I don't have any. Every cent is sunk into this house and the electric bills."

"I had a feeling they're pretty hefty."

"It'd make your balls shrivel up if you saw it."

"My balls are pretty shriveled anyway."

Another brittle laugh, followed by a hacking cough. I get up to help her, but she waves me back onto the sofa.

She says, "I can't stand being touched. Feeling another person's body heat is agony."

I'm tired of beating around the bush.

"Tell me, Ms. Thivierge, who cursed you?"

She sits back and eyes me for a minute, so I go on.

"I couldn't help noticing all the protections you had on your place. Are you afraid of someone? The person who did this to you?"

This time when she laughs it isn't brittle. It comes from deep in her throat. It's the most human sound she's made so far.

She says, "You think you're pretty smart, don't you? You're part of the Hollywood magic set, aren't you? Well, kiddo, I'll tell you exactly who cursed me: me."

It all makes a kind of sense. All of those Hollywood parties with stoned garbage wizards like Kenny; something was bound to go wrong.

"You used to do your own hoodoo at parties? What kind? I've heard about play Satanists and that scene. Was that what you were into?"

She gives me a sly smile.

"Don't make me laugh. That was those West Hollywood hippies into that nonsense. I only did one type of magic."

"What kind was that?"

She opens her eyes wide.

"Sex magic. I wasn't looking to go to the next plane of existence or any of that line. I was all about the here and now. Flesh, boy. That's the only kind of magic I wanted. And I was good at it."

"What went wrong?"

Thivierge frowns.

"I don't know. I was running the scene. It was a new ritual, so it was my fault. But for all these years, I've had the feeling that someone had it in for me. That they screwed with my tools and potions so I ended up like this."

She holds her bony arms out wide.

"The White Witch of California."

"How bad is it?"

"My condition? Anything much above thirty degrees and I'm panting like a dog. Forty is heatstroke. At fifty, I cook like a luau pig."

"Who would have wanted to do this to you?"

"I don't know and I'm not sure I want to. You're the first person who's tracked me down in all these years. How did you do it?"

"Magic, of course."

She leans forward in her chair and speaks conspiratorially.

"Well, if you've come here for lessons, you can walk right out the front door."

"I don't want lessons. You know why I'm here. Forever

yours, forever mine."

She laces her fingers together nervously before looking at me.

"How do you know about that? *Forever Yours, Forever Mine* has been buried for decades."

"To tell you the truth, I don't know anything about it. That's why I'm here. And as for how I know about it, I learned about it from Chris Stein's police file."

She looks down at the floor, frowning.

"Chris," she says. "That colossal fuckup."

"That's what I hear from people."

"What are you, a detective?"

"Something like that."

"Good luck. Half of Hollywood hated him by the end. Including me."

"Why's that?"

"The little prick tanked my career. Thirty years I worked in this business and Chris ruined me overnight. Other people too. Like that little girl who was supposed to play his kid sister."

I lean forward on the sofa.

"Wait. *Forever Yours, Forever Mine* was a movie?"

"Of course. What kind of detective are you?" She practically shouts it at me.

"It was Stein's last movie?"

"And mine, as it turned out."

"What happened?"

Thivierge sighs and steam flows from her frigid lips like there's a dying dragon down inside her someplace.

"It was a big-budget project. One of my biggest, and sure

as shit Chris's biggest. It was the movie that was finally going to put him up there with Dean and Brando. Then, in a weekend, it went to hell."

"What happened? Was somebody out to get him?"

She makes a face.

"No one ruined Chris but Chris. He was doing a lot of drugs by then. More than ever. Still going to the play parties in the hills. When the studio got wind of it, they figured that they could paper over it all with money and stories about what a young stud Chris was."

"Why didn't it work?"

"You have to remember this all happened a long time ago. Less enlightened times. When it finally got back to the studio that Chris was as interested in other men as the women, well, the executives blew their tops. I managed to talk them down and get the movie back on track. But Chris had plenty of other problems, including some woman. She was no good for him."

"How do you know?"

"She had her claws into him. The jealous type. Chris couldn't make a move without clearing it with her. An out-of-town publicity event? He had to clear it with Mommy. A late-night photo shoot? Same thing. It was revolting. They used to send each other notes and call each other at all hours of the night. You can guess how each call ended."

"Forever yours. Forever mine."

"Bingo. It got so I was sick of hearing it."

"But the movie was still going forward?"

"Sure. But then something happened between Chris and Mommy. All he'd say is she wanted something he couldn't give her. That was the end. He disappeared for days. Went on a real bender. When he resurfaced he promised to be good, but it didn't last long. That's when the thing with the girl happened. The one who was supposed to play his kid sister. Did you find that in your files, Mr. Detective?"

"This is the first I'm hearing anything about it."

She shakes her head. I don't know if it's at me or Stein. Both probably.

"The fool gave her cocaine. Fifteen years old and he was letting the kid dip into his stash. She ended up at the Cedars-Sinai ER."

"And that's when the studio killed the movie?"

Thivierge shakes her head.

"Killed everything," Thivierge shouts. "Killed the movie. Killed Stein's career. The little girl's career. And mine."

"No offense, but I know a little bit about Hollywood history. How is it *Forever Yours, Forever Mine* isn't up there with the Fatty Arbuckle scandal or Bob Crane's murder?"

"Because the studio buried it. The script, actors, crew. They used the whole movie budget. Everyone involved was paid off. The papers and TV people. I'm still living on the last of the payout they gave me. When it's gone, I don't know what I'm going to do."

I think about it for a minute.

"With all due respect, Ms. Thivierge, even paying off people, you can't keep something like *Forever Yours, Forever Mine* a secret. There had to be something more to it."

She coughs and says, "If you know so much about Hollywood, you tell me."

I remember some of what I saw a couple of years ago when

Samael was still Lucifer and he was in town dabbling in the movie business.

"Studio magicians. They had their own hoodoo team on staff."

She points a finger at me.

"Finally, you've said something smart. They wiped the whole thing out of existence. Like none of it ever happened. But it did, and I knew that if the studio could do that to the story, they could do it to me."

"So, you ran."

"Fast too. Then I got cocky and did this to myself."

Thivierge frowns again, hard enough that I think her pale face might crack.

She says, "What I don't understand is, with all the studio did to bury the story, how it ended up in a police report."

"It didn't. In the report, *Forever Yours, Forever Mine* wasn't a movie. It was in a love note. It looked like a woman's handwriting."

"It's always something, isn't it? All that money. All that magic and they miss a lousy note."

"Love is a funny magic all its own. Maybe the last piece of the affair didn't want to disappear."

She gives me an appraising look.

"I didn't peg you for a romantic."

"Mom watched a lot of soap operas while she drank her martinis."

Thivierge half-smiles at that.

"Samantha," says Thivierge suddenly. "That was her name. Mommy, I mean."

"Can you tell me anything more about her?"

Thivierge leans back and looks up, thinking.

"Who remembers these things? She was Samantha something-or-other. A pretty little thing. Probably came from money. She always had it but never seemed to do anything for it."

"If they were together back then, it would put her somewhere in her sixties now?"

"That sounds about right."

"Did anything change between them before he died?"

She raises her eyebrows.

"Lordy, did it. The Chris I knew was always into sex, drugs, and parties, but before the end, he added God and the Devil to the list. At first, I thought he'd turned into some kind of Jesus freak. But it was even stranger than that. It was almost a William Blake sort of thing. He saw something, heard something, or snorted something that changed him. I suppose he became a kind of visionary, in his own cheap way."

Zadkiel. Her again. Now she's connected to both Chris and Samantha. Was it some kind of love triangle? She wanted him to give up Samantha and when he wouldn't she killed him?

I rub my hands together and blow on them, trying to get some circulation going. Thivierge looks amused at my discomfort.

I say, "Once Chris came down from on high, was he still hustling?"

"The hustling thing seemed to just fade away. Partly because he wasn't working hard at it anymore and he'd stopped coming to parties. But mainly it was that his screwy visions scared people. You have to understand, this was around the same time as Jim Jones and other charlatans were hurting people. A lot of us became wary of anyone spewing screwy religious nonsense." When she smiles, bits of frost crack at the edges of her mouth. "What I'm saying is that he was a lot more fun back when it was just parties and sex magic. Way back when, some of us would get in disguises and go with him and Samantha to that big porn theater on Hollywood Boulevard."

"The Pussycat Theatre?"

"That's the place. I only went a couple of times, but he and Samantha loved it and would get into all sorts of trouble. That was another reason we knew that Samantha came from money. Whatever trouble they got into, she could always get them out of it. It was only when Chris tried to break things off with her that things went haywire."

"He lost his meal ticket."

"That was part of it. The stealing got completely out of hand. The little rat could get in anywhere and would leave with anything he could carry. The wretch made off with some of my jewelry. Say, if you find any emerald earrings during your investigation, let me know. I'll make it worth your while."

I think, Who cares?, but I say, "Sure, but let's get back to Samantha. She didn't live in Little Cairo, did she?"

"Yes. I think she might have. Chris was always giving her stupid little cat carvings."

"Bast?"

"You'll have to ask Chris that."

"Do you remember what Samantha looked like?"

"Oh hell. Let me think. Pretty. Brunette. A tiny thing. Always smiling, like she was in on a joke that only she knew. What else . . . ?"

Thivierge seems lost in thought for a moment, then throws up her hands.

"This is silly. I have photos from back then. There was always someone taking shots at the parties. Polaroids mostly. No one wanted to take negatives to the corner drugstore, if you know what I mean. I'm sure I have shots of Chris and Samantha."

"Can you show them to me?"

She gives me a funny look.

"Now you just sound like an old pervert. Are you sure you're a detective?"

"I'm trying to solve a murder the cops forgot about forty years ago. Isn't that good enough?"

"All right. Come down off the cross. I tell you what. You keep an eye out for my earrings and I'll find some photos for you."

"It's a deal."

Thivierge slumps back in her seat.

"I think it's about time for you to go. I'm getting tired."

"Just one more thing. Have you ever heard of the Zero Lodge?"

She puts a hand over her face and shakes her head.

"Those cretins. Yes. Chris ran with that crowd. Samantha too. You know, for all of Chris's excesses, she was the real wild one."

"Do you remember anything else?"

Thivierge turns away. "You need to go now. All this talk about the old days is bringing back memories I'd rather not dwell on."

"I understand," I say, trying to sound sympathetic. "But you'll still go through your albums?"

"I told you I would," she says angrily. "If I find anything, I'll send you a copy. Leave your address with Maggie on the way out. And that's a hint about where you should be headed right now."

I wonder if Flicker was able to buy me more time.

"Sure. But I'd appreciate it if you could do it fast. I'm kind of on a deadline."

She laughs again, and this time it's the brittle one.

"Aren't we all?" she says. "Now get out of here. I'll look for your smut this evening."

I go through the airlock fast, for both her sake and mine. I can't feel my feet anymore, but at least I got my connection to Little Cairo.

In the foyer, Maggie gives me some stationery so I can write the address of the abandoned nail salon that's the front door to the flying saucer house.

Going outside into the L.A. heat, I feel like my skin is going to crack like broken glass. It's too bad about Thivierge and the ice queen act she's been forced into. But she's survived all these years. A tough old broad. I like her. In case someone did sabotage her all those years ago, when this is over, I'll come back with Vidocq and we'll put up some better protection around her haunted mansion. Let her live out the rest of her small, cold life in peace.

IT'S LATE AT night and I can't sleep, so I walk down to Hollywood Boulevard.

Talking to Thivierge and thinking about the Pussycat Theatre brought me back to Samael. Now that I have a tight connection to his lost angel I wonder if I should have started with her in the first place. But I'm pretty good at getting things backward. And, anyway, before Chris I had nowhere to start.

What the hell is it about the Pussycat Theatre? Chris Stein partied there. His girlfriend Samantha partied there. And goddamn Zadkiel hung there too. What weird magnetism does the Pussycat possess?

They hosed the old theater down, so now it's a regular movie house playing the current crop of Hollywood crap. Nothing special about it at all anymore. Ninety-nine percent of its clientele and employees probably have no idea where they are. The place seems a lot more suited for an angel now, with dull new movies full of CG and easy morality. Angels eat that kind of stuff up. What would send the Opener of the Ways from Heaven to a classic seventies porn palace? Doc Kinski—the archangel Uriel—stayed on Earth, but he kept a low profile. But angels are a lot more like people than the Church or anyone in Heaven wants to admit. A lot of the same desires and hang-ups. Who says an angel escaping Uptown's goody-goody hosannas wouldn't want to walk on the wild side? I sure as hell would. You might be a crazy killer, but on this one thing, good for you, Zadkiel. Follow your dreams, even if they are to watch skin flicks 24/7.

It all brings me back to my other question, whether Samael really wanted me to find his angel at all or if he's playing some other dangerous game he doesn't want to get involved with. Being him, he's capable of doing both things at once. Did he really come to see me on his own or did Mr. Muninn send him with a whole other agenda in mind? They both want the war in Heaven over, but do they really believe a single angel can pull it off? I have serious doubts. Still, they might be getting desperate enough to try anything, because what do they have to lose?

When I get sick of the boulevard, I turn onto North Cherokee Avenue, to the site of the Masque club. Like the Pussycat, its heyday was in the late seventies. In fact, the club was located in the Pussycat's basement. I wish I could have seen it back in the day. Just about every punk band in L.A. played there. X. Germs. Alice Bag. The Screamers. The Weirdos.

Who knows what kind of demented stuff went on in that musical dungeon when it was open? I'd kill to know. What was it Maria said Brendan Mullen told her? "If everyone knew where all the bodies were buried, no one would dance for fear of treading over some poor bastard's face."

That's what I feel like right now: a dead slob with people dancing on my face. I'm in the middle of something but can't get a handle on any of it. Stein. The Stay Belows. Zadkiel. What the Lodge Within the Lodge really wants. Janet. Candy. How does it all fit together?

The second time an LAPD cruiser rolls by to check on me, I head home. The last thing I need right now is cop trouble.

I WAKE UP groggy after a night spent dreaming about William Blake's Great Red Dragon doing coke off Farrah Fawcett's ass in a Gothic mansion hidden under the Pussycat.

Yesterday's conversation with Thivierge has left me with a hundred more questions, but there's no way I'm going back to Ice Station Zebra for another chat. The smartest thing to do is talk to someone else who was there all those years ago. Someone who can confirm Thivierge's story about Stein's going visionary on everyone.

I dial Danny Gentry's number and the phone rings a few times before going to voicemail. But when I try to leave a message, a damn computer tells me that his mailbox is full. I wouldn't have guessed a guy like Gentry had that many friends. Or maybe he's just ducking creditors. I make sure to have money in my pocket when I ride the Hog to the Kiernan Arms.

I buzz his apartment on the building's Fort Knox front gate directory. No answer. After a couple of more long tries, I give up and go into the lobby through a shadow. I check his mailbox. It's stuffed full and there's a notice saying that he has to pick his letters up from the post office since it's too full for the mail carrier to fit anything. On the off chance something funny is going on and Gentry isn't just sleeping one off, I get out the Colt and go up the stairs to the fourth floor.

I knock on his door hard. Then harder. I twist the doorknob. It's locked. Then I knock fucking *hard*. Nothing.

Gentry's neighbor is still blasting the same teeth-grating country pop he was playing last time I was here. When the frowning dumbass sticks his head into the hall to complain about the noise I stick the Colt in his face.

"Play Taylor Swift one more time, motherfucker."

He turtles his head back into his apartment and the music stops.

I'm fed up with the whole situation. Technically, I could go into Gentry's place through a shadow, but kicking his door in is much more satisfying.

I keep the Colt up as I go through his place, room by room. I finally find him exactly where I left him last time—in a chair by the window, his Marlboros on a little table next to him. Only Danny isn't smoking. Danny is dead.

Whoever killed him has a sick sense of humor. Gentry's head is tilted back so far, another inch or two would have snapped his neck. But it wasn't the neck that killed him. Someone took that stupid plastic Academy Award that Stein gave him a thousand years ago and shoved it all the way down his throat. The poor fucker must have choked to death staring right up into the eyes of his killer.

I look around the room for anything that might give me a clue to who might have done it. But who am I kidding? I'm not a real detective. Maybe if the killer dropped an eight-by-ten and their Social Security card I could figure things out, but the room looks just how I remember it, and Gentry's door was locked.

When I look down the hall again, there's a small mob of the Kiernan's ragged tenants in the doorway staring at me.

"That's him with the gun," yells the country-pop dumbass. "Someone call the cops."

I give the place one more quick look over, and as one brave jackass advances on me with a baseball bat, I step through a shadow and come out near the bike.

I'm sorry, Danny. You had a tough life and a worse death. If I can find out who did that to you, I promise I'll make them cry.

Then I have a really bad thought.

I get on the Hog and blast across town to Chanchala Abodes.

I DON'T BOTHER knocking this time. I just get out the Colt and check the front door. It's unlocked.

The front reception area looks the same as when I was here last. But the door to Chanchala's office is open. Someone as precise as her doesn't get sloppy like that, so I level the pistol in front of me and go in.

The spare Japanese-style room is mostly the way I remember it, except for the long trail of blood spatter on one wall.

Chanchala's body is faceup on the floor, and aside from the slash of red on the wall, it looks like every drop of her blood has soaked into the carpet. I put the Colt away and kneel down. Her throat is slit in a single, precise cut that goes from ear to ear. But that wasn't enough for whoever killed her. Like with Danny Gentry, they had to add a little flourish to make the murder just a bit more awful. They filled her mouth with sand from the miniature Zen garden and stuck in the tiny rake by the handle so it sticks up like a flower on her grave.

Someone is definitely trying to cover their tracks, but they're also having fun doing it.

There's nothing I can do for Chanchala, so I get on the bike and head for Benedict Canyon as fast as I can.

I leave the bike a hundred yards or so down the hill and sprint the rest of the way to Lisa Thivierge's spook house. I know I'm too late the moment I see the place.

The front door is wide open and when I stick my head into the foyer, it must be over eighty degrees inside. Someone has turned off the air conditioner and cranked the heat up all the way.

I run to Thivierge's airlock garden room. Along the way,

I trip over Maggie's body. She has a knife in her back. There aren't any extra flourishes to her murder, so she wasn't the target. Just someone in the way.

When I open the door to the garden room, the first thing that hits me is the stink. It's like an old slaughterhouse that closed shop with meat on the hooks and blood in the sluices.

Thivierge's body isn't hard to find. She's still her in wheelchair, only now her arms and legs are tied to it. There's a space heater at her feet, tilted upward, blasting out a steady stream of scorching. Her underlying flesh is bright red, but over that is a crust of blackened skin. Her tongue hangs out and her eyes are gone. Burst sometime before or after she died. After, I hope. I've seen a lot of vicious torture Downtown, but not so much up here. Whoever is committing these murders looks like they'll have a successful career in a Hellion welcome committee.

It has to be Samantha. She's what all this has been leading to. And I have to find her fast or I get the feeling more people are going to die.

There's nothing I can do for Thivierge or the others, but maybe I could stop Samantha if I knew who the hell I was looking for. The only thing I can do now is find out everything I can about the mystery girl. And that starts with finding Thivierge's photo albums. But the mansion is huge and I have no idea where to start looking.

Not that I get the chance.

When I start out of the garden room I hear people in the house. I get behind a pillar, hoping that Samantha might have come back to check on the carnage. No such luck.

A gaggle of L.A.'s finest are coming in through the front

door, pistols drawn. I don't wait for them to find me. I jump through a shadow, get back on the Hog, and head back to Hollywood. More squad cars pass me as I go down the winding hills. I'm careful to obey every goddamn traffic law in existence all the way back to Hollywood.

My first stop is Donut Universe, but Janet isn't there, which is probably for the best. Right now, I don't need a screaming argument with someone I care about. I just grab a fritter and some coffee and hunker down in the back of the place to think things over.

All of my questions led me to Samantha. My guess is that she's the one who killed Gentry, Chanchala, and Lisa Thivierge. That's not a question. What I can't understand is how did a sixtysomething rich lady find out? And where did she get the skills to murder in such bloodthirsty ways? I know she had the money to hire a hit man to do it, but they're not exactly on Yelp. And would a straightforward killer murder three people in such baroque ways?

The murders look very personal. The killings took time and even a little skill. What the hell has Samantha been doing all these years that she's become so good at that kind of slaughter? And if it was her, maybe I'm wrong about Zadkiel's being involved. If Samantha is capable of these murders, she could have easily turned Stein into a Black Dahlia.

I wonder if I can do location hoodoo on all the Samanthas in L.A. based on age and income and . . . who the hell am I kidding? That's not what I'm good at. And I get the feeling if I ask Abbot he'll laugh in my face and pull the trigger on his own murder squad. There will go all the Stay Belows in

Little Cairo, along with how many civilians? No. I've got to work this out on my own, and do it fast. Too bad I don't have a single idea on *how*.

I shove the uneaten fritter and coffee out of the way and am about to leave when my phone goes off. I don't recognize the number, then the digits begin to move and rearrange themselves. They spell out ANSWER ME JIMMY.

I thumb the phone on and say, "Who the hell is this?"

"Oh, come on. Don't get dull on me. You know who this is."

I instantly get a headache.

"Hello, Samael. Look, I don't have time for you or your angel rescue mission right now."

"But I have good news. The week I originally gave you? Father has agreed to hold off on waving the white flag for a few more days."

I sigh and say, "I honestly don't care right now."

"I understand," he says. "You're guilty about all the mayhem you've instigated. Three dead already, and how many more to come?"

I want to punch him, but I can't reach him through the phone.

I say, "How do you know about that? I thought you were busy losing a war."

"Ouch. Kitty has sharp claws."

"Unless you have something useful to say, I'm hanging up."

"In fact, I do have something you might want to know: if you're heading back to your tacky little house to pout, don't do it."

"Why not? I have nowhere else to go and there's nothing else I can do."

"Don't do it because there's a surprise party waiting for you."

A cop car passes on the street. I watch it cruise by.

"Is it the cops or an old woman named Samantha with a knife?"

"Either would be fun, but it's neither one of them. It's your friends from the great beyond."

"Stay Belows?"

"Quite a lot of them. I don't think Flicker's little bundle of light will scare this mob."

My gut tightens.

"Is Janet safe?"

Samael laughs.

"What has that child ever done that strikes you as safe?"

I don't say anything for a minute, trying to gather my thoughts. I don't have any grand theories anymore except for Samantha. And now I'm even more worried about Janet.

"I know you know more than you're telling me. Just answer one question. Are Gentry's, Chanchala's, and Thivierge's murders connected to anything going on with the Zero Lodge?"

Imagine my surprise when Samael begins to sing.

"'All things bright and beautiful, / All creatures great and small, / All things wise and wonderful, / The Lord God made them all.'"

I keep listening, waiting for an explanation, but Samael goes silent. Now I'm both scared and pissed.

I shout, "What the fuck does that mean?"

"Time is running out."

"I'm doing the best I can, man."

He says, "Look into your heart, Stark," and hangs up.

I look into my heart and all I can see is bourbon and me punching Samael in the balls.

What does that stupid song mean? What's supposed to be in my heart?

I go over the lyrics a couple more times in my head.

"All things bright and beautiful, / All creatures great and small, / All things wise and wonderful, / The Lord God made them all."

Basically, it's saying that God made everything and everything is just great.

This thing is a damn Disney nightmare.

God made everything and everything is great.

Only . . . God didn't make everything. The angels built most of the universe. Is that important?

One more time with the lyrics.

Fuck.

I am finally and truly going to murder Samael. None of this makes sense. Him. His stupid song. Looking into my sodden heart. It's all a waste of time. It's all infuriating.

And a little light goes on in my head.

Everything Samael said, every bit of it, every stupid clue, is connected to pissing me off. And if this mess is connected, it means that everything else is connected too.

Thank you, Samael, you smart-ass sage.

I hope. But I don't have time to worry about it for another hour.

I take a bite of the fritter and get on the bike.

GETTING TO JANET'S place through the afternoon traffic is slow and frustrating. I want to ditch the Hog and go to their place straight through a shadow. But I've already taken too many chances lately. I let Gentry's neighbors see me shadow walk. Maybe the cops at Thivierge's place. Pretty much everyone in the Lodge. As anxious as I am to get to Janet, I have to think things through better and not peg the dial at 100 all the time. They're not going to listen if I show up at their apartment jabbering like an ape. I have to slow down and think. Janet isn't going to like what I have to say, so I have to go in the right way.

When I get to their place I take a breath before pressing the buzzer.

Janet's voice comes through the door speaker a moment later.

"Hello?"

"Janet, it's Stark. I know you don't want to see me right now, but please listen. I think you're in danger. Let me explain. After that, if you don't want to see me, I'm gone for good."

They don't say anything, but the lock buzzes and I go in.

The door is open when I get to their apartment. Janet stands all the way across the room scowling and with their arms folded. Not a promising beginning.

They say, "Talk fast. I have things to do."

I close the door and stay where I am, hoping the distance might relax her a little.

"Since I've been involved with the Lodge, I've been ambushed by ghosts twice. I'm only standing here now because a friend warned me about a third attack. One big enough that

I might not have been able to get out of it. You remember how scary that first attack was? Imagine that times ten."

They shift their stance a little, like they're at least listening.

"I'm sorry about all that and I'm happy you're safe, but what does it have to do with me?"

"All of the recent Stay Below manifestations have been the same. A tiny spot of light. A Thurl opens and turns sort of liquid. There's singing. The ghosts appear and then they attack."

"I know all of that. What's your point?"

"The manifestations in Little Cairo go exactly the same way. I've seen a lot of spooks in my life. But these ones come and go in very specific patterns."

They look down, then back at me.

"I don't understand what you're trying to tell me. So, get to the point or leave now."

I take a step closer and they don't pull back. Progress.

"Think back to when Kenny appeared. I think all of the Stay Below appearances—the ones in Little Cairo, in my place, in Vidocq's place, and Kenny's appearance—come from one source: Dan and Juliette."

They throw up their hands in disgust.

"If that's all you have to say, get out."

"Please listen. They're dangerous people. They've tried to kill *me* more than once, and I don't mean their hokey vampire. They almost killed you. I don't even know how many people they've killed in Little Cairo. They probably didn't mean to do it, but do you think they'd care?"

Now Janet comes to me, their face hard and angry.

"You've always had it in for them, from the first time you met them. The Lodge is important to me and you never gave it or them a chance."

"I was there three times. All three times, they did something vile, and you almost died twice. Didn't give them a chance? I didn't *kill* them because of you. But I'm telling you, Dan and Juliette are reckless and stupid and I know they're at the center all of the spook activity in L.A."

Janet shakes her head.

"That's impossible. They just learned about sacrifices the other night."

"Who says so? Kenny? Kenny's dead. Dan and Juliette? Dan said that he had a lot of experience with summoning hoodoo. He had the necromancer mask, the phurba, the horn, and knew the chants. What if he and Juliette were experimenting with summoning before but got it all wrong? What if the dove wasn't the first sacrifice? They tried it before, got it wrong, got scared, then called Kenny back so he can tell them how to do it right the next time."

"I don't believe you. You don't like them so you're coming up with all kinds of reasons not to trust them."

I'm not getting through to them at all. Time to try something else.

"Maybe you're right. But I've been wondering about your friend Cassandra. The one who was killed by a crackhead. When did it happen?"

Janet looks down at the floor.

"A little over two weeks ago."

"I thought so. That's right around the same time as the Stay Belows first appeared in Little Cairo. What if Dan and

Juliette tried to open the gate to the Land of the Dead on their own, but they needed a sacrifice?"

Janet looks at me hard.

"You think *they* killed Cassandra?"

"I wouldn't put it past them."

Now Janet smiles, but it's thin and sad.

Here comes the hard part. Something I haven't wanted to think about but has been bothering me.

I say, "You know, for someone who was supposed to be such a close friend, you seem to have gotten over Cassandra's death pretty fast."

They grab a book and throw it at me.

"I told you mourning wasn't allowed," they scream. "Just because I don't run around crying and acting out my worst impulses like you do, I'm some kind of monster? Takes one to know one, I guess. Fuck you. Get out and never come near me or the Lodge again."

I look at their eyes. Listen to their heartbeat.

"You're going there tonight, aren't you?"

"I'm not telling you."

"That's a yes. Please don't. Give me one day and I'll be able to prove everything."

There are tears in Janet's eyes when they say, "If you ever cared about me even a little, leave now. No more questions. No theories. No nothing. Just go."

I leave and they quietly close the door behind me.

The crack about Cassandra was rotten, but I had to be sure. My worst fear was that Janet might be so far in with the Lodge that they'd turn a blind eye to anything. But their heart rate and breathing didn't change like they would if they'd been lying. But that doesn't make them safe. I'm still afraid Janet is walking into something they might not be able to come back from. Vidocq talked about the mystical power in child sacrifice. The younger the better, he said. What would Janet do if they walked in on something like that? I hope they'd try to stop it. What would Dan and Juliette do then? Not to mention the rest of the Lodge Within the Lodge?

Should I go after Janet? Should I stop them? I can't. I've scared them enough for one night. Besides, what if I'm wrong? Janet was right when they said that I've had it in for Dan and Juliette. I never liked or trusted them. Then Samael comes along and sings me a little song and I'm ready to burn them at the stake. It's possible he meant something completely different and I've twisted his clue around to suit myself. Why can't angels be straight with the world for one second? This is right. This is wrong. Don't eat the apple? Then why did you even give me an apple tree? Don't give me parables and songs. Give me answers. Something I can hang on to. Am I right about Dan and Juliette? And was I wrong to let Janet go? Have I been right about anything along the way or did I get Gentry, Chanchala, and Thivierge slaughtered for nothing?

I consider going to Bamboo House and drinking myself horizontal, but that's what I always do, and where has it gotten me? Pretty much where I am now—standing in a hallway talking to myself about things and people I don't understand anymore.

I take a couple more of the PTSD pills, get on the Hog, and leave. I have to think. If I'm wrong, as I'm afraid I might be, maybe I was always better off in Hell and should have never let Wormwood bring me back. That's always been the central question of my life: Where do I belong? Here or Downtown? If I'm supposed to be here, then I have to do what I need to do to protect my friends. But if I'm supposed to be somewhere else, then everything I do could be dragging them into the Abyss with me.

I don't have time to get lost in my head like this. There's too much at stake. I need someone to help straighten me out.

I drive to Vidocq's.

HE'S IN A brandy mood today, so that's what we're drinking.

After a couple of rounds he says, "It is a dilemma, my friend. What do you intend to do?"

I swirl the sweet stuff in my glass.

"You tell me. That's why I came here."

He pushes some old books out of his way and props his feet on the coffee table.

"I think your heart and your head are working against each other. You say that Samael gave you a puzzling clue as to what has been happening, but you also say that you're not sure if you've interpreted it correctly."

"I don't know what I know anymore. People are dying. Abbot's about to flatten a whole neighborhood because I'm chasing one particular ghost. And I don't know if I'm right about any of it."

Vidocq puts up his hand.

"If you were still with Candy right now, what would she tell you?"

I think for a minute.

"Not to start punching things too quickly."

"Is that all?"

"To stop and think and make sure that I'm not just seeing things the way I want to."

"There you are. That sounds like excellent advice to me."

"But what about Janet tonight?"

Vidocq sniffs his brandy.

He says, "What about them? They've made their choice. Their loyalty isn't to you. It's to the Lodge."

"Was I wrong about Janet all this time? Were they like Dan and Juliette all along?"

"What does your heart tell you?"

"That I was wrong. That Janet was with them and never me."

I close my eyes.

"I keep coming back to this one thought: that I know everything about monsters and nothing about people."

"Does that mean you intend to leave Janet alone?"

I open my eyes and look at him.

"I have to. But every instinct I have tells me that Dan and Juliette *are* monsters."

"Yet you have no proof except for your admittedly flawed instincts."

"They sacrificed that bird and they'll do it again."

"How will you stop them without killing them and proving to yourself that you are simply a monster too?"

"Is that what I do?"

"Your image of yourself is one of a beast. A benevolent one, but a beast nonetheless. As much as this might pain you, it is also easy and familiar. It allows you to do away with deeper emotions."

"Fuck. I don't know what to do."

Vidocq leans forward and slaps my knee once.

"Stay and drink with me. By coming here, you've already made your decision. You will not run rashly after Janet based on your fears and habits. Instead you've learned something important about yourself."

"Learning is miserable. People are awful. Worrying about them is the worst."

"All true."

"When I first came back to L.A. I swore I'd never get too close to anyone. Even you. I thought that connections to people made me weak. That they wouldn't let me do the only thing I was good at—killing things."

"What do you think now?"

"That connections are a mixed bag. You and Candy make me stronger. Janet though, that's a gut punch."

"You can't kill everything bad and you can't save everyone good."

"I'm not sure who the good ones are anymore."

"Yes you are. Because *you're* one. It's just sometimes hard to admit to oneself."

"Fuck."

I just sit there for a minute and look out the window. It's pitch-black. I want a cigarette.

"You know, eventually I have to go home, only I don't know if I can."

"Worried about bad dreams?"

"That too. But the one straight thing Samael said is that there's a whole gang of Stay Belows waiting to kill me."

"Then that is a problem you can attack. Forget the Zero Lodge and their foolishness. Let us go and rescue your home."

Vidocq gets his overcoat from a hook on the wall.

I say, "You're sure you want to come with me? You've seen what those spooks are like."

As he puts the coat on he says, "All the more reason I want to go. Since that attack, I've been brewing a supply of *bannissement par l'amarante*. It won't destroy the creatures, but it should drive them away."

"Should?"

"What is guaranteed in this life?"

"Thanks, Dad. You're a bundle of comfort today."

He shows me what he's packing. There are about fifty little pockets sewn into the inside of Vidocq's big coat. Each pocket contains a potion vial that he can throw like a mini hand grenade.

I get up and manifest my Gladius.

"Let's go."

I pull him through a shadow to the flying saucer house.

When we get there, it looks like we got worked up for nothing. It's not that Samael was wrong about the Stay Belows—judging by the wreckage, they're gone now. All that's waiting for us in the flying saucer house is rubble. The spooks have had all day to get out their frustrations on the place and it looks like they took their work seriously. There isn't a single piece of furniture left in one piece. The walls are torn open in places and the insulation pulled out. The Blu-ray player is in a million pieces and the smashed TV is in the bedroom on the slashed mattress. The only good news in the mess is that the DVDs I borrowed from Max Overdrive are safe under the splintered sofa. The kitchen, however, looks like a bomb went off.

Vidocq puts away his vials and I let the Gladius go out.

"At least Samael was telling the truth," says Vidocq. "It looks as if he might have saved your life today."

"Yeah, but I don't know what I'm going to tell Abbot. How many times can I destroy this place before someone on the Sub Rosa Council gets annoyed and boots me out?"

"Abbot is the Augur. The leader. They will have to listen to him."

"Not if I can't do something for them. And so far, all I've done is wave my hands, shout theories, and get three people killed."

I find a relatively intact sofa cushion and sit down on it. Vidocq perches on the ledge where the TV used to be.

"At least you weren't here," he says. "As long as you're alive there's hope."

"You think so? I'm having my doubts."

He gives me a concerned look.

"You're not thinking of doing something rash, are you?"

I pull some stuffing from the sofa cushion I'm sitting on.

"It's nothing like that. It's just that, after this—and knowing what Abbot is about to do—I think the only useful thing left for me to do is go to Little Cairo and wipe out every single goddamn Stay Below I can find."

"Perhaps, but I think Abbot will forgive you long before you forgive yourself."

I throw a chair leg at the TV and miss.

"If you have any better ideas, please shout them out."

"We leave this for now. We'll go to Bamboo House of Dolls and you'll stay with me tonight. Tomorrow, we will figure out what to do next."

I think about it for a minute.

"I can't. I've put it off long enough. If I clear out Little Cairo myself, maybe I can save some of the civilians. If the Council does it they'll nuke everything and everyone."

We both get up and as I'm about to pull Vidocq into a shadow, he moves away.

"Is this yours?" he says.

"What is it?"

"A courier envelope."

"I don't know any couriers."

Vidocq looks it over.

"There's a return address. The sender is Janet Lawton."

I stumble through the debris, grab the envelope from his hands, and rip it open.

Something falls onto the floor.

It's an old Polaroid. A happy, naked couple smile out at me from the faded plastic. There's a trimmed tree in the background.

Across the bottom in ballpoint pen someone has written, "Chris and Samantha, Christmas '77."

The man I immediately recognize as Chris Stein. As for the woman, I take the photo under one of the few working lights to get a good look at kill-crazy Samantha.

Only it's not Samantha.

It's Manimal Mike's girlfriend, Maria Simon, but in 1977—looking exactly the way she does now.

I put the photo in my pocket and grab Vidocq.

"Forget everything I just said. We're going to a party."

THROUGH ANOTHER SHADOW, we come out into Dan and Juliette's living room. I bark some hoodoo to lock the place down tight. No one in. No one out. I get out my na'at and head down into the rumpus room with Vidocq close behind me.

There's no one downstairs. Kenny's big table is gone. The floor is covered in candles, milagros, and other supernatural baubles. Someone has pulled the boards off the entrance to the Jackal's Backbone, so I have a pretty good idea of where the table went. But not knowing why worries me.

Vidocq looks into the stone tunnel.

"Is that where we are going?"

"Yeah."

"Do you have any idea what's waiting for us?"

"A bunch of thrill-kill psychos. Also, probably, some highly agitated ghosts."

"*Merde*," he says quietly, and takes a fistful of vials from inside his coat. "Shall we go?"

I run through the tunnel into the mountain with Vidocq right behind me. As we go, I extend the na'at into a barbed whip. A good weapon for making an impression and cutting through crowds. It's times like this that I wish my angelic side was just a bit more angelic. Like, it would be nice to have wings right now. Walking through shadows is fast, but you have to have some idea of where you're going. If I start jumping through shadows down here, I could shoot right past whatever the Lodge is up to and end up with the weight lifters on Venice Beach. If I had wings, maybe I could carry Vidocq across the ceiling of the Jackal's Backbone and he could bomb whatever was happening with his vials. But I can't, so I keep running and being bitter about getting shortchanged angelwise.

It takes us a few minutes more to find the Lodge Within the Lodge party. We hang back behind a boulder and check out the scene.

At first, all I can see is people. More of them than I expected. There were six or eight at the last Lodge Within the Lodge meeting. Now the number of people is easily double that. Those are lousy odds for us, but it also simplifies things. Before, I wasn't sure how rough I would have to get. With this many potential assholes to get through, there's no holding back. Move or die, fuckers. It's that simple.

I spot Maria talking to Juliette. Good. At least I know all the bad guys are here tonight.

The way things are laid out, I can't actually make out what's happening. But I see a lot of weapons in the hands of the Lodge members. Old, brutal stuff. Heavy broadswords. War hammers. Mayan obsidian-bladed battle axes.

Trash wizard Kenny has made an appearance. Still in the House of Knives. Still being sliced and diced like pastrami. That's nice, at least. He's called up a few Stay Belows, who hang at the back of the scene. No telling what they're for but I don't like it.

I have no idea what Vidocq is thinking right now. Probably "What the hell did I sign up for?" To be fair, I wish I knew what's going on too. It would help to have some sense of it so I don't make things worse. Kenny helps me out there.

When he isn't being carved up like Thanksgiving dinner, he says, "Congratulations on a great job, everybody. Good effort. With this sacrifice, I'll be able to bring each of you into the Land of the Dead so that you see the mad truth that lies beyond judgment and the grave."

Is that what all the old weapons are for? A sacrifice? You don't need that much hardware to kill anything you can fit down here. It makes me think this isn't like the bird sacrifice but some kind of dismemberment scene. Or worse. A disemboweling, like with the guts monster back at the canyon.

I crane my neck, trying to make out what's on the sacrifice block. I don't hear any barking, so I don't think they went with Dan's dog pack idea. And I don't smell shit everywhere, so I'm guessing Juliette's horse fantasy was jettisoned too. I swear if I hear one squeak or squall that sounds like a little kid, I'm going to personally gut every one of these fuckers. Vidocq can have whatever is left.

Finally, I have an idea on how to move in efficiently and scatter the Lodge bastards. As I start whispering it to Vidocq, someone screams.

"Fuck all of you motherfuckers!"

It's Janet's voice.

A few of the Lodge members are startled by the scream and step back from the big table.

This is why they dragged it from the rumpus room. Janet is tied down on top. Manimal Mike is on the floor unconscious, probably next on the sacrifice menu.

My clever plan from a minute ago goes out the window. I bark some Hellion hoodoo and the explosion knocks the closest Lodge members into the air and over the table. The others fall back and we come in fast.

None of these bastards have ever met a crazy Frenchman who hates their sacrificing guts. Vidocq throws vial after vial of noxious potions at the Lodge psychos. When they hit the ones who didn't retreat to the far side of the sacrifice table, the vials burn them like phosphorous. Dan in his necromancer mask runs deeper into the cavern. Juliette fumbles with the phurba, drops it, and runs after him.

Janet can move their head just enough to sort of see what's happening.

"Stark!" they yell.

I swing the na'at over my head like a bullwhip and slice through the chains holding them on the table. Vidocq grabs Mike and we hustle them back out of harm's way.

Janet is bruised and bloody. They didn't go down easy but fought all the way onto the table. Good for them.

They hold on to my arm.

"I'm sorry," Janet says. "I should have listened. They're all crazy."

I'm not a told-you-so kind of guy. I point to the boulder where I hid with Vidocq.

"Wait there. We'll be back."

Mike shakes his head as he comes to. I cut him out of his bonds and take him back to where a few of the Lodge's more gutless members cower against the cavern wall. There I give him the Colt.

"Shoot anyone who moves."

"Glad to."

Vidocq moves off to torch some of the other armed Lodge members. I turn to join him, but something slams into me from behind. There's a burning, ripping pain in my side. I twist and throw an elbow behind me and send someone flying. But then someone else is on my back and reaching around to claw my eyes with their long nails.

I throw my weight back and slam us both onto the cavern floor. Whoever was on my back is seeing stars from where their skull cracked on the stones. The na'at falls from my hand, so I roll over and grab them by the collar.

It's Maria Simon.

If she—or whatever Maria is—was hurt by the fall, it doesn't last long. She swings at my eyes again with her nails. I dodge her hand and punch her in the throat. That rattles her enough that she holds still for a few seconds. Long enough for me to pull the Polaroid from my pocket and shove it in her face.

"Happy holidays from Chris."

She freezes in place. Her hand goes up a few inches toward the photo as she whispers, "Chris."

My whole side burns. I can feel blood flowing down my ribs.

I grab Samantha and say, "What are you? A vampire? A Drifter who got away? Or another spook, just a little smarter than the rest?"

Samantha, who- or whatever she is, lets out a sonic bellow in my face that's loud enough and hard enough to knock me off her. She's on her feet faster than I can move and runs into the Backbone like a goddamn cheetah.

I touch my hand to my side. There's a deep gash along my lower ribs. I look around and spot Juliette's phurba on the stones nearby. Dan, the sneaky fuck, must have doubled back. He dives for the blade. I kick it away and the bastard lands on his face. When I reach out to snap his neck, he grabs a dropped sword and swings it clumsily at me. But a clumsy sword is still a sword and I have to twist out of the way, which rips open the wound on my ribs even more.

I grab the na'at from the floor and swing it over my head a couple of times, backing Dan off. He holds the sword up in front of him defensively, and when I swing the barbed whip a third time, it snaps the sword blade in half.

The worst seems over and I'm finally ready to kill Danny boy once and for all when I hear weird, high singing.

Kenny has let loose the Stay Belows already in the cavern and a sent out a few more to join them. Dan doesn't bother saying goodbye. I want to chase him, but there will be time for that later in the mansion.

I head for the Stay Belows, but Vidocq is already there, holding them off with vials of *bannissement par l'amarante*. While he drives them back in Kenny's direction, I collapse the na'at and manifest my Gladius. Vidocq falls back and lets me hack through the ten or so spooks left and send them to oblivion.

At this point, I think the worst of it is over, but some of the ballsier Lodge Within the Lodge members who still have weapons charge us. Vidocq is beginning to run out of vials, but I still have my Gladius, so I'm pretty confident we've got this covered.

Nope.

Some of the Lodge bastards Mike was guarding managed to jump him. The ones not holding him down are with Dan and Juliette, who must have circled back and grabbed Janet to complete the ritual.

I scream hoodoo at them but have to be careful. I can't blow up or burn anybody without killing Janet. Instead, I call down a swarm of Hellion hornets on them. They're twice the size of mortal hornets and the venom in their tails is pure acid. A few stings will burn holes in you. Too many and you start losing limbs. Enough stings and you'll melt like a snowman in Malibu.

I'm close enough that I can control the hornets to go after the doom twins and the Lodge assholes while keeping Janet safe. Dan, Juliette, and their mob scatter, screaming at a real vision of Hell.

Dan takes off for the mansion again, leaving Juliette behind. The hornets drive her back across the cavern. Half-blinded and bleeding from the stings, she bounces off the sacrifice table in Kenny's direction. He sends out a couple more Stay Belows and they grab her by the arms. The hornets swarm around the three of them, but only Juliette feels the stings.

Kenny says, "You let me die, Juliette. You let me die and then you brought me back so I could be your errand boy again. Not this time. Not ever again. Do you want to see the Land of the Dead? Then come and join me."

Juliette doesn't go easy. She fights back against the Stay Belows, but in the end it gets her nowhere. Her screams from the hornet stings eventually turn to watery gurgles as the Stay Belows drag her to Kenny, where they're both ripped to shreds in the House of Knives.

The Lodge toughs holding on to Manimal Mike run off into the cavern when they see what happened to Juliette. I pull Mike back to his feet and take him to the boulder where I hid Janet. But I can't find them or Vidocq. I dispel the hornets and look for them.

Kenny has called up more Stay Belows, this time with weapons. I should be able to take out all of them easily with my Gladius, but I've lost enough blood that my reflexes aren't what they should be. I might be fine against a few mortal opponents, but these undead pricks don't fall down as easily.

They surround me and attack with broadswords and Mayan battle axes I swing the Gladius in a wide defensive circle, but no matter how many spooks I take down, it seems like there are more to take their place. I manage to hack a hole in the mob and get through so there's no one at my back, but I take a lot of shots along the way. I'm bleeding all over.

Stumbling back, I shout fire hoodoo, but they walk right through that. I can't think straight. I know there are other ways to hurt them, but my brain has flatlined. All I can think to do is put my head and down and charge back into the bunch, hacking them down before I bleed out.

As I start to put that brilliant plan into play, something noxious explodes in front of me. It smells like garlic, burning rubber, and the taste of pennies. I stumble back, my eyes watering. Someone is shouting in French. Vidocq closes in on me and the Stay Belows. His potions force them farther and farther back.

He shouts, "I'll push them back to Hell. You deal with the rest of these curs."

Vidocq gets the bunch away from me long enough that I can get a breath and clear my head. Not that it helps much.

The moment I'm clear of the Stay Belows, Dan comes out of fucking nowhere and slams me in the ribs with a war hammer. I go down on my stupid face and the Gladius goes out. I really don't want this Hollywood High, wannabe Criswell,

Hugh Hefner, snooty wine-snob piece of shit to be the one who kills me for good, but that's how things are looking as Dan stands over me with the war hammer aimed at my head.

He says, "Looks like we didn't need Janet after all. You're going to be a much better sacrifice."

I tense my muscles, hoping I'm still fast enough to roll out of the way in time.

He raises it above his head. I get ready, but I know I have a less-than-even chance of doing this right.

Something streaks behind Dan. He cries out in pain and half drops the war hammer to his side.

Something shoots by again, and this time it latches on to him.

It's Janet. They have the small automatic knife they showed me way back in Teddy Osterberg's cemetery. They've latched on to Dan's back and are stabbing him over and over again. Finally, he drops the hammer and falls to his knees. Janet keeps stabbing and all clever Dan can think to do is roll up like an armadillo and hope he grows armor.

When I can get to my feet, I grab Janet and pull them off Dan. He's fucked up but not dead yet.

I kiss Janet on their bloody cheek and say, "Thanks."

Then I get out the black blade and cut Dan's head off.

But I do it at a specific angle and in a certain way, so that when his head comes free from his body, he's not dead. He's exactly like Kasabian that first night when I came back from Hell. And just like Kasabian, Dan is screaming up a storm.

"What's happening? I'm dead! I'm dead!"

I pick him up by the hair and angle him so he can see his body lying on the cavern flor.

"No, Dan," I tell him. "You're not dead. And you're not going to die until I let you."

"What have you done?" he screams. "Kenny. Kill this fool."

But Kenny is having fun showing Juliette around the House of Knives. Which gives me an idea.

"Dan, did you know that I was the first living mortal ever to set foot in Hell?"

"What?" he says. "Someone help me!"

"I made history, Dan. Everybody down there remembers me now. And you know what? Now they're going to remember you and Juliette: the other two living humans in Hell. Enjoy your fame."

I start to throw him into the spinning vortex of blades with Kenny and Juliette but get a better idea. I give Dan to Janet. They looked shocked, then smile.

"Am I allowed to do this?" they say.

I shrug.

"It's your choice. If you want me to put Danny back together again, I'm fifty percent sure I can do it. But ask yourself this: who's he going to sacrifice next time?"

Janet looks at Dan's confused, dumb animal face and says, "I want to say that I'm not doing this because you tried to kill me. I want to be bigger and better than that. But I'm not. I'm doing this because you tried to kill me."

Holding Dan by the hair, Janet tosses him like a bowling ball into the House of Knives, where he's gobbled by the blades that will puree him, Kenny, and Juliette forever. Or until the place falls apart. I mean, it's a complicated contraption, and because of the war, nothing in Hell is getting a lot of maintenance. Still, for however long it is, Ken and the doom twins will have a cozy vacation house in the land of the dead. Just like they always wanted.

Nearby, Manimal Mike yells, "Maria!"

I look around and see Mike hunkered protectively over Vidocq as Samantha runs out of the cavern. Vidocq is still, with the phurba buried deep in his back.

Mike yells, "I'm sorry, man. I'm sorry."

I curse and grab Vidocq, Janet, and Mike and drag them into a shadow.

WE COME OUT in Allegra's clinic. A few civilians and Lurkers sit on plastic chairs in the waiting area, but I blow past them and straight into the exam room. Allegra is inside alone and at first laughs when she sees me.

"Do you ever knock, you drama queen?"

Then she sees Vidocq.

"Oh god. Get him on the table."

I lay him facedown so Allegra gets a good look at his back and the phurba.

I say, "I left the blade in so he wouldn't bleed out."

Allegra grabs a pair of medical scissors and begins cutting off Vidocq's coat.

"You did the right thing," she says.

"What can I do to help?"

"What's that in his back?"

"It's called a phurba. A ritual knife."

"What kind of rituals were people using it for?"

"Calling back the dead."

As she cuts Vidocq's shirt off she says, "Shit."

With his shirt gone, the wound looks even worse. The skin around the blade looks shriveled and crisp. Less like a knife wound and more like someone shoved a red-hot poker into him. Blackened veins radiate out from the entry point and spread all over his back. More burns or a spreading poison from the blade?

Allegra grabs a big wad of gauze and holds it near the knife.

She says, "When I tell you, pull the blade straight out. I'll pack the wound."

"Got it."

She takes a breath.

"Now."

I yank the phurba out of his back and drop it on the floor.

Vidocq doesn't bleed. His blood pools in the wound and doesn't run, but oozes from the wound, thick and oily. Green on top, like algae scum on a dying lake.

"Oh god," she says.

"Do you know what it is?"

She ignores me and says, "Everybody get out of the way."

From a set of shelves in the last cabinet, she pulls out dusty pots and jars—some of Doc Kinski's old supplies. You don't fuck around with antibiotics with a hoodoo wound like this. You go straight for the heavy stuff.

Allegra packs more gauze in the oily blood and rubs a purple salve on the skin around the entry point. From a cabinet near the floor, she takes out a globe wrapped in silk. Two shattered pieces of divine light glass—the stuff Mr. Muninn used to make the first stars. Some fell to Earth long ago and started life on this rock. Doc Kinski used the glass on me more than once. It began life and it can save it. Allegra lays the pieces on Vidocq's back and gently sets a hand on his head. After a moment, she checks his pulse. Pulls his eyelids open and shines a small flashlight into them.

Me, Janet, and Mike stand there feeling thick and useless. Allegra massages the cracked glass into Vidocq's back. After a couple of minutes, she checks his vitals again.

His body moves slightly. I hear a feeble, rasping breath. Another minute and Vidocq's eyes flutter open.

He smiles when sees Allegra.

"Hello, my love."

She puts her hand on the back of his head.

"Hey, you. For a minute there I thought we'd lost you."

"Never. In this world and whatever comes next, I am eternally yours."

She runs a hand through his hair.

"Don't talk like that. You're the one who lives forever, remember?"

He closes his eyes.

"I care nothing about forever. I care about you."

"We have you stabilized now, so don't worry about anything."

When he opens his eyes, he has a faraway look.

"Do you remember when we first met?"

"Yes. Stark brought me to meet the great alchemist who lived in a magic apartment that no one could see."

He smiles faintly.

"We were happy there together for a time, weren't we?"

"We were."

Vidocq frowns.

"I wish I could have been a better man for you. I wish I could have made it more of a home for the two of us."

"You did."

He shakes his head.

"I should have thrown away my books, my absurd flasks and potions. I should have made it happier for you."

"I was happy."

Allegra looks at me.

"Tell him, Stark."

I get up close to him so I know he can hear.

"Allegra was happy. She told me all the time."

Vidocq shifts his head around a little so he can see me. He puts out his hand. I take it.

"James."

"You scared us, old man."

He says, "The charm I put on the apartment so that people can't see it, it's permanent, you know."

"Of course it is. You did it."

"I only say this because if anything should happen to me, it would make me very happy if you returned there. It's your home. It always has been. I've merely been the caretaker."

I shake my head.

"The place is yours. Yours and Allegra's."

He blinks.

"I never had a son, you know."

"And I never had much of a father."

He squeezes my hand.

"You're a good boy, James."

He looks at Allegra and I step back.

"I'll never forgive myself for hurting you."

"That's over and forgotten," she says.

"I am forgiven then?"

"Of course."

He takes a breath. Closes his eyes.

"Thank you. You don't know what that means to me."

"You can tell me later. You should stop talking and rest."

"I love you all, my friends. And you, my darling Allegra, so much."

"I love you too."

"What I will miss are you and the stars. I would like to see them with you one more time."

"You're not missing anything. We'll see them together soon."

"Do you promise?"

"Yes."

He pulls her hand to his lips and kisses her fingers.

Allegra says, "Rest now."

"Just you and the stars."

He holds her hand.

Allegra waits for a moment.

"Vidocq?"

He doesn't move.

She shakes him.

"Vidocq?"

Nothing.

She gently begins to cry. Puts a hand on his head and rests her head on his back.

I touch her shoulder. She turns and we put our arms around each other. She cries and I just stare at the old man.

I never had a son, you know.

My eyes burn and I just stand there with Allegra. My head swims and I stumble back a step.

Allegra looks at me.

"You okay?"

"Stark is bleeding," says Janet.

"I'm fine. Don't worry about it."

Allegra pushes my coat open.

"Goddammit, Stark. No one else dies tonight."

The others take my coat off as Allegra shoots me up with a painkiller before stapling the wound closed. Then she wraps my ribs in bandages.

"I look like the fucking mummy."

"Shut up and sit down. You need to rest."

"I will soon. But not yet."

I pull Janet over and tell them, "Stay with her. I'll be back as soon as I can."

I head for a shadow as Janet says, "Be careful."

I'm pretty much numb, but the animal part of my brain has kicked in. Allegra was right about one thing. I do need to rest. But she was wrong about something else. More people are going to die tonight.

I come out in the Jackal's Backbone, near where the cavern meets the tunnel to the doom twins' rumpus room. There's no one down here. All the Lodge creeps must have run back to the mansion. That simplifies things for me.

At the tunnel entrance in the rumpus room, I lay down a little more hoodoo, sealing the Backbone from the house. Then I go back out to the road that runs in front of the place. Lodge members pound on the doors and windows, trying to get out. But the hoodoo I put down will keep them in there for a hundred years if I want. But I don't. Tonight is for settling scores. For Janet and especially Vidocq.

I stand in the driveway where everyone can get a good look at me. They scream and pound even louder. So, I bark some Hellion at them. Not the most powerful stuff I've ever conjured, but enough for the job.

The fire starts on the roof and works its way down through the attic. It takes a few minutes for smoke to drift down into the living room, but eventually a thick grayness coils down from the top of the room, reaching down into the hysterical mob like the squid Kenny conjured.

As the fire expands and the sides of the house catch, I sit on a tree stump across the road and watch the place go up.

Welcome to the land of the dead, motherfuckers. Enjoy Hell.

I take out some of the pills Allegra gave me and pop a lorazepam. Then I sit back and watch the show. The mansion is fully engulfed now. A neighbor has probably already called the fire department, but it will take them a few minutes to get here.

I sit and watch and think of the old man as sparks shoot up like fireflies in the black L.A. sky.

Soon, the distant sound of a siren is my cue to leave. But before I can walk into a shadow, my phone rings. It's Abbot.

"Stark, I'm here with the Council. You've let us down. I can't wait any longer. We're going in tonight."

I check my pocket. The photo is still there.

"Give me one hour," I say. "If what I want to try doesn't work, I'll kill the Stay Belows myself."

There's a brief silence on the line and Abbot comes back.

"One hour. Then we take over."

I hang up and walk into a shadow.

Come out in the parking lot of Donut Universe. Inside, I slap a hundred on the counter.

"Give me a dozen of anything."

I MAKE ONE more stop before heading to Little Cairo.

When I get there, the place is jumping. The Thurl is open as usual, but the spooks aren't tearing the ruined pyramids and Sphinxes apart anymore. Every single one is slammed against the edges of the neighborhood, clawing and pounding at the wards. The barrier is failing in a few places and Stay Belows can get their hands through. Spectral fingers grab at the warm L.A. air as freaked-out Sub Rosa muscle prowls around just outside the quarantine barrier, ready to pull the trigger and burn the spooks and everybody else to the ground.

None of the Stay Belows notice me as I use the black blade to dig a hole in one lawn. When it's deep enough, I dump in the donuts—an assortment of jellies and crullers. With that, I drop in a bottle of Angel's Envy rye. I hate letting go of the stuff. I hope the King Below appreciates the offering, because it's killing me.

"If you're down there, I can use all the help I can get."

Done digging, I go roaming. I don't care about the mob of spooks at the edges of the place. I only care about one, and I have a feeling he won't be with the others.

But I can't find the bastard anywhere. It looks like the power is off all over Little Cairo. I could hoodoo some light, but it would bring the other spooks right to me. No fucking thanks. Still, after wandering blind through the ruins for a few minutes I'm tempted to take the chance.

All around me, the street begins to shake. It only lasts a few seconds, but when it stops a streetlight lying on its side in the gutter flickers a few times, outlining one forlorn figure.

"Thanks, King. I'll buy you a six-pack sometime."

Stein's back is to me, so I come up to him as quietly as I can. He's swaying back and forth in time with the spooks' high, strange song. I hope Flicker is right and it comforts them, because it makes my skin crawl.

When I'm a few yards from Stein I say the magic words.

"Forever yours. Forever mine."

Slowly, he shuffles around to face me. He looks miserable. A lost dog in the rain. But he still has Samantha's last love note balled up in his dead hand. When he comes at me, it's not a charge or even a threat. It's just some sad, final impulse. He's mad at the world and Samantha for what happened to him. He's still willing to take it out on everyone alive, but he's also the most miserable dead man I've ever seen.

I say the words again.

"Forever yours. Forever mine."

This time though I take the old Polaroid out of my pocket and hold it out to him.

His dead eyes drift from me to the photo. He stares for a few seconds, then shudders. Makes a high, keening sound and gently takes the Polaroid from my hand.

I say, "Merry Christmas, 1977."

Stein looks at me.

"I saw Samantha."

He holds the letter and photo to his chest.

"She says she loves you and she's very sorry about what

happened. She never meant to kill you."

His lips move, but he doesn't make a sound. Still, I know what's he's saying. It's her name.

I'm running out of time, so I talk fast.

"She wants you to go home, Chris. She wants you to rest. Someday she'll come back to you. She wants you to know forever yours, forever—"

"Mine," he says.

Fuck me. He can talk.

He half-turns from me and says, "Heaven?"

I'm not sure if he's asking if he'll go to Heaven or saying it's Heaven having Samantha back in his arms.

I say, "Sure, Chris. It's Heaven."

He walks away, the photo and note clutched in his hands the way a kid holds a stuffed bear to keep the monsters away.

I follow him as he wanders to the Thurl. There's no hesitation when he reaches it. He's done. He's as satisfied as he'll ever be. He has Samantha back. At least her acknowledgment and apology. I wasn't lying when I said she was sorry. I saw it in her eyes and heard it in her voice when she saw Chris's photo in the Backbone. Whatever she is—vampire, witch, or Drifter—I have a feeling she's still somewhere in L.A. nursing her wounds and mourning Chris. If things were different, I might leave her to her misery. But she's the one who put the knife in Vidocq's back. That's something I can't forgive.

I'll see you someday, Samantha, and we're going to have a talk. And then I'm going to kill you.

With Stein gone—the lovelorn magnet who drew the other Stay Belows back to the world—the spooks begin drifting away from the barriers around Little Cairo and back to the

Thurl. They go one by one or in groups. Not rushing. They're no longer fueled by Stein's fury. They just amble back to the Land of the Dead—where every asshole in L.A. seems to want to go to. At least for the Stay Belows it's home. I hope they can find some peace there.

As the last one enters the Thurl, the stars seem to move a little again, like a reflection in water. I dial Abbot.

"Call off your dogs."

"You killed them?"

"I didn't need to. All they wanted was a Valentine. So, I gave them one."

"What the hell does that mean?"

"It means they're gone and you can send your goons in here to help the civilians instead of murdering them. I'm a little fed up with murder tonight, so tell your people to be nice or I'll be mad."

"Calm down," says Abbot. "I'll send in some scouts to check the area. If it's clear, we'll send in medical assistance."

"Trust me. It's clear."

"Thank you, Stark."

"Hey, Abbot. Were you ever in love?"

"What?"

"You heard me. Were you ever in love with anybody?"

"Yes. My wife."

"Good for you. I'm glad to hear it."

I hang up and go back to Allegra's clinic. There's nothing I can do to change things, but at least I can be there for a friend.

HOURS LATER, WHEN I get Allegra to try to sleep, I go back

to the flying saucer house. I'm almost annoyed that it's back to normal again. The perfection of the place is starting to drive me crazy. I appreciate that there's always good food and liquor, but I punched those holes in the wall for a reason and now they're gone. I don't know how much more of this Mr. Rogers Hell I can take.

I sleep a lot of the next day, but I don't dream at all. The slash in my ribs came from the phurba, so the healing is a lot slower than if it had been a regular knife. Plus, I have about fifty other wounds all over to deal with. Candy comes by to check on me in the afternoon and Janet comes by in the evening.

I'm in bed, covered in bandages and half-healed scars. Janet sits next to me with their hand resting on my leg.

They say, "How are you feeling?"

"Like I got gored by a water buffalo shot out of one of those circus cannons they use for clowns. You know the ones?"

They smile.

"Yeah. I've seen them."

"How is that even a job? What do you put on your taxes? 'Clown gunner'?"

Janet laughs a little.

"It's good to see you your own ridiculous self again."

"Look. About last night—"

"No. I want to apologize. You were right and I didn't listen. You saved me."

"Yeah, but I still feel weird about the whole thing. You told me to leave a couple of times and I didn't."

"It's okay."

"Is it? Look, I'm trying to understand people better, and that means not kidnapping them and not making them listen to me when they don't want to."

Janet gives me a look.

"You've kidnapped people?"

"Lots, but that's not the point. The point is that I should have listened to you and left, but I didn't, so I'm sorry."

"Stark, if you hadn't come by, you wouldn't have known I was going to the Lodge. They would probably have killed me."

I have to think about that for a minute.

"Then it's a good thing I didn't listen?"

"Partly."

"Goddamn. This understanding-people thing is harder than it looks."

They pat my leg.

"It is, isn't it? But I'll give you points for one thing."

"What's that?"

"You haven't forgotten my pronouns in days."

"I have in my head a few times."

Janet shrugs. "We all do that. I mess up other people's sometimes."

"You too?"

"Of course. People are complicated. That makes the world complicated. You're not going to figure it out in a few days."

"Punching monsters was a lot easier than this."

"You promised to tell me more about that, you know."

"I know. And I will."

They stare off into space.

"I still feel weird about what I did to Dan."

"Putting him where he belonged?"

"On the one hand, yes, but on the other, who am I to judge who deserves to go to Hell?"

"The human sacrificee gets to judge the human sacrificer. Them's the rules."

Janet cocks their head.

"Is it that simple?"

I sit up in bed.

"Sometimes. Listen, you're like most people. You think salvation and damnation are these grand, perfect systems run by flawless celestial beings with all the knowledge of the universe."

"Isn't that how it's supposed to work?"

"Maybe. But let me tell you how things really work: Hell is a carny show. Heaven is a wreck. God is recovering from a nervous breakdown, and Lucifer, well, he's the most complicated thing of all."

"How so?"

"There isn't technically a Lucifer, unless you count God because he's trying to run Heaven and Hell at the same time."

Janet frowns.

"What? I don't understand."

"Wait," I say. "It gets better. The angel who used to be Lucifer? He's a friend of mine. I'll introduce you sometime."

"I'm not sure I want that."

"He's fun in his own fucked-up way. And he always knows the best places to eat."

They pick a bit of lint off the blanket. Seeing it relaxes me. The cleaning elves or whatever aren't perfect after all.

Janet says, "You really do seem to know a lot about it. But

I'm not sure if you're telling the truth or if this is one of your funny stories."

I put a hand on theirs.

"Stick around and I'll tell you the biggest joke of all—about when I was Lucifer."

"Now you really are just telling stories."

"Maybe. But think about sticking around anyway?"

They rub my hand and nod.

"I will. I am. Do you want me to get you something?"

"How about a drink?"

"Allegra said that you don't get to drink today."

"Now you're just cruel."

They pull their lips into a single tense line.

"I'm sorry about Vidocq."

I find another piece of lint. I wonder if the elves leave them for me to find?

"He was one of a kind."

"When's the funeral?"

"Tomorrow night."

"Can I come?"

"Are you sure? You barely knew the guy."

"He saved me and died for it. I owe him. Instead of telling me about the Devil, why don't you tell me about him?"

"That I can do."

"But you should rest now."

"I will, but I want to tell you something."

They look at me.

"It's not good, is it?"

"That's for you to judge. After Vidocq died, I went back to Dan and Juliette's house."

"What happened?"

"I killed everyone there. Every single person who'd been at the ritual in the Backbone."

Janet says, "How many people?"

"I don't know. I told you I was a killer."

They put their arms around themself.

"I guess I understand. You were a little crazy right then."

"It was probably my sanest moment of the night. Can you deal with that?"

"I don't know. Let me think about it."

"Okay. I think I'm going to sleep a little."

They get up from the bed.

"I'm going to get some coffee."

"Maybe we can watch a movie later."

"That would be nice."

AROUND ELEVEN IN the evening the next day, I steal a big, flashy party bus parked down the block from the Cinerama Dome. After loading everyone inside, I drive down Highway 27 to Topanga State Park. We roll into the parking lot with the lights off because the damn place closes at eight. I hate nature, but it seems weird that people who like it only want you to see it on their timetable. I put a hex on the bus so that if someone tries to tow it they're going to be puking spiders all night.

Alessa, who grew up in the area, takes us up a hiking trail that leads to one of the tall peaks. It's not an easy walk, pushing a dead Frenchman up a mountain in a wheelbarrow—in the dark—but we make it with a minimal amount of cursing and only one scary moment when Vidocq tried to slide out of the wheelbarrow into a cavern where his stupid carcass would have fallen a hundred feet into who fucking knows where. We finally make it to the top in a little over a sweaty hour, with me and Allegra doing most of the grunt work. The others try to help, but the tripping and the muscle pulls are what we two signed up for and we see it through.

Vidocq is mummified in layers of silk and cotton sheets. I lay him out flat with his head angled facing the wild expanse of stars in the dark northern sky.

For a few minutes we all stand around looking at each other and the dark outlines of nearby mountains and cliffs. Up here, it's cooler than in the city this time of night, and a light wind blows down from the higher peaks.

Allegra gives me one of Vidocq's old books. It's small. One of those travel books the rich used to haul all over Europe a couple of hundred years ago. Get a case of these books, and you'd have all of the world's knowledge at your fingertips. I like this little book because I know Vidocq well enough to be certain that he stole a whole set from some rich French prick touring the continent who would never miss the thing. I can't read a word of French, but Allegra tells me that it's a history of Egypt, including one of the first collections of their mythology. Vidocq loved the hand-colored illustrations most of all. They reminded him of his youth, when he was a simple thief and not a doomed-to-live-forever mad scientist. I hold on to the book with both hands as I start talking, like if I don't it's going to run away like a jackrabbit.

"Vidocq always said that he didn't like being two hundred years old, but I think he was lying. After all those years, a lot of them running from the law, I think he liked where he ended up. Here. With us. He got me through a lot of bad times, before I went Downtown and after. He knew everything about me, but now that he's gone I don't think I ever knew enough about him. I never thought I was smart enough to understand his alchemical work, so I never tried to. Now I know I didn't have to be smart. He was smart. If I'd asked him more he could have explained it so I'd understand. I feel shitty that I never thought of that until now. I took him for granted. He was always going to be here. Way after I was gone. Now I can't tell him I'm sorry. He was a smart guy. A good one too. I always said that I never had a father. But that wasn't entirely true. Goodbye, old man. I'm going to miss you like crazy."

I put the book in my pocket and step away from his body. On one side, Janet takes my hand. On the other, Candy loops her arm in mine. Good thing. Looking at Vidocq lying there, I get that disembodied feeling again, like maybe if someone wasn't holding me I'd blow away on the breeze.

Allegra puts a rose and a piece of blue amber on Vidocq's body before saying anything. Her voice cracks the first times she tries to speak, but then she gets it under control.

"Vidocq was my love. We had our problems, but we'd worked them out. You know, I was this close to moving back in with him. I knew it was going to happen, but I was waiting for the right moment. Now that's never going to happen. Don't make the same mistake I made. Whatever you love, whoever you love, hold on to them tight. The world doesn't need more proud or stubborn people. We have enough of those already. Hang on to everyone around you. They're all that matter. As for Vidocq, I'm not going to say goodbye. Just good night. I'll find you in Hell or Heaven, my love."

She stops and nods, a few tears running down her face.

"Yeah. I'll find him."

When she's done, she comes over to me and says, "Do it."

I look at her, lit up under a billion little points of light.

"Don't you want to?"

She blinks a couple of times and wipes her eyes.

"Don't fuck around, man. Just burn him."

But I pull her back to Vidocq's body.

"Remember when we first met and I told you about magic? I taught you how to make fire dance across your fingers."

She opens and closes her hands.

"I haven't tried that in a long time. You think I can still do it?"

"I guarantee."

"Okay. Let's do it together."

"Yeah."

She puts her hands on the white layers of cloth.

"One . . . two . . . three."

Flames spring from our hands and move across the sheets. They catch quickly and in a few seconds Vidocq's body is burning, a ball of orange radiance against the stark peaks. A crow circles around us a few times, then is joined by a second one. After a few passes, they take off together and we disappear into the dark. Just a couple of dumb birds or a psychopomp coming to take the old man away? I'll have to ask him one day when we're all back together again.

We stay with the pyre under the stars until dawn, then let the morning winds carry Vidocq's ashes away. When it's done, we go back down the mountain and I drive everyone home to rest for a while, because the day isn't over yet.

When I get to Bamboo House of Dolls around noon there's a big sign out front:

PRIVATE PARTY. CLOSED UNTIL 2.

Fuck Hollywood is outside in my torn-up coat that I gave her. She stares at the sign all agitated, like a cat that found the kitty door into the house locked.

I say, "What are you doing here?"

She looks surprised when she sees me.

"I heard that Carlos is looking for a bar back. I was going to ask him for the job, but I guess I should come back later."

"Maybe not. Come with me."

It's strange going inside at this time of day, with no crowd and the jukebox quiet. Carlos is behind the bar and Ray is blowing up a few last balloons. There's sparkly "Happy Birthday" bunting up over the bar.

When he sees me, Carlos says, "The party store was out of wedding decorations, but I think this is still goddamn festive."

There are flowers, a cake, and paper plates on a nearby table.

I look at them both.

"It looks great."

With a hand on her shoulder, I say, "Carlos, this is Fuck Hollywood. You should give her a job."

He looks her over for a moment.

"You have bar experience?"

She shakes her head.

"No."

"Do you know how to mix cocktails?"

"Jack and Coke."

"Do you have any experience at all in the beverage or service industry?"

"I used to dance and serve drinks at the Big Red Rocket in Glendale."

"Did you bother Stark here the other night?"

Fuck Hollywood gives me a slightly panicked look.

I say, "Would I have given her my coat if she did?"

Carlos motions to her to come over.

"Let me see your hands."

She holds them up.

"They're little," he says. "And too pretty. Cleaning glasses all night is going to fuck them up. You're going to need to moisturize and take better care of them."

Her eyes widen.

"Does that mean I get the job?"

"Provisionally."

Fuck Hollywood jumps up and down a little in my oversize coat.

"Thank you. Thank you."

She grabs me in a hug, then abruptly lets go.

She says, "Sorry. That's probably inappropriate workplace behavior."

"Not today," I tell her.

Soon, the others begin to arrive.

Candy and Alessa bring Allegra and Brigitte. She's a knockout in a shiny black cocktail dress. Everyone is goofy, smiling and hugging each other. I try to stay out of range but get caught by a few cruise missiles of happiness.

Janet arrives a few minutes after that in a dark blue tailored men's three-piece suit, complete with pocket square. They, too, look amazing.

After a few drinks, Ray takes Janet and Brigitte to the center of the room, where the chairs have been cleared out. The rest of us gather around them.

Ray says, "Welcome, everybody. I know that the day started off on a somber note, but I hope it can end on a joyous and legally binding one."

He takes Janet and Brigitte's hands in his.

"Do you, Janet Peterson, take Jaroslava Schallerová to be your lawful spouse, to learn all about her so you can answer stupid questions, and to go to USCIS meetings with her until the federal government pulls its head out of its ass?"

"I do," says Janet.

Jaroslava Schallerová. I've never heard Brigitte's real name before. I sort of forgot she had one. Too late for her. She'll always be Brigitte Bardo, ace killer, to me.

Ray says, "And do you, Jaroslava Schallerová, take Janet Peterson to be your lawful spouse until it's safe for you to stay here with us without harassment, and we find the stupid bastard who narced on you and kick his ass?"

"I do," says Brigitte.

He puts Janet and Brigitte's hands together and says, "By the power vested in me by the St. Dagon United Internet Church and the state of California, I now pronounce you married."

Janet and Brigitte kiss. Candy and Alessa throw confetti at them.

When all that nonsense is over, Ray puts the marriage license on the bar. Allegra signs as one of the witnesses, then everybody looks at me.

I crook a finger at Fuck Hollywood.

"Are you a felon or anything?"

"No."

"Can you write?"

"Yeah," she says sarcastically.

"Then here's your first job. Be a witness."

She grabs the pen and signs.

"Cool. I've never done this before."

Carlos says, "Welcome to Bamboo House of Dolls, girlie. Stick around here and you'll end up doing lots weirder things than that before it's over."

I bark a little Hellion and hoodoo up a knife that I give to Fuck Hollywood.

"Whoa," she says.

"Here's your second job. You can cut the cake and serve it."

But I don't think she hears me. She just turns the gleaming white knife over in her hands.

"What kind of knife is this?"

"It's a chip from the chicken legs that hold up Baba Yaga's house. A good-luck charm. Keep it if you want. Just don't tell Baba Yaga you got it from me."

She looks at me with great intensity.

"That's. So. Metal."

We drink and eat for another hour before Carlos has Fuck Hollywood take the sign down to let in the afternoon crowd. They devour the last of the cake and buy Janet and Brigitte drinks for hours.

Vidocq would have loved it.

I GET BACK to the flying saucer house around ten. The others are still partying, but after all that's happened I need a break. I take a PTSD pill and put on some coffee in the kitchen.

When I go into the living room Samantha is waiting for me. She's perched on the back of the sofa with her wings wrapped around her like a giant bird of prey. She's wearing Thivierge's emerald earrings and still looking like she's not a day over twenty-five. So, she's not a Drifter.

She's Samael's lost angel.

"Hello, Zadkiel."

She says, "Hello, Abomination."

I lean against the wall.

"Save that 'Abomination' crap for someone who cares. You look ridiculous like that."

"You really are as thick as they say. A big mouth and no sense of the inevitable."

"Which is what exactly?"

She raises her head in the annoying imperious way angels do.

"Your death and obliteration from the universe."

I wave a hand at her.

"Please. I hear that every time I get day-old pork buns from the Lucky Phoenix."

Her voice turns sad.

"You sent Chris away."

"It was that or kill him for good. I didn't get the feeling that's what you wanted."

"No. I didn't. I suppose I owe you that much."

"You know what bugs me? It's not that you're wearing those earrings or that you're here to kill me. It's that I should have figured all this out days ago."

"What should you have figured out?"

I point at her.

"You were so good at covering your tracks for forty years that you got sloppy. You said something to me that very first time we met. It's been sitting in the back of my head ever since."

"Please tell me. What was it?"

"The story you told about Brendan Mullen talking to you at the Masque. The club closed in '78. If you'd been there back then you'd be in your sixties. But it didn't all come together until I saw your photo."

"So, Danny Gentry, Avani Chanchala, and Lisa Thivierge all died because of you."

"Because of *you* actually, but maybe if I was smarter I could have done something to stop you sooner."

"But you weren't. So, you didn't."

I look at her, trying to find some trace of the thing that once loved Chris Stein.

"What was in the rest of the note you sent Stein? The 'forever yours, forever mine' one."

She blinks once.

"That's private."

"You really loved him, didn't you?"

"Do you doubt it?"

"No. Not since I figured out what exactly happened between you and Chris. The last thing he said to me in Little Cairo was 'Heaven.' Lisa Thivierge told me his secret love wanted something from him he didn't want or couldn't give. You wanted him to die, didn't you? You're the Opener of the Ways. You told him you could get him into Heaven and you could be together forever. But he wasn't ready to go. You lost your temper and killed him anyway. You sent him straight to Hell, where he's been looking for you ever since."

She gets that haughty look again.

"You really think you're so much better than me, Abomination?"

"Yeah, I do. People can do all kinds of fucked-up things for love. I get that. But what you did . . . What happened to twist you up so much?"

"Nothing. I'm proud of what I was and what I am."

I take out one of my few remaining Maledictions and light it. I figure I can at least bother her with its Hellion goodness. After a couple of puffs she coughs. It's delightful.

"Come on. Mr. Muninn made you Opener of the Ways, but you ran off to watch *Behind the Green Door* for the next few decades. That's a little pathological."

She looks away like she's remembering something.

"That was Chris. He loved going to the movies."

"That's not what Thivierge said. She said that you were the wild one."

She looks serious.

"Chris's views on what was fun and what was possible were limited. I expanded his horizons."

"You taught him to steal. He could get through any lock. That's something else I should have picked up on, Opener."

"I guess you're not very good at your job."

"You're weren't my job. You're just trash a friend asked me

to clean up for him. Like, I was just trying to save one poor slob and there you were, trying to gut Janet like a catfish."

She smiles slyly. "Admit it. She's not Sub Rosa. She's not an Abomination like you. She's just your plaything."

I tick things off on my fingers.

"First off, you're wrong. Second, Janet's pronouns are 'they' and 'them.' You're an angel. You ought to pick up on these things."

She ignores that.

"All of your other friends are special in some way. Poor Janet is utterly, banally human. How could you possibly care for the creature?"

I look at Zadkiel hard.

"Since we're at a Dear Abby moment about relationships, I have a question for you. Were you going to do to Manimal Mike what you did to Chris? Get him to love you and then, when he finally figured out what a lunatic you are, cut him in half with your Gladius?"

"Mike is nice. But he's not Chris. I doubt I would have cut him. You, on the other hand—"

"You're welcome to try."

She gets down from the sofa and takes a couple of steps in my direction.

"I don't want to fight you, Abomination. Rather, I have a proposition for you."

"Oh good. I love making deals with crazy people."

"I'll leave Los Angeles. And if you agree to not hunt for me, I'll give you something you've always wanted."

"An Aqua Regia hot tub?"

"Your old life back."

Zadkiel holds up something small and shiny.

"Recognize this? It's an asphodel seed. Polished and cared for. Turned into a potent charm by Heaven's most powerful builders. It can give you anything you want."

"I guess you haven't heard of Amazon. They'll even bring me socks."

"Can they give you your old life? Can they give you Alice back? Think of it. Just swallow the seed and your fondest wish will come true. You can be back with your first love. You can escape Hell and all the misery it's brought you. You can be human again."

I'm not sure how far I can trust crazy pants here, but for a moment the deal is tempting. But not enough, because it's based on a lie.

"Here's the problem. I'm *not* human. I'm exactly who I'm supposed to be and I'm not interested in your deal."

She smiles and holds up a finger.

"You say that with your voice, but I can see into the greedy human part of you. I'll just place the seed on this table for when you change your mind."

She sets it on the coffee table.

"I'll admit it. The thought is tempting. A few years ago, I'd have jumped all over a deal like that. But not now. Keep your charm."

Zadkiel seems to consider this for a moment.

She says, "I have one more offer. Something I know you'll have to agree to: I'll open the gates of Heaven. Think of it. All the damned souls you care so much about finally free to make their way into Heaven and bask in the glory and love of God, the Father. I know it's what Samael wants."

"And all I have to do is let you walk away like none of this ever happened?"

"Yes. Make a wise choice, Abomination. A billion souls are in your hands."

"If I say yes, how do I know you'll do it?"

"The oath of an angel is binding."

"Even a crazy one?"

"All angels."

I think about the offer for a minute.

"If I let you go, will you promise not to make any more Chris Steins?"

"You have my word."

I look at her. I wish I could read angels better. But I can't.

I say, "Okay. I'll take the deal."

Zadkiel closes her eyes for a few seconds. Opens them.

"It's done."

"Wait. That's it?"

She cocks her head at me.

"Did you expect that there was a giant key I've carried with me all of these years?"

"I was kind of hoping."

"I'm sorry to disappoint you. However, the gates are open."

"Wait here. I need to check something."

I go through the Room and emerge in Hell, where the refugees have been huddled against the gates of Heaven Sure enough, they're open and souls are pouring through and up the celestial stairs.

After all this time. All this blood. In the end it was so simple.

I go back to the flying saucer house.

"I've got to give it to you. You told the truth. The deal is done."

Zadkiel gives me a funny look . . . and kicks me hard enough that I leave a dent in the wall on the far side of the room.

"There's one more point to the bargain."

"Wait. I agreed to what you wanted."

"But you remain an Abomination. How can I trust you?"

I hold up my hands.

"Seriously. We're done here. Go be psycho in Kansas. Become a Republican. Run for governor. I don't care. Just get out of L.A."

"I will, but you must go too."

"You mean you want to kill me like Chris. I don't think so."

"It's the only way."

"I knew it. Never trust an angel."

She manifests her Gladius. There's nothing else I can do. I manifest mine.

Zadkiel is fast and strong and I'm still not a hundred percent. She doesn't even bother trying to kill me at first. She has a good old time punching and kicking me around the flying saucer house. Furniture splinters. She knocks the TV off the wall. Pushes me back into the kitchen and kills the microwave, so I can't heat up leftovers.

That's when I lose my temper.

I swing my Gladius at her belly, but she sees the blow coming and smashes her sword into mine. The shock wave from the two divine weapons' meeting blows the kitchen to pieces.

I manage to work my way around her and back into the open space of the living room.

Zadkiel bares her teeth at me.

"When I'm done with you, I'll close the gates again. That's your punishment for being a fool, Abomination."

I do the only thing I can think of. I bark some Hellion hoodoo and set fire to her wings.

Zadkiel shrieks in pain and outrage. She spins around, bouncing off the walls, waving her wings, trying to put out the flames. Her screams are like sonic booms, and I have to put my hands over my ears before my skull explodes. The stink of burning feathers is even worse than the Malediction. She falls to the floor. Her wings are nothing but cartilage and gristle hanging from her back.

While she's distracted, I shoot in with my Gladius over my head and slash her from her throat to her waist.

Her sword flickers out. She looks at me, wild eyed, and grabs my arm. Even dying, she's strong. Zadkiel pulls me on top of her. She closes her eyes and when she opens them she gives me a last sad smile. We both lie there, beaten and aching.

"You should have murdered me before," she says.

"I was going to let you live."

She puts a bloody hand to my cheek.

"I want you to know that this is all your fault."

"What is?"

She grimaces in pain. Tears run down her face.

"I've done something awful. Just awful. You'll see."

"Did you close the gates?"

She shakes her head.

"Something much worse."

Before I can say another word she dies and fades from existence.

I fall onto my back.

What the hell could Zadkiel have done while she was lying there half-dead?

I look around. Once again, the poor flying saucer house looks like it was hit by a hurricane. A few more times like this and I'm going to get annoyed.

When I can move again, I hunt through the wreckage by the sofa until I find the asphodel seed. With it tight in my fist I shadow walk—well, shadow stumble—and come out across town.

RIGHT IN FRONT of Max Overdrive. Candy and Alessa are still partying at Bamboo House, so I'm alone with Kasabian.

I knock on his door.

"Go away."

"It's me, Kas."

"Then go far away and fuck off."

I go inside and sit down.

"Thanks for the invitation."

He's still just a pile of wreckage on his bed. He holds up his one good arm and gives me the finger.

"Make yourself at home since I'm in no condition to throw you out."

I look around and find a couple of dirty glasses.

"You have any of that Suntory left? I thought we could have a drink."

"To what?"

"Vidocq, you asshole."

He stops whining and looks serious.

"Yeah. I heard about that. I know you two were close. Sorry."

"What? No shots at me for being sentimental or a death trap? You really must be feeling low."

"Don't worry, I still think you're a prick. It's just that, unlike you, I don't kick a man when he's down."

"You're saying you're a better person than me?"

Kasabian thinks about it.

"Yeah. That's exactly what I'm saying."

"Then let's drink to that. Where's the bottle?"

"On the floor."

He's done a good job on it. The bottle is about three-quarters empty. Still, there's plenty left for what I need to do.

I pour one drink and set it on the floor by my foot. Then pour a second glass, drop in the asphodel seed, and give it to Kasabian.

I hold up my drink in a toast.

"To Vidocq. Like you and me: one of a fucked-up kind."

"I'll drink to that," he says.

We both down our drinks. Mine is smooth, with that slightly hot fruit-flavored aftertaste.

Kasabian downs his. Only his face looks funny. He chokes and coughs. Keeps coughing. Finally, he spits something into his hand. It's the asphodel seed.

"What's this?" he says.

"Nothing. It's medicine. Eat it."

He leans back on the bed and looks at me.

"After all this time, you're finally trying to kill me. What's the matter? Killing the old French guy wasn't enough for you? What's the plan? You kill me, move in here, and win Candy back? It ain't gonna work, asshole. I told you. She's gone. You're nothing to her now but a sad old mutt she's too sentimental to put down."

"Just eat the goddamn seed, Kas."

"No. I'm not going to be another notch on your belt. You want to kill me, put your gun to my head so I can look you in the eye."

I set down my glass and put my hands together.

"I promise you. I'm not trying to poison you or hurt you in any way whatsoever."

"Your existence hurts me. You walking the streets, getting drunk at a bar I can't get to, eating donuts at a shop I can't walk to. Everything about you is a pain in my nonexistent ass."

My blood pressure is going up, but I take a breath.

"You want donuts? I'll bring you some tomorrow. How many do you want? What kind? I'll fucking fill this place with donuts."

Kasabian holds out the seed.

"You think I want food from you when you try to poison me? I might be pathetic, but I'm not dumb. Get out of here," he says. "And take your poison with you."

He throws the asphodel seed at me. It bounces off my coat and under his bed.

"Shit."

I get on my hands and knees and crawl underneath. It's not pretty.

"Fuck, Kas. Have you swept under here once? It's like the

goddamn Amazon rain forest. Tumbleweeds everywhere."

He flails his one good arm at me.

"There aren't any tumbleweeds in the Amazon rain forest, you moron."

He manages to tag me a couple of times with his damn metal hand. On top of my other injuries, it really hurts.

Then my hand lands on something.

"Got it."

I come out from under the bed and blow the last of the dust off the seed.

Kasabian looks genuinely scared now.

"I'm not swallowing your fucking poison."

"I'm telling you, it's not poison."

"Then you eat it."

"I can't. There's only one and it's for you."

He looks at the seed.

"Is that from your buddy Vidocq? I bet he had all kinds of poisons around. Did he give you that to get me out of here?"

Then he does a kind of clumsy crab walk away from me on the bed.

"Or did you give that to him? Did you kill the Frenchman? You're psycho, Stark. You know that? You're a goddamn psycho."

I sit back down in the chair.

"Kas. You're eating this seed. It's not going to kill you and you're going to thank me when it's over."

"You're going to have to kill me to make me eat that thing."

"That doesn't even make sense."

He cowers in the corner where his bed meets the wall.

"Get out of here or I'll tell Alessa and she'll never let you back in here."

I consider that possibility for a minute. Then I consider another one. Candy's advice not to kidnap people. Respect their boundaries. Listen to them. But then I think of Janet. And what she said after we got back from her being the main event at a sacrifice. What comes to mind is this: Like me, Kasabian isn't exactly people. And sometimes you have to make a kid cry because they need a shot.

I grab him.

"Open your mouth, Kas."

"No."

"Open it."

"No."

This time he says it with his teeth clamped shut.

I say, "You need your flu shot."

He frowns.

"Before I just called you a psycho, but you really are one. You've gone around the fucking bend."

I lunge at him; get hold of his fat, stupid face; and start prying his jaws apart. He squirms and screams and grunts. Also, he's pounding me in the balls with his one good hand.

But, in the end, I'm stronger than him. I finally get his teeth enough apart to shove in the seed. Then I push them back together so he can't spit it out.

"Swallow," I yell. "Swallow."

He shakes his head frantically.

Finally, when I can't think of anything else to do, I grab the side of his head and bang it into the wall. When he's a little dazed, I pour whiskey down his throat. He thrashes around, and whiskey goes all over him, all over me, and all over the bed. But he finally swallows the damn seed.

Horrified, he looks at me with tears running down his face. Or maybe it's whiskey. I took some in my eye and I can't see really well right now.

"Well, that's it," he says. "The end of the line. Hell, maybe I deserve this. Killed by the monster I helped make. Yeah, that's it. You finally got the last of us. The people you crawled out of Hell to murder. I hope it feels good. You know what? I don't even hate you anymore. You're doing me a favor. Fuck this life. Even when Manimal Mike made his goddamn Tin Woodsman body for me, I've been miserable. This is good. I'm ready to go. Thank you, Stark. You're a real pal. A pile of festering puke, but a real pal."

He closes his eyes and lies back on the bed.

"Kas, just shut up and let it happen."

He opens one and says, "You're going to stay and watch, aren't you, you ghoul? I take back every nice thing I said. I don't deserve this."

"No," I say. "You probably don't."

He twists around on the bed, like he's rolling around with stomach cramps.

"Shit," he yells. "What is this stuff? Oh god. It hurts."

"Hang on. It'll be over soon."

I grab Kasabian's head as the metal armature of his body falls away. I kick it onto the floor and set him back down. He's moaning now. I can't tell if he's awake or having some kind of seizure. It goes on for a few minutes.

Eventually, he opens his eyes. He gets one look at me and puts his hands to his face.

"You prick. You followed me to Hell. Leave me alone.

Why don't you go kick Mason in the ass for a while? I hurt all over."

"You're not in Hell, Kas. You're still in your filthy fucking room. And if you want to kick my ass, why don't you get up and do it?"

He pulls his hands from his face and looks at them. Then his pudgy body. He wiggles his weirdly long toes.

I point to his foot.

"What's going on down there?"

"My toes? They're a family trait, you jerk. They're from my mother. And why are you staring at my feet?"

"Because you have them."

"Yeah. I noticed."

He looks at me, still a little suspicious.

"That's what the seed was for? To give me my body back?"

"It was a wish charm. It gives you whatever you want. Good thing you weren't hungry. You could have ended up a three-hundred-pound fritter."

He makes a face at me.

"I don't like fritters, you mook. Those are your things. I like people food. Now get out and let me get dressed."

I wipe some of the whiskey off my coat and limp for the door.

"What's with your leg?" he says.

"An angel kicked my ass tonight."

"Good."

Just before the door closes, I hear the absolute smallest "Thanks, man" ever uttered on Earth.

"Anytime, Kas."

I head back to the flying saucer house.

At least no one has cleaned it when I get there. I knock some rubble off the bed, get under the covers fully dressed, and pop a PTSD pill and a lorazepam.

I dream about somewhere far away and a different life I could have had. Should I have taken the asphodel seed and changed time to stay with Alice? A part of me wants to think that it could have worked out. Us dumb and happy together until we got old. But my whole body hurts, and my side is bleeding, and Kasabian bit my finger. When I rub it, I feel my scars.

Changing time, going back to Alice, and starting over is a pipe dream. I am what I am. A Nephilim. An Abomination. A natural born killer. Playing house a little longer wouldn't change that. I was always going to end up here. The last of my kind in the universe. At least now there are people who care about me. If I'd stayed like I was twelve years ago, I'd still be a smart-ass and a drunk and useless. Alice would have died anyway, and that version of me would have ended up alone. And he'd have deserved it.

In some ways I'll always be alone. But there are people who'll miss me when I go. Maybe they'll drag me onto a mountain and burn me so a crow can carry me back to—does it really even matter anymore? Heaven is open and Hell is obsolete. Except for the doom twins. While the other damned get to bum-rush the celestial stairs to the pearly gates, I'm keeping them in the House of Knives. It'll be chaos Downtown for a while. No one will notice they're missing.

Finally, I drop into a deep, dark sleep.

After all that's happened, I'm afraid of nightmares, but if I dream at all, in the morning, I don't remember a single one.

I WAKE UP to a great smell. When I sit up I find Samael sitting on the end of the bed sipping from a china cup.

He says, "Good morning, sunshine."

"Is that coffee I smell?"

"Did you want a cup?"

"In fact, I do."

"Sorry. This is the last of it."

I throw the covers off me and try to get up but fall back over.

"Ow."

"I take it you and Zadkiel had some fun last night."

"She beat me like I stole her car."

"Statistically, there's a good chance you did at some point."

"Please tell me that she wasn't lying. The gates of Heaven are still open?"

He takes a sip of coffee and says, "They are indeed. Damned souls are flooding in while rebel angels are flooding out. It's quite comical really. A sort of rerun of what I did with my pack of rebels all those years ago."

"Bunch of copycats."

"Unimaginative dross."

I try sitting up and this time it works. Stumbling through the wreckage, I make it to the kitchen and open a cabinet. There's a whole unopened pound of French roast on the shelf.

"You said there wasn't any coffee."

"You found some? Why don't you make us a fresh pot?"

I find a filter, shove it into the blessedly intact coffeemaker, and pour in half the damn bag of French roast.

"I hope you like yours strong."

"Like the Rock of Gibraltar," Samael says. And looks

around. “A bit of a step up for you.”

“Yeah. It’s not bad.”

“No. I meant the debris. You usually get beaten up in much worse places. You’re on your way to the big time, Jimmy.”

The coffeemaker burbles like it’s laughing at one of us, and I’m the only one covered in bruises.

I say, “Do you know how much blood I’ve lost over just the last few days? I could freeze it and carve you a new suit from it.”

Samael makes a face.

“Despite all the art, red really isn’t my color.”

“Are you here to congratulate me or just drink the last of my coffee?”

“All of the above. Well done with everything.”

I look at him.

“I always get nervous when you’re nice.”

He looks at me in mock horror.

“I’m the sincerest being in the entire universe.”

“What about Mr. Muninn?”

“The second-sincerest being in the universe, then.”

I look at him. It’s hard to tell when angels are lying, especially one who used to be the Devil, but I still give it a try.

“Did you know that Maria Simon was Zadkiel?”

He holds up a hand.

“Honestly, old man. I was as surprised as you.”

He seems to be telling the truth. But he was the Prince of Lies, so I’m not sure.

“But you did nudge me toward the Zero Lodge.”

“That I did do.”

“Because you knew Zadkiel was a member?”

"No. Because I hated them and knew that sooner or later you'd explode and kill them all."

"So, it was just a fantastic coincidence that of all the places your lost angel could be hiding, you got me to join the exact club where she was trawling for new boyfriends?"

"Absolutely."

We stare at each other for a couple of minutes.

"Liar."

He says, "How's the coffee coming?"

"Soon."

"Do you have any snacks around? I'm feeling a bit peckish."

I look around the room.

"There are cookies full of splinters and smashed corn chips."

"Corn chips sound lovely."

I toss him the bag and go back to the coffeemaker.

"What did you know about Chris Stein?"

"That you were trying to save the poor spirit from wandering the earth, smashing everything to pieces forever."

"I think I see it now. You prodded me to the Lodge to solve your problem knowing it would also solve my problem."

He rips open the bag and grabs a handful of broken chips.

"The Lord moves in mysterious ways."

"Why can't you ever just tell me these things? I don't like bastard angels and I do like steering poor, murdered, lovelorn slobs back to their eternal reward."

Samael peers at the coffeemaker.

"Done?"

"Done."

I top off the coffee in his cup but can't find an intact cup for myself, so I dump most of the sugar out of the sugar bowl and drink it from there.

Samael says, "You know why I can't always be straightforward with you?"

"Because it's more fun for you to watch me bounce off the walls?"

"There is that. But there's the other reason too."

"Mr. Muninn."

He makes a small embarrassed face.

"Father and his non-interference policies."

"Hasn't he figured out that his whole hands-off-no-matter-what policy is one of the things that screwed up the universe to begin with? At least the Earth."

"He doesn't look at it this way. Father has always been adamant about free will for humans."

I didn't dump out enough sugar. The coffee is awful. I set it down.

"How are we supposed to have free will and make our way in the universe when you people won't leave us alone?"

Samael looks aghast.

"Are you blaming *me* for all this?"

"Not just you. All angels."

He smiles and takes another sip of coffee.

"I hope you're including yourself in that company."

"No. I'm not. I'm just another clown trying to get by."

He frowns.

"Don't put on the innocent act for me. All this 'half an angel' business you're so obsessed with. 'I'm not a real angel, so none of this is my fault.' Admit it. You're right there in the muck with the rest of us. Just because you don't have wings doesn't make you any less of an angel than Michael or any of the big names."

I remember fighting the archangel at the gates of heaven a year or so ago.

I say, "Whatever happened to Michael?"

"Oh, I killed him."

"Thank you. What a complete dick."

"He really was, wasn't he?"

"The worst."

There's a sound from the other room. Abbot sticks his neck around the corner into the kitchen.

"Knock knock."

I wave him in.

"Come on in. Want some coffee? There aren't any more cups, but you can drink it from the pot."

He shakes his head.

"No thanks. I'm good."

He gives Samael a look.

"I'm sorry. You look very familiar. Have we met?"

"Probably. We've moved in similar circles over the years."

"I'm sure we've met somewhere."

Samael looks at me. I'm tired of dancing around things like this.

"Abbot, this is Samael. Samael, this is Abbot. Samael and I have worked together on some projects. Just like you and me."

Abbot smiles.

"Really? What kind?"

"For a while I was the Devil," says Samael.

Abbot tries not to look horrified. He covers it up a good 80 percent.

"Yes," he says in his most professional voice. "You used to be Lucifer."

Samael points to me.

"Technically, we both were."

Now Abbot looks at me.

"What's he talking about, Stark?"

"It's nothing. Job titles. It's like you. You're the Augur. There were ones before you and there will be ones after."

"That doesn't really answer my question."

I pop a PTSD pill and say, "Is everything okay in Little Cairo?"

He stops frowning, though not completely.

"Things are fine. We've had to administer some medical help. Modify some memories and basically repair the entire neighborhood in the last day or so, but thanks to you, the spirit infestation is over."

Samael laughs. "Infestation."

"What would you call it?" says Abbot.

"It's not that. I was just thinking about how ghosts talk about you people. It's a lot worse than 'infestation.'"

Abbot hooks a finger toward the living room.

"Can we talk in private for a moment?"

I lean on the cracked kitchen counter.

"Anything you want to say to me, you can say in front of Samael. I'll probably tell him or he'll find out the same way he seems to find out everything."

He nods.

"It's true. I'll know an hour after you tell him."

Abbot looks a little exasperated.

"Fine," he says. "It's about the house."

"Yeah. I've been meaning to ask you, who cleans it? Because I feel like I owe them some kind of tip or something."

"The house cleans itself," says Abbot. "It's the semiautonomous physical ideal of a happy home."

"Cool."

"And you broke it."

"I did?"

Abbot kicks some debris with the toe of his loafer.

"This has never happened before. I mean, we have structures like this in war zones and they don't break. But you broke this one."

Samael claps.

"Well done, Jimmy. I always said you were an overachiever."

"Listen, Stark, I don't know how to say this, but you have to leave."

"The house? You said I could stay here as long as I wanted."

"That was before you—"

"Broke the house," says Samael.

The bastard laughs like this is the funniest thing that's ever happened since the beginning of time.

Abbot says, "I'll send in a Sub Rosa crew to take care of the current mess, but the Council would really appreciate it if you could be out by the weekend."

"That's tomorrow."

"Yes."

Samael won't stop laughing.

"I'll go under one condition."

"What's that?"

"Who ratted out Brigitte?"

Abbot gives me a hard look.

"If you're thinking about killing him, there won't be anything I can do to help you."

"I promise you I won't kill him. I've had enough killing to last me this lifetime and the next."

"Careful, son," says Samael. "Lying is a sin."

Abbot looks at us both.

"I can do it, Stark. We already arranged for the man to be fired from his very prestigious job."

"The costar of her show?" says Samael. "George something." He looks at me. "He was just given the boot over some contract violation or other."

I look back at Abbot. He isn't happy that Samael follows celebrity gossip. He holds up a finger.

"If he turns up dead—"

"I told you. I'm not going to kill him."

"You better not," he says.

"What about Brigitte's situation?"

"I have good news there. I'm making headway with my contacts."

"Thanks."

"Listen, I have to get going. The cleaning crew will be here in an hour. You might want to be gone. It's going to be very loud."

"Samael and I will go get some breakfast and I'll come back for my stuff."

"I'll talk to you soon," Abbot says. He looks at Samael and says, "Good meeting you too." Then, warily, "Are you staying in L.A. long?"

"He's not the Devil anymore," I say. "And neither am I. Now, I want to get some pancakes. You can come along if you want."

"No thanks," Abbot says. "There's still a lot of work to do after a crisis like this."

He starts out but stops and looks genuinely unhappy. Says, "I want you to know that making you leave wasn't my idea. I was outvoted."

"Thanks for sticking up for me."

With a short wave, Abbot makes his way out and away from my mess.

Samael looks at me oddly.

"Do you really want to get pancakes?"

"No. Want to go scare the shit out of this George guy?"

"There's the Jimmy I love."

AT EIGHT, THE whole wedding party—plus Samael and a hundred or so artsy strangers—pile into the Starless Starlight Theater on a little side street in West Hollywood. Janet and a small band of other musicians from their school play a live original score to *A Page of Madness*—a wild 1926 silent horror movie from Japan. Over the course of the film the music morphs from a shadowy synthesized orchestra to a ferocious percussion machine, pausing in between to fill the theater with ominous industrial groans. It's so perfect that even Samael applauds unironically at the end. Afterward, everybody heads to Bamboo House to celebrate. I kiss Janet and say that I'll meet them there.

"You okay?" they say.

"Perfectly."

"Did you like the show?"

"I loved it. We all did."

Janet looks at me.

"I get the feeling there's something you're not telling me."

"I just need to get my stuff out of the flying saucer house."

"You need any help?"

"Nope. I've got it all worked out."

"Okay. But if I don't hear from you in an hour, I'm telling everyone to phone-bomb you until you come over."

"I'll be there. Don't worry."

I leave everyone and shadow walk to the flying saucer house one last time. Abbot's cleaning crew did a good job with the mess I left, but the place just isn't what it was when I moved in.

"Sorry, house," I say as I shove my clothes into a duffel bag. "No hard feelings."

Someone has piled all of the paperbacks Kasabian gave me on the bed. It annoys me that they took out Ellroy's *The Black Dahlia* from the hole I punched in the wall. So, I punch another one and put it back. Something to remember me by.

Another shadow walk and I'm home. Back to the magic apartment that I once shared with Alice and that Vidocq has been living in for twelve years. I guess I've come full circle.

Vidocq's stuff is still everywhere. I don't want to touch any of it until Allegra comes over and we figure out what to do with it all. Some she'll hold on to as keepsakes. Some will go to the clinic. Other books and equipment she'll give to Ray and some of Vidocq's friends in the alchemy underground. Not one test tube will go to waste.

I take my duffel into the bedroom and drop it on the floor. Sit down on the bed. I can still feel him here, in the smells, the crazy art and mystical charts on the walls. His clothes and some of Allegra's still hang in the closet. We'll sort that out in the next few days too. What I don't feel is a trace of me and Alice. And maybe that's a good thing. Here I am, safe in an invisible apartment that's rent free and only a few people know about. I know the neighborhood bodegas and all the best streets where I can hide the Hellion Hog. This is a chance to recover and regroup from the last few months. Kind of start over again. And it's not a bad feeling.

Still, I can't quite relax. All through the movie tonight and now in the apartment, I can't get Zadkiel's last words out of my head.

I've done something awful. Just awful.

What could the Opener of the Ways have done that's so bad? I know I'll find out. At least I have a place of my own to face it from. No Sub Rosa to answer to. No Wormwood. Nobody at all. It feels a little lonely at the moment, but the first few minutes of freedom are always like that, I think. When you have all the possibilities in the world, how to choose any one of them? From here, I have time to figure it out.

I've worked out one thing about myself and I don't like it. I always pictured myself as in control, if not of my life, of my mind. My sense of who I am. I thought I was strong. I pictured myself as a kind of leader. But I couldn't have been more wrong. I haven't controlled my life in years. Maybe ever. Mason led me around and sent me to Hell. Samael has played games with me. Mr. Muninn has used me. The Golden Vigil. Wormwood. Abbot and the Sub Rosa Council. I'm not strong. I'm not the monster who kills monsters. I'm a yappy little dog being led around by owner after owner.

I want to take a stand. Say that it stops tonight. But I've been this way for so long, I'm not sure how to change. Do I leave? Walk away from everyone and everything and start over somewhere else? Right. Who am I fooling? I can't even set foot out of L.A. without getting the shakes. I'm the weakest person I know. And the biggest fool.

Something has to change. But I don't know how to do it. Maybe being here—home again—will help me figure it out.

I DRIVE THE Hog to Bamboo House of Dolls and park it in a loading zone out front. No one bats an eye. Inside, Fuck Hollywood bounces over to me with a bourbon the moment I walk inside.

"I heard your bike."

I take the drink and say, "Keep bringing me drinks like this and I'll take you for a ride someday."

She smiles like it's her birthday and Christmas morning at the same time.

"Awesome."

I go over to where my friends are gathered. Samael is buying the drinks tonight. When he sees me, he drapes an arm over my shoulder.

"It's a good night tonight, squire. All of our problems are solved."

We toast to the good times to come.

I've done something awful. Just awful.

No. None of our problems are over. They're just different now.

Janet comes over and gives me a big kiss. I take their hand.

Something is coming and I know right down in my bones that it's going to be bad. But I also know that not me or anyone else in here tonight is going to have to face it alone. And that makes it all right. That's something to fight for. That's something to die for.

Now, though, it's just people and drinks and Martin Denny's cover of "Misirlou" on the jukebox. And that's as good a night as anyone could ever ask for.

Richard Kadrey is the *New York Times* bestselling author of the Sandman Slim supernatural noir books. *Sandman Slim* was included in Amazon's "100 Science Fiction & Fantasy Books to Read in a Lifetime" and is in development as a feature film. His other books include *Hollywood Dead, The Everything Box, Metrophage,* and *Butcher Bird*, and he also writes comics and screenplays. He lives in San Francisco.